TWO NOVELS

by Phyllis A. Whitney

Two Novels by
Phyllis A. Whitney

THUNDER HEIGHTS
and
WINDOW on the SQUARE

MEREDITH PRESS   NEW YORK

Two Novels by

Phyllis A. Whitney

THUNDER HEIGHTS
and
WINDOW on the SQUARE

MEREDITH PRESS   NEW YORK

PRINTED IN THE UNITED STATES OF AMERICA

Thunder Heights

by Phyllis A. Whitney

Thunder Heights

by Phyllis A. Whitney

CHAPTER 1

CAMILLA KING stood at the window of her small third floor room overlooking Gramercy Park and watched the last windy day of March blow itself out through the streets of New York. A gusty breeze rumpled treetops in the park, tossed the mane of a horse drawing a hackney cab along Twenty-first Street, and sent an unguarded bowler hat tumbling across the sidewalk.

Ordinarily she loved wind and storm. But how bleak and discouraging everything could look on a gray day in New York. The sky was as gray as the streets and as overcast as her life seemed at this moment.

Behind her in the little room Nettie sniffed tearfully as she packed the top tray of Camilla's trunk. This was a labor of love for Nettie. A departing governess had no business using up the parlormaid's time. But the Hodges had gone out and there was no one about to complain.

"You'll find a better place than this, Miss Camilla," Nettie said, wiping away tears with the back of her hand. "You being so pretty and clever and all."

Camilla smiled wryly without turning. "And with such a fine outspoken way about me that it has lost me the second position in a row?"

"A good thing, too," Nettie muttered. "With himself so high and mighty that—"

"It was the children I was thinking of," Camilla broke in. "They're darlings and I had to speak up against his harshness. But

Mr. Hodges said I was too easy with them and perhaps he should employ an older woman for governess."

"You're twenty-three and that's a great age!" Nettie protested. "At twenty-three I'd been married to my Tom for five years and had two babes of my own. That's the bad thing, Miss Camilla—you being so alone."

Camilla had visited Nettie's home and had seen—and envied a little—the joyous welter of family life in which Nettie thrived. She had never known such a life, but she could still remember the warm affection and gaiety of those years before she was eight, the years before her mother's death. At times, when the moment was right, her mother's image still returned to her mind full and clear and vital. Then she could remember the way Althea King had moved, light and lovely as a dancer, her dark head carried with such proud grace. She could recall the very line of her thick black hair coming to the point of a widow's peak at her forehead. Wherever Althea King was, there excitement had burgeoned. The strangeness of her death had wiped out so much. And now it grew increasingly difficult for Camilla to bring that bright image back to mind.

For the years that John King, her father, had been married to Althea, he had come out of his books and his scholar's reverie a little, and had known a quiet joy in her company. But after her mother had died in that faraway place up the Hudson, he had lost himself more than ever in his writings, his study, his teaching.

A housekeeper had been brought in to take charge of their small home and of Camilla. Mrs. Gregg was an efficient woman, but she had little feeling for children. Camilla had not cared. She had lived a free enough existence, if a lonely one. Her father had seen to her education, and lessons with him had always been a joy.

Camilla remembered him with love and tenderness. Never had she seen a man more handsome, with his poet's brow, his fine dark eyes, and the sensitive modeling of his mouth. When she thought of him now, she pictured him most often in the little room he had used for a study, with his head bent over his books. He had cared for his daughter. Indeed, he had loved her doubly, loving her mother through her. Camilla had been bitterly stricken when he had died four years ago.

The way of her growing up had given her a practical side—someone had to use good sense with a dreamer like her father. And certainly it had given her independence. But there was something of her father in her too, for there were times when her own dreamy, imaginative side took over and made her do strange things.

Now, however, she must accept only the practical in herself, so she laughed at Nettie's lugubrious words and steeled her will against despair. On a gray day like this, when she had just lost a position she needed badly—and lost it because of her very independence—despair seemed ready to seize her if she let down her guard for a moment.

"Never you mind," Nettie said, thrusting back her tears in order to cheer Camilla. "You're the marrying kind, you know. It's a good husband you need, Miss Camilla, and babes of your own."

Again Camilla smiled and did not answer. Sometimes she lingered all too readily over such thoughts, it was true. Pleasant enough dreams in the daytime, but sometimes disturbingly painful during the long hours of the night. Arms were not meant alone for holding tenderly, as one held a child. There was a demand in her for something more gladdening and all-absorbing than seemed to be the lot of the women in whose homes she worked as a governess.

From the window she saw that the hackney cab she had noticed earlier had circled the enclosure of the park twice, as if its fare were not sure of the house he looked for. Now it stopped before the Hodges' door and a man got out, holding his hat against a sudden gust of wind.

"Someone's coming up the steps, Nettie," Camilla said over her shoulder. "There's the bell—you'd better run. And thank you for helping me pack."

Nettie hurried for the stairs and Camilla stood on at the window, trying not to droop with dejection. Tomorrow, she supposed, she would be courageous again, but for the moment it was a temptation to match her spirits to the gray, unsettled afternoon and wonder where she was to turn next, whether she could ever find a position that would give her a lasting home. Or if that was what she really wanted.

If she was pretty, as Nettie said, it was of no special advantage. What good did prettiness do when it brought too easy an interest from men who could never matter to her? At the place before this,

5

the man of the house had been altogether too kind, and had wanted to be kinder. Camilla had spoken her mind and left precipitately. It was unfair that such things should happen when she knew she had done her work well and taken pride in the doing.

Was she pretty? she wondered absently. She put a hand to the dark, glossy waves of hair drawn loosely into a coil at the top of her head and puffed at the sides in the style of this last decade of the century. She knew her skin was as fair in contrast to her black hair as her mother's had been, and that the same pointed widow's peak marked her forehead. Her pink-striped shirtwaist with its bow at the high collar, and her gored gray skirt, flowing into a small train, fitted a well-proportioned figure. And she supposed that wide brown eyes, heavy-lashed, were a good feature. But prettiness—how did one know about oneself? And what did it matter anyway? A governess lived an almost cloistered life, with little opportunity to know other young people—especially young men her own age.

She turned from the window and looked at her trunk, ready now to be closed and locked, and at the cheap straw suitcase that stood beside it.

"I'm tired to pieces of this life!" she told them aloud. "I want something better than this!" She would find something better, too. She was not helpless or fearful, as a rule. And she was not without the ingenuity to make something more of her life.

There were her relatives, for one thing—those wealthy, unknown relatives up the Hudson River. She had more family than Nettie guessed, though she never heard from them, or even thought seriously of getting in touch with them. Not after the way her grandfather had treated her mother, or in the face of her father's bitter hatred of him.

John King, in his gentleness, had seldom disliked anyone. But Camilla knew that he blamed Orrin Judd for her mother's death and never forgave him. Exactly what her grandfather's fault had been she did not know, but her father's insistence that she must have nothing to do with her mother's family had made a lasting impression over the years.

Nevertheless, there they were—Orrin Judd and his daughters, in that great house up the Hudson called Thunder Heights. Her mother had told her endless stories about the place as she had

6

known it as a child. Perhaps the day would eventually come when Camilla could face these relatives, if for no other reason than to learn more about her mother. But she would not go as a beggar. Never that!

She heard Nettie breathing heavily as she climbed the stairs, and a moment later the maid was at the door, her eyes wide with excitement.

"It's a caller!" she cried. "A caller for you, Miss Camilla. A dignified gentleman, he seems—and asking for Miss Camilla King. I've put him in the front parlor. Maybe he's come to offer you a new position. Quick now—run down and see what he wants."

Camilla did not run, but she could not help a faint rising of curiosity. No one knew as yet of her need for a new position. Perhaps it was some friend of her father—though she had not imposed her troubles on them.

At the parlor door she paused so that she might enter without unseemly haste. The gentleman sat in a shadowy corner where she could not see him clearly at first. He rose and came toward her— a man in his fifties, bald except for a gray fringe of hair rimming the back of his head, and ending in two clumps above each ear. His skin had the pink, soft look of a baby's, but his eyes were a cool, wary gray. His straight, tight mouth barely smiled as he studied her. There was no approval in him.

"You are Miss Camilla King?" he asked directly. "My name is Pompton. Alexander Pompton. The name will mean nothing to you, I am sure. But I have come to ask a favor of you."

She gestured him to the sofa and sat down opposite, curious and waiting.

"You are a governess here, I believe," he said. "Are you happy in this work? Are your ties in this household very strong?"

The soreness of her last interview with Mr. Hodges was too recent for caution.

"I have no ties here at all," she said quickly. "Or anywhere else, for that matter. I was dismissed from my position this morning."

He considered her admission soberly, as if it further bolstered his conclusions about her, and she wished she had not blurted out the truth so impulsively.

"In that case," he said, "it should be possible for you to take the

7

boat tomorrow afternoon. I have gone to the liberty of procuring your passage to Westcliff in order to make your way easy."

"Easy for what?" she asked, completely at a loss.

He leaned toward her earnestly, dropping all evasion. "I have been Orrin Judd's attorney for many years, I have come here to ask you to go to your grandfather's sickbed at Thunder Heights. He is seriously ill—he may be dying."

She was silent for a moment, startled and dismayed. "But—he disowned my mother long ago. Even when she was alive he would have nothing to do with us."

"That is not quite true," Mr. Pompton corrected her. "Mr. Judd kept good account of every move his daughter Althea made over the years. Had she been in need, he would have stepped in at once, even though he and your father had little liking for each other."

"My father detested him," Camilla said. "He didn't want my mother to return to Thunder Heights when Orrin Judd finally sent for her."

Mr. Pompton sighed and ran a hand over his pink scalp as if he smoothed thick hair. This errand was clearly not to his taste. "What happened was unfortunate, indeed a great tragedy. But your father was mistaken in blaming Orrin Judd."

Camilla's fingers twisted together in her lap. "They sent for Papa after she died. He went to Thunder Heights for her funeral, and he came home ill with grief. He said her family was wholly to blame for the accident, whatever it was. He would never talk about it at all. He wanted me to remember my mother the way she was, and I've never known how she died. He said I was never under any circumstances to have anything to do with my grandfather or the others at Thunder Heights."

"Your father has been dead for several years," Mr. Pompton reminded her. "You are a grown woman. It is up to you to make your own decisions. When a man is dying there may be many things he regrets. Your mother was Orrin Judd's favorite daughter, and he wishes to see his only grandchild."

Camilla sat very still, her fingers twisted tightly. A queer, unexpected surge of excitement had leaped within her for an instant. The name of Judd was a magic one to be spoken almost in the same breath with such names as Vanderbilt, Astor, or Morgan. Though

8

in later years old Orrin Judd had pulled in his horns and, with the eccentricity in which only the very rich can indulge, had abandoned the lavish mode of living that had once been his custom. The world had nearly forgotten him, as it was never allowed to forget those others who bore great names and increased their progeny.

In none of her positions as a governess had Camilla ever breathed a word of her grandfather's identity. But she remembered once when she had been very young and her mother had pointed out a tall structure that towered over Broadway. "Your grandfather created that building," her mother said with pride in her voice. The small Camilla had envisioned a very old man with a long white beard like the pictures of Moses in the Bible, setting one brick upon another as she herself piled blocks. For a long time it had been a puzzle to her what he had done once the pile rose higher than his head. But the building had always remained for her, "my grandfather's house."

A faint smile curled her lips, and Mr. Pompton did not miss it. "You would need to stay only a day or two at this time," he said hurriedly, pressing what he took to be an advantage. "The boat trip need not interfere with your obtaining a new position in New York, if that is what you wish. I believe it would be wise not to remain longer. You would at least make your grandfather's acquaintance, perhaps bring him a last happiness. I met your mother only once, but I have seen pictures of her. Your resemblance to her is striking."

Yes, she knew that. The way she looked had always brought her father both pain and joy. But why did Mr. Pompton stipulate that Orrin's granddaughter should visit him for only a day or two? If her grandfather wanted her enough to send for her . . .

"I must warn you," Mr. Pompton continued in his solemn tone, "that you may not be altogether welcome at Thunder Heights."

Her mother's tales of the family sprang from the past into Camilla's mind. "You mean because of my Aunt Hortense? But if my grandfather wants me—"

"He may not be well enough to prevail. I'm afraid that your aunt never forgave your mother for running away with John King. But no matter—you must go and not let anything she says disturb you."

9

"Who else lives at Thunder Heights now?" Camilla asked. "I believe Mama said that Letitia was the middle sister. Has she married?"

"No, Miss Letty still lives there. She is a gentle soul, and I'm sure she will welcome your coming. Then of course there is Booth Hendricks, whom your Aunt Hortense adopted many years ago when he was ten. He must be about thirty-six now and he too has never married. There is another young man, as well—an engineer who has been a close and trusted associate of your grandfather for many years. A Mr. Ross Granger. He is now in New York on business. I expect to see him while I am here. Miss Camilla—will you give your grandfather this last pleasure? Believe me, the matter is urgent. He was ill before this heart attack—there may be little time remaining."

For a moment Camilla could not answer. The emptiness of all the years when she had longed for a family crowded back upon her. How many times she had dreamed of such a family in her young girl loneliness, and now one had been presented to her. A family whom she would not have to approach as a beggar because Orrin Judd himself had summoned her. Perhaps there were matters her father had never fully understood. Besides, she had her mother's own actions to guide her. When Orrin Judd had sent for her, Althea had gone, even over the objections of her husband. Could her daughter do less?

She smiled at her visitor in sudden bright acceptance. "There's no reason why I can't catch tomorrow's boat as you suggest."

Mr. Pompton looked more relieved than pleased. He rose at once and put an envelope into Camilla's hands.

"You will find everything in order, I believe. The boat reaches Westcliff in the late afternoon. I will send a wire ahead so that you will be met and driven to Thunder Heights. I plan to return by a later boat when my business in New York is finished."

She saw him to the door and watched him go down the steps and out to his waiting hack. The day was still gray and gusty, but now there seemed an excitement in the blustering wind. She ran upstairs breathlessly to announce the news to Nettie.

"I have a family!" she cried. "I have a family after all!" And she wrapped her arms about herself, as if she hugged the very fact to her. "Perhaps if my grandfather likes me I can stay a while, in spite of my Aunt Hortense."

Nettie had to sit right down and listen to the whole story, and she didn't leave until the Hodges were heard coming home. It wasn't necessary for Camilla to see her erstwhile employers again until she left. She had her supper in her room that night, and she could hardly sleep for thinking about Thunder Heights, trying to remember all the stories her mother had told her about the days when Althea Judd was a little girl in the great house up the river.

As a child, Camilla had pictured in her mind a great castle of a house, built on a high eminence. A house with shining turrets and windows that caught the tints of sunrise across the Hudson. She knew, as though she had stepped into it, the square antehall with marble hands that reached eerily out of the walls, and the great parlor filled with curios. Orrin Judd and his wife had liked to travel, and they had brought home treasures from all over the world. Camilla's grandmother had died while Althea was a little girl, but there had still been days of wonderful travel for her daughters.

There was an octagon staircase, too—Camilla had always loved the sound of that. It ran up two flights, and its panels of carved teakwood had come from Burma. Up on the third floor was the huge nursery, where Althea had played with her two older sisters. Camilla could imagine its cheerful fire and worn, loved furnishings.

Now that she thought of it, Camilla realized that her mother had talked more of the house than of its occupants. There had always been a soreness in Althea King that had turned away from stories of her father or her sisters. But now Camilla could go to Thunder Heights and see the bright turrets, the marble hands, the staircase, for herself.

It was not, however, the house that interested her most. A warm current of eagerness flowed in her veins, an eagerness to please her aunts and her grandfather, to love them and be loved by them. Whatever had happened in the past must be buried by the years that were gone. She was not responsible for any of it, so how could she be blamed for what was none of her doing? She would be as sweet and agreeable as it was in her to be, so that the family would delight in having her there—even Aunt Hortense who held some unaccountable grudge against her own dead sister.

She went to sleep with a smile on her lips and all her dreams were loving.

CHAPTER 2

THE FOLLOWING AFTERNOON she bade Mrs. Hodges a polite good-by, kissed the weeping children with the pang she always felt on leaving charges she had grown to love, and went out to her cab, carrying her suitcase. The trunk would follow her in a day or two. She *had* to stay at Thunder Heights for a little while at least.

She had never taken a trip up the Hudson River before, yet the river had always been a part of her memory of her mother. Sometimes the two of them had gone by horse car to the lower tip of Manhattan, where the river emptied into the harbor, and stood watching the busy water life. The Hudson had meant home to Althea King, and she had told her small daughter tales of the dreamer, Hendrik Hudson, and his ship the *Half Moon.* Stories too of the Dunderbergs and the Catskills, of Storm King, and Breakneck Ridge, and Anthony's Nose. All history, it seemed, was part of the Hudson, from Indian days to the present. Commerce had followed the vital artery and made a great nation even greater.

But Althea King had seen the river with more personal eyes. She had known the Hudson in its every mood—when its banks glowed brilliant with autumn foliage, when ice encrusted its inlets, when spring laid a tender hand upon its shores and when summer thunderstorms set the cliffs reverberating.

Yet after her marriage her mother had never again set foot on a Hudson River boat until the final summons from her father. "I want to remember," she had said, "but I don't want to turn the knife in my heart." Strange words to a little girl's ears, but her mother's passion for the river had remained, and now Camilla felt eager and alive, ready to fling her arms wide and embrace the new life that must surely lie ahead. That life was her heritage from her mother, and the river was a vibrant part of it.

Nevertheless, the river had taken her mother away, she thought with a twinge of guilt. Althea had never returned from that last journey up Hudson waters to Thunder Heights. Remembering that, she wondered what the river might hold in the future for Althea's daughter.

The boat that awaited Camilla was one of the Hudson's fastest —four decks high and gleaming with white paint and gold trim. The tourist season had not yet begun, but there was a continual flow of traffic between New York and Albany, and passengers were already boarding when she reached the pier.

The day was gray again. This was storm-brewing weather, with an electric quality in the air and a wild wind blowing—weather that carried excitement in every breath. It was cold for the first day of April, and the cutting wind sent most of the passengers scuttling for the comfort of the gold and white salons.

Since the trip would be a short one for Camilla, she had no cabin, but as soon as she had checked her flimsy suitcase, she climbed the grand staircase, her hand on the fine mahogany rail, and went into the main salon where passengers were making themselves comfortable out of the wind. She looked about, wanting nothing so tame as this. She wanted to be outside where everything was happening.

Over her hat she tied a gray veil that matched her gray *tailleur* suit, knotting it in a bow under her chin. Then she went out on deck into the very teeth of the wind. With a great tootling of whistles the boat was drawing away from the pier, turning its back upon the harbor of New York as it began its journey up the Hudson River. The paddle wheels churned a frothing wake, that sent waves rolling away to rock all smaller craft. Gulls soared and dived in the great air drafts, as if they too felt the excitement of the day.

Every manner of river craft—barges, tugs, ferries, sailboats, freighters—steamed or sailed or chugged about their individual business. As Camilla watched, she let the gale whip color into her face, breathing the fresh, tangy odor—the odor of salt air. It was as if she were truly breathing for the first time since her father's death.

Only one other passenger had dared the cold out on deck. Ahead a man leaned against the rail with his back to her, while the prow of the boat cut through choppy gray water like a great white swan among lesser fowl. He wore a sandy tweed jacket and a cap pulled over his forehead. So absorbed was he by the sights of the river that Camilla could watch him curiously without being noticed.

As she stood below him at the rail, a child of no more than four suddenly darted out of a doorway. The little girl was laughing as she ran up the deck, and Camilla, looking about for her mother to follow, saw no one. At once she hurried after the child, lest she come to harm. But the man had heard the sound of small feet running and he turned in time to see the little girl and catch her up in his arms. Then he saw Camilla approaching.

"An open deck is a dangerous place for a child," he said curtly and handed her to Camilla.

His misunderstanding was natural, and she did not take offense, but accepted the child and walked back toward the companionway just as a frantic mother rushed out and looked around in distraction.

"Here she is," Camilla said. The mother thanked her and hurried the little girl back to the shelter of the doorway. When Camilla turned, smiling, she saw that the man in the tweed jacket was watching her.

He took off his cap and the wind ruffled hair that had the glossy sheen of a red-brown chestnut. "I'm sorry," he said. "I thought she was yours, and it's a wonder I didn't read you a lecture. A child was badly hurt the last time I made this trip, and I get impatient with careless mothers."

She nodded in a friendly fashion and went to stand next to him at the rail, watching the steep cliffs of the Palisades rising ahead. She was glad he had spoken to her. Now she might ask him questions about the river. "Do you know the Hudson well?" she began.

He drew the cap down over his eyes again. "Well enough. I've lived along its banks all my life, and I've been up and down its length a few times."

"How wonderful," she said. "It's strange to think that I've lived all my life in New York City and have never sailed up the Hudson River. Today I feel like an explorer. I wish I could go all the way to Albany."

He stared off into the wind without comment, and she hoped he wasn't shutting her out. In her eagerness and exhilaration she was ready to spill over in conversation with almost anyone, but she contented herself for the moment by studying the strong line of his jaw, his straight nose and jutting brows. It was difficult to judge his age—probably he was in the mid-thirties. There was a certain ruggedness about him, a muscular breadth to his shoulders that marked him for a man of action, rather than, like her father, a man of books. She observed his hand upon the rail, long of finger and wide across the back. A hand that revealed strength and vitality. The sum of all these things interested her, made her a little curious.

"I'm going upriver to Westcliff," she said tentatively.

He looked at her more directly than before, and she saw that his eyes were gray as the river that flowed past the boat, and set widely beneath heavy chestnut brows.

"Westcliff happens to be my destination too," he admitted, but offered her no more in the way of explanation.

The wind had increased its velocity, tearing at her hat as if to snatch it from beneath the enfolding veil, pulling black strands of hair from beneath its brim. Camilla pushed them back breathlessly and laughed into the gale in sheer delight. There was something satisfying about resisting its elementary force. She would choose a storm any day to brooding safely in the shelter of a small gray room whose very walls shut her away from the tempests and clamor of life.

"I'm glad you're going to Westcliff," she told him, speaking her mind without hesitation. "I'll at least have an acquaintance in the vicinity. I don't know a soul where I'm going. Do you know the place called Thunder Heights?"

His face was not one to be easily read, but she sensed that he was startled. The set of his straight mouth was unsmiling, his gray eyes guarded as he looked away.

"Is—is there something wrong with my going to Thunder Heights?" she asked.

He did not meet her look. "Why are you going there? Surely not to look for employment?"

"No," she said. "I work as a governess and I believe there are no children in the house at present." She hesitated because she had never before claimed openly her relationship to the Judds. Then she went on with a faint hint of happy pride in her voice that she could not suppress. "My grandfather is Orrin Judd. My mother, Althea, was the youngest of Orrin Judd's three daughters. I am Camilla King."

He made no move and his expression did not change, yet it seemed to Camilla that there was a withdrawing, as if something in him moved away from her. He spoke beneath his breath, almost as if to himself.

"Another one," he said, and she sensed hostility in him.

He was judging her in some mistaken way, she was sure, though she did not know what there was in her Judd relationship to misunderstand.

"My grandfather is very ill," she hurried on. "I—I may be going to his deathbed. I believe he had a heart attack a few days ago."

This time she had truly surprised him. "A heart attack?" he repeated unbelievingly. "He has been ailing for some time, but—how do you know this?"

"An attorney of my grandfather's—a Mr. Pompton—came looking for me. He said my grandfather wanted to see me. Mr. Pompton arranged for my passage and I was able to take the boat at once."

He recovered himself to some extent, but she could see that her news had shaken him. He was studying her face now, clearly without liking.

"So you're still more of the family?" he said, and the inflection was not flattering.

His rude rejection both cut and angered her. She drew herself up with the dignity she had learned to adopt in households where she might be treated with less than the respect she wished. But before she could manage a reply, the billowing thunderheads that rode the sky burst and flung a torrent of rain upon them. Her companion would have taken her arm to help her across the deck, but she drew away and fled from him into the warmth and shelter of the main salon. He did not follow her there, but disappeared along the deck to another entrance.

She found an upholstered seat near a window where rain slashed the glass, obscuring all vision, and pretended to peer out into the

17

storm. She felt somehow disappointed beyond reason. She had been ready to like this man and accept him as a new acquaintance who might well become a friend. But the name "Judd" had turned him abruptly from her, and the realization brought with it a vague uneasiness to stem her earlier feeling of joy. She wished now that she had answered him in some way, or at least challenged him to explain the scornful tone of his voice. When she saw him again, she would do just that. If the Judds were held in bad repute, that was unfortunate, but it had nothing to do with her.

She found the remaining time before Westcliff frustrating. Longing to view the river scenery, she could see nothing for the driving rain, and though she wandered about for a while below decks, she did not see again the man she had spoken to earlier.

Not until late afternoon did the storm roll away so that a glinting of pale sky showed through the veil of gray. The decks were drenched and wet, the wind still cold, but Camilla went outside eagerly to watch the steep shores of the Hudson glide by. The river had curved sharply and seemed now to be enclosed on all sides by rocky cliffs, as if the boat had turned into some great inland lake. This she knew, must be the gateway to the Highlands. She watched, entranced, as the boat glided around the jutting crags, always finding one more opening to let it through.

Ahead on the west bank loomed a great hulking mass of mountain, its stony head cutting a profile into the sky. She could not see beyond its jutting, thickly wooded sides—still covered by the brown woods of winter—but Westcliff must not be too far ahead.

"That is Thunder Mountain," a quiet voice said in her ear.

She turned quickly to find her recent companion beside her. This time she did not wait, or give him a chance to escape again.

"May I ask why you spoke so scornfully of the Judds?" she said.

He did not seem taken aback by her sudden question. A flicker of amusement lifted one corner of his mouth and vanished.

"I should have identified myself," he told her. "My name is Ross Granger. For the last ten years or so I have worked as a close associate of Orrin Judd. Your sudden news about his illness came as a shock, since he seemed no worse than usual when I left him last week."

Her eyes widened in surprise. "Then you must be the person

Mr. Pompton wanted to see in New York. You must have missed him."

"That's possible," he said and turned back to watching the river. "You can see the house now," he added. "Up there below the mass of the mountain—there's your Thunder Heights."

The white boat, cutting through choppy gray water, was slipping past the mountain, and Camilla could see that its far slope gentled, opening into a wide, tree-grown level high above the river. She forgot that the rail was sopping wet and clung to it tightly with her gray gloves. Now she could look up and see the house for the first time.

The point of prominence on which it stood commanded an entire sweep of the river, and the structure was as fantastic and impressive as anything in her dreams. Orrin Judd had built to suit himself, as Camilla knew, and he had built with imagination, but little regard for restraint. The house was a conglomeration of wooden towers and gingerbread curlicues, with sloping roofs from which jutted gables and dormer windows. A wide veranda, arched and bracketed beneath its eaves, gave upon the river, and Camilla searched its length eagerly to see if any of the family stood there watching the boat steam past. But the veranda was empty, and so were the grounds. Shutters framed blank windows which stared at her without recognition. Plainly the house did not know her, and was not waiting for her.

The turrets were no longer bright as Althea King had described them. Storms had weathered the house to a dingy gray, left too long unpainted, and the trees crowding about gave it the look of a place uninhabited. It appeared enchanted, spellbound, there on its remote heights. Not a house, but the picture of a house, torn from the pages of fantasy.

"What a strange, wonderful place," Camilla said softly. "I think I'm going to love everything about Thunder Heights."

The man at her side made a faint, derisive sound. "If I were you, I wouldn't approach it with ready-made sentimentality. You're quite likely to be disappointed."

She would not let his words dampen her feeling about the house. Even if the place didn't know her now, it would accept her later.

How could it refuse, when she would offer it the love of a grand-daughter coming home?

"It's strange to think that my mother grew up there," she murmured.

"How did she escape?" Ross Granger asked dryly.

What an annoying person he was, she thought—without sentiment, or kindly feelings. Why had her grandfather kept him on all these years, if he thought so little of the Judds? Then, because she hated to condemn anyone in this moment of anticipation and eagerness, she relented. Perhaps he did not really know her mother's story.

"My father came to teach in Westcliff," she told him, "and my mother fell in love with him. But Grandfather Orrin had other plans for her. I suppose he didn't think much of a poor schoolteacher as a husband for his daughter. So one night they ran away to New York and were married there. My grandfather never forgave her and she only returned once—just before her death."

"I've heard several versions of that story," he said. "I came to Thunder Heights four or five years after your mother's death, so I never met her. It was always Pompton who had the job of keeping track of her, and later of you. But she must have been a bit frivolous and reckless—your mother."

Once more she sensed disapproval in his tone, and resentment prickled through her.

"I remember her as being gay and happy," she said with dignity.

Ross Granger looked up at the house on the mountain. "Frivolity seems out of place at Thunder Heights. Its gay times are long past, I'd say. You're likely to be frowned upon if you so much as laugh out loud these days. For my taste, I prefer this second house coming up here below the Judd land. That's Blue Beeches, and I can assure you its architecture is more typically Hudson River than Orrin Judd's house."

Blue Beeches, though further upriver, was below the Judd heights and closer to the water. It shone in bright yellow contrast to its more somber neighbor above. Its green shutters looked freshly painted and it stood upon the bank with the foursquare solidity of brick, as if it knew its own sound position as a family house well accepted by the community. Here there were signs of life. A woman sat rocking on the broad veranda, while three children of varying ages ran down to a small landing at the water's edge, waving eagerly as the boat went past. Ross raised an arm and returned their salute, and the children shouted and waved all the harder.

Apparently Ross Granger had friends here, among the children at least. She was puzzling over further questions to ask him, when he drew her hands from the wet rail and turned them over to reveal the gloves soaked and stained.

"Better go change your gloves before we dock. That's Westcliff coming up ahead of us."

It was exasperating to be given directions, as she might have directed a child in her charge. Perhaps he regarded her in that light—as a foolish girl who soiled her gloves and had to be looked after, however reluctantly, because he worked for her grandfather. Her indignation with him increased as she hurried below to put on a fresh pair of gloves from her suitcase. When she carried the bag up on deck, Ross Granger was there ahead of her, his own large suitcase at his feet. The dock was clearly visible now, with the clustered houses and white steepled church of Westcliff behind. On the small dock townspeople had gathered to watch the boat come in. Her companion looked down at them with interest.

"I see you're to be met," he said. "There's your cousin, Booth Hendricks, looking for you."

"Cousin?" she repeated. "Oh, you mean the one Mr. Pompton said was adopted as a child by Aunt Hortense?"

"Yes—he has kept his own name in spite of adoption. He's the tall fellow down there in the gray derby."

Camilla studied the figure of the man Ross Granger indicated. He was lean and dark, with a thin, melancholy face. Even at this distance she could see that he was handsome. He looked rather like an actor her father had once taken her to see play Hamlet at the Garrick Theater in New York. The knot of his cravat, the loop of gold watch chain across his well-cut vest, the gray derby on his head, all were fashionable to a surprising degree. Booth Hendricks would have looked at home on Fifth Avenue in New York. He seemed out of place in Westcliff. Perhaps, like her, he knew himself as an outsider. She felt sympathy quicken for this cousin by adoption, and she went down the gangplank eagerly to meet him.

CHAPTER 3

BOOTH HENDRICKS came forward to greet her. He had only a careless nod for Ross, but he held out his hand to Camilla and flashed her a quick smile in which a certain astonishment was evident.

"Cousin Camilla!" he said, his dark face glowing with an unexpected warmth. Then he turned coolly to the other man. "So you're back? We thought you might not make it in time. Can we give you a ride out to the house?"

Ross Granger shook his head. "Thanks, no," he said, his tone equally cool. Clearly there was no liking between these two. "I've business in the village first. I'll walk out as usual." He touched his cap casually to Camilla and walked away, to lose himself in the crowd.

Booth stared after him for a moment. "Did Pompton arrange for you to come upriver with Granger?" he asked.

"No," Camilla shook her head. "I met him by chance on the boat. He didn't know Grandfather was ill."

Her cousin seemed to shrug the other man aside. "No matter. The pleasant surprise of your coming is the important thing. Though I may as well warn you that you're going to be something of a shock to the family. We had no preparation before Pompton's wire. My mother says it's history repeating itself. I suppose you know how much you look like your mother?"

The flattery of frank admiration in his eyes was pleasantly soothing after Ross Granger's prickly remarks and critical attitude.

"I'm glad I look like her," she told him warmly.

Booth hailed a rig waiting on the narrow dirt road. The driver flicked a hand to his cap and drew up before them. Booth handed her suitcase up and helped Camilla into the carriage, then climbed in beside her. The driver flapped the reins, and they started off along the main street of the village.

"It's one of our little economies at Thunder Heights to keep no horses." Booth spoke lightly, but there was a sting in his voice. "Westcliff has little choice to offer in the way of hired rigs. I'm afraid you'll find us backward in a good many ways. Hardly like the gay city you've come from."

"I didn't lead a very gay life there," she confessed. "And I'm looking forward to seeing my mother's home. How is Grandfather's health?"

Booth Hendricks shrugged. "My presence at his bedside hasn't been requested. I gather he survives. Amazingly, considering his years. You should be good for him."

"I hope so," Camilla said. She went on a little timidly, longing to put something of her happiness into words. "Two days ago I never dreamed I would be coming here. I've grown up feeling as though I had no real family. But now I can hardly wait to meet my grandfather and my aunts. And to see my mother's home. I want to know everything about her. I want to ask a thousand questions and—"

The man beside her put one gloved hand upon her own, stemming her outburst. "I know how you must feel. But perhaps a word of warning at this point is a good idea. Thunder Heights isn't a particularly happy house. It's a house in which it is better not to ask too many questions. Perhaps that's one reason we are all a little disturbed by your coming. My mother and Aunt Letty won't want old sorrows brought to the surface and made acute again. They've suffered enough. Will you take my advice, Cousin, and move softly? Don't ask too many questions—at least not in the beginning."

She felt a little dashed, but she could only nod agreement. Once more uneasiness fell upon her as the carriage moved on, and she was silent, watching the road they followed.

A bank sloped toward the river on their left, with wooded hills rising above on their right. Ahead the blunt, rocky top of Thunder Mountain thrust into the sky, but the house on its slope was well hidden by the brown forest that grew all about. Spring seemed far away this chilly April day, with leaf buds still close-furled nubs along dry branches.

The road curved inland around the property of Blue Beeches, and Camilla caught a glimpse of its mansard roof among the trees below. They were climbing now, the horse moving at a walk, the harness creaking with the uphill pull. A thick, untrimmed privet hedge came into view, the leafless broom of its twigs interwoven and untamed until it had grown to a monstrous height, shielding the property behind it from the road. Rain had begun to fall again.

"We're passing the house now, though you can't see it," Booth informed her. "The driveway approaches from the southern exposure."

In a few moments their carriage pulled up before an entrance in the hedge to what had been a wide driveway. The driver got down to open a once handsome iron gate, badly in need of fresh black paint. Stone gateposts rose on either side, and on each crouched a mournful stone lion. One lion had lost the tip of its tail, the other both its ears. Just inside the gate was a large coach house, deserted now, with empty stables below.

The driveway was overrun along the sides with encroaching weeds. All about the forest crowded in, darkly bare and forbidding, its branches rattling as rain slanted through them. The approach seemed increasingly dismal, and Camilla felt the last of her eagerness melt bleakly away.

"Good luck that we're nearly there," Booth said. "I've no taste for being soaked in a leaky carriage."

The house was upon them now, looming out of the rainy dusk, huge and crouching and gray. The driver pulled up the horse, and Booth sprang down upon the carriage block and held out his hands to Camilla.

"Welcome home," he said dryly, and gestured toward the house behind him. "You'll find it carpenter's gothic at its most fantastic. Orrin had the money to build with brick, but since his beginnings were in lumber, he wanted to show what could be done with wood."

Camilla left the carriage and waited at the foot of the steps, looking up at the house, while Booth paid the driver and took down her suitcase. The structure stood at right angles to the river, with its back to the north, and a single-story wing had been attached on the land side.

Light shone in upstairs windows and through an arched fan-light above the heavy door of glass and wrought iron. But no one came eagerly to greet her, and as the clopping echo of the horse's hoofs disappeared among the trees, she was aware of a vast silence that seemed to engulf river and house and mountain. Accustomed as she was to city noises, the stillness seemed oppressive and a little eerie. She was glad when Booth led her up the steps to the front door. There he took out an enormous key, smiling at its size as he held it out for her to see.

"Always we have to be picturesque here, rather than comfortable. Grandfather Orrin sent clear to New Orleans for this door and it's heavy enough for two to pull."

A grating of metal shattered the silence, and he pushed the heavy door open so that she could walk into an antehall that was much as Camilla had imagined it. The room was large and square, with a light wood floor set in fine parquetry and an ornate plaster ceiling molded in rosettes. Except for a small rug or two, it was completely bare of furnishings, with a door opening on either side, and a wide arch straight ahead. But it was the room's curious lighting fixtures that Camilla noted with recognition. From the walls on either side, and from either side of the arched doorway ahead, marble hands protruded, each grasping a torch whose flame was a burning candle behind a glass shield.

"I see you're to be given a rousing welcome," Booth said to the silence. "Ah well, come along—I've warned you."

The arch of the doorway ahead was marble, and the smaller enclosure beyond contained the octagon staircase, with its panels of intricately carved teakwood. From a tall window behind the stairs, and from some unseen source of illumination above, light fell upon the steps. As Camilla followed Booth, a girl in a maid's uniform came running down, to bob a curtsy to them when she reached the bottom.

"This is Miss Camilla, Grace," Booth said to her. "Will you show her upstairs to her room, please."

Grace bobbed another curtsy. "If you please, mum," she said, gesturing toward the stairs.

Booth gave the girl Camilla's suitcase. "I'll see you at dinner, Cousin Camilla," he said.

She felt a sudden reluctance to leave his company and go off into the unknown reaches of the house. The lack of any welcome from her aunts had quenched her eagerness completely. Booth, at least, had been friendly. But he did not see her perturbation, and when he turned away to a door opening off the antehall, there was nothing to do but follow Grace.

Stairwell and halls were cold and drafty, adding to her feeling of chill. At the second floor Grace waited for her, and as Camilla climbed the stairs she saw that the light from above came from an oil lamp in a carved cinnabar bowl, hung beneath a wooden canopy from the ceiling of the stairwell. The octagon shaft of the stairs was set in the heart of the house, and two halls rayed out from it on each side at the second and third levels. On the second floor Grace led the way toward the river wing of the house.

"Mr. Judd has given orders you're to have Miss Althea's old room," Grace told her in an oddly furtive whisper. Then, apparently regarding Camilla more as a fellow conspirator than superior, she went on. "Miss Hortense don't like that much, but she don't dare say no, when the old—when Mr. Judd, that is, sets his mind on something. It's a real pretty room, mum. Hasn't been opened for years, so we had to rush to get it ready for you today."

She turned a pink-tinted cloisonné doorknob near the end of the hall and opened the door upon a room alive with firelight, gracious and inviting in the cold, rainy dusk. Grace set the suitcase down and ran across the room to brush a wrinkle from the dull gold bedspread, to flick imaginary dust from a two-tiered rosewood dressing table. Then she nodded toward a water pitcher and basin set on a marble-topped stand.

"The water's still hot, mum. I brought it up myself just before you came. Thought you'd want a good wash, after your trip. Dinner is at seven-thirty. Prompt, mum. Miss Hortense don't like to be kept waiting. She gets nervous." The girl watched her, as if waiting for some response to her sly hints.

Camilla paid no attention, longing for her to go. This was her mother's room and she wanted to know it in every detail. But not while a stranger watched her.

"When am I to see my grandfather?" she asked.

Grace shook her head. "Nobody's told me that, mum. Though I know Mr. Judd has been asking for you. The nurse said so."

The girl gave another uneasy bob of knee and head and went out of the room.

Once she was gone, Camilla could turn slowly and look about the lovely room that once belonged to Althea Judd. The pink marble mantelpiece above the lively fire was carved with a rose leaf design, and a small French clock of gilt and enamel ticked away upon it. The carpet was soft-piled and of a paler gold than the bedspread, the wallpaper light gray, with a gold fleur-de-lis pattern. There was a small gray and gilt French desk with a little chair to match—a desk from which her mother, who had loved parties, must have sent out many an invitation. A pink upholstered chaise longue near a French door invited one to comfortable lounging. Heavy gold brocade draperies, faded and a little shabby, had been drawn across the room's tall windows and French doors. The ceiling was enormously high, promising the cool passage of air on summer days, and a handsome plaster medallion marked the center, from which hung a gay little French chandelier, adrip with crystal.

This was her mother's room. She wanted to feel it, to believe in it, to reach across the years to her mother through it. But the room, though charming, remained remote. It was not yet ready to accept her, to speak to her.

She went to one of the doors and opened it upon a small balcony that fronted the river. It was raining harder now, and though wind swept a spatter of drops in upon her, she stood for a moment trying to make out the river, far below this high level on which the house stood. Rain and the failing light obscured her vision, however, and she closed the door, returning quickly to the warmth of the fire. Tomorrow perhaps it would be clear and she could see the view of the Hudson this house must command.

The water was steaming hot in the pitcher, as Grace had promised, with a towel laid across the top to contain the warmth. Camilla gave herself up to the refreshing comfort of bathing. The pale green cake of soap in the rose leaf dish had a delicate scent, and she wondered at such luxury in this remote place. But then, with wealth, anything could be ordered from New York. Or from Paris, or London, for that matter. What a strange economy to keep no carriage, no horses.

When she had put on a clean shirtwaist and changed to a fresh, though somewhat wrinkled, blue skirt, she lay down on the chaise longue to await the summons of her grandfather.

As she relaxed, savoring the pulsing heat of the fire, she thought of the little she knew about her Aunt Hortense. Hortense was the elder of the three sisters, with Letty the middle one. From her mother, Camilla had received the picture of a woman with an unbridled temper and an enormous vanity. There had been little love lost between older and younger sister. Once, when Camilla had been no more than seven, her mother had said casually that Hortense had suffered from a lifelong unrequited love affair with herself. The words had stayed with her, though they had little meaning then, and she wondered about them now.

A light tap roused her from her musings, and she went quickly to open the door. At a glance she knew that the slight gray figure in the doorway could not be Hortense.

"It's—Aunt Letty, isn't it?" Camilla said.

The woman's face, pale and fine-skinned as eggshell china, seemed to crumple into tiny lines, as if she were about to burst into tears. In her hands she held a small lacquered tray with a teapot and cups upon it. Too moved to speak, she held the tray out wordlessly.

Gently Camilla drew her into the room and closed the door.

CHAPTER 4

Miss Letitia Judd was somewhat less than fifty. She was of medium height, but she managed to seem tiny because of her small bones and general air of frailty. She wore her gray hair bound about her head in a coronet of braids that gave her a certain dignity and presence, even when she was on the verge of tears. Her long-sleeved dress was of a light gray material that had a tendency to float when she moved, and she wore a coral brooch at the high, boned ruching of the neck. She looked immaculately neat in every detail.

As she entered the room, a small gray tabby cat came with her, padding lightly across the carpet with an air of interest in unfamiliar territory.

"This is my friend, Mignonette," Letty said, and smiled tremulously at Camilla. "See—I've brought you some hot peppermint tea. It's just the thing for heartening one after a long trip."

She set the tray upon a marble-topped table near the fire, and not until she reached out to put it down, did Camilla note that her right arm was twisted and crooked. Her full sleeve, tight at the wrist and edged with lace, hid the deformity to some extent, and it was hardly noticeable except in the fact that she could not straighten the arm.

"My little sister Althea's daughter," she murmured, and turned to look at Camilla. While all else about Letty Judd was pale and softly gray, her eyes were a dark brown, deep and surprisingly intense, with lashes as long and dark as Camilla's own. "You are so much like her. Even that black peak of hair on your forehead.

29

And the light way you move. But there, I mustn't welcome you by crying."

She seated herself in the silk-cushioned rocking chair Camilla drew to the fire, her hands clasped in her lap so that the bend of the crooked arm seemed natural. The glow of the fire gave color to her pale, fine skin, but when she held out her left hand to the warming blaze, Camilla saw that her hands were strangely unlike the rest of her. Though small-boned, they were far from fragile. There was a strong, muscular look about them, and the skin was tanned and freckled, as if they had weathered the sun of past years and gone unprotected.

Beneath Letty's tender gaze, the lack of welcome which had been so evident to Camilla in the beginning seemed to lessen in importance. For the first time the fire began to warm away her chill, and the fragrant odor of the tea was tangy and cheering. She sat opposite her aunt while Letty poured a cupful, her crooked arm seeming to hamper her little. The gray tabby padded back across the room and looked up expectantly.

"Not now, dear," Letty said to the cat. "We're only going to stay a minute." She smiled at Camilla, as if apologizing for the bad manners of a child. "Mignonette loves all my herb teas. She joins me by having a saucerful every afternoon." She held out a cup and saucer to Camilla. "There you are—and do flavor it with a bit of clover honey. You'll find it gives you strength and courage."

Camilla spooned a little golden honey into the tea and sipped it gratefully. "How is my grandfather? When will I see him?"

At her words Letty's withheld tears brimmed over, and she drew a lacy bit of handkerchief from her sleeve, leaving a trace of lavender scent in the air about her.

"He is very weak today. Hortense won't let me go near him, for fear I'll upset him." Her dark eyes lifted suddenly to hold Camilla's own with intense pleading.

"What is it, Aunt Letty?" Camilla asked. "If there's anything I can do—"

Letty shook her head. "No, no—nothing. That is, there's nothing you can do now." Her manner became faintly agitated, and her hands clasped and unclasped nervously in her lap. "You must be-

30

lieve that what happened wasn't my fault—you must believe that I didn't intend—"

She was upsetting herself to such an extent that Camilla dropped to a velvet ottoman beside her and took the small, weathered hands into hers, feeling the wiry strength of the fingers. It was natural to adopt a protective role with Aunt Letty. Camilla felt drawn to this frail, somehow proud little woman, and she let the strength of her own youth and returning courage flow into the clasp of her hands. Her aunt looked hopefully into her eyes.

"Perhaps you've come in time. I think Papa is sorry for a good many things. It's wonderful that he has sent for you. You belong here with your family, my dear."

Unexpectedly, tears stung Camilla's eyes. Such words made up a little for the lonely years behind her. Letty saw that she was moved and tried gently to reassure her.

"Booth is delighted with you. He came to tell me how pretty you are and how lucky we are that you've come. Booth is a dear boy. A bit moody perhaps, at times, but brilliant and talented. It will be good for him to have someone young in the house."

She would have gone on, but a peremptory knock sounded at the door and she sat back quickly, withdrawing her hands from Camilla's clasp.

"That's my sister Hortense," she whispered. "It's better not to keep her waiting. She has very little patience."

Camilla went quickly to the door. Next to her grandfather, she sensed that this was the most important meeting of her visit here. More than anyone else it was her difficult Aunt Hortense whom she must please, whom she must win, if she were to become a part of this family. Smiling and eager, she opened the door to the overwhelming presence of the woman who stood there.

Camilla was not sure how she had pictured Hortense in her mind, but certainly her imagination had produced nothing like this tall, handsome, red-haired woman in elaborate dinner dress. She might have been beautiful, had her expression been less petulant and sharp. Certainly her red hair, untarnished by the years, was spectacularly beautiful in its high piled rolls and waves held in place with combs jeweled in jade. Her emerald green dinner gown was perhaps less than the latest fashion, but she wore it like a duchess, as she did the diamonds in her ears. The cut of the gown displayed firm, unwithered flesh and her figure was full and fashionable. Whether her eyes were green or blue or gray, it was difficult to tell, but one had a feeling that there was little their darting gaze missed.

She noted her sister's presence without pleasure, and Letty rose as she came into the room.

"I'll leave you alone," Letty said, and once more Camilla was aware of a certain dignity about her fragile person.

"Thank you for coming, Aunt Letty," Camilla said warmly, and accompanied her to the door. The little cat went with them and darted into the hall. Camilla turned to face Hortense, bracing herself, the eager smile a little stiff on her lips.

Her aunt was moving about the room with an air of interest, as if she had not set foot in it for a long time.

"I hope it has been cleaned satisfactorily," she said. "We had so little warning of your coming. And we don't have the servants we used to have in the old days. There's always trouble getting this spoiled new generation to stay. I never could understand why Papa wanted this room left exactly as it was when Althea was alive. It's a better room than mine—I'd have liked it for myself."

Camilla, still waiting for some greeting, watched her aunt doubtfully, uncertain of how to meet this outburst. Indifferent to her niece's gaze, Hortense paused before the tray with its cup of cooling tea, the color of pale topaz. She sniffed the peppermint odor and wrinkled her nose.

"Don't let my sister dose you with her brews. She uses little sense in such matters and they don't agree with everyone." Then, having apparently satisfied her curiosity about the room, she turned her scrutiny upon Camilla and there was open antipathy in her eyes. "So you are Althea's girl? You'll be a shock to Papa, of course. But it's his own fault for sending for you behind our backs. It has, of course, been a shock to us to learn that you were coming."

Vainly Camilla tried to think of something to say, but any opportunity for amenities of greeting had passed.

"I—I hope you don't mind my coming," she said feebly. "Mr. Pompton—"

"Pompton's an old fool," Hortense said. "Papa did exactly the same thing that time years ago when he took a sudden notion that he was going to die and he had to see your mother at once. It was Althea who died, and he's been hale and hearty all the years since, until now. Let's hope history won't entirely repeat itself."

"About my mother—" Camilla began, seizing the opening.

"The less said about your mother, the better," Hortense told her, making a futile effort to tuck a lock of red hair into the trembling mass of puffs and pompadours. "When she married and left this house, your grandfather gave orders that her name was never to be mentioned to him again. Even after he remanded that order and invited her here, her death upset us all so badly that by mutual agreement we have avoided the subject of Althea King. Of course we speak her name when necessary—but we don't *discuss* her. You understand? The memories are too painful."

Reminding herself that she must please and placate this woman, Camilla suppressed a twinge of indignation. "Yes, of course, Aunt Hortense," she said mildly.

"Good. While you look like your mother, I can only hope that you lack her wild, reckless spirit. Whatever happened to her she brought upon herself. Remember that. Come along now and I'll take you to your grandfather. But don't stay long—his strength is fading."

She swished through the door ahead of Camilla, leaving her niece to trail behind.

She led the way toward the opposite wing of the house, circling the opening of the stairs. Before a door near the corridor's end she paused.

At her knock, a nurse in a blue striped uniform, with a puffy white cap on her head, looked out at them, nodded and led the way into a large, dim bedroom. Here the fire on the hearth had burned to embers and what light there was came from a lamp set on a table near the great, canopied bed. It was a handsome room, Camilla saw as she followed Hortense through the door, with fine mahogany furniture of vast, baronial proportions.

The old man in the bed lay propped against the stack of pillows, his hair and beard grizzled with gray, his eyes, sunken above a great beak of a nose, still vitally alive in his weathered face.

"Your granddaughter Camilla is here, Papa," Hortense told him. "You mustn't talk to her for long, or you'll tire yourself."

"Get out," said the old man in a surprisingly strong voice.

"Now, now," the nurse said roguishly, "we mustn't excite ourselves. Miss Judd and I will step out in the hall and give you ten minutes with the young lady."

"You'll step out in the hall and stay there until I send for you," said Orrin Judd. "Get out, both of you, so I can have a look at the girl."

Hortense moved with a little toss of her head, and the nurse followed her. Camilla approached the bed and stood within the radius of lamplight. At her grandfather's right lay a huge open Bible on a mahogany stand. He reached out to rest one hand upon it, as if he asked for strength. Then he looked up into her face. For a few moments old man and young woman studied each other gravely.

"You're like your mother as I remember her," he said at last, and now there was a quaver of weakness in his voice. "You're my lovely Althea come back to me when I need her most."

"I'm glad I could come, Grandfather," Camilla said gently.

He sighed long and gustily, as if all the breath left to him had gone from his body. His eyes closed, and she watched him anxiously, wondering if she should call the nurse. But in a moment they opened again—the eyes of a fallen eagle who had not surrendered his freedom—and she felt their hunger searching her face.

"I should have got around to seeing Althea's girl before this. I've let so much go these last years. Too much. The house and the family with it. Bring over a chair and sit where I can look at you. I need to talk to you quickly, before it's too late."

The nearest chair was a massive piece, but she dragged it over to the bed and sat down on its velvet seat. He breathed heavily for a while before he spoke again.

"The vultures out there are waiting for me to die. But it doesn't matter if they hover, now that you're here. Between the two of us we'll fool them all, won't we girl? By the look of you, I know you can be trusted. Because you look like *her*—like my Althea. Sometimes I have the feeling that she's still around here—her spirit anyway—lively and gay, just as she used to be. Will you stay here,

34

Camilla, and help me beat the vultures? We must change things all around, you and I."

"I'll stay if you want me to, Grandfather," she said softly.

He turned in the bed and reached to a table on the far side, groping for something upon it. Camilla would have risen to help him, but he gestured her back.

"I've got it. This is the way we looked in the days before Althea ran off and married that—that schoolteacher." He seemed to have forgotten that the schoolteacher was Camilla's father.

She took the framed oblong of cardboard and held it to the light. Orrin Judd sat in a carved chair in the center of the picture, with his daughters about him. The print was yellowed by the years, but still clear. In those days he must have been a giant of a man, rugged and handsome and forceful. The youngest daughter, Althea, stood straight and lovely within the circle of her father's arm, smiling warmly at the camera. On his other side Hortense leaned against him, a hand upon his shoulder, as if she strove to draw his attention back to herself. Letty stood beside Althea, a thin, frail girl with a smile that was somehow sad. Her right arm hung at her side with no evidence of deformity.

"My three girls," Orrin said. "Their mother and I wanted too much for them. We planned so much. But she wasn't here long enough to see them grown and somehow—it all went wrong."

He was silent for a moment, and then sudden anger stirred in his voice.

"I should have forbidden the house to John King! What could *he* do for Althea—who might have had everything?"

Camilla could not let his words about her father pass. "She had everything she wanted most, Grandfather," she told him gently. "If you had really known my father, you might have loved him."

The old man stared at her unblinkingly for a moment, and she could not tell how deeply she might have angered him with her words. Then he said, "I like spirit, girl. At least you stand up to me honestly. You don't talk simpering nonsense."

He took the picture and laid it upon the open pages of the Bible, and now his gaze seemed suddenly a little vague, as if he had lost the focus of his thoughts.

"Perhaps I'd better let you rest now, Grandfather," Camilla murmured.

At once a look of alarm came into his eyes. "No, no! Don't leave me, girl. There's something I had to tell you. Something that happened—"

He had begun to gasp for breath, but when she would have left his side to call the nurse, he reached out and grasped her hand in a grip that was crushingly strong. Between rasping breaths he tried to force out the words he must speak to her.

"Trouble," he gasped. "Trouble in this house. You must watch for it, girl. There's something wrong afoot. When I'm well I'll get to the bottom of it. But for now—" he struggled hoarsely to speak, "watch—Letty," he managed and could say no more.

"You mustn't excite yourself, Grandfather," she whispered. "Rest now and we'll talk again tomorrow. Then you shall tell me whatever you want me to know."

His grip loosened, fell away. "Tired," he whispered weakly. "Althea's home is your home—you must help me save it. Don't let them—"

"Of course, Grandfather," she assured him hurriedly. "I'll stay for as long as you want me, and I'll help you in every way I can."

He seemed to hear her words and gain reassurance from them. Though he said no more, she sensed the rise of loving kinship between herself and this very old man. The blood line was strong and bright between them. They belonged to each other. She knew he read her look aright and was comforted, and she was assured that they would learn to know and value each other. But now he lay spent, and she went quietly away.

In the hall outside the nurse sat on a carved chest, resting her feet and dozing. Hortense had disappeared.

"You'd better go to him now," Camilla said.

The woman started up and hurried into the room, closing the door behind her.

Camilla followed the empty hall back to her room and sat quietly before the fire, feeling both torn and heartened. She had crossed the years so swiftly to stand at her grandfather's side, and in those few moments of interchange they had given each other their love and trust. Strange that it should be as simple as that. Yet it was a searing thing, too, because of all that troubled him, because of the regrets and sorrows that crowded upon him out of the past. She would do as she had promised. She would stay on in this house as long as he needed her. The antipathy she had seen in the eyes of Hortense Judd troubled her, and she had a sense of failure there. But the most important thing was to help this despairing old man who was her grandfather.

What he had meant in trying to warn her of some sort of trouble, she did not know. It was clear that he was filled with distrust of everyone under this roof, though such a feeling might well be no more than the product of his weakness. She must leap to no conclusions until she had talked to him further, until she knew the family better.

The French clock on the mantel marked the time as nearly seven thirty. She rose to look at herself in the dressing table mirror and smoothed back her dark hair so that the peak came into clear evidence on her forehead. Once her mother's face had been reflected in the depths of this very mirror, and it would be easy to imagine her there again, smiling out of the shadows over her daughter's shoulder. Perhaps there was a fulfilling of destiny in the coming of Camilla King to the house where her mother had grown up, and whose halls must still remember the echo of her footsteps, the sound of her voice.

A thought came to her, and she went to her suitcase and took from it a green velvet jewel case. She had nothing in which to dress for dinner, as Hortense chose to dress, but at least she might wear a bracelet of her mother's. Althea had kept only a few favorite pieces of the jewelry Orrin had given her, and now her daughter had them for her own.

The bangle was made up of gold medallions alternating with carved peach stones. Camilla fastened it about her wrist, feeling that it dressed her up for the occasion and that, wearing it, she would take something of her mother with her downstairs. There was a yearning in her to start anew with this family to which she now belonged. She wanted to free herself of her own early uneasiness and forget the unhappy warnings of an old man who was sick. This time she knew better what to expect, so she would not be surprised, or taken aback. She must show her aunts, her Cousin

Booth, how ready she was to like them, how eager for their liking in return.

With something of her first feeling of hope recovered she opened her door just as a deep-voiced Chinese gong sounded from the depths of the house. No one appeared, so perhaps the others were already downstairs. She went down the octagon staircase alone. Not knowing where the dining room lay, she opened a door toward the land side of the house and found that she had guessed right.

The others were not there and Camilla hesitated, looking around the long, wide room. Dark wainscoting ran halfway up the walls and above it pictured wallpaper presented a country scene in raspberry against cream, its busy pattern repeated to a demanding degree. The darker red carpet was figured in a design of yellow roses, faded now, and worn threadbare about the long mahogany table. The sideboard and china closet were of vast proportions to fit the size of the room. The dining table had been set with linen and Spode china, with candles alight in the branched silver candelabra at each end.

Booth Hendricks came in first, wearing informal dinner dress. The lapels of his jacket were of satin, his shirt front stiff, with pearl buttons studding it. At sight of Camilla his eyes brightened.

"What a pleasure to see someone young and pretty in this house. Are you rested from your trip, Cousin?"

"I wasn't tired, really," she told him. "I've been too excited to be tired. And now that I've seen Grandfather, I'm not so worried as I was. I didn't know how he would receive me."

"And how did he receive you?" Booth asked dryly.

"With affection," she said, and explained no further.

Letty came in, still wearing the floating gray dress that became her so well, and her eyes turned to Camilla questioningly. Camilla smiled and nodded in reassurance. When Hortense entered the room, Camilla gave her the same warm smile, but her aunt paid little heed to her. All her attention was for Booth. She took his arm and let him lead her to her place at one end of the long table.

"Have you had a good day, dear?" she asked him. "Have you been able to work?"

He seated her with a gallant flourish in which there was a hint of mockery. "What do you mean by a good day, Mother? Can any of us remember such a thing in this house?"

Hortense made the small *moue* of a flirtatious girl. "At least we've been rid of Mr. Granger's dour company for a few days."

Camilla had hardly given Ross Granger a thought since she had entered the house, but now she wondered about his place in this group.

Booth had come to seat Camilla at Hortense's left, while Letty slipped quietly into her own place across the table.

"Granger is back, you know," Booth told his mother. "He came up on the same boat with Cousin Camilla. So now I suppose there'll be the devil to pay." He smiled wryly and shrugged as he sat down at Hortense's right.

Hortense glanced quickly at Camilla. But if she meant to ask a question, she changed her mind. "In any event, since the gong has rung and he's not here, we shan't wait for him."

Tonight, in the candlelight, her hair seemed a softer red, with tints of gold brightening it. But no mellowness of light could change the unhappy drooping of her mouth, or change the hard restlessness in her eyes.

Grace, young and inexpert, brought in a silver soup tureen and placed it before Hortense. Then she scuttled back to the kitchen as though she could hardly wait to escape.

"Grace is new," Hortense informed Camilla. An emerald gleamed on her hand as she began serving soup with a silver ladle. "Our maids are always new. The village girls these days have notions above themselves, and they don't last long with me. One would expect them to be grateful for an opportunity to work for a family of our distinction. But only Toby and Matilda have stayed with us from the old days, and they are both getting old."

The silver, Camilla noted, was monogrammed with an ornate "J," and monograms had been embroidered on each linen napkin. The entire service, indeed the very room, spoke of great days of luxury long past, and the gradual decay of fine possessions. She felt a little saddened by the deterioration that she saw everywhere in the house. How shining and rich everything must have been in the heyday of the past—and could be again, if only someone cared.

39

It was not lack of wealth, but a disintegration of spirit that lay behind the neglect.

"Our mother always preferred dinner at night, instead of at noon," Hortense went on, picking up her soup spoon. "And she liked to dress for dinner, so I try to continue the custom. Such things are proper for a family in our position. Of course, since you have only a suitcase, Camilla, I don't expect you to comply while you're here."

Her aunt's delusion that the Judds were superior in position and worth to everyone else seemed rather pitiful under the circumstances, but Camilla merely thanked her for her consideration and did not mention that her trunk would be arriving soon. It seemed unlikely that Aunt Hortense would be pleased by such news.

The cream of potato soup was good, and she found that she had a healthy appetite. But as she ate she noted that Letty was watching the door and that she only toyed with her spoon.

"How long may we expect to enjoy your company, Cousin Camilla?" Booth asked, and again she sensed the light touch of mockery in his words. Perhaps directed toward those about him, or perhaps himself? She could not tell.

"That depends on Grandfather," Camilla said. "I promised that I would stay as long as he wanted me here."

Letty gasped softly, and Camilla saw that she was staring at the dining room door. Ross Granger stood in the doorway, his expression unsmiling, an angry light in his gray eyes. Hortense and Booth exchanged a quick, understanding glance.

"I see you're back—and late for dinner," Hortense said plaintively. "You know how Papa abhors any lack of punctuality."

Ross did not answer her. His bright chestnut hair shone in the candlelight as he took his place at the table beside Letty, and he thrust a lock of it back with an impatient gesture. Camilla waited for some greeting from him, some sign of recognition, but he gave her none. He seemed lost in a dark anger that set him apart from the others at the table. When Hortense filled his soup plate and passed it to him, he picked up his spoon and began to eat without paying attention to the others.

Letty coughed in gentle embarrassment, with her handkerchief to her lips, and turned to Camilla, seeking to break the uncomfortable silence.

"I've noticed your bracelet, my dear," she said. "How well I remember it."

Camilla held up her wrist, fingering the peach stone medallions. "It was my mother's. I'm very fond of it."

Hortense stared at the bracelet. "I don't know why Althea chose anything so valueless to take with her. She left behind a diamond bracelet that might have kept you all in food and shelter for a long while."

"We were never in want, Aunt Hortense," Camilla said quietly.

"How have you been keeping yourself since your father's death?" Hortense asked.

"I've been working as a governess for the last four years," Camilla told her. "There are always positions of that sort in New York."

"Do you enjoy the work?" Letty asked with interest.

"How could she?" Hortense broke in at once. "A governess is hardly more than a genteel domestic servant waiting on other people's children."

Camilla had come to the table still hoping to win Hortense, to placate her, and, if possible, reach some sort of friendly footing with the family. But the scornful words made her stiffen. Beside her, Booth watched with an amused interest that irked her further. Ross merely stared at his plate, as if he cared nothing about what went on around him.

"That isn't quite true, Aunt Hortense," Camilla said, her tone carefully restrained. "The role of a governess is an important one in any household. If the parents realize it, she can do a great deal for their children. I've always regarded the work as interesting and worthwhile."

It had given her independence too, she realized, enabling her to remain in control of her own life. That was something she would not like to lose.

Ross had been listening after all, and now he surprised her. "Good for you, Miss King!" he said. "Don't let them patronize you. Stand up for yourself."

Camilla said nothing. She was not altogether sure she wanted him on her side if it meant further alienation from the family.

"At least it's a good thing you have some sort of work to return to," Hortense said. "I suppose it's respectable enough work for an impoverished gentlewoman—which seems to be the condition brought upon you by your parents."

Booth flashed his mother a quick, ironic smile. "Oh, come now! Surely Grandfather Orrin will leave her a bit of a legacy? Perhaps she has that small hope to look forward to." He nodded kindly at Camilla. "There is still time for him to include you in his will."

Ross turned grimly to Hortense. "Yes, there's always time to change a will. I suppose that's why you wanted me out of the way for the last few days? So you could keep me from him?"

Hortense turned a furious red, but Booth only smiled. "Do you think, Granger, that we don't know how you've been trying to influence Grandfather lately? Why wouldn't we prefer your absence to your presence when we know how much you disturb him?"

For an instant Camilla thought Ross might rise angrily and leave the table, but he controlled himself and stayed in his place.

Grace cleared away the soup plates and returned with the meat course, while Letty chatted nervously about how much good today's rain had done her garden. No one paid much attention to her, and no one else spoke, but Camilla was aware of a mounting tension beneath the surface affecting everyone at the table. Hortense and Ross had behaved inexcusably, she felt. And Letty was too silent. Only Booth had tried to consider her own comfort and welfare. In any case, she shrank from this discussion of wills while Grandfather might lie dying. She remembered uneasily his warning about "vultures."

When Grace left the room again and Hortense was serving the roast beef, Ross was the first to speak.

"I'd like to know just why you had me sent off on this wild goose chase to New York," he said. "You wanted more than to get me away. What have you been up to in my absence?"

"You are insufferable!" Hortense cried.

Letty put her hands to her temples, rocking her head back and forth as if it hurt her. "Oh, please, please! Let's have peace during dinnertime at least. What is Camilla going to think of us with such talk as this?"

"One might wonder," her sister said tartly, "what she will think of *you*. I am innocent enough."

Letty looked as if she might burst into tears, and Booth turned to her gently and began to speak of the gardens of Thunder Heights in a quiet, relaxed manner. Hortense watched her son, and Ross listened without comment, his eyes upon Camilla.

It was a relief when the floating island was served for dessert and the meal finally ended. By that time, Camilla felt that her nerves were strung on fine wires unbearably tight. The antagonism in the room was almost tangible, and though she was bewildered by it, she was drawn to a high tension herself.

When they rose from the table, she would have liked to excuse herself and go upstairs to the seclusion of her mother's room, but Booth walked beside her, guiding her across the hall to the parlor, and there was no easy way to escape.

CHAPTER 5

Apparently it was the custom for the family to have coffee in the parlor after dinner. Several lamps had been lighted in the great room that ran along the river side of the house, and a wood fire crackled in the grate. The room was crowded with an overabundance of treasures from the Orient. Much of the furniture was of carved black ebony, with cushions of black satin embroidered in gold thread. There were Chinese screens and rich Oriental rugs, and on every table and shelf and whatnot stand were objects of jade or coral or brass, of Satsuma and cloisonné. The ceiling was high and the room's huge windows were oversized, requiring vast quantities of material for the acres of curtains and draperies.

"Cheerful little museum, isn't it?" Booth said to Camilla. "Can you imagine what this stuff might bring at an auction?"

Again he puzzled her. She had a feeling that his seemingly cynical manner, the callous gloss he wore, hid some depth he was not willing to display to the casual observer. He could be lightly mocking, with a certain insouciant charm, yet she sensed a passion in him that might be his real core. What drove this man, what motivated him, she could not tell, but he held her interest.

Young Grace skated in, sliding once or twice on the rugs, and managed to place the coffee service safely on a teakwood table by the fire, before darting away with the air of an escaping doe. Flames danced in miniature across the gleaming silver surface of the coffee pot, as the family drew about in stiff, uncomfortable chairs. Only Ross had absented himself, not joining the family. Mignonette,

44

the cat, awaited them by the fire, moving over just enough to be within reach of Letty's stroking toe.

"The evening ritual," Booth said as he brought Camilla her cup and offered cream and sugar. "For an hour or so every night we sit here enjoying one another's brilliant company and sipping coffee in cups that are exquisite, but too small. Fortunately there are more comfortable rooms in the house where we can withdraw later. So endure, Cousin Camilla, the time will pass."

Hortense laughed uncomfortably, as if she were not always sure how to take this man who was her adopted son. "Booth loves to tease," she said. "You mustn't believe his little jokes. Papa always thought it a good idea to draw the family together here after dinner. He liked this hour when we were girls and we've always kept it up."

Camilla thought of the old man lying helpless upstairs and remembered his sad question, "Where did I go wrong?"

Hortense ran on, as if silence was something never to be suffered for too long. Waving a beringed hand, she pointed out various objects around the room, explaining their significance and relating incidents connected with their purchase when she had gone abroad with her mother and father as a child.

"Did you go with them too on these trips, Aunt Letty?" Camilla asked, when Hortense paused for breath.

About Letty there was still a vague air of listening. Occasionally she cast a furtive glance toward the doorway, as though she did not want to be caught in her watching. She jumped a little when Camilla spoke to her, and stirred Mignonette with her toe. The little cat moved closer to Letty's chair and began a monotone of purring.

"I went to England and Scotland once after I was grown up," Letty said and reached for a basket of crocheting at her side, nervously searching it for her crochet hook. "But I was never strong enough for very much traveling."

"I was always the one with endurance," Hortense said in satisfaction, and went on to describe hardships met abroad that Letty could never have borne.

As they talked, Camilla glanced at Booth, who had taken a chair well back in the shadows. He sat with his long, elegant legs crossed and one slender hand upon the chair arm. Though his face was lost

45

in obscurity, she knew that he too listened to something that was not taking place in this room. When a footstep sounded on the stairs, he leaned forward, his eyes upon the door, and Aunt Letty jumped uneasily, startling the cat.

Ross Granger came into the room with a strong, vigorous step, and once more anger was bright in his eyes as he viewed the group about the fire with clear hostility.

"Mr. Judd was too weak to talk to me," he said. "The nurse tried to shut me out. She told me she had been given orders to keep me out of the room. By whom, may I ask?"

Hortense answered quickly. "Dr. Wheeler said Papa was not to be disturbed or worried in any way. We all know that you irritate him lately. It was I who said you were not to see him until he feels better."

"An order you knew I would disregard. I'm not the one who disturbs him—"

Booth stood up with his usual easy grace and leaned an arm along the mantel, his features somberly handsome in the flickering light.

"Look here, Granger, we know you detest us, and we've stood a good many of your insinuations because of your former usefulness to Grandfather Orrin. But you must admit that you upset him badly the last time you saw him. From what the nurse has told us, we gather that it's you who wants his will changed for some purpose of your own."

Camilla could only admire the control Booth displayed as he spoke so calmly to Ross. The latter was clearly far closer to losing his temper.

Letty's crochet hook moved in and out of her work with quick silver flashes, and she had stopped watching the door. When she spoke in a small breathless voice, the others looked at her in surprise, as if they had forgotten her presence.

"How can you blame Ross for trying to persuade Papa to change his will? Haven't we all been concerned about the same thing?" she asked.

There was an instant's dismayed silence, and then Ross pounced on her words. "So you *did* want me out of the way, just as I thought. And what was this change to be?"

Hortense said, "It's none of your business. It doesn't concern you,

Ross. Indeed, none of the affairs of this family now concern you."

"They concern me," Letty said, and again everyone stared at her. "I'm in perfect agreement with my sister," she hurried on. "What would I do with half my father's fortune, even if it were left to me, as the will reads now? My needs are modest, Ross. I should hate the responsibility of all that money."

"So you'd let your sister sign your birthright away?" Ross said impatiently. "At least I can prevent *that* move—when he's well enough to listen to me. Even if he won't follow a plan I think wiser."

"Even if he won't cut you in as repayment for your years of—ah —faithful service?" Booth asked quietly.

Listening, Camilla shrank again from the scene before her, with its talk of wills while Orrin Judd lay upstairs desperately ill. It seemed callous to a degree that she could not understand. Even Ross, who was an outsider, had been associated with Grandfather Orrin for years and must surely have some liking for the old man. It seemed heartless of all of them to be quarreling over Orrin Judd's wealth. While he still lived, all their thoughts should be for his health and well-being.

Once more Ross managed a semblance of control and addressed himself to Hortense. "I'd like to know exactly what brought on this heart attack. When I left for New York, Mr. Judd was no better or worse than he had been for months. What happened after I left for New York?"

The room was so still that a bit of charred wood falling in the grate made an explosive sound and Mignonette's purr was like a kettle boiling. Booth shrugged and sat down, dropping again into the shadows. Letty's crochet needle paused in mid-air. Hortense clasped her fingers tightly together in her lap. Tension crackled through the room.

"Well?" Ross said. "I gather that something unpleasant did happen. I'd like to know what it was."

Hortense was the first to find her voice. "Why don't you ask Letty? Booth was in the village at the time, and I was in the cellar. Letty was with him. I'm sure we'd all like to know a little more than she has told us about what really happened."

Letty's work dropped into the basket and she covered her face with her hands. "It's true, Ross—I was there. But I didn't intend—I never meant—"

"What was it you said to him, dear?" Hortense pressed her. "Or is it something that you did?"

Letty turned her head a little wildly from side to side. "No—you mustn't ask me. I can't talk about it. You must believe that I meant well."

Ross crossed the room and put a hand forcefully on her shoulder. "Try to tell us, Miss Letty. It may be important for us to know."

But Letty had begun to weep into her lavender-scented handkerchief, and it was Booth who came to her aid.

"Let her alone, Granger. Can't you see how upset she is over her father's illness? What does it matter whether we know exactly what happened? There's no undoing it. And you can't believe Letty meant him any harm. My mother likes to talk. Come along, Aunt Letty—I'll take you up to your room."

Camilla saw affection in the look Letty turned upon her sister's adopted son. His arm about her shoulders supported her, and his every movement was kind as he led her out of the room.

Ross watched them go and then glanced idly at Camilla. "An interesting family you've acquired, isn't it?" he said and went out of the room, leaving Hortense and Camilla there by the fire.

At once Hortense began to rub her brow with her fingers. "Headache," she murmured. "You had no business coming here, of course, and now that you're here . . . Most regrettable, I'm sure. If you'll excuse me?" Her words sounded befuddled, as though her thoughts followed a separate road from her tongue.

When she had left the parlor, only Camilla and Mignonette remained. The small gray tabby regarded her distantly and then stretched and yawned mightily, before settling down for another nap while the fire lasted. Camilla sat on for a little while before the orange-red embers, thinking about the tense, uncomfortable scene she had just witnessed, and about the undercurrents of conflict and antagonism that played back and forth between the walls of Thunder Heights. Why had Grandfather said to watch Letty, and what had Letty done that had helped to bring on his illness?

Suddenly she felt overcome by weariness. The long day with its emotional upheavals had left her more drained than she realized.

She was eager for her mother's room with its wide, inviting bed and air of peace long undisturbed.

Before she went to her room she paused at her grandfather's door, to see if she might bid him good night, but the nurse said he was sleeping quietly and mustn't be disturbed. She hurried down the long hall to her room, only to find the hearth cold, its comforting warmth dispelled, so that she had to undress shivering, and get quickly into bed.

She fully expected to lie awake for a long while, thinking over the events of the day, wondering about this strange household that lived together in uneasy aversion. But the bed was warm and soft with comforters and her body was utterly weary. She drowsed into sleep before disturbing thoughts could awaken her.

It was the sound of music that roused her sometime in the hours after midnight. Camilla sat up in bed, bundling a comforter around her as she listened. She could not be sure of the direction from which the mournful sound came, but it seemed to drift downward from the floor above. Someone was playing a harp, plucking the strings so that plaintive trills and chords stole through the house like a voice crying. Listening in astonishment, she could make out the strains of "Annie Laurie." Orrin Judd's mother had come from Scotland, Camilla knew, for Althea had always been proud of the Scottish strain in their blood. But how strange to play this Scottish air so late at night.

On Camilla's floor a door opened and closed, and after a little while there was silence. But the music, while it lasted, had made as lonely a sound as Camilla had ever heard. Even after the harp was still, she felt the echo of it along her very nerves, pleading, bewailing. But for what, or for why, she could not tell.

Troubled now, she could not fall asleep again, and after a time she got up and went to the heavy draperies pulled across a French door and drew them back so that she could look out into the darkness. It had stopped raining, but the night was inky black and there were no stars. With the lower mists blown away, she was surprised to see lights far in the distance and wondered about them for a moment, before she realized that they were lights on the opposite bank. That black band between was the river. The far shore seemed another world, with little connection or communication with this one. This, too, was an aspect of the Hudson. It was barrier as well as highway.

The country silence, which had seemed so surprising and all-enveloping to her on her arrival, was not, she discovered, silence at all. She heard the rumbling of a train on the opposite shore, the whistle of a boat on the river, the rustling of trees all about the house. And somewhere not far away, the rushing sound of a brook tumbling down the mountain. Spring peepers were chirping out there in the darkness, keeping up an all-night chorus of their own.

There were sounds, too, within the house. As she drew back from the balcony door, listening now to the house, the very halls seemed to stir and whisper. Someone went past her door and there was the sound of hurrying footsteps on the stairs. Had her grandfather taken a turn for the worse? Camilla wondered.

She drew on a warm flannel wrapper over her long-sleeved white nightgown. When she opened her door, she heard the sound of someone weeping softly. Her own wing of the house was empty, but the lamp still burned above the stairwell and a candle flickered in a holder on the hall table beyond the stairs. It was from that direction the sound of weeping came. Concerned, Camilla followed the cold hall to its far end.

There on the carved chest outside Orrin's door sat the slight figure of Letty Judd, crying bitterly, with her hands over her face. Her sobs had a choked sound, as if they were wrung from her against her will. When Camilla touched her shoulder gently, she looked up with tears streaming down her face.

"Is Grandfather worse?" Camilla asked. "Is there anything I can do, Aunt Letty?"

Letty was still fully dressed, with her long braids bound as neatly about her head as they had been earlier in the day. Clearly she had not gone to bed, and her face looked weary and ravaged. She shook her head at Camilla and glanced sorrowfully toward her father's door.

"He's dying," she said, "and they won't let me in."

Even as she spoke, Hortense came to the door. She too was fully dressed as she had been for dinner. Her face was twisted in a grimace that might, or might not, be that of grief.

"It's over," she said. "Papa is gone."

Camilla heard the words in blank dismay. She had not expected her grandfather to be gone so quickly—when she had only just found him.

A rising sob choked in Letty's throat. She stood up to face her sister in despair.

"You had no right to shut me out. I should have been with him when he died. It's cruel that you should have kept me away from him in his last moments."

Hortense made a futile effort to thrust back her sliding pompadour. "The sight of you upset him. He didn't want to see you. Besides, he died in his sleep quite peacefully. He saw no one when the last breath went out of him."

"I knew it would come tonight," Letty said dully. "I knew."

"I must call Booth," Hortense murmured. She seemed to waver on her feet, and Camilla moved to her side and took her arm to steady her. Hortense glanced at her in vague surprise, and then seemed to remember who she was. "Your coming disturbed him too much," she said, as if seeking a new scapegoat.

Across the hall a door opened, and Booth came out of his room. He wore a handsome dressing gown of maroon brocade, and he had paused long enough to smooth back his thick dark hair.

"What's happened?" he asked. "Is he worse?"

Hortense's lips quivered and she had difficulty controlling her voice, but again Camilla was not sure that her emotion was one of grief.

"Your—your grandfather is dead, Booth dear," she said. "I was just telling Camilla that I fear her coming—"

"Don't blame Camilla," Booth said. "I'll go downstairs and send Toby for the doctor. Or perhaps I'd better see Grandfather first myself."

With an effort, Hortense seemed to pull herself together. "Please —not now," she said. "Go send Toby for Dr. Wheeler, dear."

For an instant Camilla thought Booth might walk past his mother into the room, but instead he turned and strode toward the stairs. Hortense seemed to sigh in visible relief, and Camilla wondered why.

"Shouldn't someone call Mr. Granger?" she asked.

Hortense paid no attention to her question. "Go to bed." She spoke to Letty, but her look included Camilla. "There's nothing you can do. Miss Morris and I will stay with Papa. You'll do no good here in the cold, Letty. You're likely to be ill tomorrow."

Letty rose stiffly, like a wooden doll. "I want to see him," she told her sister. "Come with me, Camilla."

Reluctantly, Hortense let them by. Within the room the nurse was busying herself about the bed, but she drew down the sheet so that Letty and Camilla could stand beside Orrin Judd and see his face as it had been in the moment of death. To Camilla's eyes he looked younger now and somehow happier—this great fallen eagle of a man.

Letty bent to kiss his cheek, and as she reached out her hand, Camilla again saw the restriction her crooked arm placed upon such a gesture.

"Good-by, Papa," Letty whispered, and went sadly out of the room.

Camilla stood in silence, studying the proud, strong face, as if she might find there the answers to many questions. Only a little while ago he had lived and spoken to her. He had wanted something of her and had said they would talk again, when he was less tired. But now he was beyond reach, and the things he had wanted to say to her, the warning he had tried to make, would never be spoken. A longing seized her to repeat the promise she had made yesterday to help him achieve whatever it was he had wanted. If only she might reassure him again, let him know she was ready to do his bidding. But she had no knowledge of what that bidding was, and without him to instruct her, to stand beside her, there was nothing she could do.

"Good night, Grandfather. Sleep well," she told him softly and turned away from the bed.

An unexpected movement across the room caught her eye, and Ross Granger stepped out of the far shadows. Camilla stared at him in surprise.

"How long have you been here?" she whispered.

He took her arm and led her out of the room. Hortense brushed past them with an indignant glance, returning to her father's side.

"I've been here all night," Ross said flatly.

She knew now why Hortense had not wanted Booth to go into

the room. Ross must have been there against her will, and perhaps she had feared a clash if Booth had discovered him there.

"But—why?" Camilla persisted.

"It was the least I could do for him," Ross said. "Though I think he never knew I was there. Get yourself some sleep now. The watch is over."

Her throat felt choked with grief, and she could not speak. She nodded and slipped away from him down the hall.

In her room the little clock on the mantel told her, surprisingly, that it was almost five o'clock. Somehow she had thought it was nearer midnight. It seemed all the more strange that someone should have played a harp in this house at such an hour. Had the musician been Aunt Letty? Why had neither she nor Hortense undressed or gone to bed, all this long night through? And why had Ross Granger insisted upon remaining in the same room, even though Orrin Judd was unconscious?

But it was not of these things she wanted to think. Moving automatically, she put paper and wood in the grate, lighted the kindling and watched the newborn flames lick upward, eager and greedy, until the larger sticks crackled with blue and orange light. Then she dropped down upon the hearthrug, warming herself and thinking.

How strange that her grandfather's death should seem so great a blow, when she scarcely knew him. The sense of loss was an aching within her, to which she could not bring the relief of tears. If only she had dreamed that he would welcome her, how gladly she would have come to Thunder Heights long before this. She would not have let her father's prejudice hold her back. Now it was too late, and she could never do for him the things he had wanted to ask of her, because she would never know what they were.

Carefully she went over his words in her mind. He had asked her to stand with him against the "vultures" who were waiting for him to die. He had warned her against them all. He had said she must help him to save his house that Althea had loved. He had spoken of Letty. But in spite of her promise, there were no practical steps she could take.

She held cold hands to the fire, shivering. Now all her own plans must change again. She would stay for her grandfather's funeral and then take quick leave of his family. In spite of Aunt Letty, whom she was ready to love, she could not stay on under the same roof with Hortense. Her aunt did not want her here and would not invite her to stay.

Dawn was brightening the windows when at length she left the fire and went to the French door, opening it once more on the little balcony. The early morning air was clean and fresh with the wet scent of earth and new-growing things. The Hudson had turned from black to pale silver, and the sky above the hills on the far bank was streaked with delicate rose. She stood at the balcony rail, watching the sunrise fling streamers of rose and aquamarine across the sky and reflect its brilliance in the river.

At this quiet moment of dawn she sensed again the changing moods of the Hudson. How still its waters seemed now, as if they scarcely moved. Had her mother stood thus at this very window in some long ago dawn, watching the river she loved come to life with a new day? As Camilla watched, a sailboat moved serenely into view, finding some hint of breeze to puff its sails so that it drifted like a ghost along the smooth water and out of sight beyond the bend. Before the coming of steam those white birds had thronged the river. Her mother had told her of them often and of sailing in them herself. A gull swooped down toward a spit of land that thrust itself into the water just below Thunder Heights, and she heard its shrill cry.

It was as if the river called to her in a voice made up of all these things, setting a spell upon her heart. Yet now she must turn her back on it and go away forever, and she felt suddenly regretful of leaving. She could almost hear her grandfather's voice saying, "Don't run away, girl. Stay and fight."

But what battle was she to fight? And why? Now that he was gone, she would never know.

CHAPTER 6

AFTER an early breakfast that morning, Camilla put on a jacket and went through a door that opened onto the wide veranda. There were steps on the river side, and she walked down them and across wet grass. Once, here on this high ledge, there must have been a pleasant lawn between the tall elms growing on either side. Directly across the river a white-steepled little town hugged a narrow valley, and several small craft were to be seen on the water before it.

What a view there must be from the top of Thunder Mountain. She wondered if there was a way that wound to the crest. But that was no walk for this morning. She turned from house and mountain and followed a narrow brown path that wound down from the heights, crossed railroad tracks that were hidden from the house, and wandered beneath the bare trees that edged the river.

The thought of her mother had been with her often since she had come here yesterday. But now a sense of her father's presence returned as well. He had lived in Westcliff for a time. He had met Althea while he worked there as a teacher, though his real home was in New York. Where and how had they met? Camilla wondered. Had they walked together along this very path during their secret courtship, with the river flowing calmly beside them as it did now?

By now Thunder Heights was hidden by the trees, and as she walked on, the clamor of bird song rose to full voice on all sides. She came suddenly upon the noisy, tumbling brook she had heard in the night, its waters freshened by spring rains as it rushed toward the river. A little wooden bridge offered a crossing, and she went on along the path.

She followed the curving way only a little further when she came suddenly upon a man sitting on an outcropping of rock above the path. It was Ross Granger, and he was dressed for the outdoors in a corduroy jacket and trousers, his chestnut head bare to the sun.

He had not seen her, and his face in unguarded repose wore a sadness that betrayed his troubled thoughts. Beneath his eyes smudged shadows told of his long night's vigil. For an instant she did not know whether to go or stay, hesitating to break in upon this solitary moment. Then he looked about and saw her.

"You're out early," he said, standing up on the rock.

"I couldn't sleep."

"Nor I," he said.

"Why did you stay all night in my grandfather's room?" she asked him again, feeling that there were matters she must understand before she went away. Otherwise she would ponder them endlessly the rest of her life.

"I didn't want to see him bullied about a new will," he said. "I trust none of them."

"And they don't seem to trust you," she said.

His smile was wry. "Hortense took care of that. She spent the night in the room too, with Letty posted as a watchdog outside, except when she went off to play her harp. But I doubt that he was aware of us at any time."

"It seems to me," Camilla told him frankly, "that it was dreadfully coldblooded for you all to be thinking about wills while Grandfather lay dying."

Ross's expression did not change. "A man is dead for a very long time. The stipulations he leaves behind may affect other lives for generations. This was not a moment to be squeamish about such matters."

A spotted coach dog, young, awkward and big, came bounding suddenly out of the woods and ran to Ross with an air of joyful exuberance. Ross accepted his clumsy greeting, pulling his ears affectionately.

"Champion is from Blue Beeches," he explained. "He's Nora Redfern's dog. Down, fellow, I prefer to wash my own face."

The dog went gamboling off on an exploratory expedition along the edge of the woods, and Ross removed his jacket and spread it on the rock beside him.

"Come sit down a moment," he said. "I want to talk to you."

He offered a hand to pull her up the face of the boulder, and she seated herself on his jacket.

"How much do you know about your grandfather?" he asked when she was comfortable.

"Know about him?" She was not sure what he meant. "Perhaps not a great deal. My father detested everything about Thunder Heights. He never wanted to talk about it. But in spite of the way Grandfather treated my mother, I'm sure she never stopped loving him."

Camilla smiled, remembering, and told him about the building her mother had once taken her to see in New York.

Ross listened gravely until she was through. "Orrin Judd has done great things, big things. It's hard to believe that he had so little in the beginning. He was born in Westcliff, you know. His father was a country doctor. Orrin worked in lumber camps hereabout, but he had a genius for managing men and running large affairs, and he had vision. So before many years were up he owned a lumber business of his own. From that it was only a step into the building trade. Though that's a feeble term for what he wanted to do. He had no training himself as an engineer or an architect, but he learned from the men who worked for him and he was better than any of us. Perhaps he was more an empire builder than a builder of bridges and buildings and roads. He could see the future better than most men. He might have been one of the giants if he hadn't lost heart."

Camilla listened eagerly. These were things she had understood little of as a child, and when she was grown her father never talked about them.

Ross rubbed a hand wearily across his face and went on. "The time is nearly over for giants, I think. Their kingdoms grow too big and they control too many lives. America never suffers kings for long. But even when your grandfather withdrew to Thunder Heights, the world came to him. Not the social world—there's been little of that he cared for in the years I've known him. I mean

57

the business world. He wouldn't go to New York after your mother died, but he made it come to him—often through me."

"I've wondered about your place here," Camilla said.

"Sometimes I've wondered myself. My father was an engineer and his good friend, though many years younger. After he died, Orrin Judd kept an eye on me, sent me to engineering school, since that was what I wanted most. When I graduated, he put me to work on some of his projects. He came to trust me and began to want me near him. Before I knew what had happened I was doing a sort of liaison job for him, instead of following the work I wanted to do. I suppose I've helped him keep the threads in his hands, though I never planned on playing aide-de-camp to a general."

"You've given up years of your life for this?" Camilla said wonderingly.

"I don't count them as lost. He gave me a chance to learn and there were things he intended me to do later. When he felt I was ready. Besides, I loved him."

Off in the brush they could hear the dog chasing some small wild thing. The sound of rushing water, the twitter of birds was all about them. But the two on the boulder were silent.

"Thank you for telling me these things," she said. "I can see how much you've meant to my grandfather. What was the change you wanted to see him make in his will?"

For a few moments he did not speak, but sat watching as the dog bounded onto the path again, following some new and exciting scent. Then he stood up abruptly. His expression had changed, as if he grew angry again.

"My usefulness here has come to an end. The will must stand as he left it. I can't affect that now."

She was puzzled and a little perturbed by his sudden shifting of mood. "But how *would* you change it, if you could?" she asked.

The lines of his face seemed to harden, making him look older than his years. "There's no point in discussing that with you. You're a Judd too, though there's likely to be less of his fortune for you than for the others."

His words carried a deliberate sting, and she stood up beside him indignantly.

"I expect nothing at all from my grandfather," she said. "It's enough for me that he was kind to me yesterday and wanted me here."

For a moment his expression softened, and she thought he believed her. Then he seemed to think better of such weakening and laughed without sympathy.

"Do you mean that you're willing to go back to being a governess, when if you stay you may get your hands on some of the Judd fortune?"

"There's nothing wrong with being a governess," she returned heatedly. "I like to think I'm a good one. I intend to return to New York right after the funeral. The Judds owe me nothing and I want nothing from them. I came only to see my grandfather."

"Then why didn't you come before this?" he demanded. "Why did you wait till you heard he was dying before you came running to Thunder Heights?"

She felt completely outraged. If this was what he thought of her, then she did not mean to stay in his company another moment.

"Can you tell me if this upper path will take me back to the house?" she asked coldly.

"I'll come with you and show you the way," he offered.

Camilla turned her back on him and managed to get down the steep face of the rock without his help.

"No, thank you. I can find it well enough myself," she said and started up the path.

But he would not let her go alone. He jumped down from the rock and the spotted dog bounded along beside him as they turned uphill and back in the direction of Thunder Heights. Whether she liked it or not, she had to accept their company. She walked quickly, ignoring him, though now and then he pointed out landmarks by which she could find her direction if she chose to come this way again.

For example, he said, there was that weeping beech on ahead, from which she would be within sight of the Judds' house. She could not ignore the tree, for she had never seen one like it. It grew to a considerable height, but unlike other beeches, all its boughs trailed downward toward the earth, making a canopy of blue-black branches around the tree. It was as weird as something out of a witch's tale—a good landmark to remember.

When they reached the tree, her companion whistled for the dog and turned back. "I'll leave you here," he said curtly. "I'm not going in yet. You'll have no trouble by yourself the rest of the way."

He went off without waiting for any thanks she might have offered. For a moment she stood looking after him in a mingling of displeasure and bewilderment. What a strange, unpredictable, maddening person he was. Then she shrugged the thought of him aside and looked more closely about the hillside where she stood. Back a little farther it rose steeply into a cliff overgrown with wild vegetation and scrubby trees. There was a break in the brush at one point, as if a path to the top might open there. She was in no mood for exploration now, however, and hurried down toward Thunder Heights.

She had climbed well above the house, she found as she came out upon a bare, craggy place where she could overlook its gray towers. From this high rocky eminence, she could see a separation in the trees toward the north, and for the first time she had a glimpse of Blue Beeches from the land side.

The sunny yellow of the house looked brighter than ever in the morning sunlight. It shone fresh and clean, where Thunder Heights appeared drab and dingy. Looking at it, she felt an unexpected reluctance to return to the dark Judd household. Blue Beeches seemed far more inviting.

As she watched, she saw the spotted dog bound from the edge of the woods and go loping across a wide lawn. A woman came down the steps, laughing and calling to him. The breeze brought the faint sound of her voice. Camilla could not see her clearly enough to know whether she was plain or pretty, young or old. But it was clear that she had a friendly greeting for Ross Granger as he came more slowly out of the woods and joined her. Linking arms, they went up the steps and into the house.

Wondering, Camilla continued down the hill. The path from the rocky outcropping dipped briefly through the woods again and then came out on a level with the Judd house. Instead of seeking the veranda to make her re-entry the way she had come out, Camilla approached from the rear and saw that here more order and attention had been given to the grounds. A space of earth had been cleared of weeds, and there were paths leading among beds where planting had begun, with a small sundial marking the garden's center. A marble bench near the sundial invited one to rest and contemplation.

Camilla walked along one narrow path, noting bits of green already pushing their way out of the earth. As she neared the house, she looked up at the windows, but saw no sign of life, no face at any pane. Queer how dead the house always looked from the outside, even though she knew there were people within.

Grace opened the back door for her, and Camilla said good morning to Matilda, the cook and housekeeper, as she went inside. Voices reached her from the parlor, and she knew that the sad rites connected with her grandfather's death had already begun. Before she could slip past, a man appeared in the doorway and saw her. It was Mr. Pompton.

He held out his hand to her gravely. "It is sad to meet again under such circumstances, Miss King. But I'm glad you were able to reach your grandfather before his death."

"I think he wanted me here," she said. "Thank you for coming for me."

"That was his wish." His tone was courteous, but his manner seemed no more approving than it had been in New York. It was clear that her coming here was not his desire. "You will be staying on for a time now?" he asked.

She shook her head. "No longer than the funeral. With my grandfather gone, I am not wanted here."

He did not deny this, but made her a stiff bow and returned to the parlor. As she started up the stairs, Booth came out of the library to join her.

"You've been for a walk?" he asked. "Did you get no more sleep at all last night?"

"I didn't feel like sleeping," she said.

His mood seemed kinder and less remote than it had been the night before.

"A sad homecoming for you," he said. "If you stay with us a while, Cousin, perhaps we can make up for it."

She was silent as he climbed the stairs with her, not wishing to point out that his mother had given her little welcome. As they reached the second floor, Hortense came down the hall with a tray in her hands.

She wore voluminous black today, with a fringe of formidable jet twinkling across the bodice. The tray she carried held a tea service, with a quilted English cosy over the teapot, and a glass, medicine bottle, and spoon besides.

"I knew Letty would make herself ill last night," she said impatiently. "And now she has run away to the nursery again. As if I didn't have enough to do!"

Booth took the tray out of her hands. "Let me take it up to her, Mother. Camilla will help me with Aunt Letty. Pompton's downstairs, you know, waiting to see you."

Hortense gave up the tray gladly and made a vague tidying gesture that did her red pompadour no good.

As Camilla followed Booth up the stairs to the third floor, she glanced back and saw that Hortense had not gone down to Mr. Pompton at once, but was gazing after them with an air of uncertainty.

On the third floor, Booth led the way to the door of the old nursery, and Camilla opened it so that he might carry in the tray. The nursery was far from the cheerful room of her mother's stories and her own imagination. It was long and narrow, a bare, cold room. No fire had been lighted in its grate, and on this northern exposure of the house, sunshine had not reached the limply curtained windows. At the far end of the room Letty Judd lay huddled beneath a quilt on a narrow couch. Her face was swollen from crying, and she murmured faint sounds of apology as Booth approached her with the tray.

"You shouldn't bother about me, my dears," she said.

Booth set the tray down on a small table covered by a fringed red velvet cloth. "You know I'll always bother about you, Aunt Letty," he told her cheerfully. "Mother sent you some tea and medicine. We can't have you ill, you know."

At Letty's feet Mignonette lay curled in a warm, tight ball. She stretched herself, yawned widely, and regarded Booth's preparations with interest.

"I'm sorry you're not feeling well, Aunt Letty," Camilla said. "Would you like me to light a fire so it will be warmer up here?"

62

Booth answered for her. "Don't bother, Cousin. As soon as Aunt Letty drinks some tea and has her medicine, I'm going to take her downstairs."

Letty managed a tremulous smile, and there was affection in the look she gave him. "I like it up here. There are always memories to comfort me. Camilla, your mother used to play with Hortense and me in this very room."

"First your medicine," Booth said, and she swallowed the concoction gratefully.

"Balm and vervain tonic are wonderfully strengthening," she said. "I mixed the elixir myself. What tea did she fix for me, Booth?"

"I've no idea," he said, pouring a cupful with easy grace and bringing it to her. "Your herb mixtures confuse me. At least it's hot and potent."

Letty sniffed the aromatic steam and nodded, smiling. "Mother of thyme with a bit of hyssop. Just the thing. You know what David says in the Bible—'Purge me with hyssop and I shall be clean.'"

She drank deeply, and Mignonette mewed and climbed daintily over the hump of bedding made by Letty's outstretched legs.

"Give her a saucerful, Camilla—there's a dear," Letty said. "She doesn't want to be left out."

Camilla took Letty's saucer and poured tea into it, set it on the floor. Mignonette leaped lightly from the bed and lapped the hot liquid with a greedy pink tongue.

Booth watched, shaking his head. "I've never seen such a cat. Don't those mixtures ever upset her?"

"Of course not!" Letty's tone seemed overly vehement. "They don't upset me, why should they upset her?"

Booth shrugged and turned away to bring a chair for Camilla. Letty watched him unhappily.

"I know what you're thinking," she began.

"I'm not thinking a thing, except that I want to see you strong and well as soon as possible," Booth said. "The funeral is tomorrow and you'll want to be up for that. It's to be a quiet family affair, without an invasion of people from New York."

"I shall be up," Letty said and sipped her tea.

Mignonette licked the saucer and sat back to clean her whiskers tidily.

While Letty finished her tea, Camilla told of her walk that morning and of her glimpse of Blue Beeches and its dog. She said nothing about meeting Ross. She had a feeling that Booth, with good reason, would not approve of that meeting, and she had no wish to displease him.

"I'm glad you've had a look about the place, my dear," Letty said. "But if I were you, I wouldn't go too near Blue Beeches. Not that I have anything against Nora Redfern. As a matter of fact, her mother and yours were good friends in their girlhood. Mrs. Landry, Nora's mother, lives upriver now, and we haven't seen her for years —which is just as well. Nora is a widow with three children. Personally I think she is a young woman of considerable courage, but Hortense doesn't approve of her."

"Or her mother's sharp tongue," Booth added. "If you're through with your tea, I'll carry you downstairs to your room, Aunt Letty. Sad memories won't make you feel any better up here."

"They're not sad memories—they're the happiest of my life," Letty insisted. But she raised her arms to Booth.

He lifted her as if she weighed nothing, and her crooked arm went about his neck as he carried her toward the door. Camilla picked up the tray and followed, with Mignonette springing along at her heels. Just before she reached the door Camilla saw something she had not noticed when she'd entered the room. In a shadowy corner near the door stood a harp. Its cover had been laid aside, and a stool upholstered in needlepoint was drawn before it as if the musician had risen hurriedly from her playing and failed to return. So it was from this room that the harp music had issued in the dead of night.

She hurried down the stairs after Booth and waited until he had carried Letty into her room on the second floor.

"She'll sleep now," he said when he rejoined her. "Grandfather Orrin's death has been a shock to her. A shock to all of us."

"If she blames herself for something in connection with him," Camilla said, "that must upset her more than anything else."

"Aunt Letty is always ready to take on blame of one sort or another," Booth said. "And she has an imagination that gets her into trouble. Don't take her words too seriously, Cousin. I'll go down now and see how Mother is coming out with Mr. Pompton."

He gave her the quick flash of a smile that had surprised her before, always seeming unexpected in his somber face. After Ross's sharp words she warmed to Booth's kinder manner toward her.

As she went to her room she wondered about the circumstances of his adoption. Why had Hortense, who had never married and did not seem a particularly motherly person, chosen to adopt a boy of ten? And how closely was Booth tied to this family? It seemed strange that as a grown man he had been willing to live on in this gloomy household.

Camilla spent the rest of the morning in her room, not knowing what to do with herself. She had an unhappy sense of marking time between the poles of two different lives, belonging at the moment to neither one.

At noontime Letty remained in her room, Booth had gone to the village, and Ross did not appear, so she and Hortense ate alone in the big dining room. Her aunt seemed increasingly keyed up and distraught, and the black jet fringe on her dress quivered and trembled, as if stirred by the agitated beating of her heart. At least she seemed less distant than she had been when Camilla had arrived the day before.

"What will your plans be now, Aunt Hortense?" Camilla asked.

"We'll get rid of the house, of course," Hortense said. "Whether we sell it, give it away, burn it down, doesn't matter. Just so we're rid of it for good!"

"It seems a wonderful place to me," Camilla said gently. "Isn't it rather a shame to let it go out of the family?"

Hortense snorted, her pompadour trembling. "You haven't been tied to it against your will for most of your life. When Mama was alive we had houses everywhere, including a splendid town house in New York. I can still remember the parties and balls, the fun and gaiety, the trips abroad. Even after she died, Papa didn't give up as he did when Althea went away. Life was exciting, with new clothes and gay friends—exactly the sort of existence I like best. But when Althea married, Papa sold all the houses except this one, that was Althea's favorite. He behaved as though she had died and he wouldn't go anywhere, or let us go anywhere. It has been like living in a prison all these years."

Camilla felt moved by a certain pity for her. If a gay social life was what Aunt Hortense had been brought up to expect, it must have seemed a cruelty to have it taken away so arbitrarily.

"How did Aunt Letty feel about such a change?" Camilla asked.

"Letty!" Hortense waved a scornful hand. "She doesn't know what money is for. She can be happy with her harp and her garden and her cat. Given the choice, she'd probably be foolish enough to continue living under this roof in the same horribly dull way. If Papa has left money and property in her hands, she will never know what to do with it. But *I* will know. I have plans for myself and of course for Booth. There's so much I can do for him that Papa would never permit. And now I can laugh at Ross Granger. That young man has been influencing our fortunes for too long a time. The first thing I shall do is discharge him."

She was becoming excited to a disturbing degree and there were spots of high color in either cheek. Camilla sought to distract her.

"Tell me about Booth," she said.

This was a subject to which Hortense could warm. There was no mistaking the doting pride and affection that she lavished upon her adopted son.

"Booth is very talented, you know," Hortense assured her. "He's a really gifted artist. If we could live in New York, he might bring great credit to himself. But what chance has he here? Papa always hated his painting and opposed him at every step. He wanted him to go out and work in some business concern. Imagine! A man of Booth's sensitivity."

"Are any of his paintings hung about the house?" Camilla asked. "I'd like to see them."

"I have one in my room. Hurry and eat your rice pudding, Camilla, and I'll show it to you."

Her fatuous pride in Booth was evident and Camilla felt a little uncomfortable listening to her. Booth, she suspected, was completely indifferent to his adopted mother and she could not help but be sorry for Hortense.

Her aunt's room was on the second floor, across the hall from Camilla's. It was a big, dim room, heavily curtained. Camilla could feel the prickle of dust in her nostrils as she stepped into it. Hortense's love of the sumptuous had been given full play, and she had used a lavish hand when it came to velvet, satin, and brocade—

all rich materials in faded yellow, or once brilliant green. Dusty materials, gone too long undisturbed.

Hortense moved about lighting lamps on numerous tables and stands, apparently preferring lamplight to daylight.

"There!" she cried, waving a hand toward the end wall of the room. "What do you think of it?"

The painting was a large one, set handsomely in an ornate gilt frame. It was a picture of two mountain wildcats fighting. Their fiercely struggling bodies verged on the rim of a rocky cliff, with rapids frothing at its foot. A storm was breaking overhead, and the artist had painted in tawny yellows and smoky greens and grays. The result was a wild and disturbing picture.

"Papa detested this painting," Hortense said. "He didn't want to look at it day after day, and he told Booth to get it out of his sight."

Camilla could well understand that her grandfather would not want to live with such a picture confronting him in his own house. She wondered how Hortense could endure its constant violence here in her room. That Booth had painted it was significant. Camilla had sensed a depth of curbed passion in him that he did not reveal to the casual eye. It had spilled out in this picture, betraying him.

Hortense ran on eagerly. "When we sell this house and move to New York, I'll arrange for a showing of his pictures in one of the galleries. I've promised him that for a long time, but Papa would never permit it."

As she left her aunt, Camilla thought that there was far more relief than sorrow in Hortense over her father's death. Indeed, the fact of it seemed to have brought all the suppressed longings that she had stored up over the years seething to the surface. Today she was a woman driven by her rising emotions, ready to let nothing stand in her path.

Letty did not come down to dinner that night, but Hortense said she was feeling better and was sure she would be able to attend the funeral services tomorrow. Ross Granger continued to stay away, and no one seemed to know where he was, or what he was doing.

"He's probably over visiting Mrs. Redfern again," Hortense said.

67

"Why not?" Booth said carelessly. "Nora Redfern is an attractive woman."

"You know very well how we feel about her," Hortense said. "And why. Ross only does this to spite us. Never mind—he won't be around much longer, I can promise you that."

The meal was a quiet one, and Camilla slipped away when they left the table, avoiding the stiff coffee hour in the overfurnished parlor, and went upstairs to her room. In one sense she could hardly wait to be free of this house and away from it for good. Yet in another she felt that when she left she would be more frighteningly alone than ever before in her life. The thought depressed and saddened her.

She had brought a book by Washington Irving upstairs from the library, but though she got into Althea's comfortable bed and set a lamp nearby on the bedside table, she could not concentrate on the pages before her. Tonight there was no escaping her own life through words in a book.

Loneliness was a specter that sat at the foot of the bed peering at her grimly. In desperation she tried to argue it away. Being alone was no new experience for Camilla King. As a child she had often been lonely, with few children her own age to play with. And since her father's death she had been more solitary than ever. That was one reason she had sought a position as a governess who would live in the midst of someone else's family. With children needing her every moment, she had hoped to lose the feeling of belonging nowhere.

Yet none of her previous experience of loneliness had been as devastating as this. Always before there had been the secret knowledge of her family up the Hudson to dream about—a family to which she belonged through ties of blood. No matter how stern her grandfather had been to her mother, he was still her grandfather, and she had stored away the reassuring thought that the time would eventually come when she might go to him. Now Grandfather Orrin was dead, and while Letty and Hortense were her blood relatives, the fact gave her little comfort. She was not wanted here by Hortense, and Letty was a vague, sweet dreamer who could not help her. The secret hope which had long supported her was gone, and there was left in its place only a soreness and an

68

aching. Not only must she fail in whatever it was her grandfather had wanted of her, but she must also forsake a comforting hope for the future when she left this house.

She turned out the lamp and lay in the dark, thinking again of the strange things Orrin Judd had said to her. Perhaps he had felt in his last hours that an injustice had been done to Althea and wished that he could make up for it through her daughter. But no legacy could assuage this feeling she was lost to tonight. It was her grandfather's presence she wanted and the developing affection which had been promised between them.

She sighed and turned restlessly in bed. Somehow she must forget the problems of this strange household. But tears came instead of sleep, and she wept bitterly into her pillow. Wept for her grandfather and because of her disappointment in a family that did not want her here—when she had so longed to belong to her own family. Wept too for her father's gentle wisdom which might have guided her now. And most of all she wept for her mother, so tragically, irretrievably lost.

Tonight she could not even summon to mind her mother's gay image to comfort her. In this room she had lost her doubly, for the room was strange and did not know her. With her spirits at the lowest ebb she could remember, she had a gloomy presentiment that she would never know a real home anywhere.

CHAPTER 7

THE SUNLIGHT of early afternoon rayed through the stained glass window of the little church as the organist played a solemn hymn. The mourners sat with their heads bowed in prayer for the dead, and Letty, in the family pew beside Camilla, pressed her arm gently.

"We used to come here often before my sister Althea died," she whispered. "Papa gave the church that stained glass window behind the altar as a commemoration for Althea, but he stopped coming here when he lost her."

From beyond Camilla, Hortense threw the whisperer a reproving look and Letty fell silent. Booth sat beside his mother, but Ross had not been invited to occupy the family pew. Once when Camilla turned her head, she saw him a row or two back, sitting beside a pretty, brown-eyed woman—probably Nora Redfern.

The minister was a young man, and when he rose to give the eulogy for the dead, Camilla suspected that he could not have known Orrin Judd very well. His words were earnest and well-meaning, but they seemed to have little relation to the man Camilla remembered as her grandfather.

Though the church was well filled, Letty had told her earlier that many would come out of curiosity and perhaps resentment of the Judds, rather than because of any real love for her grandfather. People hereabout considered him a hard man, grown too powerful, so that he had lost his human identification with the humble who had been his friends when he was young.

When the ceremony was over the family followed the casket

down the aisle and out of the church. From her place in one of the carriages that would drive them to the cemetery, Camilla looked about for Ross in the crowd, but she did not see him again until they reached her grandfather's grave.

The cemetery lay beneath the sheltering shade of a forest that rimmed its far edge on the upper hillside. Only a few of those at the church had followed the hearse the short distance for the final burial. Letty grew tense now, and as the casket was placed beside the grave, she burst into tears and clung brokenly to Camilla. Hortense bowed her head, the conventional figure of a daughter mourning her father, but Camilla suspected that there were no tears behind her black veil. Booth had been a pallbearer, along with Orrin's doctor, the lawyer Mr. Pompton, and others, and he looked grave, if not deeply grieved. Ross, for all that he had apparently been close to Orrin Judd in life, had not been asked by the family to serve at his funeral.

Camilla saw him standing a little apart, with Mrs. Redfern at his side. His expression was guarded, betraying little, perhaps because he did not want to reveal his feeling. How much did the young widow, Nora Redfern, mean to him, she wondered, that he was with her so often?

The day was gray and cool, with more rain threatening. Camilla stood in silence beside Letty and Hortense and watched gray clouds swirl overhead with the wind at their heels. She felt no surging of grief for her grandfather now. What was being lowered into the ground had little connection with the fierce old man she had known so briefly. The eagle had long since flown its bonds.

When she looked at the earth again, it was to study the names on gravestones nearby. There, with a tall granite shaft guarding it, was her grandmother's grave. Next to that was the headstone for Althea Judd King. It was the first time Camilla had seen her mother's grave, and the tears she could not shed for her grandfather sprang into her eyes. How much her father had wanted to keep his Althea from being buried here. But Orrin Judd had had his way, and she lay in the family plot with others of her kin around her. Now Orrin, who had lost her so completely in life, would sleep nearby his dearest daughter in all the time ahead.

Near the cemetery gate, she saw Ross and Mrs. Redfern speaking to Mr. Pompton.

Letty, still weeping gently, put her hand on Camilla's arm. "Pretend not to see her, dear. Just move quickly by. Our families don't speak."

Camilla would have obeyed, but Mrs. Redfern stepped forward and held out her hand in a warm gesture of friendliness.

"I'm Nora Redfern, Miss King. If you are going to be here for a while, do come over to see me. We ought to know each other—our mothers were best friends."

Nora was tall, with soft brown hair curling beneath her tilted hat. She looked like a woman who enjoyed the out-of-doors, and the clasp of her hand was strong and direct.

Camilla thanked her and explained that she would be leaving tomorrow. She could understand why Ross spent so much time with this woman, and she watched with regret as he helped her into her carriage. Hortense had seen the interchange, and her color was high with disapproval. She whispered to Booth and his look followed Mrs. Redfern with a speculative interest. What was wrong here? And how did it happen that Ross associated with Mrs. Redfern, when the rest of the Judd household did not?

When Hortense and Booth and Mr. Pompton were settled in one carriage, and Letty and Camilla in another, Ross came over to join them, a little to Camilla's surprise. Apparently he was coming back to Thunder Heights with them.

Letty still wanted to talk on the drive home, needing to pour out thoughts that were troubling her.

"Papa was always just," she told Camilla. "He always tried to protect me, even if he didn't care much for girls who were sickly."

"He cared about you," Ross assured her gently. "You mustn't doubt that."

"He was unhappy these last years," Letty said. "And that was my fault. So much of it was my fault."

"I think you blame yourself needlessly," Ross told her. "How could you be responsible for his unhappiness?"

Letty shook her head and dabbed at her eyes with a handkerchief. "You don't know," she said darkly. "There are so many things you don't know."

Ross did not seem to take this seriously. "Perhaps it will comfort you a little, Miss Letty, if you realize that nothing could ever have made him happy again. He would never have found a way to start anew."

"That is true," Letty said wonderingly. "His life was really over, no matter what anyone did. In fact, it has been over for a long, long time, hasn't it?"

She seemed to take more cheer from this thought than Ross had expected her to.

"At least," he said, "it will be better if you don't express the way you feel about all this to any reporters who may try to talk to you."

"Reporters?" Letty echoed in dismay.

"Of course. You don't think a man like Orrin Judd can die without causing a stir, do you? There are some newsmen here already. Pompton had some trouble keeping them out of the church, and I know that Toby chucked two of them off Judd grounds this morning before I could stop him. We'll have to talk to them, of course. You'll all fare better with the press if it's done pleasantly."

"Surely no one will want to talk to me," Camilla said in dismay.

"Why not?" Ross sounded unsympathetic. "In fact, you're likely to give them the best copy. Beautiful, disinherited granddaughter! You'd better brace yourself for a siege if they get near you."

When they reached the house, she found that he was right. A group of strange young men in bowler hats had gathered near the front door, and Mr. Pompton left the carriage to speak to them, while Booth and Ross hurried the ladies into the house.

When Camilla would have left the others to go upstairs, Hortense stopped her. "You're to come to the library at once, please. Mr. Pompton wishes to see us all there. He has agreed to read us Papa's will at once."

Such haste seemed to lack decorum, but Camilla followed her aunts across the antehall where marble hands extended from the walls, and through the door of the library. Grace had set a fire burning against the misty chill of the day, and Hortense seated herself in a deep leather sofa placed at right angles to the hearth. Letty chose a small rocking chair and sank into it with a quick, nervous smile that went unanswered by her sister.

Since Camilla felt she had no real part in these proceedings,

73

whatever Mr. Pompton might wish, she took a chair in a far corner, withdrawn from the main family gathering. Ross had come into the room, and he too set himself apart from the others. He walked to one of the bookcases that lined two walls and began to study titles as though he had no other interest there.

The library was heavily paneled in dark walnut that reflected little light and gave a gloomy air to the room. A long walnut table, its legs ornate with carving, occupied the center of the room, and Booth pushed it back a little in order to give them more space about the fire. Above the mantel, commanding the room, hung a portrait of Orrin Judd.

The picture had been painted in his strong middle years, and the eagle look had been in his face even then. But only Camilla seemed to regard the portrait openly, and she had a feeling that it made the family uncomfortable.

Hortense, looking undisguisedly eager now, patted the sofa and beckoned Booth to a place beside her. Mr. Pompton turned his back to the warming fire and spread apart the tails of the dress coat he had worn to the funeral. His scalp glowed rosy in the firelight, and the two clumps of hair above each ear stood up as if they bristled in anticipation of some unpleasantness. He still looked irritated by his encounter with the press.

Watching them all, Camilla felt herself a spectator at a play. In a physical sense she would remain remote and untouched by whatever happened. When the play was over, she could rise and walk out of the theater, with no more involvement with the players.

Mr. Pompton cleared his throat and looked somewhat disapprovingly at Hortense. "You understand, Miss Hortense, that it is only because I wish the whole family to be present that we are moving with such unseemly haste."

"Yes, yes, we understand all that," Hortense said, plucking at a black lace frill on the front of her gown with impatient fingers. "Do get on with it. Then perhaps we can return to our sorrow."

He threw her a suspicious look and explained that one of the firm instructions Mr. Judd had given was to the effect that there was to be no formal mourning period. He had wanted no one to pretend grief, or to dress in black, or avoid social duties.

"As you know," Mr. Pompton continued gruffly, "Mr. Judd sent me to New York a few days ago to find Miss King and ask her to come to Thunder Heights. While I was away on this mission, and without my knowledge or advice, he drew up a new will."

Camilla sensed the quickened attention of the room. Hortense glanced at Booth with an air of triumph.

"He must have listened to me," she whispered.

"Or else to Granger," Booth said, glancing around at the man who stood before the bookshelves.

Ross continued to page through a volume he had taken down, and if the change of wills was news to him, he gave no sign.

"The new will," Mr. Pompton said, "has been legally drawn and witnessed."

He began to read aloud, and Camilla caught the wording of the first bequest.

"'To my eldest daughter, Hortense Judd, I leave the family Bible, with the hope that she will learn from its wisdom.'"

Hortense sniffed, her impatience growing. "If Papa has doled out everything stick by stick, this is going to take us all day."

"Believe me, madam, it will not take very long," Mr. Pompton said, and continued with the task in hand.

To his second daughter, Letitia Judd, he had left the treasured photograph taken of himself and his three daughters. Letty nodded in pleasure and her tears began to spill again.

"I shall treasure it too," she murmured.

Hortense threw her a look of scorn for such simple-minded gratitude.

Several small sums had been left to Toby and Matilda, and to others who had worked for Orrin in the past. His bequest to Ross was a strange one.

"'In view of the years of trusted service given me, I wish Ross Granger to be permitted the occupancy of the rooms above the coach house for as long as he cares to use them.'"

Ross did not look around, or acknowledge the request in any way. What a strange thing for her grandfather to do, Camilla thought. Surely Ross's quarters in this house must be more comfortable than such an arrangement would be. Besides, if his work for Orrin was finished, he would be leaving soon.

When Mr. Pompton paused, Booth looked quickly at Ross, and Hortense put a hand on her son's arm, as if to restrain him.

Clearing his throat, Mr. Pompton continued. "'To Camilla King, daughter of my youngest daughter, Althea Judd King, I bequeath this house of Thunder Heights and all the property therein.'"

For an instant the words meant nothing to Camilla. Then, as she began to grasp their meaning, she was so astonished that she did not hear what followed. Mr. Pompton had to repeat the fact that Orrin Judd had left, not only Thunder Heights, but his entire fortune and business holdings to Camilla King, who was herself to be the sole executor of the will.

Camilla's shock and bewilderment were like a mist through which she struggled for some landmark simple enough in its meaning for her to grasp. She was aware of Hortense's gasp and the startled silence of the others. Even Ross had turned and was watching her. With an effort she forced herself to listen and understand the meaning of the stipulations Mr. Pompton was reading.

In order to inherit this house and fortune, Camilla King would have to live at Thunder Heights, preserve it in good state and continue to care for the rest of the family as long as they chose to live in the house. They were to live on the present allowances given them. If any member of the family chose to leave Thunder Heights, he was to receive nothing at all thereafter. Nor was Camilla to receive anything if she chose to leave.

The full meaning of the burden her grandfather had placed upon her was clear now, and Camilla rose uncertainly to her feet.

"I don't understand why Grandfather did this. He must have made this will before I came here—"

"He was insane when he made it!" Hortense cried hoarsely.

Mr. Pompton shook his head. "Madam, Dr. Wheeler would quickly vouch for his sanity. I regret the fact that he did not consult me about this will. Perhaps he would have done so if he had lived. Then I would have warned him that such stipulations were too general and difficult to fulfill. They can be regarded only as Mr. Judd's wishes. I doubt that a court would uphold them."

Hortense recovered herself abruptly. "Why didn't you say so at

76

once? Of course we will fight this in court. The whole thing is preposterous."

"If you will allow me a word—" Mr. Pompton bent his disapproving gaze upon her, "the stipulations could probably not be enforced. But the main body of the will remains sound. Mr. Judd has left everything he owns to Miss King, and I doubt that you could touch that in a court. What she does with it is her own affair. She may go or stay, care for her aunts or not, as she pleases—the inheritance is still hers."

Hortense had begun to breathe deeply, harshly, as if she restrained herself with difficulty. Letty was watching Camilla in bewilderment, as if she did not altogether understand what was going on. The sardonic look was once more in Booth's eyes, though he took no active part in what was happening. Ross was regarding her sharply, his arms folded across his body.

How could she possibly accept this legacy? Camilla thought. A small sum of money she would have received gratefully. But not this, when so clearly the true rights to it lay elsewhere.

"What happens if I refuse the legacy?" Camilla asked.

Mr. Pompton looked faintly skeptical, as if he found it hard to believe that she would do such a thing.

"Since there is no other legatee," he said, "the same thing would happen as would happen in the event of your decease. The money and property would revert to the next of kin."

"To Aunt Hortense and Aunt Letty?" Camilla asked.

"Exactly." Mr. Pompton reached among his papers on the table and drew out an envelope.

"Then I'll refuse it!" Camilla cried. "I have no right to it. And I don't want the burden and responsibility of it."

"Bravo!" Booth cried. "We have a heroine in our midst."

Mr. Pompton wasted not a moment's glance in Booth's direction. He crossed the room to Camilla and held out the envelope. She saw that her name was written upon it in a wavering hand and that it had been sealed with red sealing wax and imprinted with the initialed emblem of a ring.

"This letter is from your grandfather," Mr. Pompton told her. "I do not know its contents. When Toby brought this new will to my office while I was away, he brought the letter also. It was to be given you only in the event of your grandfather's death."

Camilla took the letter almost fearfully, turning it about in her hands.

"The girl has refused the legacy," Hortense said sharply. "Is anything else necessary?"

"I cannot accept a refusal hastily given and without due thought," Mr. Pompton said. "It is my duty to see that some attempt be made to carry out Mr. Judd's wishes. Perhaps you would like to take the letter away and read it, Miss King? It is not necessary to do so here under our eyes."

She accepted the offer quickly. "Yes—yes, please. I'd like to do that. I'll return as soon as I've read it."

She did not look at the others as she left the library and crossed the hall to the parlor. Someone had left a cloak over a chair, and she flung it about her shoulders as she hurried toward a veranda door.

It was not raining now, but the air was heavy with moisture as Camilla leaned upon the railing, looking out over what had once been a fine lawn. Beyond and below lay the river, wreathed in fog, with misty swirls drifting among nearby trees. From the water came the low mooing of a foghorn on a boat.

All these things she was aware of with her senses, without knowing that she was aware. She steadied herself with one hand upon the damp rail, holding in the other the sealed envelope she dreaded to open. How could she follow her grandfather's stipulations and live here, knowing that the family would resent her and want her away, knowing they must hate her because they were tied to her for as long as they chose to accept her charity? Under such circumstances, could she even count on Aunt Letty to befriend her? If she accepted this inheritance she must give up her own freedom and the sense of independence that meant so much to her. She would have to give herself to Thunder Heights. Forever. The prospect was frightening.

She took her wet hand from the rail and looked at it absently. A memory of the river boat and Ross Granger turning her hands palm up swept back. What did he think of this strange turn of events? But what he thought did not matter. She had the feeling that she ought to make up her mind before she read her grandfather's letter. Yet how could she know her own heart and mind so swiftly?

With a resolute gesture she lifted the envelope and broke the seal.

My Dear Granddaughter (the letter began):

You do not know me, which is not your fault. Nor do you know that I have long followed your fortunes and watched you from a distance. I am aware that you have been a loyal daughter to your father, and that since his death you have conducted yourself with good sense and courage. You are able to work with pride for your living, and this is a trait I admire.

I have thought more than once of asking you to come to Thunder Heights for a visit, so that the two of us could become acquainted and so that you might forgive an old man for his sad mistakes of the past. It may already be too late.

Recently I have had a severe shock, and it may be that this time I shall not recover. Those who live under this roof with me I do not trust. I know now that the things I have built and worked for must not go into their hands, to be wasted and flung aside. What I have built is sound and good. I want it to remain with someone of my own blood who will be loyal to me.

You are the only possible answer to this desire of mine. For this reason I am changing my will. Thunder Heights will be yours. Restore it, my dear. Make it what it was in your mother's day. I have no wish to turn my two elder daughters out of this house, so I must ask you to keep them for the rest of their lives. And Hortense's adopted son, Booth, as well, though I have no personal liking for him.

Keep my daughters loyal to this house and to their name. Give neither of them anything if they move away. On this point I am adamant.

The business problems are large ones—I lack the strength to go into them now. We will talk about all these matters, and I will explain my distrust, my hopes, my fears to you. Then you will be armed and guided when the time comes.

By the time you read this, I hope we will have long been good and trusted friends. I will be able to go in peace, knowing that what I leave behind rests in responsible hands. Do not fail me, Granddaughter.

Your loving grandfather,
Orrin Judd

Camilla read with a growing sadness and with an increasing sense of being trapped. The will she might put aside and refuse to consider. This letter—the last wishes of a man whom she had learned, even in so short a time, to love and respect—must be considered solemnly.

Folding the letter, she put it back in its envelope and looked out again upon the swirling mist. The brown grass below the veranda was wet, but she went down the steps and across it with little heed for shoes and skirt hem. She walked between the old elms that bordered each side of the wide lawn, noting that leaf buds were showing along every limb.

She paused at the rim of a steep hill that dropped away in a thick stand of trees, concealing the steel ribbons of railroad track below. Here she turned about so that she could look up at the house and at the dark mountain towering behind. How grim the structure looked—as grim and forbidding as the stony cliff above. The weathered gray of the house seemed dingier than ever with wet mist clinging to its towers. The weed-choked clumps of thin grass added to the picture of woeful neglect.

How could her grandfather, who loved the house, have let it go like this? He must indeed have been driven far along a road of despair and hopelessness. Perhaps in writing his letter he had tried in some degree to retrace his steps, to mend what he himself had broken. If the weeds were destroyed and grass planted, this might again become a beautiful lawn. The house cried for repairs and fresh paint to make it once more a show place on the Hudson.

An odd, unexpected excitement ran through her—almost a sense of exhilaration. It lay within her power to make such changes if she wished. The realization was sudden and heady. What if she accepted her grandfather's trust? What if she set about bringing the house out of its bad years and back into such glory as it had once known long ago? Might this not be a splendid and satisfying thing to do? Orrin Judd had wanted Althea's daughter to breathe new life and hope into Thunder Heights. He had believed that she could do this very thing.

Could she? Did she dare accept not only the trust, but the challenge?

Someone came out of the house and stood upon the veranda, watching her. It was Letty Judd. She wore black today, but the material was soft and light, and a silk scarf about her shoulders softened their thin contour. Her injured arm was held tight across her body. Standing there at the head of the veranda steps, she seemed strangely of a piece with the house—a part of all the mystery it stood for. Letty Judd was a woman filled to the brim with secrets.

But though Camilla's sudden vision of her in that moment was clear, she refused to be daunted. She lifted her skirts so they would clear the wet grass and ran back to the steps, her face glowing and eager.

Letty saw the look and held out her hands in pleading. "Don't stay here at Thunder Heights. Let the house go. Let all of us go. That's the only wise choice, the only safe choice."

Camilla hesitated at the foot of the steps as distrust flicked through her mind. If she gave up this fortune and went away, Letty would inherit half, along with her sister Hortense. Yet Letty had disclaimed all interest in the money, and Camilla put the thought away almost as swiftly as it had come. This, she knew, was one of the dangers of accepting such a fortune—that she might become suspicious and distrustful, as her grandfather had been. And she did not want that.

She went up the steps and took Letty's hands in her own. "This is your home, Aunt Letty, and you shall live in it as long as you like, and with everything you need or want. Help me to make something good out of Grandfather's wishes."

Letty regarded her sadly. "You're going to stay, aren't you? I was afraid you might. You have the look of your mother about you— of Althea when she had a notion between her teeth and meant to carry it through, no matter what. No one ever changed her mind when she looked like that. It's a dangerous trait to inherit, my dear. It won't be easy for you to stay here."

Camilla smiled at the thought that she might indeed have a notion between her teeth, and that she might even like it.

"Come back to the library with me," she said, and drew Letty into the house.

No one had stirred in the walnut-dark room. Mr. Pompton stood with his back to the fire, his hands clasped behind him under lifted coat tails. Hortense sat bolt upright on the sofa, her fingers intertwined in her lap. Booth leaned beside her with an air of being faintly amused, as if nothing of consequence hung in the balance. Ross seemed again wholly absorbed in books on a shelf and he did not turn when Camilla entered the room.

She could feel the warmth in her own cheeks, sense the brightness of excitement which must stamp her appearance.

"I've made my decision," she told Mr. Pompton. "I'm ready to accept my grandfather's legacy and his stipulations. I shall remain at Thunder Heights."

CHAPTER 8

A LOG on the fire crumbled into ash, throwing up sparks as it fell. For a moment there was no other sound in the room.

Then Mr. Pompton began to gather up his papers with a dry rustling that betrayed neither displeasure nor approval.

"Exactly," he said, as if he had expected all along that she would make no other choice.

"My grandfather's letter—" Camilla began, but Hortense interrupted her by standing up. She looked pale and stricken.

"Help me to my room," she said to Booth, and he gave her his arm and led her to Letty, who stood watching in the doorway.

"Aunt Letty will take you upstairs, Mother," he said, and came back into the room.

In the face of Hortense's precipitate exit and Mr. Pompton's remote and impersonal manner, something of Camilla's first exhilaration had begun to fade. But Booth, at least, spoke to her kindly.

"I'll admit that I hadn't expected matters to go in this direction," he said. "Forgive us, Cousin, if we don't seem altogether happy. It's rather a shock to my mother to find herself in the position of being dependent upon a niece she hardly knows. I only hope we can accept Grandfather Orrin's wishes with good grace." He smiled wryly. "As a matter of fact, you'll probably do better justice to the handling of Grandfather's fortune than my mother would. Certainly better than Aunt Letty. Or, for that matter—Booth Hendricks. So, for whatever it's worth, you have my support, Cousin Camilla."

He held out his hand and she put her own into it, touched and surprised. She had not thought that Booth would react like this.

Ross Granger shoved his book back on the shelf and looked around at them. There was nothing of conciliation or acceptance in his face.

"This is all very touching," he said. "But you must admit that the situation could hardly be more ridiculous."

"You might explain that remark, Granger," Booth said.

Ross threw him an irritable look. "Do you mean you don't find it ridiculous that all of this"—he waved a hand to encompass the Judd fortune—"has been left unequivocally in the control of an inexperienced girl of twenty-three?"

"You can always resign, you know," Booth put in, his eyes brightening as though he enjoyed this moment of clash.

For an instant Ross stared at the other man wrathfully. Then Booth shrugged, smiled at Camilla and went out of the room. Before Ross could speak again, Mr. Pompton cleared his throat and addressed Camilla.

"If you are willing, I'll come to see you as soon as I have things somewhat in order. There are various legal matters we must go over together. In the meantime I'll say good day. If you wish, I can make a statement to the press on my way out and take the reporters off your hands."

She thanked him, and when he had gone she looked uncomfortably at Ross. He appeared thoroughly angry, and she had no idea what to say to him, how to deal with him.

"I'll make no pretty speeches," he said curtly. "You have my resignation, of course. I'm sure you'll have other advisers who will work for you more cheerfully than I would. I'll try to be out of your way in a week or two."

His angry disapproval was so unfair that she did not want to let him go out of the room without offering some defense.

"Would you like to read my grandfather's letter?" she asked.

He shook his head. "No, thank you. It's sure to be the letter of a weak, defeated old man—not of the Orrin Judd I knew years ago. Reading it would not change my feelings about what he has done."

"I didn't ask for any of this—" Camilla began, but he would not

84

stay to listen. He walked out of the room as though he dared not trust his temper and closed the door behind him.

Alone, Camilla sat at the library table and looked up at the portrait of her grandfather. She felt sick and shaken. This was going to be far harder than she had expected. Her spirits had plummeted from that moment of high elation when she stood looking up at the house, thinking of the changes she might bring to it. Only Booth had spoken to her gently and tried to hide something of his own disappointment. Letty had advised against acceptance. Hortense was distraught and indignant, and even Ross, who was not one of the family, was angry with her.

She felt helpless and appallingly alone. Tears came before she could find strength to fight them back, and her head went down on her arms.

It was Ross who returned to find her there. He came into the library and stood beside the table while she made futile dabbing gestures at her eyes.

"There's no help for it," he said. "You'll have to talk to the reporters. They're not satisfied with Pompton's dry-as-dust evasions. What's worse—Booth is out there now, antagonizing them further. It's you they want to see, and you can't blame them for trying to do the job they've been sent here to do."

She stared at him, panic rising in her. "But—how would I know what to say? I—I've hardly grasped this myself. And—I must look terrible."

A flicker of amusement showed unexpectedly in his eyes. "You do," he said. "Your nose is red and your eyes are puffy. But you can be forgiven, since you've come from your grandfather's funeral. It's just as well if someone manages to look grief-stricken. Shall I bring them in?"

How hard and insensitive he was. She knew by his face that he would probably call the reporters in, whether she agreed or not. It was difficult to make a request of him, but she could not face them alone.

"Will you stay while I talk to them?" she asked.

"I'll stay," he said. "But you're in charge now, and you'll have to manage this yourself. The sooner you take hold, the better it will be for you."

Her feeling of panic increased, and he must have seen it in her eyes, for he softened a little.

"Look—we'll set the stage, shall we? Sit over here with your back to the light. That will give you an advantage. Take a few deep breaths and just try to be yourself. There's no great damage you can do, really. Most of the damage has been done by the situation itself."

As he went to summon the newsmen, she realized that she was gripping the arms of the chair with all her strength.

She was relieved when Booth returned with Ross and the five or six reporters who accompanied them into the library.

"Why did you agree to this?" Booth whispered, taking his place beside Camilla's chair. "I'd have got rid of these fellows for you in a few more minutes."

There was no time to answer him. The group of newspapermen had ranged themselves around her, and she saw their curious glances as they took in the room's details and studied her.

"How do you feel about being Orrin Judd's heiress?" one of them asked.

She knew her lips would tremble if she tried to smile, and she answered stiffly. "I can only hope to be worthy of the responsibility."

The questions began to come quickly then. Why had Orrin Judd chosen her, when he had never sent for her before? Was it true that he had long ago disinherited her mother? What did he have against the other members of the family that he had treated them like this? Was it true that she was a governess?

They were not polite questions, and they were not intended to spare her. Once, sensing Booth's indignation, she put a hand on his arm so that he would not burst in angrily. Ross had gone to stand before the fire, as Mr. Pompton had done earlier, taking no part in the proceedings, and making no effort to come to her aid.

When the rapid questions confused her, Camilla put her hands up in protest. "There's so much I don't know. Perhaps it would be better if I tell you the little I do know about how I come to be here."

They listened and scribbled notes as she related simply, sometimes haltingly, what had happened from the moment when Mr. Pompton had come to see her in the house in Gramercy Park. All that

86

she told them was the truth, though there were many omissions. She had no intention of giving any hint of the atmosphere in this house, or of the things her grandfather had said to her. She did not mention his letter. It lay in her lap, and once when she touched it inadvertently, she remembered its contents and felt strengthened. She had her grandfather's words and trust to hold to, though she might have nothing else.

When the reporters asked about her plans for the future and how she meant to run Orrin Judd's enterprises, she managed a rueful smile.

"You must know that is a question I can't answer now," she said. "But at least I have plans closer to home. I want to do this house over completely and make it the wonderful place it must once have been."

They liked this and took her ideas down as she talked. There was only one more sharp question near the end of the interview.

"What about your mother's death?" one young man asked. "There was some tragedy here—years ago, wasn't there? She was pretty badly smashed up in an accident, as I recall. Didn't your father—"

Ross broke into the interview smoothly. "You've had the time I promised you, gentlemen, and I think you have your story. Let's not torment the young lady unnecessarily."

His manner was courteous but firm as he saw them to the door and out of the house.

"You were wonderful, Cousin," Booth said, bending over her. "And more sensible than I. It's in my blood, I suppose, to hate reporters, since we've fared badly with them in the past."

Now that the ordeal was over, Camilla felt weak with relief. Her knees were trembling as she stood up. Beyond Booth she saw Aunt Letty in the doorway.

"They've bothered you enough, my dear," Letty said. "Come upstairs now and lie down. No, Booth, not another word."

Gratefully, Camilla went with her. She had nothing to say to either Booth or Ross Granger.

When Letty had gone, Camilla lay on her bed in the darkened room, trying to command her own thoughts, to formulate some sensible plan of action.

These first days would be the most difficult to get through, she assured herself. Once the family grew accustomed to the idea of having her here, once they came to know her and accept her, it should not be so hard. Surely they would be pleased when she made plans for the house. Hortense had longed for a gay life. Why couldn't it be gay enough for her right here at Thunder Heights? If Booth wished it, why couldn't he go to New York and arrange for a showing of his paintings? She could do so much for all of them, once they accepted her and began to trust her.

Her immediate task was to win them, to be patient and never angry, no matter what anyone might say or do. The business affairs she could do nothing about. Mr. Pompton would handle those, and she must trust him as her grandfather had undoubtedly trusted him. In spite of his attitude toward her, she wished that Ross Granger were not going away, because he too had been trusted by her grandfather. She could not, however, ask him to stay.

She had no desire at the moment to go downstairs to face the others, and when Grace came tapping at her door with a supper tray, she was relieved.

"Miss Letty fixed it herself," Grace said, setting the tray on the marble-topped table before the hearth.

When Camilla sat down to the tray, she found a brief note propped against a cup. It was from Letty.

Don't come down to dinner, dear. Let us talk this out among ourselves. Everything will be better tomorrow.

Lovingly,
Aunt Letty

She was grateful for the respite and happy to have her meal quietly here in her room. She went to bed early and fell asleep at once, waking now and then to the rumble of a train that seemed to come from the earth beneath the house, or to the whistle of a boat, or foghorns on the river, only to fall quickly asleep again.

In the early morning she came wide awake, to find sunlight glowing beyond window draperies, and she sprang out of bed to let it in. The air was brisk and cool, but there was no sharpness in its touch as she opened the balcony door. She looked out across the river toward the morning sun, feeling rested and no longer fearful.

"This is mine!" she thought. "I need never look for a home again as long as I want to stay here. I belong to this now. I have a family." They might not want her here at first, but she belonged to them and eventually they would accept her.

When she had washed and dressed, she hurried downstairs, hungry for breakfast and eager to begin the day. Yesterday had been sad because of the funeral and frightening because of all the new, strange things that had been hurled at her when she was unprepared. But today she felt strong and unafraid. She would laugh at Ross's scowls and coax Aunt Hortense into good humor. She would find ways to make Aunt Letty happy, and she would show Booth her gratitude for his unexpected kindness.

Once more the dining room was empty, and for the moment she was glad to be alone so that she could marshal her plans before she talked to anyone. She had brought paper and pencil downstairs with her, and she set them beside her plate and began to jot down reminders to herself. Unobtrusively, if possible, she must learn to know the entire house. She must inquire into the possibility of hiring gardeners, carpenters, painters, so that the work might be appraised and started as soon as possible. There must be additional household help. Yet with all these changes she must move quietly and without seeming to jerk the reins from the hands of others. She must remember to consult Aunt Hortense, draw her into her plans, move gently until the others could see that only good would come of having her here.

No one joined her at the table as she finished breakfast, though Grace said Mr. Granger was up early as usual, and had gone over to Blue Beeches. He, at least, she would not have to consult, Camilla thought, and undoubtedly Thunder Heights would enjoy a less ruffled atmosphere when he was gone. Yet when she thought of Ross it was always with a tinge of regret. Under other circumstances they might have been friends, and it was sad to see a possibility of friendship lost.

When she had finished her second cup of coffee, she took her newly jotted list and descended from the kitchen to a landing at the back door. From the landing the stairs dropped in a second steeper flight to the cellar below, and she followed them down.

The main room of the cellar, at the foot of the stairs, was a large one, lighted by high windows that rose above ground. A huge cookstove indicated that the room had once been the main kitchen of the house. What a busy, exciting place this must have been in the great days of Thunder Heights, before the new wing had been built to accommodate a smaller upstairs kitchen.

Camilla followed a corridor that ran the length of the cellar, looking eagerly into one room after another. There were storerooms of various kinds, and finally a room with high stone walls and an air of chill that indicated a larder.

Its door opened inward and stood ajar. These days butter and cream were kept in the ice chest upstairs, serviced from the village, so another use had apparently been found for this room. Along the wall facing the door were rows of shelves lined with dozens of small glass-stoppered jars and corked bottles. A marble slab had been set into a work shelf below at waist height, and a mortar and pestle rested upon it.

All these things Camilla saw at a glance as she stood sheltered by the door, unaware until she moved into the room that she was not alone. At her right, standing before a further row of shelves, was Aunt Hortense. This morning she wore a voluminous green negligee trimmed with yellowing lace. Her red hair, done up in rag curlers, was hidden by a white cap with coyly placed green velvet bows. She had not heard Camilla's quiet step in the doorway, and as Camilla hesitated, she reached up to a shelf and took down one of the labeled bottles.

"Good morning, Aunt Hortense," Camilla said, and her aunt whirled about, nearly dropping the bottle in her hands.

"Don't startle me like that!" she cried. "I didn't know anyone was about."

"I'm sorry," Camilla said. "I didn't see you till I stepped around the door."

She moved toward the shelves and looked up at them with interest, reading the labels. Here were Letty's herbs. The usual cooking herbs: thyme, chives, basil, marjoram, parsley, summer savory—all dried and pulverized, or left in leaf form, all labeled. On another shelf were the medicinal herbs: angelica, chamomile, hyssop, and many more. There were infusions and elixirs and

distillations, as well as the dried herbs. As Camilla studied them, Hortense replaced the labeled bottle of tansy she had taken from its place.

"My sister Letty's hobby," Hortense said, her nose wrinkling a little as if she did not wholly approve. "It gives her something to do. But she indulges in too much experiment. I prefer to pick my own mixtures and avoid hers. I came down for something for my stomach and nerves. I hardly slept a wink all night. Is there anything you're looking for down here?"

In the bright morning light, Hortense's skin looked gray and a little withered. Her eyes that were not altogether green, nor altogether blue, had a look of cold resentment in them as they rested upon Camilla.

"I'm not looking for anything special," Camilla said. "I thought I would start at the cellar and begin to know the house. I hope you don't mind. When you feel up to it, Aunt Hortense, I'd like to consult you about so many things."

Hortense sniffed. "I'm certainly not up to it now. Not after the several shocks I've had to endure in the last few days. And after a miserable night. How did you sleep?"

"Soundly," Camilla said. "I hardly stirred till morning."

"She didn't bother you then? She didn't come to your door and try to get in?"

"What do you mean?" Camilla asked. "No one came to my door."

"A good thing. She might have frightened you. I've always wanted to lock her in at night, but Papa wouldn't hear of it."

"What are you talking about?" Camilla asked in bewilderment.

"My sister Letty, naturally. When she is disturbed she often walks in her sleep. And we never know what she may do next. I found her climbing the attic stairs last night and I had a time getting her back to bed."

Hortense reached for a jar of peppermint tea leaves, lifted out the glass stopper and sniffed the fragrance. Then she dropped a spoonful of the leaves into the teapot she had brought downstairs, added another spoonful from a jar of rose hips, and picked up the pot. As she reached the doorway, she paused.

"I should think you would be *afraid* to stay on in this house," she said.

"Afraid? Why should I be afraid?"

Hortense shrugged. "You might ask Letty sometime just what it was she gave Papa to drink the night he had his attack." She walked out of the larder, leaving Camilla to ponder her words in astonishment.

CHAPTER 9

IN THE DAYS that followed, spring began to move brightly up the Hudson valley. Forsythia spilled its yellow spray, and enterprising crocuses and jonquils poked their heads through the bare earth of winter, announcing a change of seasons. About the house there were changes as well.

Camilla went vigorously and determinedly to work on her plans for renewal and repair. Booth laughed in good nature at her efforts, though he told her plainly that he could see no point in her desire to refurbish the house. Let it fall to ruin, he said, and then they would be rid of the burden and could live somewhere else in more fashionable style.

Nevertheless, he obligingly helped her find carpenters and set them to work. Old Toby obtained help in the village for work about the grounds and went at it with a will. Toby, at least, was all for restoring Thunder Heights to its former glory, pleased at the notion of lording it over the new help. He became something of a Napoleon in his attacks upon weeds and scrubby undergrowth. He planted with a lavish hand—grass and flower beds and new young trees to replace those that were old and dead.

An extra kitchenmaid was hired as well, leaving Grace free for upstairs work, but Camilla quickly discovered that indoor household help was difficult to find. Thunder Heights had a reputation that would have to be lived down. This Hortense, who was in need of a personal lady's maid, had to do without, since Camilla was unable to find anyone to work for her.

With Letty's help, Camilla checked slowly through every room

93

in the house, to make sure of all that must be done. Letty was sweet and co-operative and refused her nothing, but Camilla had the uneasy feeling that she too did not believe in what they were doing. Except when Letty was in her herb room downstairs, or outside in her garden, she worked vaguely, as if with fog that blew through her hands as she measured it and would be nothing when she was finished.

Hortense remained hostile to all plans and would take no part in them. There was, Camilla quickly discovered, a convention to which all those in the house, masters and servants alike, bowed in convincing pretense. The pretense was that Hortense ran the house, gave the orders, made all plans, settled all problems. But it became evident in Camilla's first week that it was Letty who quietly executed these matters behind Hortense's back, even while she too gave lip service to her sister as mistress of the house. Camilla might have found something touching about this little game of pretend in which Letty protected her older sister from realizing the emptiness of her rule, had it not been that this sort of thing got in her way when she wanted to act without bowing to the wishes of Aunt Hortense. Camilla intended to make things happen *now,* and she found she could not wait until Hortense had been placated and coaxed into the new pattern. She tried not to oppose her openly, but she could not follow the example of the others if real changes were to be made.

One morning when Camilla found Hortense alone at breakfast, she tried to talk to her and draw her into some active role in the new plans for the house. But her aunt remained sharply antagonistic.

"If you had any sense," she said, "you'd let things alone. This house has seen too much of tragedy. Don't tamper with it. Don't wake it up, or you'll bring more down on our heads. There are times when I think it has a malevolent will to destroy us all. I don't want to see it repaired and renewed."

Camilla paid little attention to her words. The problem of Hortense was one she still hoped to solve, but it could be postponed in the face of matters more urgent.

Ross Granger, too, remained remote from all that was going on, though not to the extent of refusing to help if some immediate need arose. More than once he looked over repairs that were being made and made suggestions that saved time and waste. But he acted seldom and with evident reluctance. Often he carried his books and papers over to the comparative quiet of Blue Beeches, where there was less pounding and shouting, and where he was apparently welcome, as he worked to wind up his own part in Orrin Judd's affairs.

Camilla's first consultation with Mr. Pompton took place more than a week after the funeral. On the morning before Ross Granger was scheduled to leave, she received the lawyer in the library with a mingling of hope and hesitation, not sure whether or not he might try to stop her from spending money on the improvements she wanted to make. She was prepared to oppose him firmly if she had to. A sense of confidence was growing in her as she found that her orders were obeyed, her wishes deferred to—at least by those she employed.

Mr. Pompton had other matters on his mind, however. He droned on in monotonous detail about investments, holdings, interest, and other affairs of a similar nature, until Camilla's head spun and she felt increasingly confused. Then he relented and let her know that there was little she need do about any of these matters at present, except to sign a few papers. Mr. Granger, he said, had been Orrin Judd's lieutenant for years and he undoubtedly understood all the larger business affairs, which were not Mr. Pompton's province. Mr. Granger had formed a liaison between Thunder Heights and New York, and she could inform herself about these matters through him.

"But Mr. Granger is leaving tomorrow," she said in surprise that Ross had not let him know.

Mr. Pompton smoothed his pink scalp, unperturbed. "And when will he return, Miss Camilla?"

"He's not coming back," Camilla said. "He resigned from this work right after the funeral."

The attorney stared at her as if he did not believe his ears. Then he got up and strode back and forth across the room several times. When he sat down again, he had clearly made up his mind.

"You must not accept Granger's resignation, Miss Camilla. Later, perhaps, when someone else can take his place. But at the moment you cannot do without him."

As Camilla listened, he made very plain the reasons why she could not let Ross Granger drop her grandfather's affairs. Her first dismay began to fade as she heard him out, and she felt faintly relieved. Even though Ross had avoided her lately, his presence in the house had been reassuring. The fact of his being here had more than once bolstered her courage. She did not know quite why this was so, since she and Ross seemed seldom to be together without conflict or irritation. Nevertheless, at the moment she felt only relieved to hear that his continued presence was necessary.

When Mr. Pompton finished, Camilla rang for Grace and sent her upstairs to summon Mr. Granger from his room. He left his sorting and packing and came down to the library with his bright hair on end and a smudge of dust along one cheekbone.

"Please sit down," she said, and plunged in before she could frighten herself by thinking what might happen if he refused. "Mr. Pompton has just made me understand how indispensable you are in Judd affairs. Must you really leave us, Mr. Granger?"

He did not seem surprised. "Your cousin Booth and your Aunt Hortense don't want me here. And I certainly haven't meant to force my services on you."

Mr. Pompton coughed impatiently. "Stop play-acting, Granger. You know she can't move a finger without you."

Ross's straight mouth relaxed into a smile. "Miss King has been moving very fast in a number of directions without me."

"Women's matters," Mr. Pompton scoffed. "Supervising pots of paint and getting seamstresses in to make new draperies. Planting grass and clipping back the underbrush." He slapped the table before him impatiently. "What does she know about the Judd projects that are now in the making? These can't be dropped in midstream."

"I'd like to learn," Camilla said quickly.

Mr. Pompton and Ross Granger exchanged glances that were clearly despairing.

"You must stay, Granger," Mr. Pompton said. "You owe it to Orrin Judd."

Ross glanced at the portrait over the mantel. "I suppose it's impossible to leave without making some attempt to help. For a time at least."

"Then you will stay?" Camilla asked, and found that her tone sounded meeker than she had intended.

Ross hesitated for a moment longer, before he gave in. "All right —I'll stay. But not under this roof. I'd have moved out long ago, if Mr. Judd hadn't insisted that I be where he could call me the instant he wanted me."

"He left you the use of the rooms over the coach house in his will," Pompton said. "That was a bribe, wasn't it? To give you what you wanted, so you'd stay on and assist Miss Camilla?"

"Perhaps." Ross smiled wryly. "Or else it was meant to infuriate Hendricks."

Camilla looked from one to the other. "I don't understand. Why should it infuriate Booth?"

"Mr. Hendricks has his studio in those rooms," Mr. Pompton said. "He dabbles at his painting there."

So that was where Booth went when he absented himself from the house.

Camilla considered the matter, still at a loss. She did not want to antagonize Booth by putting him out of rooms he liked to work in. At the same time, she did not dare to lose Ross, and he was clearly firm about getting out of this house.

"There's no immediate hurry, is there?" she asked. "If you'll give me a little time, I'll talk to Booth and persuade him to work somewhere else."

Ross quirked a doubtful eyebrow, but did not object to a delay. Mr. Pompton gathered up his papers, found still another for Camilla's signature, and then went off, shaking his head doubtfully.

"I'd better get to my—unpacking," Ross said when Pompton had gone.

On impulse Camilla held out her hand to him. "Thank you for staying. I know you didn't want to."

He took her hand, bowed over it remotely and went out of the room without further comment.

Left alone, Camilla wondered about the best way to approach Booth. Perhaps Letty could help her on this, since she and Booth seemed on affectionate terms.

Camilla found her in the rear garden. Her aunt knelt at her work, the sleeves of her gray dress rolled up and her hands gloveless as she handled the soft brown earth, preparing it for planting. So this was why Letty's hands were not the pale, protected hands of a lady, but had a sturdy look of usefulness about them.

Much of her work seemed to be done with her left hand, but she brought her right hand frequently into play by bending her body forward to accommodate the stiff arm. Her rolled-up sleeve revealed to a pitiful extent the misshapen right arm, thin and twisted. As she drew near, Camilla saw with a pang of dismay the ugly, welted crescent of a scar on the inner flesh of the arm.

At that moment Letty heard her. The bent head with its silver coronet of braids came up, and at once Letty pulled down her sleeve to cover the scarred and crooked arm. The gesture seemed more automatic than distressed, as if it were something she did out of long habit, to save the sensibilities of others. Her smile of greeting for Camilla was affectionate.

"Spring is the exciting time of year," Letty said, sounding as exuberant as a girl. "There's something about the smell of earth warming in the sun that's full of wonderful promise. I can almost feel things beginning to grow."

"I can at least see them beginning," Camilla laughed, and sat down on a flat rock at the edge of Letty's garden. "There's green everywhere you look today. Are you planting flowers, Aunt Letty?"

"No—herbs. Toby raises a few flowers, and I've planted a white narcissus fringe along the edge of the wood up there. But it's my little friends the herbs I like best. Look at coltsfoot there—already blooming. He's a bold one. That means warm days are on the way. He comes up as quickly as a dandelion, and just as bright and yellow, with his thick leaves close to the ground."

She gestured toward the plant beside her, and Camilla reached out to touch a leaf and turn it over, revealing its white, woolly underside. Watching Aunt Letty, listening to her, Camilla felt once more impatient with Hortense and her unkind insinuations. It was not Letty in this household who was to be distrusted.

"They're all so different, these herb people," Letty went on, more talkative now than Camilla had ever seen her. "Sage has leaves like velvet, while some herbs have leaves shiny as satin, or prickly, or smooth, or tough. Of course they're not much when it comes to flowers, yet the garden can look gay as a carnival when my herbs are in bloom. You'll see, later on."

Her bright, intense gaze, strangely young, lifted to meet Camilla's look frankly.

"I'm glad you're going to stay with us, my dear. At first I thought the only answer for you was to let the house go. But perhaps I was wrong."

"I hope so," Camilla said soberly.

"Of course you mustn't live the way we've lived." Letty prodded the earth with her trowel, continuing her work. "I mean shut in with each other, turning our backs on Westcliff and all our neighbors. Booth has a few friends he meets away from the house, but that's not enough. You could open the house, if you wanted to— make it like it was in the days when we were young and your mother was alive."

Camilla moved on the rock and drew her knees up, clasping her hands about them. "That sounds like fun, but there's so much to be done first, and it's still hard to believe in what has happened to me. I haven't begun to get used to it yet. Yesterday, when I was going through my trunk after it arrived from New York, I found myself wondering how I could remake some of my clothes, so they would last another season."

She laughed out loud, remembering her own foolish behavior. Suddenly, as she puzzled over the problem, it had come to her that she might have all the new clothes she wanted. Whereupon she had rolled up a bundle of her old things, rejoicing in an outburst of reckless abandon, and packed them off for charity. A gesture which left her with hardly a stitch to her back until the matter was corrected.

Letty laughed with her gently, as she told the story. "Perhaps you'll let Hortense help you with your planning of new gowns."

"Of course," Camilla promised readily. "Let's plan a new wardrobe for all three of us."

Letty nodded a little absently and returned to her work.

In a little while, Camilla knew, she must bring up the subject of Booth, but it was so pleasantly peaceful here in the herb garden that she wanted to postpone that problem for the moment. She wondered about Letty as she watched her work. It would be interesting to know what thoughts went on behind her present tranquility. She did not look like a woman who would walk in her sleep, or ever intend the slightest harm to others. Did she ever guess how her sister maligned her?

In the picture Grandfather Orrin had left, Letty's right arm had looked as straight as her left, so the crippling must have occurred after she was grown. What had caused the ugly scar that welted her arm? And why had so sweet a person as Letty never married?

"A normal social life would be good for Hortense, too." Letty paused, trowel in air. "She has been hungry for gaiety for a long time."

"Yet she doesn't approve of what I'm doing," Camilla pointed out. "She says the house is born to tragedy and we must let it alone, or be destroyed by it."

Letty sat back on her heels to gaze up at the dark towers above them. "I know what she means. Once death has stepped into a house it leaves a shadow."

"Every old house knows death," Camilla protested. "Why should we mind that? Grandfather was an old man and he must have lived a full life. Perhaps we shouldn't grieve too much for his going."

The silver braids about Letty's head shone in the sun as she bent over the bed where she was working, crumbling earth idly in her fingers. Her silence was only a cloak for her thoughts, Camilla knew, and she spoke to her softly.

"You're thinking of my mother, aren't you, Aunt Letty? That she died in this house—died too young. Will you tell me what happened? When those reporters were here, one of them mentioned her. He spoke of her being—smashed up. Why shouldn't I know the truth, whatever it was?"

Letty's brown eyes, so warm and unlike her sister's, rested on Camilla's face for a moment and then flicked away. In that instant Camilla glimpsed in them something of—was it fear? There was a long silence while Letty dropped seeds into the earth and patted them down, moving on along the row, not minding the earth stains on her skirt. A robin, fat and red-breasted, hopped close enough to pull a worm from the far side of the herb bed. There was a warm odor of earth and sun and pine needles in the air, and Camilla thought she had never been in so quiet and peaceful a place. Peaceful except for the glimpse of quickly hidden uneasiness she had seen in Letty's eyes.

While her father had refused to speak of Althea's death because of his own pain, and his desire to keep his daughter from unnecessary hurt, the silence which surrounded Althea's death at Thunder Heights had in it something more. Something that savored of concealment, of a fearful reluctance to have the truth known.

It would be no use, Camilla knew, to repeat her question. The time for the answer to be given her was not yet ripe. In as matter-of-fact tones as she could manage, she began to speak of Booth's studio over the coach house and of the fact that Ross, if he were to stay, must have the use of those rooms.

Letty listened, nodding thoughtfully. "Of course we can't afford to lose Ross Granger if he is willing to stay. Booth will have to give up his studio. But he won't want to, you know. And he can be difficult when he chooses. Perhaps I had better speak to him."

For just a moment Camilla was ready to accept Letty's offer. For all that Booth had been kind, she had a feeling of strangeness about him. He had never shown anger toward her, yet she had a sense of dreading his anger. Nevertheless, she put aside her feeling of readiness to rely on Letty. If she was to make her home at Thunder Heights she could not sidestep the difficult tasks. This was something she must solve herself. She had come to Aunt Letty only for advice.

"I'll speak to him myself," she said.

There was approval in Letty's look. "You're right, of course, dear. Perhaps you might offer him some other place when you tell him about this. Why not—the nursery? It's big enough and the light is good up there. Booth only moved his workroom out of the house because Papa came to dislike the smell of paints and turpentine. But I don't think the rest of us will mind it up at the top of the house."

"Thank you, Aunt Letty," Camilla said. "I'll go talk to him now."

But still she did not spring up at once to go in search of Booth. "I saw your herb collection in the cellar the other day," she went on idly. "You must have given a great deal of study to the subject to put up all those different things."

Letty nodded. "I love to mix my tisanes and infusions. Herbs have so much to give when you understand them. I used to treat most of the villagers in the old days, whenever they got sick. They trusted me more than they did the doctor. There was a friendly rivalry between Dr. Wheeler and me at one time. Of course I don't do that any more."

Camilla studied her aunt's face with its fragile bone structure and hint of inner strength. "Why did you stop, if you helped people and if you enjoyed nursing them?"

Letty did not answer at once. She pressed earth over seeds she had dropped and smiled down at them fondly.

"You have to be careful about planting herbs. They're likely to come up—every one—and grow elbow to elbow like city folk. So we have to give them room in the planting."

Camilla waited, and after a moment Letty went on, not meeting her eyes as she spoke.

"Hortense didn't like what I was doing. She didn't think it was a fitting occupation for a Judd."

"Why not start again, Aunt Letty?" Camilla asked.

"It's too late," Letty admitted sadly. "Too late for so many things." She bent her head, so that only her silvery braids were visible.

There was no point in postponing her unwelcome task any longer and Camilla stood up. "Do you know where Booth is now?"

"I saw him going out toward the coach house this morning," Letty told her. "He's probably still there. If he's angry with you at first, don't mind. I'll get him to come around."

"I'll get him to come around myself," Camilla said with a resolution she did not entirely feel. She walked around the house and took the driveway in the direction of the stable.

CHAPTER 10

As she approached, the coach house could be seen ahead near the gate. Here, too, an unconventional imagination had been at work in the design. It looked almost like a miniature of the main house, with its own turrets and gables and the barge-board bracketing that was typically Hudson River.

She found the barnlike lower door ajar and saw that it was somewhat the worse for weathering. More repairs would be needed here, as well as fresh paint. From the open doorway she could see a steep flight of stairs running upward to the floor above. She did not approach them at once, but moved among the dusty stalls and examined the big room where a carriage had once been kept. Dust and cobwebs lay over everything. Only the stairs had been swept clean. An old set of harness hanging from a nail rattled as she struck it in passing and Booth's voice challenged her at once from above.

"Who's down there?"

She went quickly to the foot of the stairs. "It's I—Camilla."

He came to the head of the stairs and looked down at her. "A pleasant surprise! Come up, Cousin Camilla, and see my workshop."

Holding to a rickety handrail, she mounted the stairs and took Booth's extended hand. He drew her up the last step, and she stood blinking in the bright, spacious upper room.

Booth wore a long gray linen duster revealing smudges of paint, and he held a palette in one hand. An easel had been set up in the center of the room with a nearly finished painting upon it.

"You're just in time for coffee, Cousin," Booth told her. He set the palette down and brought an armchair for her, dusting it before she seated herself. "My housekeeping's not of the best, but I don't like servants moving my stuff around."

When she had taken the chair, he stepped to an alcove, where a coffee pot had just started to bubble on a small stove. The fragrance of coffee was laced by the odors of Booth's paint materials—a combination Camilla did not find unpleasant. While he busied himself with the coffee, she studied the painting on the easel.

Once more she was caught by the violent power of Booth's work. This view was one of the Hudson, with what must surely be an exaggerated Thunder Mountain rising from the bank. Black storm clouds boiled into the sky above, and the whole was a moment held suspended in a flash of lightning. At the foot of the precipice Hudson waters churned to an angry yellow in the sulphurous light, and a tiny boat was caught in the instant of capsizing and spilling its occupants into the water. Booth had endowed the painting with a wild terror that made Camilla's scalp prickle.

"Are your pictures always so violent?" she asked.

Booth set the coffee pot down and came over to her, interested at once in her reaction to his work.

"So you see what I've tried to catch? The moment of danger! The very knife edge of danger, where there is life one moment and possible death the next."

She could see what he meant, and even sense the fascination such a moment might have for him as an artist. But she wondered what might drive a man to preserve such moments repeatedly on canvas. The picture she had seen in his mother's room had portrayed the same "moment of danger."

He saw the question in her eyes. "Can there be any greater excitement in life than the moment just before a man solves the last mystery?"

There seemed a dark elation in him that was disturbing. From the first she had sensed about him a strangeness that she did not understand, and which she remembered when she was away from him. Because it made her uneasy now and a little self-conscious, she left her chair to wander about the room, examining other paintings that leaned against the walls.

"Your mother spoke of arranging a show for you in a New York gallery," she said. "Why don't you go ahead with that now?"

He returned to the stove, filled a cup from the coffee pot and brought it to her. "I suppose I could—if I cared enough. Grandfather Orrin never approved of my painting. He didn't consider it a man's work. Not that I cared. I paint for my own amusement."

Amusement was a strange word for a product so gloomy. She sipped her coffee and moved on about the room, pausing to study the scene of a fierce cockfight, in which the feathers of the birds were bright with blood as they met in deadly combat. The next picture was an unfinished painting of a woman who struggled to hold a rearing horse, its hoofs flailing not far from her head. Her face had not been completed and the background was a vague blur, but the wild eyes of the horse, its distended nostrils and bared teeth, had all been carefully depicted.

Booth noted Camilla's arrested interest and crossed the room to turn the picture against the wall. "I don't put my unfinished work on view," he said.

There was almost a rebuff in his manner, and she glanced at him, puzzled. What haunted this man? What drove him and made him so strange? Darkly strange and strangely fascinating.

She returned to her chair, moving it so that she need not stare at the painting of the capsizing boat with its little human figures flung out over the torrent.

"Your model has courage," she remarked. When he said nothing she went on. "I've always loved to ride. Do you suppose I could buy a horse hereabout and ride again at Thunder Heights?"

Booth sat down upon a high stool, hooking his heels over the rungs. "Why not? Grandfather Orrin's not here to forbid it."

"Why wouldn't he keep horses when he had a coach house built?"

Booth drank a swallow of coffee, hot and black. "We hardly needed them, since we had few places to go. The world came to Orrin Judd when it had to, and it could hire its own hacks."

She knew he was evading her question, but she could not bring herself to challenge him.

"If you're seriously interested, Cousin," he went on, "I'll keep an eye open for a horse that's been trained to the sidesaddle. I think I can find you a good one."

"I'll appreciate that." She finished her coffee, wondering how to bring up the subject of Ross Granger and these rooms.

He gave her an unexpected opening. "I suppose you'll plan to clean up the stable below and keep your horse here when you get one? There's room for a stableboy beyond that partition."

Camilla forced herself to the topic in hand. "Did you know that Mr. Granger has agreed to stay on for a time? Mr. Pompton says we can't do without him. He has been my grandfather's eyes and ears for so long that there's no one to take his place."

She stole a look at Booth as she spoke and saw that he had stiffened.

"I was afraid we wouldn't be easily rid of him. I suppose you've come to tell me that I'm to move out of these rooms and let Ross Granger take over his—inheritance? Is that it?"

She could feel herself flushing. "Perhaps we could fix up the old nursery as a studio for you. The light there should be better than you have here, and it might be more convenient to do your painting inside the house."

"I suppose this is a plan Aunt Letty has suggested? You were afraid to come here and ask me to move, weren't you, Cousin?"

"I came," she said simply, not caring to admit her reluctance.

"So you did. But what if I tell you I don't choose to move? What if I tell you I don't care for the nursery?"

She looked away from the rising anger in his eyes. "I don't blame you for not wanting to move, when the place has been yours for so long."

"Your sympathy touches me, Cousin," he said, and began stacking his finished paintings against the wall. "All right then—I'll move. But please understand—I'm not doing it to suit Granger's convenience."

She set her cup and saucer aside and went to stand beside him. "You needn't hurry. Mr. Granger can wait. I'm sorry it has to be this way."

His look softened unexpectedly and he smiled. "I believe you mean that, my dear. Don't worry, I'll cause you no embarrassment. But remember that I'm doing this for you, not for Granger."

"Thank you," she said, and turned toward the stairs, retreating instinctively from his gentler mood, lest he ask more of her than she was ready to give.

He did not let her go alone, but came with her toward the house. As they followed the driveway, he slipped her hand into the crook of his arm, as if he wished to reassure her. Camilla was sharply aware of him close at her side, moving with his air of restrained vitality, as though the dark power that flowed through him was held for the moment in leash. What might it be like if he once lifted his self-imposed restraint? An odd sense of excitement stirred her.

As if he knew her reaction to his nearness, he tightened his arm so that her hand was pressed against his side.

"Tell me, Cousin," he said, "how does it happen that a young woman as attractive as you are has gone unmarried in New York?"

"I have never known very many men," she admitted, and tried to quicken her step.

He held her to the slower pace, and she knew he was amused by her quick confusion and the warm color she felt in her cheeks. Booth Hendricks puzzled and dismayed her, and as often as not he filled her with a sense of—was it attraction or alarm? Perhaps a mingling of both, for it might be dangerous to grow too interested in this man.

"We must mend this lack in your life," he said. "Unless you know a variety of men, you're likely to be too vulnerable to attention from almost any man."

He went too far, but she did not know how to reprove him, was not even sure that she wanted to.

When they neared the house the sound of carpenters working on a scaffolding above the front door reached them, and Camilla looked up at the new repairs in satisfaction.

"The house looks better already. I'm eager to see it painted."

Booth's look followed her own with indifference. "I'm afraid I agree with my mother that it's a waste of good money and energy. But if it pleases you, Camilla, if it makes you happy, then I suppose it serves a purpose in our lives."

He released her hand from his arm and left her at the foot of the steps, going off in one of his abrupt withdrawals, so that it seemed all in an instant that he had forgotten her. She went into the house troubled by a curious mixture of emotions. At the moment she was not at all sure how she felt about Booth Hendricks.

Letty met her in the upstairs hall. "Did you see Booth? How did he react when you suggested a change of studios?"

"I know he didn't like it," Camilla told her, "but he tried to be kind. I suspect that he's angry with Ross. I'm relieved to have the interview over."

Letty was studying her with quick understanding. "You look upset, dear. Why don't you lie down in your room for a little while and let me bring you a tisane to make you feel better?"

It was easier to allow Aunt Letty to minister to her, than to resist or refuse to be doctored. But when she was in her room again, she could not lie quietly on a bed. Her visit to Booth's studio had been upsetting in more ways than one. She had sensed in him a bitter anger that might one day explode into the open. When it did, she hoped it would not be directed against herself. Or did she hope for just that? Did she want to be involved with Booth at whatever cost to herself?

She was still walking restlessly about the room when Letty tapped at the door. As Camilla opened it, Mignonette streaked in first, leaving Letty to enter more slowly with a tray in her hands.

"Here you are, dear," Letty said. "There's hot toast in that napkin and a bit of rose petal jam. Let the tea steep a minute, and it will be just right."

"Thank you, Aunt Letty," Camilla said, grateful for her consideration and affection.

Letty patted her arm lovingly and hurried away. For once Mignonette did not follow her mistress. She came to sit before the small table that held the tray, looking up at it expectantly.

Camilla laughed. "You're staying for your saucerful, aren't you?"

The little cat mewed in plaintive agreement.

"All right," Camilla said, "I'll pour some for you, but you'd better be careful—it's scalding hot."

She filled the saucer and set it on a piece of wrapping paper on the hearth. Then she poured a cupful for herself and stirred it, waiting for it to cool, sniffing the sharp aroma that was a little like that of the daisy, and not altogether pleasant. Mignonette was already lapping daintily around the cooling edges of the liquid, and Camilla watched her in amusement. A strange taste for a cat. Letty must have fed her tisanes when she was a kitten, that she had grown up with so odd an appetite.

Feeling that she must drink some of the tea whether she liked it or not, Camilla raised her cup. The cat made a choking sound, and she looked down to see that Mignonette was writhing as if in pain. While Camilla watched, too startled to move, the little cat contorted her body painfully and rid herself of the tea she had just lapped up so greedily.

Camilla set her teacup down and ran to the door to call Letty. It was Hortense, however, who came down the hallway.

"Letty's gone downstairs. What is it?"

"Mignonette is sick. I just gave her a saucer of tea and she's throwing it up."

An odd expression crossed Hortense's face. She cast a single look at the cat and then picked up the untouched cupful of tea. She sniffed it and shook her head.

"I'll take care of this," she said and picked up the teapot as well to carry away.

Camilla poured water into the saucer for Mignonette and began to fold up the paper. In a moment Hortense was back.

"You mustn't let my sister dose you with these things," she said. "She overrates her knowledge of medicinal herbs, and it's best not to give in to her whims. What if you had drunk what was in that cup and hadn't the faculty of getting rid of it as Mignonette did?"

She went off without waiting for an answer, and Camilla regarded the cat doubtfully. Mignonette was trying weakly to clean herself, and she looked up at Camilla with an air that might have been one of entreaty. Camilla picked her up gently and carried her downstairs in search of Letty.

Grace said Miss Letty was in the cellar larder, and Camilla went down the lower stairs. She found Letty at work cleaning shelves, with Booth assisting her in a desultory fashion. They were taking down bottles and jars, wiping them and replacing them in neat order.

Camilla held out the cat. "Mignonette drank some of my tea

just now and it made her painfully sick for a few moments. She really frightened me. Though I think she's recovered."

Letty turned and Camilla saw the color drain from her face. She almost snatched the cat from Camilla's hands and held her close, stroking the small body tenderly. Camilla had never seen Letty angry before, but now she fairly bristled with indignation.

"No one gives Mignonette anything without my orders," she cried. "Never, never do such a thing again!"

Camilla heard her in astonishment and found no answer.

"Perhaps," Booth said quietly, "we had better think of Camilla. Did you drink any of the mixture, Cousin?"

"No." Camilla shook her head. "Aunt Hortense came in when I told her the cat was sick, and she took the pot and cup away and emptied them. I hadn't even tasted the tea."

Her words seemed to bring Letty to herself. While she did not release her hold on Mignonette, she gave Camilla a weak and apologetic smile.

"I'm sorry, dear. Mignonette means so much to me that I—I was cross for a moment. It was most inconsiderate of me."

Booth was watching her, his gaze alert and questioning.

"What was in the tea, Aunt Letty?" he asked.

Holding the cat to her shoulder with one hand, Letty hurried to the row of shelves behind the door and took down an empty jar. "Why—it was just my usual marjoram and mint mixture. I used the last of it—see."

Booth took the jar from her hands and removed the cover, sniffing before he gave it back to her. "Are you sure? Sometimes I wonder how you tell all these leaves and powders apart when you're working with so many ingredients."

"It's quite simple," Letty said with dignity. "I know the appearance of each one as well as I know the faces of those about me. And every scent is different too."

She put the empty jar back on the shelf, and Camilla noted idly a vacant place on the same shelf a little farther along, where a bottle had been removed from between two others.

"Tell me, Aunt Letty," Booth said, "did anyone else know you were going to fix this pot of tea for Camilla?"

For just an instant Letty's gaze wavered. It was nothing more than a flicker, yet Camilla sensed in it indecision and hesitation. A shock of distrust that was close to fear flashed through Camilla, leaving her shaken and apprehensive.

Then Letty was herself again, and if she had experienced a moment of doubt in which she had seen a choice of action before her, the fact was quickly concealed by her more usual manner. Had she thought in that instant to conceal blame, or to place the blame elsewhere? In any case, she did neither.

"I'm sure it wasn't my tea that upset Mignonette," she said. "I tell you what—I'll fix you some fresh tea, dear. It won't take a minute."

Camilla started to refuse, but Booth broke in smoothly. "Make some for me too, Aunt Letty. The three of us can have a pot together. I've had a bad morning."

He glanced at Camilla, his look faintly mocking, as if he dared her to refuse. His mood had lifted strangely into something laced with excitement, and far from reassuring to see.

Letty made the tea, heating water on the stove out in the main room of the cellar, where a fire already burned beneath a simmering mixture. There were several straight chairs about a round table in the big room, and they sat down to drink a mint tea that Letty had flavored with leaves of fragrant balm. Mignonette, apparently none the worse for her experience, trustfully took a saucerful from Letty's hands. But only in the small cat was there any trust, Camilla thought as she sipped the fragrant tea. Letty's eyes did not meet her own, while Booth's gaze met Camilla's all too readily. She felt a little sick with distrust, so that she could hardly swallow.

Before they were through, Hortense came downstairs and regarded them in astonishment.

"Do join us," Letty said almost gaily, but her sister refused.

Booth slanted an oblique look at his mother. "You shouldn't have thrown out that pot of tea so quickly. It might have borne looking into. Could you tell whether anything was wrong?"

"They all smell vile to me," Hortense said. "That cat was at death's door. What affected the cat might have killed Camilla."

Letty busied herself with Mignonette, and one would have thought by her manner that she had heard nothing of the talk going on about her. Yet there was a rigidity in the movement of her head that told Camilla how intently she listened. It seemed as though some duel went on below the surface among these three— as though each knew something Camilla did not know, and each suspected the other two.

Camilla let the rest of the tea cool in her cup. The bitter taste in her mouth gave it a flavor she could not endure.

That afternoon at Ross's request, Camilla had a talk with him in the library. After what had happened to Mignonette, she was in no mood to discuss business matters, but Ross insisted and she lacked the strength to oppose him.

They faced each other beneath Orrin Judd's picture, and Camilla found it difficult to attend to his words. She would have preferred to pour out her own doubts and bewilderment, but Ross, she suspected, would dismiss such notions as feminine nonsense. His own manner was as correct and impersonal as Mr. Pompton's would have been, and such a bearing did not invite confidences.

"Did you have any trouble getting Hendricks to agree to move out of the coach house?" Ross began.

"None at all," Camilla said. It was not to Ross that she would admit her confusion about Booth.

He studied her with a skeptical air, as if he were ready to discount anything she might say. She blinked in the face of such scrutiny, finding him no more an easy person to be with than was Booth. Or did most men leave her ill at ease? she wondered, thinking of Booth's words. Not vulnerable—merely uncomfortable.

She made herself meet Ross's eyes and take the lead. "Why are you so anxious to move out of the house?" she asked.

"Frankly, I don't want to be under the same roof with your Aunt Hortense or her son. I'm sure no love is lost between us and we'll be glad to avoid chance meetings that wear on the nerves when we meet constantly about the house."

"What about mealtime?" Camilla asked. "Won't you be joining us then?"

"Only for dinner," he said. "I can manage the rest myself. The coach house is set up for light housekeeping, and I can work straight through the day out there, with plenty of room for office space. But this isn't why I wanted to see you. If I'm to stay on here for a time, I'll need to know your wishes in various matters."

Camilla nodded. She had no idea what he expected of her.

"If you choose," he went on, "you can make final decisions from here, just as your grandfather used to do. Even though he remained at Thunder Heights, he never let the reins go slack. It's to be hoped that you'll follow in his footsteps."

His face was expressionless, but Camilla could hardly believe that he meant what he was saying.

"How could I possibly—"

He broke in at once. "Or you can go down to New York yourself and meet the directors of his business holdings and discuss problems with them whenever you like."

Now she was sure he was baiting her. "I can't make decisions concerning matters I know nothing of."

"I agree." He nodded as though her answer satisfied him. "A few days ago you said you wanted to learn about your grandfather's affairs. If you like, we can meet for a time every day so that we can go into them together."

She could imagine him as a stern, remote tutor, and herself as his humble student. The prospect did not please her.

"Isn't there another choice? Since you understand all this so well, can't you make the necessary decisions and talk to the businessmen in New York?"

His smile was cool. "You've mistaken my identity," he told her. "I'm Mercury, not Jove. I've played messenger for your grandfather, and on occasion I've advised him on engineering projects. But I've never made final decisions. I doubt that anyone would listen to me."

Camilla gave him a sidelong glance, once more aware of his look of vigor, as if he were made for an outdoor existence and never for the work of a clerk—or a messenger.

"You'd have to begin at the very beginning," she said with a sigh.

"Shall we start tomorrow morning at nine, then?" he said.

When she nodded, he stood up, as if only too eager to escape her presence. Whether she liked it or not, a period of tutelage lay ahead, with Ross Granger as her mentor.

CHAPTER 11

Now a tidal foam of cherry, pear, and apple blossoms surged north along the Hudson. This was a joy not to be experienced to any such extent in New York, and Camilla reveled in the pink and white beauty. She found a favorite spot beneath the plumes of a flowering peach where she could often sit overlooking the Hudson, watching the busy river traffic. Here petals drifted on every breeze, settling about her on the young spring grass.

Escaping the house and its submerged antagonisms, she could make herself forget the episode of Mignonette's poisoning. Or at least she could convince herself that in so lovely a world such forebodings as grew out of the incident were foolish. These days she felt an increasing, comforting affinity with the river.

With Ross's occasional help, she was learning to identify by name some of the boats that passed. She knew the cargoes of the flat barges, and the freighters that plied their way up and down the Hudson. She might have preferred her instruction from Booth, but he had little interest in the river.

It was unfortunate that her business conferences with Ross were less amiable than her river discussions and that the tension between them increased. At first he tried conscientiously to make clear the complicated details on construction that he set before her. But with no background for understanding the vast reaches of the Judd building empire, and no natural flair for the figures and blueprints Ross laid before her, she was soon weltered in confusion and, at length, boredom. When she tried to talk to him about her own eager plans for the house and the grounds, he shrugged them aside as being of no consequence. This, more than anything else, infuriated her. Why should he expect of her talents that she did not have, and ignore the real gifts she felt she was bringing to Thunder Heights?

The outdoor painting was nearly finished, and she could regard the old house with new pride. She had refused to have it painted a frivolous yellow, like Blue Beeches. Silver gray seemed to suit its seasoned quality, and now its turrets gleamed a clean, pale gray against the surrounding green of the woods, with the roofs a dignified darker gray. The house had lost none of its eerie quality in the painting and there was still a somber air about it, but at least it was handsome again, as it had been in its youth. Camilla had already had the satisfaction of seeing passengers on the river boats look up at the house and gesture in admiration.

Yet all this Ross ignored, as though she were a child playing with toys and not to be taken seriously. He thought it a waste of time and money to trouble about the house when there were matters of moment at stake. The real quarrel between them, however, came over the bridge.

Perhaps the matter would not have brought on such a crisis if she and Ross had not been particularly at odds with each other that day. Their disagreement came over the improvements she insisted upon for the coach house. So far Booth had not found a saddle horse for her, but Camilla wanted the stable to be ready for one when it was found. The invasion of his premises with pounding and sawing and the noise of workmen had irritated Ross. The place had been all right, he said—let it alone!

As a consequence he was shorter than usual at their morning sessions in the library, which had become their schoolroom. When he mentioned the bridge out of a clear sky one morning and said they must soon go seriously to work on this as an important future project, she asked flatly why they should consider building a bridge across the Hudson, with all the enormous expense and complications such an undertaking would involve. Mr. Pompton was urging her to sell more and more of her holdings and invest the money in other ways. He thought it foolish of Ross to try to teach her anything of her grandfather's business affairs, and she was ready to agree with Mr. Pompton.

Ross contained himself and tried to be patient about explaining the matter.

"Camilla, you must realize that for miles up and down the river, there is no way for people and commerce to cross, except by ferry. How do you think this country can continue to grow, if those who have the means and the imagination shun their responsibility? Can't you see what such a bridge would mean to the entire Hudson valley? And can't you imagine how it would look?"

His hands moved in a wide gesture, as if he built before her eyes a great span of steel and concrete. He had come to life as she had never seen him do before. She had not thought of him as a man who could dream and the realization surprised her. Nevertheless, she could not go along with so staggering a project.

"Did Grandfather think such a plan practical?" she challenged.

Ross looked thoroughly exasperated. Perhaps all the more so because for a moment he had let down the guard he seemed to hold against her.

"He was certainly for the idea in the beginning. I'll admit he lost interest in a great many things in the last few years, and perhaps he was no longer as pressingly keen on the bridge as he was at the start, but I'm sure he never gave up the idea completely. The legislature in Albany is interested. I've appeared before committees more than once. And we're in a position to underbid the field when the time is ready for action. But a great deal of preparatory work must be done. The location we will recommend must be settled on. Materials must be selected well ahead of time, construction contracts worked out in advance—oh, a thousand details must be taken care of before we can even present our story for a final contract."

He reached into a briefcase and drew out a sheaf of engineering drawings he had brought into the library.

"Here—you might as well see what I'm talking about," and he spread before her the detailed drawings for a suspension bridge across the Hudson.

None of them had any meaning for Camilla, but she could recognize the gigantic nature of the project, and she could well imagine the myriad difficulties it would represent. Perhaps her grandfather would have taken to the task eagerly in his younger days, but she could well imagine his shrinking from its complexities in his last years.

"For one thing," she said, trying to sound reasonable, "I don't see why such a bridge hasn't been built before, if it's really needed. Would it justify the amount of traffic it would handle?"

"With that reasoning," Ross said, "no one would ever try anything that hadn't been done before. But of course we've looked into that very question, and I've been able to convince the authorities that the bridge is needed. However, we'd be building for the future as well. You don't think traffic is going to remain at the horse and wagon stage, or even be confined to trains and boats with the motor car coming into use, do you? Roads and more roads are going to be needed. And bridges to connect them, as we've never needed bridges before!"

He almost fired her with his enthusiasm. She had never seen him so eager and alive and persuasive. The picture he was painting was one to stir the imagination. Yet her grandfather, who knew a great deal about such things, had held back, had not been ready. His reasons had probably been good ones, and not merely the reasons of a man grown fearful and tired. She could not know. And since she didn't know, she could not take so reckless an action as to let Ross go ahead on this.

She rubbed her temples wearily with her fingertips and drew back from the papers Ross laid before her.

"If such a bridge needs to be built, let someone else build it," she said. "With Grandfather gone, it's not for us."

Ross stared at her for a moment. Then he scooped up his papers and went out of the room without another word. Camilla knew how angry he was. For a long while she sat on at the library table wondering despairingly what to do.

Then a slow, resentful anger began to grow in her as well. Somehow Ross Granger always managed to put her in the wrong, and she would not have it. He was not going to involve her in the frightening responsibility of building bridges. Only recently there had been a terrible disaster where a new bridge had collapsed, killing a great many people. Remembering the dreadful stories and drawings in the newspapers, her will to oppose him strengthened. There could be no bridge built under the Judd name unless she gave her consent, and she did not mean to give it.

After that, matters went badly between them. The morning "lessons" became painfully formal, with Ross performing a duty in which he plainly had no interest, until they finally ended altogether. Camilla had a feeling that he might resign again at any moment, and she was resolved to let him go. He, more than anything else, was the fly in her ointment these days. Even Mr. Pompton agreed with her about the bridge, when she told him of it a few days later.

It was a good thing there were other satisfactions for her. Letty had found two skillful seamstresses and Camilla had sent for dress goods and household materials from New York, throwing herself into an orgy of sewing. A whole new wardrobe was being prepared for her, as well as a new wardrobe for the house.

Hortense had been indifferent to an offer of new clothes for herself. In her own eyes she was dressed in the grand styles she had admired as a girl, and she preferred them, she said firmly, to the ridiculous way women dressed today. As for Letty, she was satisfied with her own soft, drifting gowns, and Camilla had to admit that they suited her.

Having new clothes was a pleasure she had never been able to indulge to such an extent before, and she was feminine enough to enjoy it wholeheartedly.

Lately she had caught Booth's eyes upon her admiringly more than once, and she had been pleasantly aware of his approval. Since the day when she had gone out to the coach house to talk to him, she had continued to be drawn to him in an oddly uneasy way. She was not altogether comfortable with him, but she could not help but feel flattered by his admiration.

One late afternoon in May Camilla sat on the marble bench in the rear garden, savoring the fragrant company of Aunt Letty's "herb people." She could always find balm for her spirits here, and things to think about as well. It pleased her that she was learning to identify the herbs and could watch their progress with recognition.

Lungwort had followed coltsfoot, with early blooming flowers of pink and blue. Wild thyme spouted between the stones around the sundial. The bee balm was growing quickly, and Camilla loved to pinch off a thin green leaf and rub it between her fingers for the lemony scent. Rosemary, Letty said, belonged to warm climates and always faded away in pained surprise at the first touch of winter. But she loved it and planted it anew every spring—so it was up again now, with its narrow leaves breathing more fragrance into the garden.

It was good to sit here and breathe the sweet and tangy perfumes, pleased that she was beginning to separate one scent from another.

She had worked hard inside the house today, helping the seamstress with the rich materials that had come from New York and which were now bringing new life to the dreary interior of the house. Rose damask draperies in the parlor would give the room a softer, more gracious look. The dining room wallpaper was now a cool, pale green that didn't give her indigestion every time she looked at it. The draperies there were to be a rich golden color—luxurious and expensive. She could imagine their folds as they would hang richly at the dining room windows, and satisfaction flowed through her over what she had accomplished and still meant to accomplish.

The feeling swept her weariness away. She mustn't waste what remained of the afternoon light. Her gaze, roving possessively, pridefully over the house, moved to small windows beneath the main roof. So far she had never explored the attic. Why not have a look at it now, while daylight lasted?

After one last breath of the fragrant garden, she went inside and up two flights of the octagon staircase. At one end of the third floor wing, a narrower, enclosed flight led to the attic. She found candles and matches and climbed the final steep steps that ended in the low-ceilinged area above.

Up here the air was dusty and dim, but she lighted two of her candles and set one of the small holders on a shelf, retaining the other to carry about. Beneath the eaves of the house, she was more conscious of the irregularities of the roof than she had been on the floors below. Overhead the ceiling beams slanted upward here, and down there, at sharp angles, with the dormers and gables that cut up the roof plainly evident. A room that must have been a servant's bedroom had two dormers overlooking the front of the house, and along one side of the room, just beneath the ceiling slant, was a long row of clothes hooks. Perhaps some long ago lady's maid, ironing her mistress's starched petticoats and lace-trimmed drawers, had hung them on those hooks as she finished them.

Another room held old trunks, and Camilla raised the lid of one, to be greeted by the pungent odor of lavender buds and other mixtures of herbs in small bags, used against moths. Clothes of a style long past were stored here. Garments which must have belonged to her grandfather and grandmother, and undoubtedly to Letty, Hortense, and Althea as well.

She moved on to a smaller room at the back of the house, carrying both candles now. Here she had to stoop to avoid dusty beams overhead, and a strand of cobwebs brushed across her face. There was another smell here, besides the stuffy odor of dust and the tang of herbal bags—the smell of leather. Holding her candle high, she saw that leather harness of various types had been tossed over the beams. These must have belonged to the day when Thunder Heights had kept its own horses and carriages. She reached up to touch dry leather, cracked and rough beneath her fingers. No care had been given these things in years.

Circling a post in the middle of the room, she came upon a saddle which had been set apart from the rest of the gear. It lay across a slanting beam within easy reach, a single bright stirrup hanging toward the floor. It was, she saw, an elegant sidesaddle with elaborately embossed silver trimmings, and a silver horn for milady to hook her knee over. She had never seen so beautiful a saddle and she held up a candle to examine it more closely.

A thin film of dust lay upon the surface of the leather, but not so thick a layer as covered other objects in the attic. A spider had spun a web in the dangling stirrup, but it was no more than a filament. The dark leather shone richly, reflecting the light of Camilla's candle, and when she touched it she found the surface smooth as satin and uncracked. The silver mountings and the stirrup were faintly tarnished, but not sufficiently so to reveal years of neglect. Someone had been coming up here regularly to care for this particular saddle. She searched further and found the silver-mounted bridle that matched the saddle; it too had been cared for over the years. There were other sidesaddles and bridles, stored carelessly, without attention. Only these things had been treated lovingly.

Camilla took the polished bridle from its hook and held it in her hands, listening to the small chime of dangling metal parts. What fun if Booth could find a horse for her soon and she could use these things herself.

Returning the bridle to its hook, she moved toward the stairs, but on the way a wooden chest caught her eye. It was of a pale, oriental wood, with brass handles and a brass lock. She raised the lid and looked inside. This time the odor that greeted her was the pleasant scent of camphor wood. With a sense of growing excitement, Camilla lifted out a pale gray top hat that a lady might wear while riding. Beneath, carefully wrapped, were a pair of patent leather riding boots. Finally, she drew out the habit itself and held it up with an exclamation of delight.

It was the most beautiful ash-gray riding habit she had ever seen. The style was one of bygone years, but the draping was so graceful, so truly right, that it could surely be worn in any period. Had this habit belonged to her mother? she wondered. Somehow she could not imagine Hortense or Letty wearing it. As she turned it about, she saw that on the right breast a horseshoe had been embroidered in dark gray silk against the pale ash of the material. Within the horseshoe were embroidered the letters *AJ*.

Standing there with the heavy folds of material in her hands, it was as if she had come unexpectedly upon the very person of her mother here in this attic. An old sadness and longing swept through her, and she held the gray habit to her heart as if she clung to a beloved presence. In the swift pain of remembering, she could recall details of her mother's face that she had not thought of in years. She could even catch in memory the faint violet scent that had always clung about her.

She could not bear to leave this habit in the attic. Quickly she bundled it up, then picked up the hat and boots and blew out the candles. Back in her room she laid the garments upon the bed, where she could examine them more carefully.

To her distress, she found that a muddy stain ran down one

side of the habit, with a jagged tear in the skirt. How strange that these things had been put away without being mended or cleaned. But she would care for them now. She would clean and repair the habit and try it on. The thought was exciting.

It was almost dinnertime now, however, and for the moment she laid the things aside regretfully. Later she would slip away to her room and put on the habit.

All through dinner she hugged her secret to her and waited impatiently to escape. She paid little attention to the desultory conversation, though when Booth mentioned that he was thinking of a trip to New York, she encouraged him.

"Why not?" she said. "Why don't you take some of your paintings with you and see if there's any possibility of holding a show?"

Booth shrugged the suggestion aside and said he was thinking in terms of seeing a play and perhaps looking up old friends.

Ross said, "I'll give you a business errand to take care of while you're in town."

Booth agreed indifferently, and after dinner Ross followed him into the parlor to explain what he had in mind. Camilla, glad to be free, left them and hurried upstairs.

A full-length mirror had been set into the door of the French armoire in Althea's bedroom, and when she had put on the habit —even to the boots, which were only a little tight, and the top hat that sat so debonairly on her black hair, she approached the glass with an odd hesitance. Now that she was fully dressed in these things that had belonged to her mother, she was seized by a fear that she would fall too far short of what Althea had been. Perhaps her image would mock her for daring to mimic her mother. She drew a quick breath and faced the mirror.

The girl who looked back at her was someone she had never seen before. The full gray skirt was caught up gracefully to reveal high-heeled patent leather boots, and the ugly tear and stain were lost in the folds. If the leather of the boots had cracked a bit across the instep, that did not matter. The long-sleeved jacket, with its diagonally cut closing, molded her body, outlining the full curve of her breast, the soft rounding of her shoulders, emphasizing her small waist where the jacket came to a point in front. Camilla had tied the darker gray silk stock about her throat and fastened it with a bar pin. The tall hat was pale gray like the habit, and bound with a wide gray veil that hung down in floating streamers behind. If only she had a crop to complete the picture, and more suitable gloves than these of her own, what a dashing figure she would make. But there was more to her appearance than the costume alone.

For the first time she could recognize beauty in her own face. She could not judge for herself whether it was beauty of feature, or simply that of the high color in her cheeks, of the sparkle of bright eyes beneath long-lashed lids, the look of eagerness and anticipation which gave her a new vitality.

She moved before the mirror, stepping and turning lightly, and knew that her movements were lithe and graceful—as they told her Althea's had been. Did she really resemble her mother so very much? Would she light a room when she entered it, as her father had said his Althea could?

A longing to show herself to someone seized her. Perhaps if she went downstairs and walked into the parlor dressed as she was, she might learn the truth about herself in the faces of others, in the look of eyes that would tell her whether or not she was as lovely as her mother had been.

She opened the door of her room and listened. In the distance downstairs she could hear the murmur of voices. They were still in the parlor—an audience waiting for her to astonish them. Even Ross Granger, whom she would love to confound, was still with them. And Booth, of whose disturbing presence she was always aware. Eagerly she ran toward the stairs and paused at the first step to gather up her skirt in graceful folds. Light from the stair lamp in its high canopy above spilled down upon her, and she found it regrettable that no one stood at the foot of the stairs to see her descent.

She ran lightly down and went to the parlor door, stepping into a glow of lamplight. There she waited quietly and a little breathlessly for those in the room to look up and see her.

CHAPTER 12

Hortense, the green jade stones in her combs gleaming in her red hair, was reading aloud. Letty listened and crocheted, while Booth sat staring at his own long-fingered hands. Ross had spread some papers on a table and was marking them with a pencil. It was he who saw her first and there was no mistaking his astonishment, even his reluctant admiration.

Booth was the next to glance around and see her. He sat quite still, but there was shock in his eyes. The very tension of his body made itself felt in the room, and Letty looked up and rose to her feet with a cry, dropping her crocheting. For a moment she stared at Camilla in something like horror. Then, without warning, she crumpled to the floor. Booth recovered himself and hurried to her side.

Hortense was the last to move. She put down her book and stood up, frowning at Camilla. The frayed ruching of lace upon her bosom moved with her quickened breathing.

"Go upstairs," she ordered, her voice rising. "Go upstairs at once and take off that habit."

Camilla heard her, too surprised to move. She did not in the least understand the consternation she had caused.

Aunt Letty moaned faintly as Booth held Hortense's ever-present smelling salts to her nose.

Hortense threw her sister a scornful look. "Don't be a goose, Letty. It's only Camilla dressed up in Althea's old riding habit." Then she spoke to Camilla. "My sister thought Althea's ghost had

124

walked into this room. You had no business frightening us like that."

Camilla tried to speak, but Booth looked at her and shook his head. It was Ross who got her out of the room. He left his papers, and took her quietly by the arm. She went with him without objection, and he led her across the antehall into the library.

"Sit down and catch your breath," he said. "You look a bit shaken yourself. They probably frightened you as much as you frightened them."

She turned to him in bewilderment. "I don't understand what happened. Why should seeing me in my mother's riding habit upset everyone so much?"

He sat beside her on the long couch, and a frown drew down his brows. "I can't tell you all the details. I came here some years after your mother's death. But I've been able to put together a few of the pieces. I suspect, from the reaction in there tonight, that your mother was wearing this very habit on the night she died. I know she went riding just before dusk, with a storm coming up —which seems a wild sort of thing to do. She rode clear up Thunder Mountain and must have reached the top when the storm broke. The thunder and lightning probably frightened her horse, and it ran away. She was thrown, and the horse came home with an empty saddle."

Camilla reached up with fingers that trembled and drew the pin from her hat. She took off the hat and set it on the couch beside her. Then she pushed her fingers against the place where a throbbing had begun at her temples.

"I didn't know," she said softly. "No one would ever tell me the truth."

Ross went on in the same quiet tone, with none of his usual irritation toward her in evidence. "When your grandfather knew she was missing, he went up the mountain to look for her. He knew that was her favorite ride. He found her there on the rocky crest and brought her home. She was dead when he found her. She must have struck her head against a rock when she was thrown."

Camilla fingered the long tear hidden by the heavy folds of the habit, and tears came into her eyes.

"My father would never talk about what happened. When he came home after her funeral, he was like a different person for a long while. But why should he have blamed Grandfather Orrin for her death?"

"I can't tell you that," Ross said. "There was something queer about her riding out so late that afternoon, with a storm about to break. I don't know any more about it than I've told you."

Camilla sighed unhappily. "I can see what a shock it must have been for Aunt Letty and Aunt Hortense when I walked into the room just now. It was a terrible thing to do. I'll go upstairs and take these things off."

"It wasn't your fault," Ross said, his tone surprisingly gentle. "You couldn't possibly know the effect you'd have on them. Don't worry about it."

His unexpected kindness brought tears, and she covered her face with her hands. She had seemed so close to her mother earlier tonight, and with remembrance all the hurt of losing her had come rushing back, to be painfully increased by what had just happened.

Ross touched her shoulder lightly. "I'm sorry. Perhaps I shouldn't have told you."

"I had to know!" she cried, and looked up at him, her eyes wet.

He rose and moved uncomfortably about the room. Perhaps he was impatient with her tears, she thought, but she could not stem them.

"Look here," he said abruptly, "you need a change from the burdens of this house. You've been taking on too much. Nora Redfern has wanted me to bring you over for tea some afternoon. Will you go with me if she sets a day?"

Camilla looked at him in surprise. This was certainly a change from his recent attitude toward her.

"You n-n-needn't feel sorry for me!" she choked.

There was no mockery in his smile. "Believe me," he said, "I waste no pity on you. But perhaps I sympathize more than I've let you see. You've been without a real friend in this house, and yet you've kept yourself busy and reasonably happy, and you haven't given up trying to crack the guard set up on all sides against you.

I may not approve of your actions, but I admire your courage. I don't want to see it broken."

He went to the door and stood listening for a moment. Then he turned back to her.

"They've taken Letty up to her room. Why don't you slip upstairs before Hortense sees you again?"

How unpredictable he was. He opposed her at every turn, laughed at her plans for the house, scolded her. Yet now he seemed gentle and thoughtful. Almost like a—friend. Tremulously she smiled at him.

"I—I'm very grateful for—" She wanted to say more, but the words would not come, and she moved helplessly toward the door.

When she reached the second floor, Booth came to the door of his room, as if he waited for her. He had changed to a velvet smoking jacket of dark maroon. Cuffs and lapels were of a lighter red satin, and the effect was one of romantic elegance which fitted Booth so well. The look of shock had gone out of his eyes and he studied her coolly, and not without admiration.

"Althea's riding habit becomes you, Cousin. Though I must say you stirred up a nest of old ghosts tonight and startled us all."

She had no answer for that. She did not want to be drawn out of the quiet mood the change in Ross had induced in her.

"How is Aunt Letty?" she managed to ask.

"She'll be all right. Mother is putting her to bed, and she's already sorry she behaved as she did. Though I can understand how she felt. You look even more like your mother than we realized."

When she turned away because he made her uneasy and she had nothing more to say, he stopped her.

"Wait a moment, Cousin. I want to show you something." He gestured to the room behind him. "Will you come in?"

Booth had a small den adjoining his bedroom, and it was into this he invited her. She stepped uncertainly into a room where lamplight shone warmly on brown and gold surfaces, a room attractively furnished with pieces that were genuinely old, and with a touch of Moorish opulence about them. He drew forward a Spanish chair with a velvet seat and leather back, and brought a small carved footstool for her feet. When she was seated, he stood for a moment studying her face with a strange intensity that made her uncomfortable. If he saw the streaking of tear stains he did not mention her weeping.

"It's hard to believe," he said. "You are so much like her."

While she watched him, puzzled, he picked up a picture which had been set with its face against the wall and brought it to her.

"Do you remember this?"

She saw it was the unfinished painting of a girl and a horse that he had taken away from her so abruptly when she had visited his studio. But now she saw something about the picture that she could not have recognized before. The faceless girl who stood struggling with the horse wore a riding habit of ash gray and a high top hat with floating gray streamers of veil.

Camilla looked from the picture to Booth's dark face, and he nodded in response.

"Your mother posed for this when she came back to Thunder Heights before her death. She loved to ride, and she was an expert horsewoman. I didn't want to paint her tamely, without action, and she thought a pose like this exciting. Though of course I had to do the horse from imagination. After what happened, I never finished it."

"I wish you had been able to finish it," Camilla said. "If you'd done her face, it would bring her back to me a little."

He set the picture against a table where he could study it. "Why shouldn't I finish it now? Why shouldn't I give you her face as she was when she was so vitally alive?"

He came to her quickly and put a finger beneath her chin, tilting her head to the light. "From life. Will you pose for me, Cousin?"

The thought gave her an intense pleasure. To help him finish her mother's picture was almost like a fulfillment.

"I'd love to pose for you, Booth," she said. The prospect of working with him so closely left her faintly excited. It was not only because of her mother that she would look forward to posing for him. Perhaps now she would have the opportunity to know him better, to get past the strange mask he so often wore and learn what the man himself was like.

"Good!" He held out his hand, as if to seal a bargain, and she found the touch of his fingers oddly cool and dry. "We'll begin tomorrow, if you're willing. You feel better now, don't you? The tears are over?"

So he had noticed, after all. She nodded. "Ross told me how my mother died. It must have been terrible for you all that night. And for Grandfather especially. You were here then—what happened afterwards?"

"I wasn't in the house when they brought her in," Booth said. "When she didn't come home, I took another horse and followed the path along the river to see if she had chosen that trail. One of the stableboys had already gone after Dr. Wheeler, so he was here when Grandfather carried her in. There was nothing to be done. Grandfather went out and shot the poor beast that had thrown her, and later he got rid of every horse he owned. That's why we've had no carriage, no riding horses for so many years."

Camilla heard him sadly. "As if that would bring her back."

"You won't be afraid to ride, after what happened here?" Booth asked.

"Because my mother met with an accident? Of course not. It would be foolish to give up riding for that reason, when I'd love it so in country like this."

"You'd better break it gently to Mother and Aunt Letty that you mean to buy a horse," he said. "I haven't told them I was looking for one. Grandfather set them both against horses after what happened. They used to ride, too, but they never did again."

He came with her to the door and catching her hand, held her there a moment. "I want very much to paint you, Camilla."

There was a rising excitement in his voice, and she felt again the strength of his dark appeal striking an echo in herself. She turned hurriedly away and went down the hall, hoping he had not read her response.

When she opened the door and looked again at Althea's room, it was to see it with new eyes. In the beginning the room had seemed to reject her, to hold her away as if she did not belong there. But the strangeness was gone, as if the room had warmed to her, as it had not done before.

Had her grandfather carried Althea here to place her upon this very bed? Had she lain here in death, her lovely body still clothed in the very habit her daughter wore tonight? It must have been that way. Perhaps this was why the room seemed different now. She knew its secret, knew its sorrow, and because she knew she belonged to it.

She took off the habit and spread it gently upon the bed. Tomorrow before she posed for Booth, she would clean away the stain as best she could, and mend the rent in the cloth. It was *not knowing* that had troubled her for so long. Now she knew the worst there was to know, and in embracing tragedy and making it part of her own knowledge, it became less instead of greater.

She would not allow her mother's accident to frighten her. As soon as it was possible to find a good horse, she would ride these hills herself. She would mend her mother's riding habit and wear it with love and pride and joy. But first of all, she would wear it in posing for Booth.

After breakfast the following morning she worked for a while on the habit, then put it on and went upstairs to the nursery. It was fortunate that Ross had given up her education in Orrin Judd's affairs, since this would leave her mornings free to pose for Booth.

He was waiting for her in the big bare room that he had changed very little. He needed only a few essentials for his work, he said, and had added no new furnishings. An old table for his painting equipment was adequate, and he wanted no rugs he might spill paint upon. His easel occupied a place where the light was good, and he posed Camilla facing him.

"We'll leave the face for the last," he said. "I want to get into the mood of the picture again before I touch that. Today I'll pose you standing, so that I can do further work on the color of the habit, and catch the way the folds of material hang."

His mood was bright and incisive this morning, and she felt in him an eagerness to be at work once more on this picture. His hands were light when he touched her, turning her this way and that, seeking to match the pose of the woman in the picture. Though his manner was impersonal, Camilla was sharply aware of him, and the very fact made it difficult for her to assume the pose he wished.

When he got to work at his painting, she was more comfortable because then he seemed to forget her as a woman, so that something of her self-consciousness faded.

The utter quiet of posing for him now opened her mind to a flood of saddening thoughts. Though she could not see the picture from where she stood she could remember it all too well. Fourteen years ago Althea Judd had worn this habit in warm and vital life. She had begun posing for this very picture that Booth would now finish with her daughter for a model. Just such a rearing, fighting beast as Booth had depicted in his picture had flung Althea from her saddle, killing her. *Should* the picture be finished? Camilla wondered suddenly. Or should it be hidden away and forgotten forever?

"You're tired, aren't you?" Booth said. "I mustn't weary you. Sit down a moment and let yourself go limp."

She realized that her body ached with its effort to hold her pose, and she was glad to relax and pull her thoughts back from their futile path.

He brought a chair for her, and she sat down in it gratefully. Now as he worked on without reference to her as a model, she could watch him as she had seldom had the opportunity to do. His thin, proud nose, his faintly arrogant mouth and gloom-ridden eyes were disturbing in their melancholy. Yet elation had kindled him this morning, and he painted for a while as if his strokes were sure and the picture promised well.

It was a shame, she thought, that a man who was so keenly an artist should be buried in a place like Thunder Heights. What did he ask of the future? Why had he remained here, when there could be so little within these walls to make him happy? She wished she might question him, but she had never quite dared.

"Why don't you plan a trip to New York soon?" she suggested, following the trend of her thoughts along a fairly safe course. "Perhaps you could take Aunt Hortense with you and give her a whirl in the city."

For a few moments he did not look at her, or answer, but worked in concentration with his brush. Then he set his palette down and came to stand before her, studying her intently.

"How eager you are to make us happy, Cousin. And how frustrating you must find us when we resist. I doubt that we're meant to be a happy family, so don't break your heart over us."

"I can't help worrying," she said. "I've come here unasked by any of you, and Grandfather's no longer here to make the rules. I know I've never been welcome as far as your mother is concerned. But isn't there something I can do that would please her?"

"If taking her on a trip to New York will please you, I'll do it, Camilla. You're the one with a capacity for happiness that mustn't be dampened. Who knows, perhaps it really would do her good."

"And you, too," Camilla said.

His laughter had a dry sound. "I'm content with my work. As long as it goes well, there's nothing more I'll ask of you for the moment. Shall we get back to it again? Do you suppose this time you can try for more life in your pose? It's the body beneath the gown that matters. Folds of cloth are lifeless in themselves."

His hands were light on her shoulders again, turning her. He was so close that his touch was almost an embrace, and she had a curious desire to run from it, as if there was a need to save herself in time from the dark forces that drove this man. But she held herself quiet and submissive beneath his hands, allowing him to turn her as he wished.

He stepped back and looked at her, clearly not pleased with the result. "No," he said, and his tone was no longer gentle. "You haven't caught it. You're merely a pretty young woman in a riding habit, posing in a studio. And that's not enough."

There was a sting to his words that brought her head up in an instinctive challenge. At once he stepped toward her and put his fingers at her throat, just under her chin. How cool his touch was. As if all the fire in this man burned at the core and never came to the surface.

"That's it—keep your head high like that. Be angry with me, if you like." The pressure of his fingers was suddenly hard against her flesh. She drew back from his touch in confusion, and he shook his head at her ruefully.

"You must help me in this, Cousin. I want you to be, not merely an attractive girl, but a beautiful, angry, spirited woman, struggling furiously with a horse that must not be allowed to get out of control."

His description made her feel awkward and inadequate. "But you're not painting my face today," she reminded him. "What does my expression matter?"

"I wish I could make you understand," he said more quietly. "Whatever is in your face will be reflected in the lines of your body. As your body comes to life, so will your garments reveal spirit. After all, I want to paint a woman, my dear. The woman you are, if you will let yourself go. You should have seen Althea when she posed for this picture. I was only twenty-one at the time, and she was an inspiration. I'll confess I found her irresistible."

With every word, Camilla felt less spirited and less fascinating. "I'm not my mother," she said defensively. "People are always telling me how exciting she was, but I know I'm not—"

His two hands on her shoulders stopped her as he shook her almost roughly. "You must never talk like that! You have more than your mother had, if you'll only realize it. Your bone structure is better—the planes of your face are finer, keener. There's a fire in you too—I've glimpsed it at times. But you keep it banked. Your mother had a confidence you lack. With confidence, a woman can be anything."

He let her go and turned back to his work table.

"We've done enough this morning," he said. "I've upset you, and I didn't mean to. Let's try again tomorrow."

She did not know what to say to him, how to answer him. How could she be for him what she knew very well she was not?

He looked up from cleaning his brushes and saw her standing there helplessly. The quick flash of a smile lighted his face.

"There," he said, "I've hurt you and I'm sorry. It will go better tomorrow. You'll see. The fault isn't yours, so don't distress yourself. If I can't make you see what I want, if I can't bring you to life for this picture, then the blame is mine. Will you forgive me, Cousin, and let me try again tomorrow?"

She nodded mutely in the face of his kindness and went quickly out of the room and down the stairs, feeling shaken and bewildered. How foolish she had been to think posing for Booth's picture would be a simple and wholly pleasant experience. In a strange, contrary way it had been almost like having him make love to her. The method was indirect and rather exciting, and made her wonder what move he might make next. Made her wonder, too, how she might receive it.

CHAPTER 13

As Booth predicted, the posing went better for a few days after that. But more, Camilla felt, because Booth tried harder to put her at ease, to give her confidence, than because she really rose to the perfection he wanted from her.

Now Letty came in to watch while he worked, and as a result something of the personal climate between artist and model which had come into uneasy existence that first day was lessened. Now Camilla was aware of it only in an occasional look Booth bent upon her, in an occasional touch of his hand.

He made no objection to Letty's presence, and did not seem to mind it. She would sit near a window, crocheting, with Mignonette curled at her feet, seldom speaking, offering little distraction. Once during the morning, she might leave her chair and go to stand behind Booth, studying the picture as he painted. Only then did her presence seem to make him faintly uncomfortable. Once Camilla thought he might speak to her impatiently, but he managed to keep any irritation he felt to himself. After a moment Letty returned quietly to her chair, as if she sensed his mood, and she did not look at the picture again for several days.

One morning when Booth stopped the posing session early, Letty invited Camilla to her room.

"If you've nothing pressing to do," she said, "perhaps you'd like to help me with a task that may interest you."

Ever since the day when the saucer of tea had made Mignonette sick, Camilla had experienced a constraint when she was with Letty. She had reproached herself for this feeling, considering it unjustified. She did not want to listen to Hortense's dropping of hints, and yet the actuality of what had happened remained as a bar to the friendship she had previously felt for Letty. There was no reason to avoid her, however, and perhaps it might even be possible to return to more comfortable ground with her aunt, and clear up some of the things that were troublesome, if they could have a good talk.

This was the first time she had been invited into Aunt Letty's private retreat, and she looked about the small room with interest. In one corner a second floor tower bulged into a circular addition to the room, with windows all around and a padded window seat. The wall over the bed sloped beneath a slanting roof, and the entire expanse of the angled wall was covered with pictures of one sort and another, so that only a trace of sand-colored wallpaper showed between them here and there.

While Letty knelt to pull a box from under the bed, Camilla studied the pictures on the slanting wall. Some of them were clearly Hudson River scenes—both sketches and engravings—but there were also scenes from abroad, glimpses of castles and mountains, glens and lochs.

"This looks like Walter Scott country," she said to Letty.

Her aunt was lifting folders and envelopes from the box and piling them on the bed. "It is. Just a few memories of a lovely year I spent in Scotland when I was a young girl."

"And did you meet a young man in the Highlands and give your heart away in the proper romantic fashion?" Camilla asked.

Letty smiled, but there was a flush in her cheeks. "Oh, I met several, and perhaps I did give my heart away for a little while. But Papa didn't approve, and I took it back after a time. It was nothing very serious. Perhaps I always had too many story-book heroes in my mind, to be satisfied with the men I met in real life."

Camilla curled herself up comfortably on Letty's bed, wanting now to pursue this topic.

"What about Aunt Hortense? Why has she never married? Did no young men ever come to Westcliff?"

"Oh, they came," Letty said. "Papa's name was always enough to bring them. But Hortense had an unfortunate faculty for wanting only what someone else had."

"What do you mean?" Camilla asked.

Letty's gaze seemed to turn upon something far away in the past. "There was one man who came to Westcliff—I can remember him as if it were yesterday. He looked as I imagine a poet might look. And he could quote poetry too—in a voice that sounded like one of our mountain streams, sometimes whispering, sometimes thundering."

"My father's voice was like that," Camilla said. "I always loved the way he read poetry."

"Yes, I know." Letty's silver braids bent low over the papers she was sorting.

The tone of her voice startled Camilla. "This was the man Hortense fell in love with?"

There was sad assent in Letty's sigh.

"Was he a schoolteacher?"

"Yes, dear," Letty said. "I see you've guessed. It was your father Hortense loved, and she would have no one else."

"So that's it?" Camilla was thoughtful. "Did my mother know?"

"Hortense took care to let everyone know. She didn't behave very well, I'm afraid. She always claimed that he would have married her, if Althea hadn't stolen him from her. Of course that wasn't true. He never looked at anyone but Althea. She was always the lovely one—the lucky one. They fell in love at their first meeting, and since Papa wanted someone else for Althea, there was nothing to do but run off. Althea told me that night and I helped her get away. Papa never forgave me for that."

There were tears in Letty's eyes.

"I never knew," Camilla said. "Poor Aunt Hortense."

"It has been difficult for her. When she looks at you she sees two people who hurt her, two people she has never forgiven. You must help her to get over that, my dear. Be patient with her."

Camilla leaned back against a poster of the bed. For the first time she was beginning to understand the intensity of disliking she had seen in Hortense's eyes. What insult it must have added to injury when Orrin Judd had left his fortune to the daughter of Althea and John King.

"Was it because Aunt Hortense knew she would never marry that she wanted to adopt a child?" she asked.

137

Letty's hands moved vaguely among the papers she had heaped on the bed. "That was so long ago. I—I don't remember the details. I suppose she must have felt there would be an emptiness in her life without a child. We needed someone young in this house. I was glad to see Booth come. He was such a solemn, handsome little boy, and so determined about what he wanted."

"Why didn't she adopt a baby?"

Letty shrugged. "I only remember that he was ten when she brought him here, and he was already quite talented as an artist."

"But what an odd thing to do," Camilla said. "Surely if a woman wanted a child, she would want one from babyhood on."

For some reason Letty seemed agitated. Once more she was ready for a flight from the unpleasant. "It all happened so long ago—why trouble about it now?"

"Because of Aunt Hortense," Camilla insisted. "I want to find some way to make her happy here at Thunder Heights, and if I'm to do that, I ought to understand her better than I do."

Letty changed the subject firmly. "There's been enough talk about the past. That isn't why I asked you here. I thought you might like to help me sort my collection of herb receipts. I can't make head or tail of things the way they are."

Letty gathered up a handful of loose sheets on which clippings had been pasted in long yellowing columns, and dropped them in Camilla's lap.

"What I'd like to do is to separate the medicinal information from the cooking receipts and catalogue them both. And I'd like to sort the receipts into categories so that when I want one for mint jelly, I don't have to hunt through a mixture like this."

Knowing other topics were closed for the moment, Camilla set to work with interest. Now that she was acquainted with the herbs in Letty's garden, the next step to their use was fascinating. She read through a receipt for Turkish rose petal jam, and one for marigold custard. There were directions for making saffron cake, for rose and caraway cookies, and tansy pudding. Sometimes Aunt Letty had written her own pertinent comments in the margins, or her own suggestions for changes in the ingredients.

"I should think," Camilla said, her interest growing, "that you would have enough material here for a book about herbs. You've grown them and worked with them for years and you're a real authority. Other people should be interested in what you have to say."

"Do you really think I might do something with all this?" Letty's eyes brightened.

"Oh, I do!" Camilla warmed to the idea. "All you need is to sort it out and make a plan for presenting it. I'll help you and—"

There was a knock at the door and Grace looked into the room. "If you please, mum, there's a note for you," she said and handed a blue envelope to Camilla.

When she had gone, Camilla opened it and read the note. It was from Nora Redfern. Would Miss King permit Mr. Granger to bring her to tea at Blue Beeches one afternoon next week? Nora was looking forward to knowing her better.

Camilla held out the note to Letty. "How very nice—I'd love to go."

Letty read the note doubtfully. "I don't know. We haven't been on speaking terms with Blue Beeches for a long while, you know."

"What is the trouble between the two families?" Camilla asked.

"Mrs. Landry, Nora's mother, and your grandfather had a quarrel years ago. Naturally we took Papa's side and we haven't been friendly with her since."

"But all that can't be Nora's fault. Ross seems to like her." Sometimes, indeed, Camilla had wondered just how much Ross liked the attractive young widow.

"We've all regretted that," Letty said. "Papa never approved of the way Ross made friends with the Redferns. Under the circumstances, it was inexcusable."

Never before had Camilla heard Letty sound so uncharitable. Her attitude seemed more like what might be expected from Hortense.

"I'll be sorry to go against your wishes," Camilla said gently, "but I'd like very much to accept this invitation."

For a moment Letty looked as though she might offer further objection. Then she sighed and began to gather up her papers and notes and thrust them back into their box.

"Wait," Camilla said, "—we must talk about your book."

Letty shook her head. "I'm not in the mood now, dear. Some

other time, perhaps." She looked sad again and increasingly troubled.

"A few moments ago you thought the idea a good one," Camilla said. "Why have you changed your mind. Surely not because I'm going to see Nora Redfern?"

Letty pushed the last batch of clippings into the box and fastened the lid. Then she looked up at Camilla.

"You know what they whisper about me, don't you? They say I've tried to poison people. If I were to do a book on the subject of herbs, all the whispers would spring up again."

She looked so forlorn that for the moment pity thrust doubt from Camilla's mind. Aunt Letty had burden enough to carry with her crippled arm.

"I think we must pay no attention to such gossip," she said. "It's too ridiculous to heed."

Letty's smile was tremulous. "Thank you, my dear." But she pushed the box resolutely into place under her bed, and Camilla knew that for the moment at least the subject was closed.

When she returned to her room, she sat down at her mother's desk to answer Nora Redfern's note. But her thoughts would not at once relinquish the thought of Letty. One part of her—more heart than mind—wanted to trust in her wholeheartedly. That day when Camilla had talked to her grandfather he had said, "Watch Letty." Surely he had meant to take care of Letty, to watch out for her. But something more questioning in Camilla held back and reserved judgment.

Resolutely she put these disturbing thoughts aside and picked up her pen to write an answer to Nora Redfern. She wrote her note rapidly, accepting the invitation. It would be good to escape from Thunder Heights and visit Blue Beeches next week.

That evening Booth told her that it was hopeless to continue with his painting. Something had thrown him off his course and it would be better to stop for a while. If Camilla were still agreeable, he would accept her offer of a trip to New York for himself and his mother, and they would leave as soon as Hortense could get ready. It was a plan Camilla readily encouraged.

A day later, on the morning they were to leave, Grace tapped on Camilla's door. Mr. Booth, she said, requested a moment of her time in the library.

Camilla hurried downstairs and found him pacing restlessly about the room. He turned with something like relief when she entered.

"Good! I wanted to see you for a moment, Cousin, before Mother comes down."

He stepped to the door and closed it after her. Camilla watched him, puzzled. He looked handsomer than ever this morning, and more than ever the gentleman of fashion. He wore a black coat, gray checked trousers, and gray spats. His gray gloves and top hat lay upon the table.

"We'll get to work on the picture again as soon as I return," he said. "It isn't just because I'm out of the mood for painting that I'm making this trip. It's because of my mother."

"I hope the change will do her good," Camilla said politely, still wondering what lay behind his words.

"She's not going to New York for the change," Booth said. "She's going for the sole purpose of trying to upset Grandfather Orrin's will. I thought you ought to know. She means to see a lawyer of greater eminence than Mr. Pompton and learn what steps she might be able to take."

Camilla nodded gravely. "She's entirely within her rights, of course. I really can't blame her."

"You're more than generous, Camilla. I hope you know that this is none of my doing. Frankly, I think she has no chance of success, and I've urged against the step. But she won't listen to me."

"Thank you for telling me," Camilla said.

He held out his hand, and when she put her own into it, he did not release her at once. It was a relief when Hortense came sailing into the room, flinging the door open with an air of indignation at finding it closed.

She was elaborately gowned for travel. Her skirt was of mauve broadcloth, and she wore an elbow-length cape of black broadcloth, with a high, satin-trimmed collar and huge buttons. The straw hat that tilted over her forehead was wreathed in violets and bound in violet ribbon that clashed with her red hair. An exotic Parisian perfume floated generously about her person.

"I hope you'll have a fine time in New York," Camilla told the impressive figure.

From high piled violets to mauve skirt hem, Hortense seemed aquiver with energy this morning. She ignored Camilla's good wishes and nodded to Booth.

"The carriage has just pulled up to the door. We'd better be going if we're not to miss the boat."

Booth picked up his hat and gloves, but Hortense did not move at once from the doorway.

"I know this is the opportunity you've been waiting for," she said to Camilla. "You may as well make good use of your time while I'm away."

"I'm afraid I don't know what you mean," Camilla said.

"I mean that this is your chance to prove what a housekeeper you are. Matilda and Toby are going upriver to visit Matilda's sister. The scullery maid has the day off, and Letty is turning out the linen shelves upstairs, with Grace's help. So you may do exactly what you like with the rest of the house."

Hortense spoke with the air of a great lady conferring a favor, but Camilla could only stare at her in bewilderment. As she well knew, it was Letty who quietly kept things running, in spite of Hortense's high-handed gestures. Certainly she had no intention of trying to take these duties out of Letty's competent hands.

"I don't want to interfere with the regular routine," she said mildly.

"I've thought from the first that your education has been neglected in household matters," Hortense said, sniffing a little. "I doubt if you can so much as bake a decent loaf of bread. However, the house is yours for the moment—if you choose to take advantage of the opportunity."

"Thank you, Aunt Hortense," Camilla said and suppressed a desire to smile.

Her aunt swept toward the door. Booth arched a dark eyebrow at Camilla and followed his mother without comment. Camilla went to the door and watched him help his mother into the rig.

"Have a pleasant trip," she called as the carriage pulled away.

Hortense said nothing, but Booth turned his head and waved. Camilla stood for a moment looking thoughtfully after them. It was a little ironic that she was paying for this trip to New York so that they might seek legal advice on taking everything away from her. Not that the fact disturbed her. If she lost all this, she would only be back where she was before she came here. She would have lost nothing. There was a twinge of bitterness in the thought.

She walked a few steps across the drive and looked up at the front of the house. It stood gray and strong against the mountain. There was no sign of dilapidation now, no worn, unpainted surfaces, no broken shutters. It was still a house of secrets, a brooding house, but this was part of its character. There was an impressive grandeur about it, now that it was no longer falling into disrepair and apologetic in its ruin.

Was it true that she would not mind if Thunder Heights were taken from her?

She went up the steps and into the antehall. As usual the marble hands reached out to her, but now their gesture seemed almost a welcome. It was as if the house was ready at last to give itself into her hands.

The malevolent influence, whatever it was, had been lifted. With only Letty upstairs, there seemed no longer any resistance to her presence. When Hortense had said the house could be Camilla's for a time, she had spoken more truly than she knew.

A sudden feeling of release and freedom swept through her. Today was truly her own to use as she pleased. There would be no suspicious eyes watching her, no hand turned against her, whatever she chose to do. Why shouldn't she pick up Hortense's challenge and prove that she could bake a loaf as well as the next woman?

The bread box was nearly empty—she had noticed it this morning. By now she had watched Matilda several times at her baking, and she believed she had the hang of it. It would be fun to fill that box and fling Hortense's words back at her.

She went to get the starter dough from the ice chest. Then she collected her ingredients, and the bowls and utensils she would need. She would not, she decided, work in the kitchen. She liked the larder downstairs where Letty often worked. It was a cool, pleasant room, and there was a ledge with a marble slab that made a good working surface. She went downstairs with a feeling that this was a morning to sing at whatever she did.

Yesterday Aunt Letty had been down here making the green herbal soap that Camilla had found such a luxury in her room, but now everything was neat as a whistle, the way Letty always left it. Camilla set out her things and started happily to work. Into the bowl went her lump of starter dough, sifted flour, and milk. When she had stirred the whole sufficiently with a long-handled wooden spoon, she covered the yellow crockery bowl with a cloth, as she had seen Matilda do. Now it must rise before she could have the fun of kneading it.

Feeling pleased and successful, she wandered idly about the room, studying the neat labels Letty had lettered so carefully, sometimes taking down a bottle to sniff the contents and replace it. On the shelf that stretched behind the door, she saw that the jar which had contained a mixture of marjoram and mint leaves had been refilled, and she took it down to smell the pleasant minty scent. Further along the shelf there had been an empty space the other day, and it had now been filled by a bottle containing a pale liquid of some sort.

The label on the bottle read *Tansy Juice*—a name that had a pleasantly old-fashioned ring. Perhaps she had read about tansy in a book, Camilla thought. She took down the bottle and removed the stopper. The odor was sharp, with a faintly resinous quality and at once she was reminded of the odor of the tea Letty had brought her a few days ago. She would not forget that odor readily —it had reminded her of daisies, as this odor did too. Perhaps Letty had added tansy to the tea that day, since she liked to experiment with unusual flavors.

Camilla put the bottle back and wandered upstairs to see how the linen-sorting was progressing. Grace was standing on a stepladder, while Aunt Letty handed stacks of pillowslips up to her to be set on a high shelf. She looked at Camilla and smiled.

"Did Hortense and Booth get off all right?"

Camilla nodded. "Booth told me the real purpose of their trip to New York."

Letty glanced at Grace. "I know. But don't worry, dear. I doubt that a thing can be done. I tried to argue against it, but I'm afraid my sister seldom listens to me. What are you doing with yourself today?"

Camilla did not want to admit to her breadmaking until she had something to show for it.

"I've been wandering around. I was down looking at your herbs for a while. What is tansy used for, Aunt Letty?"

"I have a wonderful receipt for tansy pudding," Letty said. "I believe you were looking at it the other day."

"I noticed a bottle of liquid labeled 'tansy,' " Camilla said, "and I was curious."

"Yes. I crush a few leaves for juice now and then. When the oils are used for perfume, the leaves have to be distilled, but for cooking we just use their juice. Or sometimes the dried leaves."

A remembrance of that faintly unpleasant scent had stayed with Camilla. "Is tansy anything you might use in a tea mixture?"

"Yes." Letty nodded. "I often put in a pinch of leaves, or a few drops of the juice."

Camilla watched the work for a little while, but another pair of hands was not needed, and she wandered downstairs and outside to the river front. Across the river a train rumbled along the water's edge and she watched it out of sight around a bend up the Hudson.

It was a shame both sides of the river had been scarred by steel rails. How pleasant it must have been when everything was open country, or dreamy little towns, and all the transport followed the water itself.

Thinking of transport made her think of Ross and his notions about a bridge. More than once lately he had returned to the subject, and it had become a sore point between them. A bridge, she thought, her eyes upon the river, would not leave the scar of a railroad track. A bridge might be a thing of beauty, as a railroad bed could never be. Nevertheless, she would not give in to him. She would not become involved.

At the foot of the hill, beyond the tracks, a spit of land cut out into the river. It, at least, had the edge of the water to itself. She had never been down there, and she began a descent of the steep bank, digging her heels in, so that she wouldn't slip in loose earth and dry leaves, holding onto branches to let herself down slowly.

In a few moments she had reached the tracks and was out of sight of the house. The shining rails stretched away toward Westcliff in one direction, and out of sight around the foot of Thunder Mountain in the other. She crossed the ties and in a moment was in the stiff grass of the lower spit of land. Here she could walk out beneath a huge willow tree to a place where at high tide Hudson waters lapped a small stony beach. Here there was the ruin of an old wooden dock, and a small boathouse, its roof long ago caved in. The salty smell of the mud flats when the tide was out reached her on the breeze from the river.

She scrambled onto the broken dock and then skirted the crumbling boathouse, exploring. Down here shrubbery grew thick to the very edge of a narrow, pebbled beach, and the wild growth had almost engulfed what men had built upon the river's edge.

Her foot slipped in a muddy spot, and she caught at a thick bush to keep herself from sliding. As she pulled herself to dryer ground, her eye was caught by an object deep in the forked branches of brush. Curiously, she pushed the scrub aside and reached in. To her surprise she pulled out a flexible stick a foot or so in length with a blackened silver head attached to it.

Though the silver was tarnished and dented, she could make out an embossing in the form of tiny chrysanthemums. The wood of the stick was black and strong, and propped there above the earth, it had resisted the effects of rot, though it had been scratched and scarred by long weathering. A leather thong, rotted through, hung from one end.

She realized suddenly that the sorry object she held in her hands was a woman's riding crop. To whom had it belonged, and how had it been lost in so odd a place? At any rate, she would carry her find home, clean it up and polish the silver. Then if it didn't look too bad perhaps she could carry it when she went riding. Undoubtedly someone at the house would know to whom it had belonged. Her mother, perhaps? She could imagine Althea carrying such a crop when it had been polished and beautiful.

CHAPTER 14

A‌FTER she had taken the crop to her room and tucked it into a drawer, she went downstairs to the larder. Removing the cloth, she looked at the dough and found it a sodden, inert mass in the bottom of the bowl. By now it should have puffed considerably, but it had not risen at all. In fact, it looked sticky and wet and incapable of rising. Probably it needed more flour. She scooped it out on the marble slab and added flour, kneading it in. But now the mass turned dry and crumbly, so she dribbled in a little water and kneaded again. There seemed no way to get it right.

Her hands were sticky with wet flour, and her confidence began to ebb. She had the horrid presentiment that this lump of grayish dough was never going to rise at all. Her dream of triumphantly producing a delectable loaf at dinner was just that—a dream, and discouragement seized her. There was more to breadmaking than met the eye, and undoubtedly Hortense Judd was right about her household talents.

The cellar seemed suddenly a lonely and depressing place. How still it was down here. How empty. She could hear no fall of footsteps from upstairs, no sound of voices, and the chill of stone walls seemed more damp than pleasantly cool. Before her in the bowl lay the grayish lump—and for all that it had not risen, there was a great deal more of it than she had intended in the beginning.

What on earth was she to do with this mess? She could imagine Matilda's annoyance if she found that her kitchen had been invaded and perfectly good ingredients wasted—to this end. Undoubtedly she would report the matter to Aunt Hortense, and

Camilla could imagine Hortense's scorn and Booth's amusement. There was nothing to do but dispose of her clandestine efforts where they would not be discovered.

Quickly she transferred the inert weight of dough to the cloth with which she had covered the bowl, and turned up the corners, wrapping it well. Then she took one of Aunt Letty's garden trowels from the tool room and marched resolutely up the stairs and outside.

Through the herb garden she ran toward the woods, where Aunt Letty had planted white narcissus in a winding border at the edge of the trees. She followed the path she had taken back from Blue Beeches that first day when she had met Ross Granger and he had come home with her. Now she knew the perfect hiding place for her unpleasant burden. When she had climbed the rocky eminence and reached the weeping beech tree, she found she was still within sight of the house, but she knew the thick, drooping branches would hide her from view. Smiling, she slipped between them into the shadowy seclusion of the open space around the blue-black trunk of the tree.

The shelter was like a child's secret playhouse. Had her mother played here as a little girl? Camilla wondered. The big dark leaves and thick branches shielded her all around and she was completely hidden. She knelt on brown earth, softened now by spring rains, and began to dig with her trowel. It would take a fairly large hole, she discovered, to hide all evidence of her culinary crime. So absorbed was she in her digging that the sudden crackling of branches being parted came as a startling sound. She looked up in dismay to see Ross Granger peering at her through the wall of her shelter.

"What's wrong?" he asked. "I saw you scurrying up here like a fugitive. Are you digging for buried treasure?"

What she was doing seemed suddenly ridiculous and childish— not at all a role becoming to the mistress of Thunder Heights. She regarded him uncomfortably, unable to think of a reasonable explanation for her actions, fighting an impulse to laugh out loud and further label herself a child.

He glanced from the hole to the covered bundle and the smile left his face. "Oh? That's not Mignonette, is it?"

This was too much. She covered her face with her hands to stifle her laughter and sat helplessly back on her heels. At once he picked up the trowel and knelt beside her.

"Don't worry—let me take care of it. You turn your back, and I'll have it buried in no time at all. If it's the cat, this will devastate Letty. What happened anyway?"

She lowered her hands, and when he saw she was not crying, but laughing, he dropped the trowel and stood up, clearly annoyed.

"The—the only thing that—that died," she choked, "was—oh, look for yourself!"

He stirred the bundle doubtfully with his toe and the cloth fell back to expose the lumpish gray contents. "What is it?" he asked.

She wiped her eyes with a handkerchief and thrust back her tendency to hysterical giggles. "You looked so funny and sympathetic! And now you look so suspicious! I—I was just trying to make bread. Aunt Hortense and Booth left for New York right after breakfast. Everyone's gone from the house except Aunt Letty and Grace, who are working upstairs. Before she left, Aunt Hortense said I couldn't even bake a decent loaf of bread. So I wanted to prove her wrong and confound her with my skill when she came home. But the only one I've confounded so far is myself."

He started to grin, then to laugh out loud, and the tendency to giggle left her abruptly. It wasn't that funny. His amusement was altogether too unrestrained, and she did not like being the butt of his laughter.

He caught her eye and sobered. "Now you're angry with me. But you thought the situation funny yourself until I laughed. If you'll stop scowling at me, I'll help you out."

"Help me out?"

He picked up the trowel again and quickly enlarged the hole. Then he dumped the sodden dough into the grave and covered it, stamping down the earth.

"I don't suppose you want a headstone?" he said.

Camilla had gained time to recover a semblance of poise and she stood up and held out her hand for the trowel. "Thank you, Mr. Granger. Though I really could have managed by myself."

"Oh, we're not through," he said cheerfully.

She looked at him in bewilderment, and once more the amusement in his eyes faded. He was regarding her with an odd tenderness that was almost like a caress. His tone softened.

"Don't think I don't know what a hard time you've had in that house. You've had everyone fighting you, including me, and giving you very little help in your effort to do something to save the old place. To say nothing of the people in it. Orrin Judd would have been proud of you, Camilla. I think you're wasting your time on the unimportant and on what can't be changed. Which makes me very sorry—because I like to see the young and brave and—and foolish—succeed."

The climate between them had changed in some subtle way. There was a long breathless moment while she looked into his eyes and time hung queerly suspended. She was aware only of their closeness in this tiny space, hidden from the world by branches all about, aware only of him, as he was of her. *This is what I want,* she thought. Something in her had known from the first moment she had spoken to him on the river boat that someday it would be like this, and that when the moment came she would not retreat. She had fought him and resented him, and raged within herself because of him. But now nothing mattered except that his strong fine head with the bright chestnut hair was bending close, and there was a question in his eyes.

She raised her own head without hesitation and went quite simply into his arms. He was not gentle now. His mouth was hard upon her lips so that they felt bruised beneath its touch. Her body ached under the pressure of his arms, but she did not want the pain lessened. When he raised his head she would have put her arms about his neck and risen on her toes to rest her cheek against his own, admitting everything—all the wild feeling that surged through her, all the wanting so long held in check because there was no one to want. Her movements were those of one spellbound, as though she had no will of her own, and could bow only to his. But he took her by the shoulders and held her suddenly away, his eyes grave, his mouth unsmiling.

"You *are* something of a surprise," he said.

The words were like an unexpected slap, and the blood rose in her cheeks as though the blow had been a physical one. There was a moment of consternation while she stared at him in helpless dismay. Then she turned and would have run straight away from him, but this time he caught her hand.

"Come along," he said as calmly as though nothing had happened between them. "I told you we weren't through. We've work to do."

Brooking no resistance, he led her down the path toward Thunder Heights. She could not struggle against him without indignity, so she went with him, shocked and angry and confused. When they reached the back door, he did not release her hand, but came with her up the steps and into the kitchen. There he looked about confidently, while she watched him, completely at a loss.

"With your permission, I'll wash my hands," he said. "You still want to bake bread, don't you?"

To Camilla's astonishment, that was exactly what they did. Spellbound once more, she obeyed him, afraid to wake up and face what had happened, afraid to acknowledge the emotion that had swept through her there beneath the beech tree. Under his skillful instruction, she began the process of breadmaking all over again, and he was as matter-of-fact when he asked her to scald the milk as though that exultant moment between them, with the shock of its aftermath, had never been.

"To be good," he told her, "a batch of bread should be made with a large portion of love and cheer mixed in. At least that's what my Aunt Otis always used to say. She had the cheeriest kitchen I've ever seen. There were always yellow curtains and yellow tea towels all around, so that if the sun wasn't really shining, it would seem to be in her kitchen. Aunt Otis raised me, and she used to say there was no reason why a man shouldn't know how to bake bread, when breadbaking was good for the soul. She was right too."

Camilla listened in wonder, her sense of shock lulled for the moment by his words and his companionable presence. She did as he told her, and the dough seemed to come to life under her hands.

"Where is your home?" she asked him, curious now to know all there was to know about this man.

"It's on the river—but down along the Jersey bank," he said.

It was easy now to ask him questions. "Did you grow up there? What of your mother and father?"

"My mother died when I was born, and my father was mostly away in his work as an engineer. As I've told you, he was Orrin Judd's good friend and worked on many a project for him. But Aunt Otis had me in hand while I was growing up."

Looking at the breadth of him, at his bright hair and the mouth that was smiling now, but which she had seen looking firm and stern, Camilla thought silently that his Aunt Otis must have done a very good job indeed. A shiver like a warning sped along her nerves, but she did not heed it. Whether he regretted kissing her or not, she wanted to be with him, to be near him, and that in itself was something new and frightening.

"Now," he said, "you'll need to put this in a warm place to rise, leave it alone for a couple of hours and—"

She clapped a hand to her mouth. "That's it! I left it to rise in the cellar where it's cool. Of course the yeast never started to grow."

He nodded at her, grinning. "Think you can carry on success-fully now? You can knead it after it rises—that's for better texture —and let it rise again. Another kneading and it's ready for baking. Can you fire the stove all right?"

"If I can't, I'll get Grace to help me," she said.

Plainly he was going to leave her now, with so much that was still unexplained between them. Yet she could ask him no further questions. You could not say to a man, "Why did you kiss me, if you didn't mean it? Why did you invite me into your arms if you didn't want me there?"

"I'll go back to my work now," he told her, "and you needn't admit you've had any help. After all, you did the whole thing your-self, so you're entitled to the credit."

Her mouth felt stiff and her lips would not smile easily. She could only nod in silence. He put out a hand and touched her shoulder lightly. Then he was gone by way of the back door.

She could hear him whistling as he rounded the house, returning to the rooms he preferred to keep so far from the house. The sound was a cheerful one, but she did not know whether to laugh or to weep.

A little to Camilla's relief, Ross did not appear at dinner that night, but sent word that he was going to the village, so Camilla and Letty dined alone. With Hortense's restraining presence re-moved, Letty was ready to chatter, but Camilla felt subdued and pensive, and she listened in a silence that was only half attentive.

There were a few moments of excitement over the bread she had baked. Matilda, coming home from her visit, had found the fresh loaves and admired them generously. Letty said this was the best bread she had tasted in a long while, and Camilla must cer-tainly show Hortense what she could do when she returned from her trip.

Camilla accepted their compliments in her preoccupied state and kept her secret. The thought of Ross was never far away, and she did not want to be alone lest she give herself wholly to dream-ing about what had happened.

After dinner, they avoided the parlor ritual, and Camilla fol-lowed Letty and Mignonette upstairs.

"Something's troubling you, isn't it, dear?" Letty said when they reached the door of her room. "Would you like to come in and keep me company for a while?"

Grateful for the invitation, Camilla seated herself on a window cushion in the circular tower that made an addition to Letty's small room. Sitting there, high among green branches that pressed against the windows, she felt like a bird suspended in a swinging cage. She could glimpse the river shining far below in the twilight. It was a peaceful spot, and she tried to let her mind go blank, let her feelings wash away in the quiet green light.

Letty made no attempt to question her, or draw her out, but went contentedly to work on her collection of receipts.

"I've decided to think about your suggestion for a book after all," she said. "Whether I try to have it published or not, it will give me satisfaction to compile it."

"I'm glad," Camilla told her, pleased to see her aunt busy and interested. It was a shame that the shadow of such a lie should be allowed to hang over her head. Mignonette sprang onto the win-dow seat and began washing her face with an energetic paw. Camilla pushed her over idly, to pick up a book the cat was sitting on. It was a fat volume and seemed to be a medical dictionary of herbs. The pages fell open and she read at random, her interest only half upon the words.

Sage tea was good for sore throats, it appeared. Summer savory might be used to cure intestinal disorders. Sesame was a mild laxative and could be soothing when applied externally. The action of thyme was antiseptic and antispasmodic. Tansy . . . her interest quickened at the name. Tansy could be rubbed over raw meat to keep the flies away, and its leaves were useful in destroying fleas and ants. It was a violent irritant to the stomach, and many deaths had been caused by it.

Camilla looked up from the pages, watching Letty in silence for a few moments as she worked with her papers.

"You said the other day that you used tansy in puddings," she said at length, "and sometimes in tea. But this book says that it's poisonous."

Letty did not look up from her sorting. "It is if one uses too much of it. The Pennsylvania Dutch make poultices of the sap, and they used the leaves in tea in treatments for the stomach. It's all in the quantity used."

The bottle of tansy juice had been there on the shelf and available, Camilla thought, and a jar with tansy leaves. There had been a strong scent of daisies about the tea that had made Mignonette ill. Though of course Aunt Letty had admitted to a touch of tansy in the mixture. She wanted to ask more questions, but she could not in the face of the suspicion Hortense had tried to cast upon Letty. She could not look at Letty and believe her guilty. If anyone was to be blamed for that tea, it was probably Hortense. Had Booth known what his mother had tried to do? she wondered, remembering the look she had caught between them that morning in the cellar.

Letty spoke evenly, quietly, still not looking up. "It's very easy to pick up a few facts and put them together in the wrong pattern. I never let myself do that if I can avoid it, my dear. Too much harm may be caused by a mistaken interpretation."

Camilla glanced at her, startled. "Sometimes I think you're a little fey. Sometimes you almost read my mind."

"It's my Scottish blood, I suppose," Letty said without smiling. "Sometimes I have a queer feeling of knowing when something is about to happen. As I did the night Papa died. And there have been other occasions too. The night your mother rode out to her death was one—" She stopped and shook her head. "I mustn't think about these things. They give me an uncomfortable feeling. I don't want to be queer and—and fey."

Camilla left her window seat and went to sit beside her.

"If there's anything queer about you, Aunt Letty, then it's a nice sort of queerness to have," she assured her aunt.

She began to help Letty with her sorting, and the green light faded at the windows as night came down. The sky to the west might still be bright, but the shadow of Thunder Mountain had fallen upon the house, and here night had already begun.

As the evening wore quietly on, Camilla began to feel lulled and peaceful. Letty was right—she mustn't allow groundless suspicion to grow in her mind. She must live in this house and accept the people in it. She could not afford to question what lay behind every action, or she would find no peace here at all.

She did not remember the little riding crop she had found until she returned to her room. Then she got it out and carried it back to Letty.

"Look what I found in the shrubbery today," she said, and held out the black crop with its tarnished silver head for Letty to see.

Letty stared at it without recognition for a moment. Then she rose from her work and came to take it from Camilla's hand. The color went out of her face, and she sat down abruptly.

"Where did you find this?" she demanded.

Camilla explained how she had climbed down the bank and walked out upon the spit of land that extended into the river. How she had seen something odd caught in the brush and had found the riding crop.

Letty brushed at her face as though cobwebs clung to it. "No," she said. "No!"

"Do you know whom the crop belonged to?" Camilla asked.

"Of course," Letty said. "It belonged to my sister Althea. Papa had it made for her when she first started riding."

"I saw the saddle with the silver mountings in the attic," Camilla said. "Was that hers too?"

"Yes. Papa brought the saddle and bridle from Mexico."

"Someone has been going up to the attic to care for the leather and polish the silver," Camilla said.

"Papa did that." Letty spoke in a low voice. "After Althea ran away and he was so angry with her, he used to go upstairs sometimes and sit with those riding things she loved. Once when I went looking for him, I heard him talking to them as if she had been there. He was questioning and scolding—all in the manner of a man who couldn't understand what had been done to him. He wouldn't let us mention her name, but he used to steal up there and take care of her things, so that the leather wouldn't dry out, or the silver tarnish. Even after her death, he went right on caring for them. I think it brought him some sort of comfort."

Camilla could imagine her grandfather climbing the attic stairs with his head bowed, going to his sorrowful task. Perhaps in some strange way he had recovered his daughter in love and pain as he worked over her things. The picture was sadly touching.

"Perhaps I can bring my mother's saddle down from the attic and use it again," Camilla said. "Perhaps she would like to have me wear her habit and use her things."

Letty started to speak and then fell silent.

"Why were you startled when I showed you the crop, Aunt Letty?" Camilla asked. "Was my mother carrying it that evening when she went out to ride for the last time?"

Letty rose and went to the window of the little tower room to look out toward the river, shining now in the pale light of a rising moon.

"I don't remember," she said. "I'm not sure."

"No, of course she couldn't have carried it," Camilla mused. "Not if she rode up Thunder Mountain. Not when I've just found the crop down near the water's edge. Even if she dropped it, it could never fly so far out in the river."

Letty nodded as if relieved. "You're right, naturally." She seemed to brighten a little. "I can't imagine how it ever got there. It's very strange. But probably not important."

Camilla took the crop back to her room, but she felt restless and not at all ready for sleep. The moment she settled down and was still, all the thoughts she wanted to put away from her would come rushing back. Perhaps a walk would quiet her, still her thoughts. Softly she slipped through the hall and down the stairs, finding her way in the light from the canopied lamp above.

The servants were in their quarters in the kitchen wing by now, and the house seemed lonely and empty. She opened the heavy door with its iron grillwork, and went outside. The night was soft and cool, and moonlight flooded the world, though the park expanse before the house was dark with the thickness of trees.

Silently she drifted across the grass, not following the drive, but running straight through the park in the direction of the gate. Her urge to run in the moonlight, in the cool night air, was without conscious purpose, and she did not pause until she saw the lights of Ross's rooms above the stable. Then she came to a breathless halt, shrinking back into the deep shadow of an oak tree, watching the patches of light.

Memory swept back on a flood of warmth, to engulf her being. She could hold her thoughts at bay no longer. In memory she could feel Ross's arms about her, she could raise her head and feel his kiss hard upon her mouth. He would be part of her dreams tonight, and she knew no way to rid herself of the thought of him. That he had chosen to put her so quickly aside, that his impersonal manner had told her how much he regretted his impulsive act, seared as though it had just happened.

A shadow moved across a square of light, and Camilla came to herself abruptly. What foolish thing was she doing here—spying upon him out of the shadows! Eager as a schoolgirl for the sight of her love.

Her love.

She did not want it. She had not asked to love this man, but there it was—hurtful and real and not to be lightly dismissed. She turned and ran back through the trees, letting herself quietly into the house, scurrying upstairs to the retreat of her own room.

There was once more an exultance in her, and a torment as well.

CHAPTER 15

IN THE MORNING the exultance was gone. Camilla awakened feeling as tired as though she had not slept, but her eyes were clear, her thoughts brittle and sharp with self-judgment.

How could she have been so trapped by gentle dreams last night? In the morning light she could look at herself and remember something she had told Booth. She had not known many men. It was true that she was easily vulnerable. Whether it was Ross or Booth, the warm longings that were part of her youth reached out toward a male counterpart in an instinctive answering. Love? How could she have been so foolish? What could she know of love? If she were honest with herself, she must admit that there were times when she had been equally attracted to Booth.

Today there were other things to think of. Regardless of Letty's remark about misinterpretation, she must face the possibility that someone in this house had added a poisonous potion to Letty's tea. Since it was hardly likely to be one of the servants, nor could it be Ross, who was an outsider, the tamperer must be one of the three within this house: Hortense, Letty, or Booth. This morning, with her mood so newly cool and hard, she could even regard Letty with serious doubt, though Hortense was to be more easily suspected.

At any rate, she must get to the bottom of what had happened and discover whether someone had tried deliberately to harm her. If one attempt had been made, there might well be others. By daylight she could be brave and strong. But she knew the shadow of fear that night could bring, and she did not want to live her life in such a shadow.

Yet when she met Letty that day, she could find no means of taking hold of the problem. The moment she moved toward it, Letty seemed to slip mistily away from her probing, and she could not bring herself to question her directly.

She dreaded her first meeting with Ross. If he showed amusement toward her, if he referred in any way to what had happened between them, she would not know how to meet him with her pride intact. Her fears were unfounded, however. He was courteous, though distant, and it was hard to remember that he had worked so cheerfully beside her in a kitchen yesterday. She could not help a certain anger, but she told herself that it came more from hurt pride than from any real emotion on her part.

In the days before Hortense and Booth came home, Ross was completely matter-of-fact toward her. He placed business matters before her as usual, and did not hesitate to show his disapproval when she seemed unenthusiastic about projects that absorbed his attention.

On the afternoon when Hortense and Booth were to return, Ross reminded her of the invitation to tea at Nora Redfern's tomorrow. But she had a feeling that he regretted his original impulse in urging such a visit.

If it had not been for the fact that Camilla longed to make Nora's acquaintance, she might have pleaded some excuse to escape the invitation. But she found that she was looking forward to the occasion more than she had expected to. She would have an opportunity to wear one of her enchanting new afternoon frocks. She would look her very best, and be serenely remote and indifferent to either criticism or approval on the part of Ross Granger.

It was with a sense of regret that she heard the sound of the carriage bringing Booth and his mother back to Thunder Heights. Now the quiet, friendly hours she had spent with Letty would come to an end, and disquieting influences would be at work in the house again.

Nevertheless, she went to the door to greet them, and her first look at the travelers told her that as far as Aunt Hortense was concerned, the trip had been a failure. Booth appeared to have enjoyed himself thoroughly and was ready to talk about what he had seen and done in New York. Hortense was clearly angry and frustrated, impatient even with Booth, and hardly civil to Letty and Camilla.

The next morning Booth was ready to take up his painting again, and this time all went well.

As he worked, Letty came in to join them again and sat down nearby to watch. Once Booth paused to ask a direct question of Camilla.

"What has happened to you, Cousin, since I've been away?"

Camilla was startled. "Happened? Why, nothing much. I've baked bread and helped Aunt Letty with her receipts. The new draperies are up in the parlor. Nothing much else."

For a few moments Booth worked intently on the face of the girl in the picture. Then he flashed the smile that always seemed so unexpected in his dark, sardonic face.

"It was none of those things I meant, Camilla. Even though you're very quiet today, there's something that was lacking before. I can see more than Althea in you this morning."

"I don't know what you mean," she told him, and had nothing more to say.

Letty looked up from her work to glance at her in mild surprise, and Camilla was suddenly afraid that her aunt might add some comment of her own.

"Why don't you play for us while I'm posing, Aunt Letty?" she said hurriedly. "I've never really heard you play your harp."

Perhaps Letty sensed a plea behind her words, for she put her work aside. "Very well—if Booth doesn't mind."

"I've always enjoyed your playing, Aunt Letty," he said gallantly, but his eyes were still on his model, and Camilla sensed a quickened interest and curiosity in his look.

Letty went to the harp and drew off its cover. The fingers of her left hand moved easily on the strings, but she had to bend her body forward to reach them with her crooked right arm. After a few chords she began to play, and the music was nothing Camilla had ever heard before. It had a wailing, melancholy sound, as if the contented, busy Letty Judd of everyday vanished when she sat down to her harp. In her place was a woman lost and tragic. The music seemed to sing of longing and of wasted, empty years with an intensity that was frightening.

Booth looked up from his painting somberly. "You're hearing the music of Thunder Heights, Cousin. It speaks for us all, doesn't it? Trapped and damned and without hope. That's why Mother hates to hear Aunt Letty play. The music tells too much about the things we try to hide from one another."

Letty's fingers were still on the strings. She rose to cover the instrument without a word and slip quietly from the room.

Booth worked in silence for a time, and when he spoke again, it was of another matter. "As you've probably guessed, my mother found no encouragement on her mission to New York. It's possible that the will might be broken. At least the lawyer she consulted didn't try to discourage her as a client. But it seems that it would cost a fine penny—and where is the money to come from? She can hardly ask you to finance her effort to take a fortune away from you, can she, Cousin? It makes for a difficult situation."

Camilla watched him guardedly. "You don't sound as if you minded."

"Why should I mind?" He shrugged graceful shoulders. "I live a more comfortable life under the new regime. While I'll admit that the money would be easier come by in my mother's hands than in yours, Cousin, I've suffered very little."

He worked on for a while longer and then laid aside his brush. "That's enough for today. It's going well. A change of scene has done me good. And the change in you is stimulating. I shan't give up wondering what caused it. Camilla, I haven't forgotten your wish to find a good saddle horse. I shopped around a bit in New York. But so far I haven't found what I think you might like."

She was relieved to have him speak of horses. "I don't know that I'm that particular. I'd love to buy a horse and go riding soon."

"Trust me a little longer, will you?" he said. "You deserve the best."

Again the faint note of mockery was back in his voice, but she ignored it. She was glad when the posing was over. On and off during the last half hour she had been thinking about the tea at Blue Beeches this afternoon, and she was eager to get away and look through the frocks she might wear.

Somehow it grew increasingly important that she seem beautiful and remote and self-contained to Ross Granger. He must be made to forget that Camilla King had ever moved in so headlong a fashion into his arms. Today she would be out of reach and yet —delectable.

There was still a hurt in her that wanted to pay him back.

The dress she decided upon was of pale blue Chinese silk, trimmed with touches of ivory lace. It was a thin, delicate dress, and she found it satisfying to appear in something that was far from serviceable, and not at all suited to a governess. When she had put on her mother's bracelet of medallions and peach stones and turned before the armoire mirror a few times, she was ready.

Letty came in to admire her just before she went downstairs, and her aunt was warm in her praise.

"I haven't seen anyone looking so pretty and appealing since Althea lived in this house. You'll do us credit, my dear."

Camilla gave her a quick, loving hug, wondering at the perversity of her own thoughts that could at times hold anyone as endearing and guileless as Aunt Letty under suspicion.

As she ran down the octagon staircase, she listened pleasurably to her own silken froufrou, and sniffed the aura of light apple blossom scent with which she had surrounded herself. How lovely it was to feel young and unexplainably happy. Though there was danger in this, lest she forget how out-of-reach she meant to be with Ross.

She was smiling as she stepped into the antehall and was faintly disconcerted to find Booth watching her from the library door.

"Charming!" he said. "And surprising to find a lady of fashion at Thunder Heights."

She could not resist turning about before him, displaying her new frock at its most fetching angles. There was an eagerness in her, a hunger for approval—and masculine eyes were more satisfactory in meeting that need than feminine.

"Your escort is waiting for you outside," Booth said. "I'm sorry I'm not the one who's taking you to visit Nora."

She smiled at him, warming toward everyone today, and went outside. Ross stood at the foot of the steps, and as she came out he turned and stared at her, his startled look gratifying. He would find in her today neither the little governess he had met on the river boat, nor the stubborn heiress who quarreled with him so often.

Nor would he find the ingenuous girl of the beech tree. Today she meant to be—Althea's daughter.

Ross recovered from his surprise all too quickly and made no comment on her appearance. She found, however, that he could play the gentleman as smoothly as Booth when he chose. They followed the path that led to the lower level, and crossed the railroad tracks to walk along the bank just above the river. Ross held branches back from brushing her, and helped her up and down steep places in the path as if she were really as fragile as she wanted to believe herself today. Sometimes she wondered if he were laughing at her, just a little, behind his rather elaborate gestures, but she was too happy and confident to mind.

Once they stopped to watch a fleet of little sailboats gliding past on the surface of the smooth blue Hudson, and Camilla followed them out of sight, feeling that they added to the carefree aspect of the day.

The first glimpse of Blue Beeches was always reassuring. It sat foursquare upon its high basement, its generous veranda open toward the river. On a slope of lawn at one side of the house Nora's two older children were playing a game of croquet, while their nurse sat with the youngest, watching. The spotted dog, Champion, saw the visitors and came bounding across the grass toward them. Ross accepted his effusive greeting with affection and held him away from Camilla.

"He misses his master," Ross said. "As we all do. Nora's husband died just over a year ago. Ted Redfern was one of my good friends. I've been trying to help Nora with some of her business problems ever since. She has a lot of courage. I hope you'll be friends."

There was a note of tender affection in his tone that made Camilla glance at him quickly. Was his feeling for Ted Redfern's wife more than that of a friend? She did not like the pang that stabbed through her at his words. It bore too close a resemblance to an emotion that went by an uglier name. She would not be jealous of Nora Redfern!

A maid showed them into a huge parlor with moss green wallpaper and softly cushioned furniture. Everything looked a little frayed and worn, as if the room had never been closed to the children. Over the mantel, seemingly cut through the huge chimney above the fireplace, was a circular window. Blue sky and fleeting clouds could be seen through its high double glass, while the interior flues separated to circle round it.

Nora joined them after a brief interval, flushed and a little breathless. Her brown hair had been swept back from her forehead without any vestige of a pompadour, and tied with a black velvet ribbon at the nape of her neck. The marks of a hasty brush were still upon it. She wore a frock of dark silk that suited her in its simplicity.

"Do forgive me for keeping you waiting," she said, holding out a hand first to Camilla and then to Ross. "I had Diamond out for a ride and I lost track of time. Not that forgetting about time is anything new for me. Ted used to say it was never any use buying me watches because I'd always forget to look at them."

She noted Camilla's interest in the unusual window and smiled.

"My grandfather designed that window when he built the house. In his day there was always a stuffed bird kept between those double panes of glass. But I like to see the sky."

Nora had an engagingly friendly manner, and under other circumstances Camilla would have been drawn to her warmly. But now she found herself a little watchful, a little too much aware, for her own comfort, of every glance that passed between Nora and Ross. She did not want it to be like that—it simply was.

The maid brought tea in a handsome Sèvres service, with watercress sandwiches and frosted cakes on a three-tiered stand, and Nora settled down comfortably for conversation.

"I remember your mother well," she told Camilla. "When I was quite small she used to come here often to visit my mother. Mama lives upriver now. I wrote her that I was going to invite you over, and she wants me to tell her all about you. By the way, when are you going to open up the house again?"

"Open it up?" said Camilla. "I'm not sure I know what you mean."

"Only that when you have it fully refurbished, you must give a party and bring back the old days. How gay it used to be! I can remember coming home from across the river late one night with my parents and seeing Thunder Heights lighted from top to bottom, with Japanese lanterns strung across the veranda and all about that high lawn above the river. We could hear the music clear from the other side. Often here at Blue Beeches there were nights when we could catch the sound of music and laughter."

Letty too had urged her to open up the house, Camilla remembered. "I'd like to give a party," she said, her interest rising. "Perhaps we could invite people from up and down the river who used to know the family. Would you come, Mrs. Redfern? And perhaps your mother?"

Nora hesitated. "Mother would come in a moment—though I'm not sure that would be a good idea. She is pretty outspoken, you know, and there's no telling her what not to say. Besides, your aunts would be angry if you invited her."

"But why?" Camilla asked. "What happened to break up the friendship your mother had with my family at Thunder Heights?"

"Let's not spoil the afternoon with old quarrels," Nora said. "Perhaps your coming will make the difference and we can all be friends again."

"If we give a party, we'll want you both," Camilla insisted. "I should think Aunt Hortense would love the excitement of a party. And I know Aunt Letty would like to see the house opened up for the sake of the rest of us, though I'm not sure she would really enjoy it herself."

"I'm afraid she gave up that sort of thing after her arm was so badly injured," Nora said. "She wouldn't wear evening dress after that, and for a long while she was terribly self-conscious."

"No one ever mentions her injury," Camilla puzzled. "When was she hurt? What happened?"

"She was thrown from a horse," Ross said. "Just as your mother was. It occurred before I came to live at Thunder Heights."

Nora nodded. "It was after Althea had married and gone away. Hortense and Letty used to ride a good deal in those days. Orrin gave Letty a mare that had a maverick streak they weren't aware of. Letty was thrown and dragged. The mare went half crazy, and in her kicking and stamping Letty's arm was stepped on and broken. She might have been killed if Hortense hadn't been riding with her that day. Hortense rescued her and got her home. But the arm never set properly, and the mark of the hoof left a scar she has carried ever since."

"The Judds have had bad luck with horses," Ross said. "With

two such accidents, it was no wonder that Mr. Judd would have no horses on the place."

Nora looked quickly at Camilla, almost with a question in her eyes. But before she could put it into words, one of her children came running in. He was a sturdy little boy, with his hair on end, and his face dirty.

"I won! I won!" he shrieked, and flung himself in triumph upon his mother, croquet mallet and all.

When she had applauded him, wiped his face, and sent him back to play, she did not return to the subject of Letty's accident.

"Where do you go riding?" Camilla asked as Nora refilled her teacup.

"Today I followed the river," Nora said. "But my favorite rides are back in the hills. I think I'm happiest when I can ride up through the woods and come out on top of Thunder Mountain."

"I've been thinking of getting a horse," Camilla told her. "I loved riding as a child in the parks in New York. And it would be so much better here."

"In spite of the Thunder Heights jinx when it comes to horses?" Nora asked.

"I don't believe in jinxes," Camilla said quickly.

"In that case, you needn't wait until you buy a horse. Borrow one of mine. I'd be glad to loan you Diamond. He was Ted's horse, really, but I've trained him to the sidesaddle. You may have him tomorrow, if you like. I'm leaving with the children to visit my mother upriver for a few days. Ross can take one of the other horses and go with you. I often loan him a horse when he wants to ride."

Unable to hide her sudden pleasure at the thought of riding with Ross, Camilla glanced at him quickly and saw clear reluctance in his eyes. She rushed into words to hide her hurt.

"Surely it's not necessary for me to have an escort!"

"Indeed it is," Nora assured her. "We can't have you going out in the hills alone until you know your way. It's all wooded mountains back there, with trails crisscrossing. You can lose yourself easily when you get away from the river. You'll take her, won't you, Ross?"

166

"I'm going down to New York in a day or two," he said. "But perhaps I could manage it tomorrow."

His lack of enthusiasm was obvious, and Camilla would have refused his company if Nora had not settled the matter with the quiet assurance of a woman who knew that what she asked of a man would not be refused.

She felt only relief when the tea hour passed and she could rise to go. She did not want to remain in Ross's company a moment longer than she had to, now that she felt sure where his interest really lay. All her earlier happiness in the day, all her confidence in herself, was evaporating. She had not, after all, proved herself Althea's daughter. Althea had been irresistible.

On the way back to Thunder Heights, Ross continued to be silent and preoccupied. It was almost as if he had forgotten her presence, and she felt further piqued into calling him back.

"Did you know," she asked, "that Aunt Hortense's purpose in going to New York was to try to break Grandfather's will?"

"I'm not surprised," Ross said. "It was to be expected that she'd try. If I were you, I'd break it myself and pack Hortense and Booth out of the house straight off."

She brushed indignantly ahead of him, heedless of a briar that caught at her dress. "Even if no one else cares, I feel bound by what Grandfather wanted me to do. I'm not free to dispose of his property in any way I might wish."

"You're being sentimental," Ross said. "Why not give those two the money and let them go? You'd be better off in the long run. Orrin Judd was trying to bring back the past. He was trying to undo old mistakes and revenge himself on those he distrusted at the same time. You must live in the present—the future. Don't be a fool."

They were nearing the house now and she began to hurry. "If I'm a fool, I'll be one in my own way. At least my conscience is my own. And—you needn't trouble to ride with me tomorrow. Perhaps I can ask Booth—"

He surprised her by reaching out to catch her by the wrist. She felt the medallions of her bracelet press into her flesh with the strength of his grasp.

"I'll ride with you," he said, his gray eyes angry. "Don't try to change your plans now." Then he dropped her hand abruptly and strode away from her toward the house.

What was the matter with him? She could not altogether suppress a sense of satisfaction that she had at least stirred him to anger.

Very well, she *would* ride with him tomorrow. But she would go as the mistress of Thunder Heights, and she would keep him strictly in his place. She would show him, once and for all, how little he meant to her. Today she had not succeeded very well.

When she went up to her room, she was shaken by a queer sort of fury in which disgust with herself mingled with her anger against Ross. Who was she? What was she? Today she had flung herself through a ridiculous gamut of emotions, from high hope and elation to a disappointment that was out of all proportion to the cause. Why? Because she cared more about Ross Granger than she was willing to admit, even to herself? And because she was beginning to feel that his affections were well occupied elsewhere?

She sat down at Althea's dressing table and looked into Althea's mirror. A black-haired girl with dark eyes that were angry, and a soft mouth that was all too tremulous, looked back at her.

"What would *you* have done?" she whispered, and her question was directed not to herself, but to a long ago image that had appeared in this mirror. But if the shadowy face of her mother looked over her shoulder, it did not speak, or counsel her. Only Nora's words sounded again in her mind. "Why don't you open up the house?"

Perhaps she would do just that. Fling open the windows and doors, open them wide to a more normal life in which gaiety had some part. A life that would bring new faces, new friends to Thunder Heights. She would tell the others about her plan right after dinner tonight.

CHAPTER 16

WHEN dinner was over that night and Ross had gone back to his rooms above the coach house, the family gathered on the veranda to enjoy the evening air after a warm day. Behind them the parlor glowed with light, but here on the veranda they could sit in the semidarkness—a quiet, not very companionable group. Into the separate silences Camilla dropped her suggestion.

"Let's give a party," she said.

Letty looked surprised, but said nothing. Hortense murmured, "What for?" and Booth said, "Why not?" in lazy amusement.

Camilla went on in a little rush, speaking more to Hortense than to the others. "Today Nora Redfern was telling me about the way it used to be at Thunder Heights. About the parties Grandfather used to give when you and Aunt Letty were young. We could at least make a beginning and wake the house up. This veranda must be big enough for dancing—"

"It is," Letty said quickly. "Many's the time we used to dance out here in the summertime. Do you remember, Hortense?"

"I want to forget," Hortense said.

"But I'll need your help," Camilla pointed out. "Don't you think a party would be fun on a lovely summer evening?"

"My mother adores parties," Booth said dryly. "She's told me a good many times how she used to shine at them. And how much she missed them."

Hortense gave him a look that was just a shade less doting than usual, but offered no objection.

169

Camilla talked on about how they could set tables on the lawn, and hang Japanese lanterns—just as they'd done in the old days. And surely friends of the family, people who had known her mother and Letty and Hortense when they were young, could be invited, along with their grownup children. Thunder Heights was beginning to look so beautiful—they must show it off, gain it a new reputation for gaiety and hospitality.

Someone came around the end of the house as she spoke, a dark shadow among the trees. As he reached the veranda steps, Camilla saw that it was Ross. He spoke to her directly.

"What time do you wish to go riding tomorrow? I forgot to ask."

The silence that fell upon the veranda was like that of a breath being held. Camilla was aware of Letty's faint gasp, of Hortense's stillness, of Booth's quick, intent look.

"Will nine o'clock in the morning be convenient for you?" Camilla asked stiffly.

"I'll have the horses here at nine," Ross said, and went away as he had come through the grove of elms.

"What horses?" Hortense demanded when he had gone.

"Nora Redfern offered me a saddle horse to ride tomorrow, and Ross is going with me to show me some of the trails."

"Nora Redfern!" Hortense cried. "Have you no sense of propriety that you must strike up a friendship with this woman? How can you—"

Letty slipped out of her chair and drifted across the veranda to Camilla's side. "I know you said you wanted to wear Althea's things, but I didn't think you really meant it. Don't go riding, dear. Please don't go riding."

Camilla smiled at her reassuringly. "Aunt Letty, I know how you must feel about horses, but I think I'm a fairly good rider and I want to be a better one. Booth has promised to find me a saddle horse, and then I mean to go riding every day when the weather allows. And as for Nora Redfern, I enjoyed my visit with her this afternoon, and I hope we'll be friends. I see no reason why I shouldn't borrow one of her horses until I have my own."

Letty rested a hand that trembled on Camilla's shoulder. "You don't understand, dear. Papa said there was never to be a horse at Thunder Heights again. He made us all promise that we would give up riding forever."

She unhooked her right sleeve at the wrist and started to roll it up, but Camilla caught her hand, stopping her. "Don't, Aunt Letty. I know. But just because there have been accidents before, doesn't mean there will be another one. I love to ride, and it would be foolish not to enjoy it again."

"Bravo!" Booth applauded, clapping his hands together lightly. "I have no use for faint hearts. The riding habit suits you, Cousin. I say wear it and go riding tomorrow. And give your party. A little excitement about this place will be welcome. If we don't have it, we may well—explode."

Letty went back to her chair and sat down without a sound. Camilla could not see her face in the dim light, but there was something unnerving about her stillness, as if she held some rush of shattering emotion in check. Hortense stood up and walked to one of the parlor doors.

"Ride, then," she said listlessly and went into the house.

Booth yawned and held the back of his hand over his mouth. "These emotional scenes are wearing. That is, when the emotion is suppressed. I'd rather see tears, an outburst of temper, some flinging about in good feminine fashion."

Letty's silence remained complete, her face expressionless.

"At least, Cousin, you've won your point," Booth said. "No one will lift a finger when you go riding tomorrow. I must say I find it generous of Mrs. Redfern to loan you her horse and even suggest that Granger go riding with you. She must be very sure of herself."

His meaning was clear. "A remark like that is uncalled for!" Camilla said sharply.

"Is it?" The mockery had gone out of him. "Perhaps I want to see your eyes opened in time, Camilla."

"Mrs. Redfern's husband has been dead hardly more than a year," Camilla reminded him. "And Ross was his very good friend."

"All the more reason for what is happening," Booth said. "A lonely, saddened woman, and a man who had a great affection for the man she loved. I don't blame them. It's natural enough. But I would hate to see you grow too interested in Granger."

"I can take care of myself," Camilla said stiffly.

Letty coughed gently, but said nothing, still lost in her remoteness. When Camilla rose to go inside, Booth stopped her, his hand light upon her arm, his voice unexpectedly tender.

"I'm not sure you can take care of yourself, Cousin. But I'd like you to know that you can count me your friend."

She was moved in spite of her hurt, and she gave him an uncertain smile as she went into the house.

That night Letty played her harp again.

Camilla heard the eerie music stealing through the house as it had done on the night when Grandfather Orrin had died. Was this music perhaps the emotional release Letty needed—something to keep her from going to pieces when some inner strain became too great for her?

Tonight no door opened, no footsteps sounded in the hall, no one stole upstairs to silence the music. After a time Camilla fell asleep, and when she wakened some hours later, the house was as still and hushed as if no mournful harp music had ever drifted through its corridors. But now, in spite of the silence, she had the feeling that something had changed in the very climate of the house. The harp music had saddened her, but there had been nothing truly frightening about it. In the hush that now lay upon the house—as if the very walls held themselves still to listen—there was something new, something fearful. Into this silence stirred a whisper of sound, as if someone moved in the hall nearby.

Camilla sat up and reached for the matches and candle beside her bed. The candle flared and smoked in a draft from the balcony's open door, then settled to a pale, steady flame. Her attention was fixed upon the corridor door to her room. With a cold washing of fear through her body, she wondered if she had really locked that door tonight.

As she watched, she saw the cloisonné doorknob move almost imperceptibly. An unseen hand turned it softly and carefully as far as it would go, but the lock held and the door did not open. Slowly, softly, as Camilla stared in fascination, it turned back to its original position. The faintest sound of a sigh reached her from outside the door, followed by silence.

Camilla slipped out of bed and into a wrapper. For a long moment she stood with her ear against the panel, listening with all her being, but there was no sound of a footfall to disturb the stillness of the house. Whoever had turned the knob might well be standing just outside the door, waiting. If she opened it, the unseen intruder might spring quickly inside.

But the silence seemed not to be a breathing silence. She had the feeling that whoever had stood there had moved so stealthily away that the hall carpet had hidden any retreat. Her own fingers could not move so secretly. There was a click as she unlocked the door and pulled it open a crack.

No one stood in the hall outside her room, but now she heard the sound of a creaking step on the stairs above. She looked boldly into the hall and was in time to see the white of a flounced nightgown moved out of sight up the stairway.

She did not hesitate, but ran barefooted toward the stairs and up them to the floor above. Letty was there, drifting smoothly ahead of her down the corridor toward the attic stairs. In one hand she carried a candle, and as Camilla watched she opened the door to the stairs and vanished up them.

Troubled, Camilla hurried after. Aunt Letty was not to be feared, and clearly she was sleepwalking again. She must be stopped and brought back to her own bed, but she must not be startled awake. This must be done gently.

Letty had climbed to the attic by now, and she did not turn as Camilla came up the stairs behind her. She seemed to know exactly what she wanted here, and went at once to the small rear room where Althea's saddle rested over a beam. There she set the candleholder upon a shelf and took the shining stirrup into her hands. Though her eyes were wide open, Letty felt blindly along the stirrup leather until she came to the saddle itself, and her hands followed it to the jutting silver horn. She seemed to be touching all these things, searching them out, as if her hands found some reassurance in contact with them.

Camilla stood silently watching her, wondering what she must do. She wished now that she had called Hortense, who knew how to handle these sleepwalking spells. Before she could decide whether to speak to her aunt, or touch her arm to lead her back to bed, Letty picked up her candle again, went past Camilla without seeing her, and started downstairs.

Softly Camilla followed, and Letty returned to her own room without further exploration and closed her door. In all probability she had gone safely back to bed. Shaken and mystified, Camilla went to her room, and when she had locked the door, she stepped out upon the balcony. The night air was cool and fresh to her hot cheeks, and there was no tinge of horror there.

What hidden thoughts and sorrows roused Letty to make her walk in her sleep? And why would she go to the attic and seek out Althea's saddle? A remembrance of Grandfather Orrin's words once more returned sharply to her mind. "Watch Letty," he had said.

Below the balcony Camilla heard the rustling sound of something moving. Was there someone else abroad on this strange night? But the sound, she decided, was no more than an elm branch brushing the side of the house. Starlight dusted a silver patina over Thunder Heights and shimmered on the surface of the river.

The thought of her ride tomorrow returned, and with it all the things she wanted to shut away. In particular the words Booth had spoken about Nora and Ross. She had been angry with him at first, but his words had only strengthened her own conviction of the affection that lay between those two.

Booth had been right—she must not let herself be hurt. Her wayward feelings must be turned back from the path of disaster.

She went to bed and lay awake for a long while.

In spite of her disturbed night, she was awake early the next morning. The sun, rising brightly in a golden sky across the Hudson, carried out the prophecy of the night. It was a beautiful morning for riding, and she felt eager to be away from the house and out in the hills.

A little to her surprise, Aunt Letty came down for breakfast, looking somewhat subdued.

"I'm sorry you were upset about my riding," Camilla said.

Letty smiled at her with forced brightness. "You mustn't let my foolish fears spoil your plans. This will be a good day for riding—a safe day." She paused to tell Grace she would have just a little toast and a cup of coffee.

"What do you mean—a safe day?" Camilla asked.

"It's not storming," Letty said. "You must never go riding in a storm."

Clearly she was thinking of the horse that had thrown her sister —the horse that had been afraid of thunderstorms. If the idea had become an obsession with Letty, there was no point in trying to argue her out of the notion.

"I love storms," Camilla said. "I even like to be out in them. But I don't think I'd deliberately go riding in a thunderstorm, if that's what you mean."

Letty was staring at her with a wide, misty gaze. "You're so much like your mother. I hope you haven't an affinity for thunderstorms, as your mother had."

The fey quality was evident in Letty again this morning. Her delicate, fine-skinned face had a faraway look about it, as if she moved in wreaths of mist in spite of the sunlight. It might be just as well to call her back to more earthly considerations, Camilla thought, and asked about her garden.

"The nasturtiums are thriving this year," Letty said, rising readily to the bait. "Perhaps they're not really herbs, but I love the way they brighten the garden all summer long. In the fall I can use the seeds for pickling. And have you seen my honeywort? The yellow buds are already blooming, though they never really open, you know. Not that it matters, when the leaves are so shining and beautiful."

When she talked about her garden, she was shining and beautiful herself, Camilla thought. One forgot the twisted arm, the ugly scar hidden by her sleeve.

When breakfast was over, Camilla went upstairs to dress for her ride. She put on her mother's habit and boots. The gray top hat with its floating streamers of veiling was as fetching as ever, and she liked the look of it on her dark hair. When she was ready, she opened a drawer and took out the little black riding crop, with its polished silver head. This would make the final perfect touch. Today she would carry it when she went riding, just as her mother had once done.

She went into the hall, to find Hortense at the top of the stairs, filling the cinnabar stair lamp with oil. She had drawn the great bowl down on its pulley, and Camilla waited until the lamp had been filled and returned to place beneath the carved canopy high over the stairwell. Hortense heard her and turned, her greenish eyes venomous this morning.

When Camilla would have passed her to go downstairs, Hortense put out an arresting hand. "I suppose you heard Letty playing her harp last night?" she asked in a whisper.

"I heard her," Camilla said.

"Hush! She's waiting for you at the foot of the stairs. I don't want her to hear. I hope you realize that the harp playing was your fault. She only plays at night when she's unhappy and upset. You've treated her with a complete lack of consideration."

Hortense was hardly the one to accuse others of a lack of consideration, but Camilla did not point out the fact as she started downstairs. And this was not the time to mention the sleepwalking.

"Aunt Letty and I had breakfast together," Camilla said. "She seemed quite all right then."

"We can expect more sleepwalking," Hortense persisted. "That will be your doing too."

"I'm sorry," Camilla said and would have continued on her way, if Hortense had not suddenly seen the riding crop in her hands.

"Where did you get that?" she demanded.

Before Camilla could answer, or knew what she intended, Hortense snatched at the crop. She only succeeded in knocking it out of Camilla's hand, and it went over the banister to fall with a clatter to the floor below. Hortense looked after it in dismay for a moment, then shrugged and went back to her own room.

Camilla ran down the stairs to find that Letty had picked up the crop and was holding it as she watched Camilla descend. She stood tapping the ragged end of the leather thong across her palm in a nervous gesture.

"You look lovely," she said. "Have a wonderful ride, dear. I'm sure everything will be fine this morning."

"Thank you, Aunt Letty," Camilla said, and held out her hand for the crop.

Letty did not give it up. "Will you leave this with me, please? I'd rather you didn't carry it, dear."

"But—why not?" Camilla asked.

"Perhaps—" Letty hesitated, "—perhaps I'm more sentimental

about this little riding crop than I am about the other things. Leave it with me, Camilla."

Puzzled though she was Camilla gave in. Letty held the door open, and Camilla went out into the bright morning.

"Have a nice ride," Letty repeated softly, and closed the door behind her.

Moved by an increasing sense of uneasiness, Camilla stood on the steps, waiting for Ross. She heard the neighing of a horse, and a moment later he appeared, coming up from the river path and around the house, riding a roan mare and leading Diamond, saddled and bridled. Nora's favorite mount was a dappled gray—a handsome, high-stepping creature, with a white diamond blaze on his forehead.

"I hope you can manage this fellow," Ross said. "Grays are supposed to be unsuitable mounts for ladies because their dispositions are unstable. Though I'm not sure I hold with the legend. Nora handles him beautifully."

His words sounded like a challenge, and Camilla felt quite willing to pick it up. She fed Diamond a lump of sugar, stroked his nose and talked to him for a few moments. He seemed to accept her readily enough, and from the mounting block she put her left foot into the stirrup, turning her body so that she went lightly up to hook her right knee over the horn of the sidesaddle. Diamond took a skittish step or two and then, sensing firmness in her hands, did as she wished him to. She smiled at Ross from the saddle, feeling pleased and triumphant.

"Where would you like to ride, Miss King?" he inquired formally, holding to the role of one who had been given a task to perform and meant to carry it out correctly to the letter.

Camilla turned Diamond away from the river, her smile stiffening. "Let's go up Thunder Mountain. I've been wanting to get to the top. Do you know the way?"

"Of course." He went ahead along the drive toward the road, accepting the suggestion as an order which gave him no choice.

She touched Diamond with her heel to catch up, and they rode out side by side between the stone lions that marked the gate in the great privet hedge.

The air was brilliantly clear, with a bright blue sky overhead, but not too warm for comfort. Camilla loved being on a horse again. This high seat above the world, with the feeling of Diamond's smooth-flowing strength beneath her, gave her a heady sense of power.

They overtook an elderly farmer driving a cartload of vegetables to market, and he looked up at them. For an instant he gave Camilla a shocked stare and then touched a finger to his forelock in recognition. Camilla almost laughed out loud in delight as they rode past. Surely he remembered Althea Judd, and he must have been carried back through the years at the sight of her daughter.

She urged Diamond into a canter, and Ross kept pace with her, though now he rode a tail's length behind, still acting the role of groom. He did not take the lead again until they neared the opening to a narrow road up the mountain, when he called to her and trotted ahead.

CHAPTER 17

THEY WENT single file beneath the trees, winding upward at a gradual pace. Riding along with branches interlacing just above her head, and the river, blue as the sky, sometimes glimpsed below, she could almost forget Ross in sheer physical happiness.

Once he turned his head and spoke to her over his shoulder. "Here's something for you to see."

She followed him into the wide scar of an open place which had once been cleared through the woods. It dropped away in a steep slope of mountain to a rushing stream below. The stretch was overgrown with scrub now, and along the edges of the scar mountain laurel glowed in the bright pink and white blooming of spring.

Ross reined in the mare as Camilla drew up beside him. "When your grandfather was young and worked in lumber, this was a pitching place," he said.

"Pitching place?" Camilla repeated the unfamiliar term.

"They used to snake the logs down the old road and get them started on this slope, where they could pitch them to the stream below and send them down to the river."

Camilla sat very still in the saddle, breathing the spicy scent of the woods about her, listening to the noisy voice of the stream. She could almost see Orrin Judd as he must have been in the strength of his youth—a young man who belonged to the forests and the hills, reveling in this outdoor work.

"Let's go on," Ross said abruptly.

The path wound back into the woods behind the rocky eminence of the mountain, and the climb grew steeper. When they emerged suddenly upon an open space at the top, Camilla had not realized they were so high. She rode eagerly toward the stony head of the mountain, where it towered above the river, dropping steeply away in a face of rocky cliff.

Ross put a hand on Diamond's bridle. "Not too near the edge," he warned. "Sometimes he takes notions into his head."

"I want to stand near the edge," Camilla said, and she slipped out of the saddle without waiting for Ross's help, and let him take the reins from her. While he walked the horses back toward the trees to tether them, she climbed a slope of rock and sat down on a boulder near the very lip of the cliff.

Up here the wind blew strong and free, whipping out the streamers of her gray veil. Below and a little to the north lay the village, its white church steeple like a toy tower on a child's house of blocks. Across the river the unknown town opposite seemed a world away and beyond it rolled the hills clear to the blue haze of New England mountains. When she turned toward the north she could see the outline of the Catskills far away on her left. At her feet the sheer face of the cliff dropped toward the river.

"Can we see Thunder Heights from here?" she asked Ross as he came to the foot of the rocky incline where she stood.

He shook his head. "Not from this spot. Only the face of the cliff can be seen from below. The trees jut out lower down to hide everything else."

"It must have been near here that my mother was thrown from her horse," Camilla said softly.

"This was the place," Ross admitted, and said nothing more.

He climbed up to stand at the edge of the precipice, looking over the dizzy drop to the river. She could study him now, as she had done that day on the river boat, before she had ever spoken to him. He had seemed less remote from her then than he did today.

Suddenly he pointed. "Do you see the long white boat coming down from Albany? That's the *Mary Powell*. She's not young any more, but she's still queen of the river boats. Listen—you can hear her whistle."

A clear, silvery sound reached them from the river, and Camilla watched the white boat move past their prominence, gliding smoothly as a queen of swans.

"I worked aboard her once when I was a boy," Ross said. "She always seems like a member of my family. It will be a sad day when they take her off the river."

"You love the river, don't you?" Camilla watched his face, forgetting the boat.

"I belong to the river," he said simply. His eyes followed the *Mary Powell* as she disappeared around a bend. "Do you see the place downriver where opposite banks seem to reach out to each other?"

Camilla looked in the direction of his pointing finger. "Yes, I see it."

"That's where your grandfather meant to build his bridge," Ross said. "When he was keen about it in the beginning."

The bridge again. As always it stood between them, as if it were indeed a steel barrier already built. But she did not want to bicker today.

"Why do you care so much about that bridge?" she asked.

He did not answer her directly. "When I was a little boy my father took me on a trip to see Niagara Falls. But it wasn't the falls I looked at, once I was there. It was the railroad bridge John Roebling had built across the gorge. I thought it the most miraculous and beautiful thing I'd ever seen. While I stood there staring with all my eyes, a locomotive pulled a train of freight cars across the span and it stood under all the immense weight without a quiver. And yet to me it looked as fine as though it were strung of cobwebs, instead of great suspension wires. I fell in love with a bridge that day, and it's a love I've never gotten over. I suppose that's something no woman could ever understand."

She was beginning to understand a little as she listened to him and watched the light that had come into his face. She had not dreamed that he felt like this.

"I grew up knowing I would build bridges someday," he went on. "Little bridges, at first—and one day a big one. With a design and innovations of my own. Of course John Roebling made it easier for all bridge engineers when he invented the wire rope that strings the great suspension bridges. He did what had never been done before, and we've been using his method of making wire cables ever since. His methods of anchorage too. He did a lot for bridge-building long before he designed his masterpiece—the Brooklyn Bridge."

"My grandfather knew how you felt about all this?" Camilla asked.

"Of course. That's why I care so much about a bridge here across the Hudson—because he meant to give me the job of building it. When I was ready. He set me at smaller projects in the meantime —I've one good-sized bridge to my credit upstate, but it's not across the Hudson. With this bridge behind me, I'd be ready to build bridges anywhere. I've even built a working model here in these hills. You'll see it in the woods up there if you go back a little way. I've tried some innovations of my own there. With workmen to help me, of course. It's a real bridge, though small."

Camilla listened in growing surprise. Why hadn't he told her these things in the beginning? Why had he always presented the project of the bridge as a business proposition alone?

"Those designs you showed me," she said, "—are they of your making?"

"They are," he answered curtly. "But I shouldn't have expected you to understand them, or have the vision your grandfather had."

"Tell me something else," she went on. "In what way did you want Grandfather to change his will? What was the thing you wanted in opposition to what Hortense wanted?"

His tone was cool as he answered her. "I wanted to see everything left in a trust, where the family couldn't get their hands on the money and tear down everything he'd built."

"With you as executor?"

Anger flashed in his eyes. "That wouldn't be a job to my taste. There were men in New York he could have chosen. That way perhaps the building of the bridge would have been assured, and the continuation of the construction empire he had built. When he wanted to leave something to me, I told him I'd not accept it. I wanted only this, and I might have won him over if he hadn't begun to think sentimentally of his lost granddaughter."

"I see," she said soberly. "I won't oppose you any longer. Build your bridge. Do as you like about it."

He stepped down from the rock with a violent movement, as if he wanted solid ground beneath his feet. Anger blazed through him.

"Do you know why I'm going down to New York as soon as possible?"

She could only stare at him, seeing no reason for this sudden anger.

"I'm going to find a job of the sort that I can stomach," he told her. "I've had enough of Thunder Heights and working for women. I'll be back to wind up my work here. Then I want to get away."

She scrambled down from the rock a little awkwardly in her boots. "But why do you want to leave when I've just said you can build your bridge? Build a dozen bridges, if you like!"

He looked as if he wanted to shake her. "Do you think the building of bridges is something you can toss out as a sort of largess? 'Build a bridge, if you like. Build a dozen bridges!' Because *you* have the money to pay for them? As if a bridge were a toy! As if you could buy me with a bridge. Because I was foolish enough to—" He broke off and walked back to the horses with a long angry stride, leaving her to follow if she pleased.

What had he been going to say? Because he had been foolish enough to kiss her? She was suddenly angry herself. When he cupped his hands to help her into the saddle, she accepted his touch icily, but she liked it no better than he liked touching her.

Diamond started at the flick of her heel and took off in a dash for the woods. She turned him in the direction of home as they reached the path, but she did not look back to see whether or not Ross Granger was following. She could give Diamond his head now, since he knew the way, and she kept well in advance of her companion. Sometimes she heard the mare's hoofs on the trail just behind, but not once did she turn her head.

Diamond disliked taking the turn to the Judd house, and Ross went past her on the driveway. He dismounted first and came to help her from the saddle. She dropped down into his arms, and for an instant she was as close to him as she had been that day beneath the beech tree. Her heart thudded wildly, but he let her go and stepped back as if he disliked all contact with her. She ran up the steps and beat a tattoo with the knocker on the front door. He was gone before Grace came to let her in, and Camilla walked into the house feeling keyed to a furious pitch.

Hortense came out of her room as she climbed the stairs.

"I see you've broken no bones," she said.

Camilla went by her without a word, not wanting to betray the intensity of feeling that shook her.

Hortense spoke to her retreating back. "I was in the village this morning, and Mr. Berton at the livery stable tells me he has a bay mare for sale."

Camilla paused and turned around. "Yes?" she said.

"What on earth has upset you?" Hortense asked. "You look mad enough to sour cream."

"What about a bay mare?" Camilla demanded.

"Only that she's been trained to the sidesaddle, and I thought you might be interested—since you're set on having a horse. I told him to send her over this afternoon for you to see."

"Thank you," Camilla said stiffly. "I'll look at her."

She hurried on to her own room, got out of her riding things and flung herself upon the bed. Already her muscles were feeling the effect of this first ride, and she knew she would be stiff and sore tomorrow. But it was not the soreness of her body that troubled her now.

Why must her feelings toward Ross Granger always kindle her to anger? Why must she be furious with him, when all the while—she pulled her thoughts back from the path of danger. This was a road she would not follow!

Before long he would leave Thunder Heights for good. He would no longer be here to sting her with his scorn and criticism. Never again would she ride with him up the mountain trail, or slip from a saddle into his arms. He would build his bridges and he would do it without her help. So why was she not pleased at the prospect?

She turned her cheek and found the pillow wet with tears. That wouldn't do at all. She got up and bathed her eyes, put on a fresh frock and went downstairs to join the family for the noonday meal. She was finishing her dessert, when one of Mr. Berton's stableboys arrived with the mare Hortense had mentioned. Grace came in to say that he was holding her for Miss Camilla's inspection at the coach house.

Glad of something new to occupy her attention, Camilla took some lumps of sugar from a bowl on the table and turned to Booth.

"Will you look at this horse with me?" she said.

Booth had watched her curiously throughout the meal, and she knew he saw more than she wanted him to. But while his eyes were bright with speculative interest, he kept his manner matter-of-fact.

"I'm no expert, Cousin," he said. "But for whatever it's worth, I'll give you my opinion."

When they went out the front door, Letty followed them down the steps and called Camilla back.

"Don't buy this horse, dear," she said.

Camilla felt in no mood to listen to Letty's whims at the moment, but she made an effort to be patient. "Why don't you think I should buy her?"

Aunt Letty put a hand to her breast. "I—I have a feeling about this horse. I can't explain it sensibly. I just know that she's wrong for you."

Letty, undoubtedly, would have premonitions about any horse that might be brought to Thunder Heights, but Camilla was unwilling to listen.

"I'll look at her, and perhaps try her out. If she suits me, I'll buy her, Aunt Letty," she said.

She did not wait for further words from Letty, but went quickly to join Booth and walked with him toward the stable.

"So the Judd temper is up," he said softly. "That means trouble is brewing. There'll be a storm at Thunder Heights, or I miss my guess."

Camilla kept her face averted and walked on without answering him.

When they reached the stable, she saw Ross in the doorway, looking on idly, as Berton's stableboy walked the mare up and down the drive. She did not want him there, watching, but there was nothing to be done about it.

The mare was a dainty, flirtatious creature—a smooth bay in color, with one white sock. Her name was Firefly.

Booth looked her over carefully, approving her lines and good health, but he shook his head over the white sock. "White feet on a lady's horse are a bit fast, you know," he told her. "Though I suppose since it's only one foot—"

"I shan't be stopped by that," Camilla said tartly. Indeed, she would *like* to be thought fast. She would like to be thought anything but what Ross Granger seemed to see when he turned his gaze upon her. He believed her simple and foolish, and he had said as much.

She approached the mare and held out a lump of sugar on her palm. Firefly looked at her askance for a moment, and then thought better of her hesitation. She snuffled up the sugar with velvety lips and no unladylike snorting and blowing. Ross watched, and Camilla, for all that she was sharply aware of him, did not glance his way.

"I still think I can do better if you'll wait awhile," Booth said. "But if you're anxious, this horse will do well enough."

"I'll try her out," Camilla decided. Toby had come over to watch, and she sent him for the silver-mounted sidesaddle in the attic.

While they waited, she turned from the others and walked Firefly along the drive, gentling her and talking to her in a low voice. The little mare seemed to respond, and by the time saddle and bridle had been brought and she was ready, Camilla felt that they were becoming friends.

Her stiffening muscles rebelled a little as Booth helped her into the saddle, but she did not permit herself to wince. She rode the mare around the drive, trying out her paces and her response to the rein. She seemed an altogether feminine creature, confident of her own charms. For all her delicate, ladylike ways, she was not above taking a few skittish steps now and then, as if to assert her independence and attract attention. She would, Camilla felt, be perfect in every way—spirited enough, but obedient to the touch, and ready to be friendly.

When they rode back toward the stable, she found Ross waiting for her in the driveway. He put a hand upon Firefly's bridle and halted her.

"I wouldn't buy her," he said. There was no anger in his voice now, no emotion of any kind. He had simply put himself once more in the position of her adviser—and she would not have him there.

"I like her very much," she told him. "Why shouldn't I buy her?"

"I'm not exactly sure," Ross said. "There's something about the way she rolls her eyes—I don't think she's to be trusted."

At another time she might have listened to him. But Ross had hurt her too often. He had laughed at her offer to let him build his bridge, and had even grown angry at her words. All the hurt he had done her rose to oppose anything he might advise. But before she could speak, Booth came over and took the bridle from Ross's grasp. A certain excitement had come into his face.

"Miss King is capable of making up her own mind, Granger," Booth said. "I think it's time your interference around this place came to an end."

Ross relinquished the bridle at once, but he stood his ground without so much as glancing at Booth.

"Don't buy her, Camilla," he repeated.

The way he spoke her name was unsettling, but she did not mean to hear the plea in his voice.

"You sound as fearful as Aunt Letty," she told him lightly. "I really don't believe Firefly is as frightening as all that."

Booth laughed. "There you have it, Granger. And, after all, your advice hasn't been asked."

The antagonism between the two men was close to flaring into the open. But Ross turned his back on Booth and looked up at Camilla.

"I'm leaving for New York by the late afternoon boat. Is there anything you'd like me to do for you in the city?"

She shook her head mutely, and Ross turned his back on them and went into the stable.

"It's easy to judge the caliber of his courage," Booth said, his words carrying after Ross's retreating figure.

"I think there's nothing wrong with his courage," Camilla said, her tone unexpectedly sharp. "You had no business behaving in so outrageous a way."

She slid out of the saddle without Booth's help and spoke to the boy from the stable. "Will you ask Mr. Berton to come to see me, please. I will probably buy the mare. Leave her here for the time being—the stable is ready. And do you suppose you could find me a boy in the village to take care of her?"

His eyes still round with excitement over what had happened, the stableboy agreed to try, and set off for Westcliff. Camilla led Firefly into the stable herself, soothing her when she stepped uneasily among strange surroundings. Booth took off the saddle and put her into her stall. There was amusement in his eyes when he turned back to Camilla.

"So that's the way the wind blows?" he said oddly as they started back to the house.

Before Ross left for New York that afternoon, the purchase of the mare had been transacted. The price was surprisingly moderate, though Camilla had been prepared to pay more. A boy was hired, and the lower part of the coach house once more became a stable. This was a beginning, Camilla thought. Later, when Letty and Hortense were once more accustomed to a horse at Thunder Heights, perhaps she would buy a carriage, and carriage horses as well.

She did not see Ross again, except briefly, just as he was leaving. He passed her on the stairs after he had come in to bid Letty goodby. He was courteous enough, but distant, and she had a sudden impulse to plead with him not to go. If he stayed, she knew she would again be angry with him, and he with her, but she had a feeling that without him there would be no one here upon whom she could wholly depend.

But she could not put any of this into words. "Have a good trip," she told him, and held out her hand.

He took it briefly and thanked her. In a moment he would be gone.

"Will—will you be back in time for our lawn party at Thunder Heights?" she asked in an unexpected little rush of words.

"I hadn't thought about it," he admitted. "Nora is coming, isn't she?"

Camilla could only nod. If he came only because of Nora . . .

"I'm not sure I'll be there," he said, and she could not bring herself to urge him.

He went quickly down the stairs and out the front door.

The next morning, disregarding her stiffness, Camilla went for her first real ride on Firefly. The little mare was a delight, and Camilla took her up the mountain trail again, feeling it familiar now.

The air was calm today, and even up on the rocky top of Thunder Mountain, there was no wind to tear at her hat and veil. She drew rein on the wide treeless plain of the bald top, and sat quietly for a while, to give Firefly a breather and look out over the tremendous view. But somehow the place was filled with memories of Ross, and in a little while she turned back to the trail. This time she followed it on along the side of an incurving hill to see where it might lead. As long as she avoided the back trails that wound inland, she could easily keep from getting lost.

Today she had no sense of buoyancy as she rode, no feeling that she might shed the dark influences of Thunder Heights up here in the hills. All the worries and problems of the house seemed to ride with her. There were so many small things to add up disturbingly by now. There had been the matter of the tea, to which she had found no answer. There were the hints that something untoward had brought on her grandfather's heart attack. There was Letty's odd behavior about the riding crop, Hortense's open dislike of Althea's daughter, to say nothing of Booth's strange attitudes which Camilla did not understand at all. Each segment of the puzzle, however, remained just that—a segment. She could not glimpse the pattern which made up the whole, and of which all strangeness at Thunder Heights was surely a part.

The trail wound inward through a thick stand of pines, and then emerged beyond in the open. Now she could look across the intervening cove of blue water far below, with the railroad trestle cutting across it, to the hill on the opposite side. Surprised by what she saw, she reined Firefly in.

There, crowning the opposite hill—a less impressive prominence than Thunder Mountain—rose what looked strangely like the ruins of an ancient castle. There was the castle tower, crenelated at the top, with a stretch of broken wall falling away behind. The stones looked weathered and old, as if they had withstood wind and storm for hundreds of years. But this was the Hudson valley, and not a countryside given to age-old castles.

She wanted to ride on along the hill and examine the ruins at close hand, but the stiffness from yesterday's ride still troubled her and a glance at her watch, fastened to the breast of her habit by its fleur-de-lis pin, told her it was nearly time for the noon meal at Thunder Heights.

Firefly was willing enough to head for her new home, and they followed the mild incline that led back beneath the trees until a path forked suddenly ahead of them. Camilla could not resist the invitation to explore.

"We'll just follow it a little way," Camilla told the mare. "Just to see what direction it takes."

The new fork dipped toward a stream that she could hear not far away, and when the woods opened to a small clearance, Camilla reined Firefly in. The path went down an incline to the place where a small bridge hung above the stream, leading across to the other side.

But this, as Camilla recognized at once, was no ordinary woodland bridge. It was as beautiful a little suspension bridge as she had ever seen, and she knew at once that it was the model Ross had told her about. Though it was only a miniature compared to a bridge that would cross a river, the cables dipped from the posts that anchored them on either side into gleaming crescents spanning the stream, with other supports dropping in thin strands to hold the planked path of the bridge in immobility. Camilla rode the little mare across its length and back again, and the bridge did not sway or jolt beneath Firefly's dainty hoofs.

She knew she had glimpsed a bit of Ross's dream—a glimpse that was far more vivid to her than any number of diagrams on paper. It gave her, too, a clearer picture of the man. A picture that twisted at her heart. Ross had rejected her from the first, and she must not think of him.

She turned back toward Thunder Heights, knowing she must put this vision of his, this dream of his bridge, away from her, and forget it, as she must forget the man.

CHAPTER 18

A WEEK LATER Hortense went off on another trip. This time she went alone and not very far. She mentioned her intention casually —that she was going across the river to visit friends, and that she would stay overnight. No one objected, or even commented, and she left for the ferry from Westcliff early in the day.

Letty spent the morning in the downstairs larder, boiling freshly picked horehound plants to make the juice for horehound candy— useful for colds and coughs through the winter. While the horehound mixture simmered, she prepared marigold petals to be mixed with other herbs for seasoning. Leaves of mint, tansy, and thyme had been set out for drying, to find their way eventually into small bags to be used for scenting linens and blankets, and for keeping insects away. Camilla worked with her, helping where she could, learning under Letty's skillful instruction.

It seemed to her that Letty looked a little wan today, but that was perhaps due to the unusual heat of last week. This morning it was exceedingly hot and close for June, and when Letty had worked for a while she began to complain of a headache.

"Let's go outside," she said. "This is one of those days when I can't breathe within walls."

Camilla brought notepaper and pen and ink to the herb garden and sat on the grass in the shade of nearby woods. Using a bread-board for desk, she continued the writing of invitations to the lawn party. Letty rested listlessly for a little while, and then began to cut branches of yellow tansy to fill a pewter jar. Now and then she glanced anxiously at the sky as if she saw some portent there.

Once Camilla paused lazily in her writing to admire the herb garden spread at her feet. "June's a lovely month for herbs. I know what you mean about the garden beginning to look like a carnival. Individually the flowers aren't very impressive, but they're wonderful in a mass."

Thyme had spread its purple blossoms around the sundial, and coriander was dressed in white, shining against gray-green leaves of sage. Bees darted above the scarlet balm, while butterflies preferred the purple. Letty sat down to rest a moment on the marble bench near the sundial, rubbing a finger between her brows to lessen the pain.

"How is Booth's painting going?" she asked. "I haven't looked in on you lately."

"I'm not sure," Camilla said. "Sometimes he seems keyed up and eager to work and pleased with what he's doing. Then the next day he will be dissatisfied and do it all over. I think he'll never finish at this rate. Aunt Letty, why did Hortense go across the river today?"

Letty sighed. "I'm afraid she has gone to see another lawyer, dear. She doesn't give up very easily, you know. She's still looking for some way to break the will."

Camilla was silent, and Letty picked a sprig of mint where it encroached upon the bed of thyme, her thoughts drifting back to her garden.

"How greedy mint is! It would take the whole garden for itself if I let it." She crushed the leaves between her fingers, and the scent was pleasant on the warm air. "I think it's going to storm," she said abruptly.

Camilla looked up at the bright cloudless sky. "Why do you think that? There's not a thunderhead in sight."

"There's a feeling," Letty said. "It's so hot and still and breathless. Don't go riding today, dear."

Camilla laughed. "I hadn't meant to, but you almost tempt me. I'll have to prove to you one of these days how safe Firefly is."

"Ross didn't trust her either," Letty said.

Ross! Camilla thought. Ross was gone and she had firmly dismissed him from her mind. There had been no word from him since he left. That was a book that would be closed shortly, and she did not want to so much as ruffle the pages.

"Tell me, dear," Letty said. "What do you plan to do with yourself from now on?"

Camilla was silent for a moment. She knew only too well what Letty meant. What was she to do with herself for all the rest of her life? Where was she to find the fulfillment and joy that should be a part of living? When would she ever be loved as a woman hungered to be loved? But she could not say these things to Letty, and tried to answer her brightly.

"It seems to me I'm busy from morning to night. And with the lawn party ahead I have hardly time to catch up with all I want to do. What do you mean?"

Letty was not deceived. "Life," she said quietly, "is loving and marrying and having children. You haven't so much as touched the edge of life as yet. How can you manage it if you bury yourself here? Don't you think about these things?"

Did she not, indeed? And when she thought of them, she saw Ross's face all too clearly, and she did not want to see it at all. She shook her head impatiently and stood up.

"There's time for all that. If you don't mind, Aunt Letty, I'll go back inside. The heat is worse out here than it is in the house."

"What is it you're running away from?" Letty asked.

Camilla stared at her, not answering, and after a moment her aunt went on.

"Once I thought there was plenty of time. But when I look back the years are gone and my life with them."

"I'm sorry," Camilla said softly.

"Don't be," Letty told her. "I've known contentment and happiness a good deal of the time. Though it's of a different sort than I might have had. A lesser sort, perhaps." She rose from the bench and came close to Camilla. "Don't make the mistake I did, dear. The mistake of closing the door on life."

For all that she could be so vague and misty and tremulous at times, Letty saw the truth all too clearly when she chose to. But these were things Camilla did not want glimpsed in her own life, matters she could not discuss. She turned away and went quickly into the house.

As the day wore on, the air grew ever more still and stifling, with the sun burning fiercely through a haze that seemed to magnify the heat. Late that afternoon relief was promised in thunderheads that loomed across the Hudson, bringing gusty winds to tear at the house and set its old timbers creaking. Wind rattled the shutters, wailed down the chimneys of Thunder Heights, and heat fled before the damp onslaught of the wind. All through dinner the buffeting seemed to increase. Nevertheless, the storm held back its expected torrents and was for a time only wind and sound.

Except for the wind noises, dinner was a quiet meal. Letty ate little and spoke not at all. Booth seemed lost in moody silence. Camilla, deep in her own tormenting thoughts, made no bid for conversation. Thoughts stirred to uneasy life by Letty's words.

Letty's headache had grown in severity, and after dinner she excused herself and went up to bed, refusing Camilla's offer to get her something to ease the throbbing. Camilla watched her go anxiously, and Booth saw her concern.

"She often feels like this when it's about to storm," he said.

The weather had a different effect upon Camilla. She slipped away from Booth and went outside to the ledge above the river. There she stood for a long while in the open, where wind whipped her skirts and buffeted her with rough fingers. Out here, with this exhilaration of the elements all about her, she could lose something of her depression, her loneliness.

Below her the river churned into choppy gray waves, and on the heights above trees thrashed their branches and moaned in the wind. How far above, invisible in the gusty darkness, the stony head of the mountain seemed tonight. Had it been on such a night that Althea had ridden to the crest? Camilla wondered.

She could understand the invigoration her mother might have found in so wild a ride. The racing black clouds overhead, the cold thrust of the wind, even the stinging slap of the first rain against her face—all these were exciting, stimulating.

Cold needles of rain pricked through the thin stuff of her shirtwaist, and she turned reluctantly back to the house. From the lawn Thunder Heights looked dark and somber and cheerless. No one had lighted the swinging lamp above the stairs tonight—that was usually Hortense's charge, and Letty must have forgotten. Lamps had not yet been lit in the parlor, and the dark windows had an eerie look. Camilla remembered her first feeling about the house when she had seen it from the river—that it was a place enchanted and spellbound.

It drew her now, in spite of herself, and she moved toward it just as thunder clapped against the mountain and went echoing from hill to hill up the valley of the Hudson. She did not glimpse Booth in the shadows of the veranda until she reached the steps. His presence startled her. How long had he stood there, watching her?

"It's time you came in," he said. "Don't tempt the spirit of the mountain."

Thunder rumbled nearer now, and lightning flashed, illuminating black towers, striking brilliance from blank windows. Then darkness swept down again, all the more blinding in contrast. Camilla went up the steps, still feeling the strange lure of the house. As she reached the door, Grace came to light lamps in the parlor, and Booth followed her in, locking the French doors against the storm.

How hot and close it seemed inside, once the wind was shut out. Hot and close and alive with rattling sound.

"Perhaps Aunt Letty would like someone with her tonight," Camilla said. "Perhaps I'd better go upstairs."

"Wait," Booth said. "There's no need to go to Letty. I've given her one of her own witch brews and she'll sleep through it all and feel better in the morning. Stay with me awhile, Cousin. It's I who don't want to be left to my own company."

She had no desire to be alone either, in this creaking, whispering house. She sat down in a chair from Malaya, resting her hands upon its ornately carved teak arms. It was too warm for a fire to be lighted, but she missed the bright leaping of flames on a night like this. A fire always made this museum of a room seem more cheerful. Tonight it was a room of oppressive shadows, abounding in its own secrets.

Booth did not take the chair opposite her, but moved restlessly about, tinkling a brass temple bell from India, picking up an ivory elephant and setting it down again. She had the feeling that he wanted to talk to her, and she waited for him to begin. Something in her listened to the storm, tensing to the thunder and vivid flashes of lightning. The fury seemed to be lessening a little now —rolling away toward the Catskills. Rain still lashed against the windows and roofs, but the wild vitality was ebbing.

Booth continued his uneasy prowling, and she watched his finely chiseled head as it moved from lamplight into shadow, to emerge again, the face visible in all its dark intensity. Drawn as she had been more than once in the past, she began to wonder about him. It was as if his somber presence made a focus of its own, matching the storm in a strange concentration of energy.

"Why do you stay here, Booth?" she asked. "Why haven't you left this house and found yourself a better life out in the world? What is there for you here?"

Her words brought him about to face her. He leaned against the mantel, one arm stretched along its marble surface.

"How little you know me, Cousin! You don't even know that everything I've wanted in life is contained in this one household, and always has been. Contained, but held beyond my reach. For the moment, at least. But not forever. No, I think not forever."

His eyes were bright with a mirthless laughter that was troubling to see.

"What is it that you want of life?" she asked him.

He ran an appreciative hand along the graceful fluted edge of the marble. "To be a gentleman," he told her. His sardonic smile flashed for an instant and was gone as suddenly as the lightning. "To be a gentleman, to live like a gentleman, to enjoy myself as a gentleman. This has been my purpose for as long as I can remember. Does it astonish you?"

It did indeed.

"I suppose," Camilla said, "that I've never thought of the matter of being a gentleman—or a lady—as being an end in itself."

"That's because you never lived as a child hating your father's butcher shop, longing to get away from the look and smell of it. You didn't grow up watching ladies and gentlemen from a distance, having coppers tossed to you in an offhand manner, being treated as an underling."

He left the mantel and flung himself into a chair, watching her face now, as if he looked for something in it.

"What are you thinking?" he demanded. "What are you feeling about me?"

She sensed a surging need in him, something that reached out to her, almost in pleading.

"Why, surprise, mainly, I suppose," she said, trying to answer him honestly.

"You mean because I've succeeded so well that you'd never have guessed my miserable origin?"

She shook her head. "No—only surprise that anyone should feel as you do. I suppose that all my life I've known people in different walks of life, and if I liked them, their background made no difference to me. It must be easy enough to adopt a veneer of polish, if that's what you want. But how can that be an end in itself?"

"It can easily be an end," he said, "if it coincides with everything you wanted up to the time when you were ten years old. And if it is what you were taught from that time on."

"Aunt Letty told me you were adopted when you were ten," Camilla admitted. "Sometimes I've wondered about that. Aunt Hortense doesn't seem exactly—" she hesitated, not wanting to hurt him.

"Don't you know why she brought me here? Don't you know why she snatched me out of my humble beginnings and made a gentleman out of me?"

There was something hard in his tone and Camilla was silent.

He went on evenly, coldly. "She had lost the man she'd set her heart on—your father. She didn't intend to marry and have children. But she wanted to make sure that a good portion of Orrin Judd's fortune came her way. She thought that presenting him with an heir of sorts would safeguard the money she wanted in her own hands. My father was happy to be rid of me. My mother had died the year before and left the whole brood of us to him. Miss Judd had a look at me, talked to me, found that I was bright enough and eager to be part of a different world. I'd shown some talent for painting even then, and she thought me a likely boy to present to her father, who was all for humble beginnings. Unfortunately, old Orrin and I never cared for each other—though she wouldn't see that. Your Aunt Hortense has always believed only what she wanted to believe. She imagines that she has been a doting mother.

But all her doting developed after I was twenty and she found she liked a grown young man at her beck and call."

Camilla made a small gesture of distaste, of disbelief. Booth laughed.

"It's not a pretty story, is it? Can you imagine Hortense mothering a boy of ten? And of course she wouldn't take a small baby. She felt I was at least old enough to be of little trouble. I might have run away once or twice, if it hadn't been for Letty. It was Letty who mothered and loved me and brought me up. Of course when I was older I began to see very well which side my bread was buttered on. Sooner or later the old man would die. And whether he left me anything for myself or not, I would have Hortense eating out of my hand and whatever she had would be mine. I've never for a moment lost sight of that. Everything I want is here at Thunder Heights."

Camilla listened, her sympathy aroused, for all that she felt a little sickened. He had, she suspected, deliberately put everything in the worst possible light, driven by some strange need for self-inflicted punishment. The phrase "edge of danger" came to mind. In telling her these things, perhaps he moved a little closer to that edge of destruction that so fascinated him, tantalizing and tormenting himself with his own words.

"How sad and—pitiful," she said softly, more to herself than to him.

He smiled, and his dark face sprang into that strange beauty that she had surprised in it before.

"Scarcely pitiful, Cousin. Though you must admit that my plans and hopes went awry for a time when you appeared on the scene and we discovered that you were to inherit everything that might have come to my mother."

"I should think you would have left then," Camilla said. "I can understand why two women like Hortense and Letty might feel they couldn't leave a security they had depended on all their lives. But you—"

"Tell me, Cousin," he said, "have I been unkind to you? Have I made you feel that I resented and disliked you?"

"No. No, not at all. You've been far kinder to me than Hortense has been." Or than Ross Granger had, for that matter.

"Perhaps I stayed because of you," he said, and there was a gentleness, almost a tenderness, in his voice.

The storm had come rumbling back upon its own tracks, and Camilla saw the blinding glitter of lightning. The windows shivered in an almost instantaneous crash of thunder, and this time she winced.

"A close one," Booth said. "That was on the mountain above us, I think." He went to one of the long doors to peer out through the lashing branches of an elm tree. When he turned and looked at her across the room, his gaze was long and searching.

She was suddenly aware of how closed off they were in this room. She was aware, too, of a change in Booth, of a quickening in him as he watched her. Something in her own blood stirred in response to the urgency she sensed in him.

Because the knowledge left her shaken, she rose uncertainly and walked from the parlor into the antehall. Candles had been lighted in the outstretched marble hands, but the octagon stairway beyond lay in shadow without the usual illumination from above. Intermittently the tall window above the stairs flickered with lightning. All the dark secrets of Thunder Heights seemed to center in the heart of that weirdly lighted stairway, and she dreaded walking up it.

In the moment that she hesitated, Booth came through the door to find her there. Perhaps she had wanted to hesitate, knowing he would come.

This time he moved toward her with assurance and took her into his arms, kissed her full on the mouth. His lips were cool in the hot and stifling house, and the shock of their touch brought her to herself. She thrust him away, in spite of the response that throbbed in her own blood. Thrust him back instinctively, lest his darkness engulf them both.

For an instant he seemed taken by surprise, as if he had not expected her to resist. Then he drew her roughly against him and kissed her again.

"Never fight me, Cousin," he said as she tried to turn her head away. "Always remember that—never fight me!"

There was a warning in his voice that made her cease her struggling. She went limp in his arms, resting there inert, until he put her quietly away from him.

"Haven't you known the attraction you've had for me from the first, Camilla? There's no cousin relationship between us—that's a pretty fantasy. Don't you know that you are why I've stayed in this house? That I've stayed because I wanted you and mean to have you?"

She found herself moving backwards from him, toward the stairs and possible flight. She no longer feared the darkness. She feared Booth Hendricks more. Or was it herself she feared—the response he had aroused against her will?

"You were drawn to me in the beginning," he persisted. "It was clear enough. What turned you away? I suppose you'll tell me it was Granger?"

"No," she whispered. "Ross Granger is nothing to me."

He laughed with a queer exultance. "Do you think I haven't seen the way you look at him? Not that I mind. There's all the more satisfaction when a formidable opponent is beaten. I don't underestimate Granger, believe me. But I think you both under-estimate me."

She had reached the stairs, and she turned and fled up them through the flashing light, with the thunder drowning out any sound of pursuit. She did not look back until she reached the door of her room and flung it open. In a flash of lightning the hall behind her stretched empty and livid. Below, in the heart of the house, she heard a ringing shout of laughter. Booth was amused by her flight, by her fear of her own emotions, but he had not followed her upstairs.

She closed the door and locked it, stood trembling against it in the warm safety of her room. But before she had found matches to light a candle on the stand near the door, she stood alone in the darkness, welcoming the soft gloom that hid her.

Never before had she felt such shame and fear. Not alone because of Booth, but for herself. She knew now that her own loneliness must be watched. It was true that she had always found Booth attractive. But was she, who had been so rudely rejected by Ross Granger, now responding to Booth out of her own need, and because he needed her? Was her fear of becoming like Letty, dry and brittle as herb leaves on a shelf, to drive her to desperate action?

Her hands shook as she lighted the candle. Was it even possible that Booth was what she wanted, after all? Certainly they shared a good deal—a lonely background and the insecurity of the past. What was it then that held her back from him? What was it she distrusted? Booth Hendricks could be artist or devil. She did not know which.

Now she was afraid in this house as she had never been afraid before. She was seized by forebodings that she could not put aside. Booth would not easily be stopped in his purpose. And his purpose was to have her. Only then would he achieve all he wanted of Thunder Heights. Had she the strength to stand against him? Would she always want to?

CHAPTER 19

IN THE MORNING she dreaded the moment when she must come face to face with him again. When she went downstairs to the dining room, Booth was there, as if he waited for her. He stood near the bay window overlooking Letty's herb garden, but he stood with his back to it, as if he were studying the room.

"Good morning, Camilla," he said cheerfully as she paused at the sight of him, trying to hide her dismay. He hurried to draw out her chair, a faint mockery beneath his good manners, as if he knew very well how she felt about seeing him.

"I've been admiring this room," he said. "You've done wonders with it. I can remember how many depressing meals I've eaten in the old room under Orrin Judd's eyes, with dark wallpaper and draperies adding to my depression. You've been good for this house."

She had nothing to say to him. She stared at her plate, avoiding his eye as Grace brought coffee and oatmeal. He was smiling as he took his place beside her.

"Did you sleep well?" he asked.

She nodded and began to eat in silence. How could she pretend, as he seemed to be pretending, that everything was as it had been before he had kissed her last night?

Plainly amused, he passed her cream and sugar, set the honey bowl by her plate. Then he picked up a knife and made a mark on the tablecloth with the rounded end of it.

"Attend, my dear. I have a problem for you to consider. A theoretical problem. Do you see this line I've drawn? Let's say it represents the life span of a man. The salt cellar here is his birth, the napkin ring his death. Do you follow me?"

"No," she said. "I don't know what you're talking about."

"I haven't explained myself yet," he told her. "The point is this—at certain places in the life line there are forks in the road, choices a man may take. Or a woman. One road may be a pleasant one, with opportunity and safety and very little excitement. The other choice may spell danger, disaster, perhaps. You see the dilemma? The choice of roads a man makes depends, I suppose, on what he is. While I'm not sure there is any conscious choice involved in the matter, I'd like to think there is."

Camilla broke a piece of toast and buttered it, added a dab of honey, avoiding the waxy bits of comb embedded in the amber. She said nothing at all.

He watched her, smiling. "Last night I'd have sworn the honey could melt any wax. What is it, my dear? Do I fail to interest you this morning?"

"I don't know the rules of the game you're playing," Camilla answered.

"I was merely seeking your advice in a serious matter. Which road shall I choose, Camilla? Which way shall I follow?"

"What choice have you decided to make?" she countered.

"I'm not sure that I've decided. In this case both ways tempt me. A man may have his work, even at Thunder Heights. But I am a man who needs more than sufferance, Camilla, and a paid income."

She had no answer for him. When Letty came through the door, she looked up in relief.

"Good morning, children. How well I slept last night!" Letty said. "I didn't waken once. It seems strange that the thunder didn't disturb me, as it usually does."

"Booth gave you a sleeping draught, Aunt Letty," Camilla said.

Letty took the chair Booth pulled out for her, and the look she turned upon him was suddenly intent. He spoke before she could question him.

"Camilla is right, dear. I didn't want you to suffer a headache all night long. I know what a Spartan you can be, and I thought I could spare you that for once. Besides, I wanted to be alone and unchaperoned for once with Cousin Camilla."

A flush came into Camilla's cheeks, and Letty glanced at her and then away. "I see," she said. She turned her attention to breakfast and asked no more questions.

Booth picked up a spoon and crisscrossed the lines he had made on the tablecloth, raising a dark eyebrow quizzically at Camilla as he did so.

"I think I'll do no painting today," he said. "I have a feeling my model is not in the mood."

"But you've only a little more to do on the picture," Letty said. "I'll be glad when it's finished."

"You've never liked that picture, have you?" Booth asked, but Letty did not answer.

They were still at breakfast when Hortense returned from her journey across the river. Booth went to the door to help her with her bag. Camilla heard them talking in the distance, but Booth did not return.

"What happened last night?" Letty asked when they were alone in the dining room.

"Nothing," Camilla said, not meeting her eyes. She wanted no one to know what had happened. "The storm seemed to key him up. I went to bed early."

"Good," Letty approved. "Sometimes I think Booth's high moods are almost as difficult as his low ones. It's best to leave him alone until he gets over them."

When Hortense came in to join them for breakfast, it was clear that this second trip had brought her no more success than had her journey to New York. Her manner was disgruntled, and she seemed unwilling to speak to anyone. Camilla was glad enough to excuse herself from the table and leave her two aunts alone.

Preparations for the lawn party were moving ahead by now, and answers to the invitations were beginning to come in. The affair was to be next week, and there was still a great deal to be done. A big box of Japanese lanterns had been sent up from New York. Caterers had been hired for that day to assist Matilda in the kitchen and help serve refreshments on the lawn. Camilla threw herself into the work of preparation and planning and put away from her the disturbing thoughts that wanted to crowd in. These things she would think about later. Not now.

Some of the little tables that would be used on the lawn needed painting. This was something she could assist with herself. Late that morning she went downstairs to the cellar to find brushes and paint in the room that had once been Grandfather Orrin's workshop.

As she came down the steep flight of cellar stairs, she saw Booth ahead of her and paused, not wanting to meet him alone. But he had not heard her and he moved with purpose toward the larder. When she saw him go into the room where Letty kept her herbs and cooking materials, Camilla darted toward the door of the tool room next door and stepped inside. She would get her things quietly and slip out before Booth emerged. She was curious, however, and wondered what he was doing down here.

As she groped for the things she wanted in the dim room, she heard him utter an angry exclamation: "So! I thought you might be down here."

For an instant she thought in dismay that he had discovered her. Then he went on in the same angry tone.

"You're up to your old tricks, aren't you?"

There was a smothered cry from someone in the larder, and Camilla heard the crash of glass, as if a jar had been dashed to the floor.

"I've warned you not to try that again," Booth cried. "Do you want to find yourself in prison?"

The murmured reply was lost to Camilla's ears, though she pressed close to the wall, trying to hear.

"Tansy!" Booth said and the word lashed like the snap of a whip. "Enough of it can kill, as you very well know. Are you such a fool that you think they wouldn't uncover so clumsy a trick? Clear up that mess and don't try it again."

Once more there came a soft mumbling reply in a voice Camilla could not distinguish. She shrank into the dark space behind the tool room door as she heard Booth stride toward the stairs and spring up them as lithely as the tomcat he often reminded her of. The cellar door closed sharply above, and a soft brushing sound began in the next room.

Camilla slipped out of the workshop and fled upstairs and outside, escaping to the serenity of the herb garden. Here there was brightness and warm, perfumed air. Bees hummed around the balm, and all was quiet and peaceful. Yet not altogether so. For the very herbs in this garden had powers she could not know and did not trust.

She shivered in the warm air. What was she to do? How was she to live with the undercurrent of dark purpose that existed in this house? Hortense or Letty—which one? Oh, not Letty, surely not Letty! Booth would never have spoken so roughly to the woman who had given him love and trust over the years. Or would he, if he were angered? How little she really knew of Booth. And what of his own frightening purpose?

Here in the bright sunlight she tried to tell herself that it was a purpose she need only ridicule to destroy. He could scarcely marry her against her will. Yet she had felt the intensity of single-minded purpose behind him. "Don't fight me," he had said, and there was something in the words that terrified her, even in retrospect. All the more so because a portion of her fear was of herself.

In the days that followed she began to dread the event of the lawn party. How was she to carry it off with the gaiety she had intended? How was she to pretend a pride in Thunder Heights and a desire to throw it open once more to the world, when all the while she knew the very core of it to be sick with evil?

Strangely enough, there was a change in Hortense, and this too made Camilla uneasy. Was it a result, perhaps, of Booth's warning to her in the cellar that day? Or would he have spoken so to the woman who held his fortunes in her hand? At any rate, Hortense became almost cheerful about the coming party and actually began to take part in the preparations. She displayed an interest in the identity of the guests who had accepted and went through the answers Camilla had received, exclaiming about this one and that. She would look forward to seeing old friends, she said, and was pleased that some of those from the best old families had accepted. Only one name caused her displeasure. When she came upon the note Nora Redfern's mother had written, she brought it indignantly to Camilla, who was once more painting lawn furniture.

"Do you mean that Mrs. Landry has actually accepted your invitation?" she demanded, waving the bit of notepaper under Camilla's nose.

Camilla had spread newspapers on the big veranda overlooking the river, and was kneeling there before an upended chair, a pot of green paint beside her.

"Why shouldn't she accept?" Camilla asked, brushing long green strokes down the leg of the iron chair. "Mrs. Redfern is coming, and she says her mother and mine were the best of friends when they were young. They seem to have no wish to keep up an old feud."

"Humph!" Hortense's snort made her red pompadour tremble. "And did she tell you that Laura Landry was horribly rude to us after Althea's death and came near making a public scandal?"

"A scandal about what?" Camilla asked, concentrating on her work.

"Laura took your father's side," Hortense said. "And of course all John King wanted was to make trouble—as we very well knew. He felt he had been slighted by his wife's family, and he wanted his little revenge."

"That doesn't sound like my father." Camilla set her brush down and gave her aunt her full attention. "Just what are you talking about?"

"I've no intention of dredging up something that had no basis in fact in the first place," Hortense said, showing signs of hasty retreat. "But you can take my word for it, Camilla, that Mrs. Landry was extremely rude to Papa and that he told her she need never set foot in his house again. The same went for your father."

Hortense had begun to stride up and down the veranda in her agitation, and Camilla watched her soberly. Once this woman had been in love with John King. How had it been for him—for them all—when he had come back to Thunder Heights for Althea's funeral? What reception had he received?

She asked her question suddenly. "Were you still in love with him, Aunt Hortense? I mean when he came back that last time?"

Hortense whirled about, and the long silver chains she wore about her neck swung and glittered. "In love with him! I have despised your father for more years than I can remember. He led me on when I first knew him, and I would have married him if

207

it hadn't been for Althea and her sneaking ways. It's a good thing I didn't so demean myself, since his true character was revealed when he ran away with her." With that she flounced into the house before Camilla could answer her.

Camilla hurried now with her painting, and as soon as she could pause she went in search of Letty. She found her in the upstairs sitting room, working on a pile of soft lavender material she was making into one of her drifty dresses for the lawn party. Camilla asked point-blank about what trouble there had been between Grandfather Orrin and Nora Redfern's mother. How had it involved John King?

Letty glanced vaguely up from her sewing, and Camilla could almost see her pulling her mists about her, to shut out what she did not wish to consider.

"That was all so long ago," she began, using her favorite retreat.

Camilla persisted. "Aunt Hortense says that Grandfather told Mrs. Landry never to set foot in this house again. And now Hortense is upset because I've invited her to the party."

"Perhaps she won't come," Letty said.

"She has already accepted. Aunt Letty, surely you know what happened between her and my grandfather."

Letty's needle never paused as it moved in and out of her work. "Laura had some foolish idea about what happened to Althea. I don't recall exactly what it was."

Camilla reached out to cover the lavender material with her hands, so that the sewing must stop.

"Are you against me too, Aunt Letty?" she asked.

Letty's lips were trembling. "Please," she said, drawing the goods out of Camilla's hands. "I must hurry if I'm to have this dress ready in time. If you like, dear, I'll play the harp for your guests at the party. Would that please you? I could play all the old Scottish airs Papa used to love. I think they might enjoy my music."

It was no use, Camilla knew. She rose without further pleading and went to the door. At once Letty dropped her work and came after her.

"Don't be angry with me, dear. I've begun to wish there was to be no party. I wish Mrs. Landry weren't coming. I—I'm afraid of what may happen. Please be careful, Camilla. Be very, very careful."

CHAPTER 20

DELIBERATELY and with an effort of will, Camilla focused her attention on her coming duties as hostess. The lawn party must be a success for Thunder Heights, no matter what lay beneath the surface.

The additional servants came in the day before the party to help with preparations. Hortense was in her element, giving orders right and left, while Letty quietly countermanded those that were too absurd.

Before the servants arrived, Letty had locked the door to the cellar.

"If any of you need anything, come to me for the key," she told the rest of the family. "I'd rather not have strangers moving around downstairs."

It was clear that she was thinking of her precious herbs. Hortense remarked that she was being ridiculously cautious, but no one really objected and the key remained in Letty's pocket.

The day of the lawn party presented clear and sunny skies—a perfect day. The guests would not begin to arrive until four, and at three thirty Camilla and Letty, dressed and ready, sat down on the veranda to rest.

The little tables and chairs set about on the lawn were fresh in their leaf green paint, and Japanese lanterns had been strung the length of the veranda, and from tree to tree on the lawn. At dusk Thunder Heights would be a beautiful sight. Letty's harp waited at one end of the veranda, with a stool drawn up to it, so that she could sit there and play for the guests when the time came.

And there were fiddlers coming from the village later on to play the old dance tunes, and even a modern waltz or two.

"After all," Camilla said, "this is a country party. We aren't trying to imitate New York."

She wore a new summer frock of frilly muslin with sleeves that pushed up in soft puffs. Letty's lavender dress was soft and drifty, and the scent of lavender floated about her when she moved.

Booth had absented himself from the house for most of the day, admitting that he detested domestic preparations. He would rather appear with the guests and enjoy himself without responsibility. In these last days Camilla had found his eyes upon her whenever she looked up. He said little, as though he could afford to bide his time, and even though his persistent attention made her uncomfortable, there was a perversity in her that almost welcomed it. If Ross had no eyes for her, at least someone else did.

Only one thing had disturbed this day of the party. Mignonette had disappeared, and no amount of calling brought her to view. For a while Letty did not seem especially perturbed. "She'll turn up eventually," she said. "She's much too clever to let anything happen to her."

Only now, as they sat rocking on the veranda, did she begin to fret a little.

"It's not like Mignonette to stay away so long. She's very fond of me, you know."

"Do you think you might have shut her in the cellar when you locked it yesterday?" Camilla asked.

"No, because she was around early this morning. And I haven't been down there since I locked the door."

A voice sounded within the house, and Letty stopped rocking. "Hortense wants you, dear. I do hope she hasn't overdressed for this afternoon. She wouldn't tell me what she meant to wear."

Camilla went inside, to find Hortense at the foot of the stairs striving ineffectively to set spikes of larkspur into a brass bowl. Her gown, as Letty had feared, was on the elaborate side. It was her favorite emerald green color—a somewhat threadbare satin, with an old-fashioned bustle. The skirt was looped up at the side to show a panel of yellow, embroidered in black. Her pompadour was anchored soundly with the little combs studded in green jade.

Somehow her elegance of a day long past seemed a little pathetic, and Camilla found herself moved by a pity she did not show.

"Oh, there you are!" she said as Camilla reached her side. "No one has fixed any flowers for the post stand here at the foot of the stairs. I thought this brass bowl would do, but it's not deep enough. Do run down cellar and get me a china vase that will be deep enough. Here—take this brass atrocity with you."

The brass bowl was large and heavy and Camilla took it in both hands. Letty gave her the key, and she hurried through the busy workers in the kitchen and down to the landing door and pushed it open. As she stepped down upon the first step something dark leaped wildly past her up the stairs and out the door. Alarmed, Camilla jumped and dropped the bowl. The leaping creature was only the lost Mignonette, but the harm had been done. The bowl bounced out of her hands and down the stairs with a frightful clatter, and Camilla stood looking after it in dismay.

As her eyes grew accustomed to the dim light, she saw that the bowl had done an extraordinary amount of damage in its heavy progress down the steep stairs. The third step, just below where she stood, had splintered and collapsed completely. If she had stepped upon it without looking, she would have been pitched helplessly to the concrete floor, a good twelve steps below. The stairs had no rail, and nothing could have saved her from a dangerous fall.

There was so much noise in the kitchen above that no one had heard the clatter of the bowl, or come to investigate. Camilla stepped carefully over the broken step and made her way to the foot of the stairs. One or two of the other steps had been faintly dented by the bowl as it bounded down, but only the third step, on which she must have dropped it, had been completely shattered.

What had happened puzzled her. The bowl was not so heavy as to cause such serious damage unless the step had already been rotten and ready to collapse. That seemed unlikely. Someone would surely have noticed it. The stairs were of the open kind, and she walked underneath, where she could look up at the shattered step. The board had broken in the middle. One side had fallen through and lay at her feet. The other side still hung in splinters from the steps above.

She picked up the broken tread and studied it. The wood did not look rotten. The splinters of the break looked clean and far from powdery. The step had not rotted through. It was possible that it had been deliberately broken from above, then pushed back in place, to trap the first unwary person to set foot upon it. If Mignonette had not been imprisoned in the cellar and come leaping out to startle her, if Camilla had not dropped the bowl upon the step, triggering what certainly looked like a trap—she would have been flung all that steep flight to the cement below, with nothing to stop her fall.

Her knees had begun to tremble in reaction, and she found a chair and sat down. Anyone who had put weight on that third step might have been seriously hurt. But a deliberate trap would not be set for just anyone. She knew that step had been prepared for one person alone—Camilla King. Yet how could that be? How could anyone know that she would surely be the one to step on it? Carefully, bit by bit, she thought back over what had happened.

Yesterday Letty had locked the door. Yet she herself might have run up and down these stairs a dozen times since if she'd chosen to. Unless it had been prepared at a time when it was unlikely that she would be coming down them again. But how could anyone know that Camilla King would come down them at exactly the right moment?

The pattern grew clearer by the moment. Hortense had sent her down deliberately on an errand. She had waited for the prescribed moment and conceived an errand that would send just one person down these stairs—to disaster.

"Camilla! Camilla, are you there?" That was Hortense now on the landing before the cellar door.

She had only to be silent, Camilla thought, and see what happened. If Hortense came down cautiously, stepping over the broken stair, she would know the answer. She could see her green skirts up there now, see her foot coming down to the top step. Camilla jumped up and called to her aunt.

"Be careful, Aunt Hortense! There's a broken step. Watch out or you'll fall." She had not possessed the steel nerves to try the experiment, lest she risk Hortense's life.

Hortense gasped and drew back her foot. Camilla picked up the brass bowl and went to the bottom of the stairs.

"This bowl saved me from a bad fall. This and Mignonette. Someone must have shut the cat down here by mistake and when she leaped out she frightened me so that I dropped the bowl and it broke the step. Odd, isn't it, Aunt Hortense, that a step should break so easily?"

Hortense said nothing. She was staring at Camilla in horrified silence, and Camilla could not read the cause of her horror. Was it because of her own narrow escape—or because Camilla had discovered the trap?

"Wait there," she said. "I'll get you the other vase."

She went to the shelf where extra vases were kept and picked one out with strange care. It was as though it were easier to concentrate on the matter of the right vase for a spray of larkspur, than to think about how nearly she had met injury, or even death.

By the time she returned to the stairs, her knees were steadier, but she knew her cheeks were flushed, her eyes bright.

"Here you are," she said, climbing the stairs and stepping carefully over the dangerous place. She put the vase into Hortense's limp hands. "I must lock the door so no one will make a mistake and come down these stairs until they're mended. I was lucky, Aunt Hortense. This is the second time Mignonette has practically saved my life."

Seen in the light of the landing, Hortense's face looked as though it had caught something of the reflected color of her dress.

At that moment the knocker rattled on the front door, and Camilla spoke quietly to her aunt.

"The first guests are arriving. Hurry and fix your larkspur. And don't worry about the step now, Aunt Hortense. We have a party to get through."

But as she followed Hortense through the kitchen and back to the foot of the stairs, her mind was busy with the three corners of a triangle. It could have been Letty, who had the key to the cellar. But access through a window would have been equally possible, and Mignonette could have come in unnoticed by a window. In that case it might have been Hortense. Or the entire plan, including instructions to Hortense and the fixing of the step, could have been managed very easily by Booth.

She could not find the answer now, for there was Nora Redfern at the door, and with her a plump, rather dowdy woman with an air of confidence and authority, whom Nora introduced as her mother, Mrs. Landry.

Laura Landry's handclasp was strong and friendly. "I insisted upon coming early," she said, "so that I could have a bit of a visit with Althea's daughter before the others arrived."

When Grace had taken hats and wraps, Camilla led the way through the parlor and out upon the veranda, where Letty still sat rocking peacefully.

Camilla slipped the cellar key into her hand. "Be sure no one goes downstairs, Aunt Letty. There's a broken step that might injure anyone who didn't see it. It's only thanks to Mignonette that I escaped. She was in the cellar after all."

Momentary alarm flashed in Letty's eyes, and then she was rising to greet Nora Redfern and Mrs. Landry. The key had been hidden, and there was no telling what she thought about the broken stair. If there had been a long-existing animosity between Thunder Heights and Blue Beeches, it was not evident in Letty's gracious reception of the two women.

Camilla turned toward the veranda steps and saw Booth at the foot of them watching her. "Congratulate me!" she said to him brightly. "I came very near killing myself on the cellar stairs a few moments ago. It was only by luck that I saw the damaged step and saved myself."

Did something flicker in his eyes? She couldn't be sure. He had taken her hand to draw her down to the lawn, and his manner seemed truly solicitous.

"You must be careful, Camilla. I'll have a look at the bad step later on."

Then he too was greeting Mrs. Landry and Nora in his usual suave manner, and if he had ever plotted disaster to Camilla King, there was no reading it in his face or bearing.

She walked across the lawn with Nora and Mrs. Landry for a view of the river, and there was no further opportunity for her to be anything but a hostess. Mrs. Landry was more interested in her than in the river, however.

"You're as pretty as your mother was," she said. "Perhaps prettier. But there's a difference. Your mother had a daredevil streak that could get her into trouble. You look a bit more sensible."

Was she sensible? Could she be, with this trembling at the pit of her stomach that never quite ceased, that urged her toward a blind terror that she must hold off at all costs?

"I'm not sure that's a compliment," she told Nora's mother, and miraculously the trembling did not show in her voice. "I'm so glad you've come, Mrs. Landry. I know you and my mother were good friends, and there's so much I want to learn about her."

But now other guests began to arrive, and there was no opportunity for more talk. Soon there were little clumps of ladies and gentlemen all about the lawn. Hortense and Letty and Booth moved among them, greeting old friends, meeting younger members of river families, whom they had not met before, and all three seemed at ease, slipping easily back into old ways.

Once Hortense stopped beside Camilla, glowering a little. "You know why these people have come, don't you? The old ones are here out of curiosity. To see what we've done with ourselves. The young ones are here to have a look at you and decide whether you'll make a good match for one of their own crowd."

Camilla laughed with a touch of bitterness. There was a time when this party would have seemed like wonderful fun to her and she would have taken part in it wholeheartedly. But that was before the shadow of Thunder Heights had crept across her spirit.

As always, the sun vanished abruptly behind the overhanging hill, though the colors that streaked the sky seemed brighter than ever because of the black silhouette of the mountain. The house stood aglow with lamps, and now servants were lighting the candles in the Japanese lanterns, so that lawn and veranda were soon rimmed in jewels of blue and green, red and yellow. Down toward the river, against the blackness of the bushes, fireflies lit small darting lanterns of their own in the warm night.

On the veranda the fiddlers from the village struck up a tune, and the young people ran up the steps to enjoy a reel. Camilla found herself handed breathlessly from partner to partner. Once she saw the lighted shape of a boat passing their promontory on the Hudson, and knew that the passengers must be watching, perhaps with envy, the festivities at Thunder Heights. Sometime, long ago, she had wanted that very thing. Now it seemed an empty illusion.

When the musicians changed to a waltz, someone touched Camilla's arm and she turned to look into Ross Granger's face. In the happy shock of seeing him, all doubts fell away. The rush of joy that went through her was rooted deeply in pain, but for the moment the joy was uppermost. She no longer questioned her own heart. This was her love and would always be, whether he cared for her or not. In him lay all safety and strength—a haven from peril. The very shape of his chin, the carriage of his head gave her confidence to face whatever she must face. She went into his arms and made no effort to hide the joy in her eyes.

"I'm sorry I'm late," he said. "I hope I'm still welcome. You invited me, you know."

"Oh, you are, you are!" she cried, and joy was there in her voice as well, with only a small stab of pain in her heart.

He held her gently as they danced, and she felt a kindness in him that had been lacking when he went away. Perhaps he had missed her just a little too.

"Did you find what you wanted in New York?" she asked, and held her breath against the answer. "Are you going away soon?"

"I'm not sure," he said. "There are some things I must finish here first."

"Work for my grandfather?"

"Work for you. How have things gone while I was away?"

"Badly," she whispered. "Terribly! I want to see you. I must see you!"

"That shouldn't be difficult. I'm here."

"You don't understand. I must see you away from the house. Where no one will watch me, or hear us."

"Wherever you say."

She thought frantically. "Tomorrow morning at the cemetery, then. Can you meet me there at ten?"

"Of course," he said.

The waltz had come to an end, and she went reluctantly out of his arms, feeling that she gave up all safety until she could be in them again. Now the throbbing of pain and loss came uppermost and joy subsided.

Refreshments were served at the little tables on the lawn, and Camilla, moving here and there as hostess, was drawn at length to Mrs. Landry's table, to sit down with her and Nora. Up on the veranda Letty had taken her place at the harp and begun to play the old tunes of Scotland. There was a good deal of Scottish blood in the Highlands of the Hudson, and she was listened to with delight, and sometimes with tears, on the part of older members of the group.

Laura Landry was neither Scottish nor sentimental, and she liked better to talk than to listen.

"Nora tells me you're a good rider," she said. "And that you've bought a horse of your own. I'm glad to hear it. We all rode in the old days. Althea especially."

"I know," Camilla said. "I found her gray riding habit in the attic, and I wear the whole costume—top hat, boots and all. I think sometimes the older people around the countryside think I'm her spirit come back to ride Thunder Mountain again. Mrs. Landry— were you at Blue Beeches when my mother was thrown and killed?"

The plump, assured face creased into lines of pain. "I was here when Orrin Judd brought her down from the mountain. Booth came looking for her at Blue Beeches, hoping she hadn't taken the mountain trail. So I came right over and waited here at Thunder Heights."

"I've heard there was some sort of scene after they brought her down," Camilla said.

"You mean I made a scene. You needn't be delicate about it. I did. Althea was too good a rider to be thrown, no matter what that horse did. I felt there was something wrong—more to the accident than met the eye. I wanted it looked into."

"I understand her horse was frightened by the thunderstorm," Camilla pointed out.

"That always seems one of the strange things about what happened," Nora put in. "That Althea went out on Folly in the first place."

"Not if you knew Althea as I did," Mrs. Landry said. "That part I can accept. It was the wild sort of thing she would do. But as you know perfectly well, unless she is taken by surprise, it's practically impossible to throw a good rider from a sidesaddle. After all, if your knee is over the horn and your right foot hooked behind your left calf, you're locked into the saddle and nothing is going to budge you. Althea would have secured her seat and fought her horse to a standstill. The horse didn't live who was too much for her. And I said as much to Orrin Judd. But it was the wrong time."

"What do you mean?" Camilla prodded.

"He was wild with grief, and he thought I was trying to make trouble of some sort—to blame him. He was blaming himself as it was for not having got rid of the horse long before. There wasn't anyone I could talk sensibly to, until your father got here. He saw what I meant, but by that time it was impossible to get through to Orrin. He took to his bed, except for the funeral, and they stood about him, holding everyone else away. The three of them—Hortense and Booth and Letty. I don't suppose Orrin would have believed us anyway."

"Believed what?" Camilla asked. She felt cold and her hands were clammy.

"Believed that what happened was not wholly an accident," Mrs. Landry said flatly. "Your father believed it, but there was nothing he could do. No evidence of any sort."

"But—but why? I mean why would anyone have wanted to harm my mother?"

"Your grandfather sent for her when he was ill, and once he saw her again he knew where his affections lay. He was at outs with the rest of the family by that time, and he felt Althea had been treated badly. So he was going to change his will. I gather that he meant to do the same sort of thing he did in the will which left everything to you. But he tossed it in their faces. He let them know what he intended ahead of time. So two days before Althea was to leave for home, the horse threw her. Only I don't believe it."

Camilla heard her out in sick dismay. It all sounded so horrible—and so possible. She could believe these things now, as she might not have believed them when she had first come to Thunder Heights. She could believe because she knew what it was like to be the hunted one.

"The thing I've never understood," Nora said, "was why old

Orrin waited so long before he sent for you, Camilla. If his feelings had changed toward Althea, why didn't he want to know her daughter?"

"John King took care of that," Mrs. Landry said. "I remember him as a gentle person, with great kindness and sensitivity. He won all our hearts in the old days. But when a gentle person is angered it can be a fearful thing to see. He swore Orrin Judd would never have his daughter, and that neither of them would ever set foot in Thunder Heights from that day on."

Camilla spoke softly. "And he kept his word as long as he lived. Now I understand why he would never talk about what happened to my mother. Now I can understand why his sickness over her death was more than ordinary grief."

Mrs. Landry reached across the little table to cover Camilla's hand with her own. "This is why I had to see you. You must never make the misstep your mother made."

Camilla nodded mutely.

She had forgotten her guests for a time, and she looked around dazedly. Letty had not chosen to join them for refreshments and was still at her harp. Hortense had taken over the duties of hostess in the grand manner and was moving about among the tables with an air of doing what she had been brought up to do. Ross had disappeared after his waltz with Camilla and was nowhere to be seen. Camilla's eyes moved uneasily from face to face, now searching for only one. She found it at length. Booth had withdrawn a little from the scene. She saw him on the far side of the lawn, leaning against an elm tree, the light from a lantern flickering across his dark face.

He was watching her. She met his eyes across the expanse of laughing, chattering people, and she could not look away. It was like the exchange of a lover's gaze, she thought queerly. He was waiting for her. Waiting for the time that he would hold her in his arms. She was aware of the cold sweat upon her palms, and she reminded herself quickly that Ross had returned. She was not alone any more. Tomorrow she would talk to him, tell him everything. He would know what to do.

CHAPTER 21

It was well into the evening when the last guests had left and the Japanese lanterns had been extinguished. Camilla went upstairs, only too ready to drop the role she had been playing and let down her guard. Now she could be afraid, if she wanted to be afraid. And she could think about what she must say to Ross Granger tomorrow morning. She must plan an ordered recital, so that he would believe her and not dismiss her words as nonsense.

When she reached her room, she found that the door she always left closed stood ajar. For an instant the feeling she had experienced in the cellar, staring down at a broken step that might have pitched her headlong, swept over her again. Fear was like nausea in her stomach, and she did not want to go in. She pushed the door wide and stepped just across the threshhold.

But it was only Letty, waiting there in her room. She sat in the little rocker before the cold hearth, still dressed in her frock of misty lavender, rocking gently back and forth, and twisting a bit of lavender in her fingers. Mignonette slept comfortably in the middle of the bed, none the worse for her imprisonment in the cellar.

Camilla closed the door and went quickly into the room. With the nausea subsiding, she could almost chatter in relief.

"Did you enjoy the party, Aunt Letty?"

Letty sniffed the lavender absently. "I want to talk to you, dear."

"That's fine," Camilla said. "I'd like to talk to you, too. Mrs. Landry told me something about—about my mother's death. I think you should know what she said."

"I do know." Letty closed her eyes and waved the lavender beneath her nose, as if to gain strength from its pungent odor. "That's why I must talk to you. I know what Laura Landry believed at the time. And in part she was right. But only in part. Sit down on the ottoman, dear. Come close so I needn't speak loudly."

Camilla drew up the big footstool and sat down, almost touching Letty's knees.

"Mrs. Landry doesn't know what happened that late afternoon when Althea went riding on the mountain. She doesn't know that it was I who sent her to her death."

Camilla waited in silence and without belief for her to continue.

"Perhaps you don't realize that the horse that nearly killed me several years before was the same horse that killed Althea."

Camilla heard her in surprise. "No, I didn't."

"She was a mare named Folly. As beautiful a little mare as I've ever seen—delicate and good-mannered and affectionate. She was my horse, Camilla, and I loved her dearly. Until I found out that dreadful day, I never knew that she had a wild streak in her that made her go crazy in a thunderstorm."

"She threw you then?" Camilla asked.

"No. I had dismounted to look at the view. There was a storm coming up, and the whole Hudson valley was a queer livid color, with thunderheads boiling up and lightning flashing in the distance. It was frightening and very beautiful. Hortense was riding with me that day, but she didn't get off her horse. She was impatient to get home. I stood on a rock to put myself into the saddle, and just as I set my foot in the stirrup there was a clap of thunder that might have startled any horse. But Folly was more than startled. She went mad. My foot was caught and she trampled on my arm trying to get free of me, dragging me until my foot came loose from the stirrup. Folly ran away, and Hortense managed to get me home."

Letty's voice was quiet, empty of all emotion, but her fingers twined together tightly as she went on.

"I was very ill for a long time afterwards. The doctor feared a brain injury, as well as the broken arm that never healed properly. Papa would have shot Folly, but in spite of the way I was hurt I loved her, and I pleaded for her all through my delirium. To soothe me, he promised that she could live and I could keep her as a pet, providing no one ever rode her. I know she never meant to harm me, and she remained my friend after I was well. But none of us rode her again. All this, of course, was after Althea had gone away and married."

"When my mother came here on that last visit, didn't she know that Folly wasn't supposed to be ridden?" Camilla asked.

Letty bowed her head. "She knew. Booth told her, when he tried to stop her that day."

"Booth?" Camilla repeated softly.

"He had been painting her, you know. But they didn't hit it off very well, and I think she never liked him. She posed for him, but she made fun of his painting. She was always gay and I think she only meant to tease, but she made him angry. She told him she was a better woman than the girl he was painting in the picture, because she would have had that rearing horse in hand and ridden him if she wanted to. Booth said the horse in the picture was my Folly and that she was a dangerous animal—a killer.

"I was there at the time, and I can remember the way Althea laughed and said she would ride her. And she would do it right then. I heard the whole quarrel between them. I tried to make her understand that a storm was coming up, and she said that was exactly the point she wanted to make. She was a good enough rider to handle a horse under any circumstances."

Letty paused, shaking her head sadly.

"She was always like that—even as a little girl. The moment anyone told her she couldn't do something, that was what she must do."

"Where was Grandfather while this was going on?" Camilla said.

"He had been ill—that's why he had sent for her—and he was in bed upstairs in his room at the time. Booth had been painting outside on the veranda to get the best light. Althea was wearing her habit for the picture, and she laughed in his face and ran down the steps and off toward the stable. I wanted to go to Papa then, but Booth said not to disturb him. I think Booth was really upset by Althea's outburst. Perhaps he thought Papa would blame him. He was so often in the wrong with his grandfather. He said he would go after her and stop her, keep her from riding."

"But he didn't, did he?" Camilla said.

Letty was silent for a moment, as though she were trying to

remember something. "He tried. I sat there on the veranda waiting, with the sky growing darker, knowing there would be an early dusk, due to the storm. I waited for Booth to bring her back to the house. But after a while he returned alone with a red slash across his face where she had struck him with her riding crop. They had quarreled out there in the stable."

"Couldn't you have sent someone after her?" Camilla asked.

"The only one who could have handled her in a mood like that was Papa. I should have gone to him then. But I knew he would be wild with Booth, and I was afraid he might even put him out of the house for good, if he knew about this trouble with Althea. So I sat there and did nothing. I can remember my thoughts at the time. Remember them so well. I was thinking that Althea was always the beautiful one, the gifted one, the lucky one. She had led a charmed life, and nothing could happen to her. So I sat there and let her go to her death. And all the while there was a voice speaking to me inside, telling me that this time something would happen. But I wouldn't listen."

Letty's calm had begun to dissolve, and she was weeping gently, a scrap of lavender-scented lace to her eyes.

"You mustn't blame yourself," Camilla said. "The fault was Booth's, not yours. Grandfather couldn't have stopped her either by that time, and he was ill."

"No, no!" Letty looked up at once. "It was not Booth's fault. Even though she had struck him, he was worried and upset about her. I can remember the way he strode up and down the veranda, watching the storm blow up, helpless and frustrated because he could do nothing."

"Do you think he might have been acting?" Camilla said. "Mrs. Landry thinks there was something—deliberate about what happened."

"Mrs. Landry is a gossip," Letty said, her tone unusually sharp. "A troublemaker. As I know very well, she tried to make a great deal of trouble afterwards."

"When did you go to Grandfather?"

"When Folly came home with an empty saddle. Booth heard her gallop into the drive, and he ran out to catch her and put her into her stall. Then he sent a groom out to search for Althea, and came running to the house to let me know what had happened and that he would go out searching himself. That was when I went to Papa. When it was too late. He got out of bed and had his own horse saddled. And he rode up the mountain where he thought she was sure to have gone. Booth was out looking for her too, but he chose the wrong route. He thought she might have taken the easier road along the river. He couldn't believe she would be so foolish as to go up the mountain on a crazy horse in the storm. But that is what she did. And it was on the mountain top Papa found her."

"Where was Hortense?" Camilla asked.

"She had a headache and went up to her room to lie down. She didn't know what had happened until they brought Althea home."

A silence settled upon the room. Letty wept softly, her handkerchief to her eyes, while Camilla sat lost in unhappy revery. A rising wind whispered in the chimney, and Letty looked up uneasily.

"Listen to the wind. It's beginning to blow again. I don't want to stay alone tonight, Camilla. I don't want to get up in the night and go walking about the house."

"You needn't," Camilla said quickly. "Stay here with me. The bed is plenty big enough for two, and I'd like someone to keep me company tonight."

Letty began to speak again in a rush of words, as though she wanted to hold nothing back. "I've suffered for so many years because I didn't act. I could surely have found a way to stop Althea if I had really tried. So I am the one who is guilty. I'm the one Mrs. Landry has a right to blame, if she blames anyone. But you see that I couldn't remain silent forever. A few months ago I tried to tell Papa exactly what had happened. I wanted to gain his forgiveness. But he was so badly upset by what I told him that it brought on his last attack. So I was responsible for his death too. And for his changing of his will—because after what I told him, he said he could never trust any of us again."

That all this unhappiness had existed behind Letty's quiet serenity was disturbing. Yet there was no real comfort Camilla could offer. Any reassurance would sound hollow and meaningless. True, Letty's self-blame was exaggerated out of all proportion to reality, but Camilla knew better than to try to dissuade her in her present distraught state. Later, perhaps, at a calmer time, they could talk about these things, reason them out sensibly.

"I'll go get my night clothes from my room and come right back." Letty rose and slipped out of the room, a slight, frail figure in pale lavender, moving in a faint aura of lavender scent.

Later that night, when the lamp was out and the room dark except for a bar of moonlight from the balcony, Camilla lay awake and quiet beside her aunt. Tree branches soughed in the wind all about the house, and she lay very still, waiting for Letty to fall asleep. But Letty's breathing remained ragged and uneven, and it was Camilla who slept first.

Once during the night she wakened uneasily and stretched out her hand to find Letty gone. But when she stirred and reached for a candle and matches, Letty spoke from the rocking chair by the hearth.

"I'm here, dear. Go to sleep. I'll keep watch. Don't worry about me. I have so much to think about."

And Camilla fell asleep again and did not waken until morning. When she sat up in bed, she found that Letty had taken her clothes and returned to her own room.

But she had other matters to think about now. Today she was to meet Ross at her grandfather's grave. In Ross she centered all hope of escape from the frightening dilemma in which she found herself. She had no actual evidence of any kind to offer him, but she thought he would listen with sympathy to her story. And perhaps he would tell her what to do.

When the time came she gathered an armful of flowers and set off on the road to the village. The day was once more hot and still. Distant clouds in the east seemed to hang motionless, and the morning steamed with humid, oppressive heat.

The cemetery drowsed on the hillside in the warm June sun. Slowly Camilla climbed the path that led to the burial plot of the Judds. She always felt a sense of peace and friendliness in this place. Here all storms had quieted, and those who slept held no rancor against the living.

A tall stand of yew trees shielded her from view of the road, and she sat on the grass beside Orrin Judd's grave and took off her big straw hat. Other than those who lay beneath the stones, no one awaited her. The old man who tended the graves nodded from a distance and went about his own work. All else was still and somnolent in the sun. When the flowers she had brought were arranged, Camilla tucked her white skirts about her, leaned her cheek against her propped-up knees, and closed her eyes.

She knew, however, the very moment when Ross reached the cemetery gate. Though she heard no more than his step, no more than the creaking of a hinge, her quickening senses told her it was Ross. She sat up eagerly and waited for him.

He climbed the path and she watched him come toward her, saw with love and pride the broad strength of his shoulders, the clean length of his stride. But it was his face she sought most eagerly, so that she might read in it his mood toward her. There seemed no antagonism in his look this morning, but only the gentleness she had sensed in him yesterday. Her heart began to thump raggedly, and she had to remind herself of the purposes which brought her here to talk to him.

"A pretty picture you make," he said, "there on the grass in your white dress."

He dropped down beside her, stretching out to his full length, leaning on one elbow. She could not bring herself to destroy the peace of the moment with the words she had to speak, and he did not ask her purpose in bringing him here. It was as if he, too, wanted to preserve this moment of companionship between them.

Idly he began to tell her about shad fishing at night on the Hudson, when the run had been on, and how he had gone out one evening with Toby and they had filled their nets with silver shad and brought the fish home to Thunder Heights and Blue Beeches. She listened with pleasure, wishing that she might go out on the river with him another year.

Then, when she felt lulled and quiet, he sat up so that he could look into her face. "You were afraid of something yesterday, Camilla—what was it? Why did you want to meet me here?"

She began to tell him then what had happened—all of it. About the tea that had made Mignonette sick. About the night when Booth had said he wanted to marry her and she had run away from him. About the words she had overheard in the cellar, and finally about the broken step.

He listened grimly and discounted none of what she told him. She saw the dark blood rise in his face as he listened, saw the anger in his eyes.

"There's only one thing to do," he told her when she came to an end. "You must get away from the house. Break your grandfather's will and do as you please. You have no real obligation to any of these people. They'd never given a thought to you. If you must, settle something upon them so your conscience will be free. But get away from Thunder Heights yourself and don't come back. It's the only way."

"If I went, I could keep nothing of the money or property. I would leave everything behind with the house. If I couldn't live up to Grandfather's wishes, then I would have no right to any of the inheritance he left me."

There was a light in Ross's eyes that she could not read. "Do you really care? Do you want it? You lived without it before—you can again."

"That's not the important thing," she said helplessly. She had hoped he might understand. Knowing that he did not, she felt defeated. She could not put into words her feeling about all this. How could she make him hear the echo of her grandfather's sorrowful voice? How could she convey her tenderness for Letty, whom she could not abandon? Or her conviction that she must somehow pick up life in her mother's place? The ties that held her to Thunder Heights were intangible and emotional. They could not be held up to the cold light of reason.

He saw refusal in her face and sighed. "I was afraid you'd feel this way. It's ridiculous, of course, but the choice is yours and I shan't try to dissuade you. But if you're to stay, you must safeguard yourself and you must do it at once."

"How?" she asked. "What do you mean?"

"You must make a will. Pompton's in New York now, but he'll be home tomorrow. See him then and tell him what you want."

"What good would a will do? If anything happened to me, everything would go to Hortense and Letty. In a will I could make no other arrangement."

He reached out and circled her wrist with his fingers. "Oh, yes you could. In fact, that's the whole idea. The will must leave everything you have to charity—with no more than a bare pittance for Letty and Hortense. And you must let them know the wording of the will as soon as it has been safely drawn up. Then you'll be safe. You'll be worth a good deal to them alive, and they're likely to guard you tenderly."

"They would hate me for it. At least Hortense would. And Booth. How could I go on living at Thunder Heights in an atmosphere like that?"

"How can you live there anyway?" He dropped her hand impatiently, and she could see that he was growing annoyed with her again. "There's no choice, apparently, that is acceptable to you. Don't you understand—this is the only safe move for you to make! That is, unless you do as I first suggested and give the whole thing up."

"I can't," she said. "I can't do that."

"Then think about the matter of the will," he told her. "But do something about it soon. They must realize you might take such a step, so they're unlikely to wait, once they're sure you're suspicious. These—accidents—may grow more deadly."

Camilla plucked a blossom of white clover, twirling it between her fingers. She felt painfully torn between conscience and duty.

"I'd better get back," Ross said. He got up and stood looking down at her.

She stood up beside him, not wanting him to go, but knowing no way to hold him here. The anger had died out of him and there was only pity in his eyes now—and something more. He stepped toward her as if he could not help himself, and she was in his arms where she had been once before, held close to his thudding heart, clinging to him and weeping.

"My dear," he said. His hand was on her hair, and he held her head against him for a moment before he bent and kissed her lips. There was only tenderness in his touch now, only a great sadness.

"Why must you go away?" she wailed. "How can I live if you go away?"

"You must know I can't stay any longer," he said gently, his lips against her hair. "I've given ten years to your grandfather, but they were years of preparation. Now I must get on with my work. I believe I'm ready for it now."

"Build your bridge here," she whispered. "Build it for Grandfather. Build it for me."

"And if I did?"

"Then you could stay nearby. For all the time you were building it you would be a part of my life."

"But after that I'd be gone," he said. "As you've just told me, you're tied to Thunder Heights, Camilla. You could never come with me to all the places where I'll go. It's better to end this now. It would hurt us all the more later. I didn't ask to love you. Indeed, I've fought against it."

She clung to him more tightly than ever. "No, no! We mustn't ever be apart again. Ross—I'll do as you say. I'll give up the inheritance and go wherever you wish. If only you want me with you—that's all I ask."

He kissed her again. "You know how much I want you. But in the end you'd never forgive yourself, or forgive me. I was angry when I asked you to throw away what you feel is your responsibility. It's not a sacrifice I could accept."

He put her out of his arms, as he had done once before, but this time his hands were gentle and there was pain in his eyes.

"Stay here in the cemetery a little while longer," he said. "Then we won't be seen together outside. It won't help you if the Judds think you've met me here secretly." He started away from her and then turned back for an instant. "Please be careful, Camilla," he said and hurried off toward the gate.

She stood stricken and helpless, watching him go. What was she to do? What was the answer for her? To know that he loved her and wanted her brought a mingling of pain and joy with the knowledge, but pain was uppermost, and she could not tell where to turn.

When she heard the gate creak and knew he was gone, she went to stand for a little while beside the grave of Althea Judd King. How young she had been to die. Yet she had known the fullest meaning of happiness. She had lived with her love and borne him a daughter whom they both had loved. And now that daughter stood beside the place where Althea lay and knew that something of herself must die too soon, as surely as the body which lay beneath the granite slab had died too soon. But in Camilla it must die without the taste of happiness or fulfillment.

Once more her thoughts turned to that stormy night on the mountain and all the dark puzzle of what had happened there. If she could find the full answer to these things, might she not find as well an answer to the problem of her love? Why she should feel this to be a possibility, she did not know, but the conviction was strong within her.

If Althea had been too good a rider to be thrown, how had Folly freed herself and come home with an empty saddle? And what had happened between Althea and Booth out there in the stable before she had ridden off in the storm? Why had she struck him with her riding crop? What was the basis of the angry quarrel that had flared between them?

She thought again of the crop as she reached the stone lions that marked the gateway to Thunder Heights. How could it possibly have fallen into those bushes? Could Grandfather have tossed it there despairingly after the accident? Yet Grandfather had taken loving care of Althea's riding things in the attic. And why had Aunt Letty taken the crop away, kept it out of sight, said nothing to the others about the finding of it?

None of these questions could be answered, and it was the present she must face, not the past.

CHAPTER 22

Luncheon that day was a solemn meal, with only Hortense and Letty to keep her company. Letty said Booth was working upstairs on his picture. Only a few touches to the background remained to complete it, and he wanted to work straight through, while the mood was upon him.

"I'll take him something when we finish," Letty said. "I'm glad he's working again. I'll be happy when this painting is finished."

There was something in her tone that made Camilla glance at her. "Why will you be happy?"

"It's as Booth says—I've never liked it," Letty said. "It's too painful a picture to be endured. I can't look at it without seeing Folly's rearing hoofs, striking at me. Just as they must have struck at Althea."

"Do you suppose she dismounted the way you did?" Camilla asked. "Do you suppose that is how she was thrown?"

Hortense said brusquely, "Do talk about something else. We can do without such a gloomy subject with our meal."

They finished the meal in silence.

Afterwards, when Letty had fixed a tray for Booth, she asked Camilla to come upstairs with her to his studio.

"He wants you to see the finished picture, dear," she said, when Camilla looked as though she might refuse. "I think he wants you to be pleased with it."

Camilla would have preferred never to look at that picture again. She felt as Letty did about it, but she had no reasonable excuse to offer. And she could not avoid Booth all the time. Not if she was to continue living in this house.

Up in the nursery, he had set his easel facing the long windows along the north wall. When they came in he had finished the last brush stroke and was standing back to study the picture with critical eyes.

"I've brought you something to eat, dear," Letty said, and set the tray on a table.

Booth hardly glanced at it. His look was on Camilla. "It's done," he said. "Come and tell me what you think."

Letty slipped a hand through Camilla's arm, and they approached the easel together.

With the background completed, the violence of the scene seemed to hurl itself at the beholder. Folly, rearing with wild hoofs, was a deadly sight. Her ears were laid back, her nostrils dilated, her lip curled above vicious teeth. But the girl who stood clinging to her bridle was almost laughing in exultance, as if she had thrown herself into the furious satisfaction of taming this rearing beast. Althea herself would surely have applauded such reckless courage.

Camilla, staring at the picture, could not be sure whether the face in the picture was her own or her mother's, but she knew that the wild emotion the artist had caught in the woman's storm-lighted face could well have been Althea's.

"I think I've never looked like that," she said to Booth.

"But I can imagine you like that, after seeing Althea angry," he said.

Letty had stepped closer to study the picture's details. The background of stormy sky had been completed, and the dark, stony ground beneath the feet of horse and girl had been painted in detail. The scene was clearly the bald top of Thunder Mountain, with the edge of the cliff dropping off not far away. The girl in the picture had dropped her riding crop in her struggle with the horse and it lay a short distance away in the left foreground.

Letty uttered a soft exclamation. "You've painted in Althea's riding crop!" she cried.

"It's a good touch, don't you think?" Booth said. "I needed something to fill that empty spot."

232

"But the crop was never found up there," Letty said softly.

Booth shrugged. "Aren't you taking this too literally? After all, the entire scene is something I made up. I started painting it before I ever knew what would happen to Althea."

Letty said, "Wait for me here, Camilla. I'll be only a moment."

She hurried off and Booth smiled at Camilla. "What's the trouble these days, Cousin? You hardly came near me at the lawn party yesterday."

She wanted to say, "There's the ugly matter of a broken step between us. And how will you explain that?"

But she remembered Ross's warning and suppressed the words. She would not be safe in this house until a will had been made. And she could not go to Mr. Pompton until tomorrow. In the meantime caution was her safest defense. If Booth did not know that she suspected him, she would be far safer than if he did.

"I was busy with our guests," she said quietly. "I had no time for members of the family."

"Yes," he said, "I saw the attention you were paying to Mrs. Landry. I suppose she tried to fill your ears with old scandals out of the past?"

Before Camilla could answer, Letty had returned, carrying in her hands the little riding crop with its head of silver chrysanthemums. She held it out to Booth.

"Here you are," she said.

Booth took it, and the queer, electric excitement kindled in his eyes. *The moment of danger,* Camilla thought. The crop had meaning for him—that was plain.

"Where did this turn up?" Booth asked.

"Camilla found it. She can tell you where."

Booth turned the crop in his hands, examining the polished silver cap, the leather thong that had rotted through.

"Suppose you tell me, Cousin," he said.

The roof of Camilla's mouth felt suddenly as dry as her lips. Booth was watching her. Letty was watching Booth, and there was an undercurrent of sick excitement in the room. Camilla touched her lips with the tip of her tongue and began to speak.

"When I climbed down to that spit of land that strikes out into

233

the river below Thunder Mountain," she said, "I found the crop caught in a crotch of brush."

"As if it had been flung there," Letty puzzled. "But where could it have been thrown from, I wonder? Not from the top of Thunder Mountain—the spit is too far out for that."

"And why, if Althea had carried it up there, would she have thrown it over the cliff?" Booth said easily. "I'm sorry there's been such a mystery about it. I can tell you what happened."

"If you knew, why didn't you tell us sooner, dear?" Letty asked. "Why didn't you tell us when Papa kept wondering about the crop and looking for it to keep with the saddle and bridle?"

"I didn't tell anyone," Booth said, "because Althea struck me across the face with the crop, and that was not something I cared to tell. I took it out of her hands, and she mounted Folly and rode away. I carried the crop to the lawn above the river and flung it out as far as I could throw. Into the water, I thought. I intended that she would never strike anyone with it again."

Letty's sigh was a soft release of breath, as if she had been waiting in dread for his explanation. She took the crop from him and held it out to Camilla.

"You may have it now, dear. Carry it the next time you wear Althea's things. I'm sure she would want you to have it."

"I'll carry it this afternoon," Camilla said. "I've had no time for riding lately. But I've wanted to explore those queer ruins that look like a castle over on the next hill."

"That will be nice," Letty said. "Booth dear, do come eat your lunch."

"You're right about the ruins," Booth said. "They are those of a castle. But they're man made. A few families along the Hudson got the notion years ago that they would give the river a look of the Rhine. They thought a few expensive castle ruins would be picturesque—but the idea never caught on. When I was a boy we used to use Castle Dunder for picnics, didn't we, Aunt Letty? It's a good spot for a view."

He had turned his attention to the food before him, and Camilla smiled at Letty and slipped away from the room. There was in her a growing urgency to be out on Firefly again, riding through the hills. Away from this house she would be safe just that much longer.

She could use the entire afternoon for riding and exploring the ruins. Then there would be only dinner, the evening, and one last night to get through. She would lock herself in, perhaps ask Letty to stay with her again. And in the morning she would go to Mr. Pompton's office in Westcliff and await his coming. Ever since she had talked to Ross this morning the need for action had been building within her. She was no longer undecided as to what she meant to do. Somehow, ever since she had looked at the finished picture of girl and horse, she had known that she must fight for her life. She must act swiftly while there was still time, and while Booth was without suspicion of what she meant to do.

The riding crop lay on the bed where she had tossed it, and as she dressed in Althea's gray habit, she glanced at it now and then. Booth's explanation had been glib and logical, but she did not believe it. He might fool Letty, who loved him as a son, but he could not fool her. His story of what had happened to the crop was a lie. She had seen it in the exultance in his face, in his supreme confidence that he could step to the very knife edge of danger and back away in time to save himself.

Yet, even while instinct told her that he was concealing something about the crop, her mind drew only a blank when she tried to think what it might be. Why had he painted the crop into the picture unless it had really lain there on the ground near Althea when she had struggled with the horse? Had he done it deliberately, playing with danger? Or had he done it from memory, without thinking—with an artist's unconscious observation of every detail?

But there was no way in which Booth could have been on the mountain to see what had happened. He had come in to tell Letty that Althea had refused to listen to him and that she had gone out alone into the rising storm. Then he had remained at Thunder Heights until her riderless horse had come home. After that he had roused the house and sent out searchers. Orrin Judd had gone up the mountain. Booth had chosen the river path for his search. He had never been near the mountaintop that night at all. There was no way in which he could have affected what had happened to Althea. Nor could he have seen the crop on the ground at her feet. That is, if the crop had really been there, and was not merely the imaginative touch Booth claimed it to be.

When Camilla was dressed and ready for her ride, she went to Letty's room and tapped on the door. Someone moved inside, but there was no answer and she knocked again. To her surprise, Hortense opened the door, and Camilla saw that she had been crying.

"I was looking for Letty," Camilla said.

Hortense stared at her in antipathy. "All the trouble that has come to this house since Papa died is due to you. Why don't you go away?"

"Do you know where Letty is?" Camilla repeated.

"I don't want to know. I came here to make her understand something, and she flounced out and left me. You'll have to look for her."

Camilla met Grace on the stairs, and the girl said Miss Letty had gone down to the cellar. Camilla hurried down and found that the broken step had been repaired. Nevertheless, she stepped cautiously as she went down the steep flight. Letty was in the larder, and she glanced up as Camilla came in the door.

"Rosemary and lavender make a lovely tea," she said, busy with her jars of herbs. But Camilla saw that her hands were trembling.

"Did you know," Camilla asked, "that Hortense is upstairs in your room?"

"I know," Letty said. "She came in to see me just now, but I walked out and left her there, I didn't want to listen to the things she had to say."

"About me, Aunt Letty?"

Letty waved the question aside. "Her nonsense doesn't bear repeating. I see you're ready for your ride, dear."

"Yes. I'll go out in a little while. But I wanted to talk to you first, Aunt Letty."

"You, too?" Letty sighed. "I came down here to be busy and peaceful."

Camilla wondered if she dared tell Letty about the will she meant to ask Mr. Pompton to draw up tomorrow. There was nothing greedy about Letty and her advice might be worth seeking, if she were not in one of her vague and evasive moods. But first there were other things to be said, and there was no use trying to approach them delicately.

"I think you ought to know," she said, "that the step that might have killed me yesterday was deliberately tampered with. I'd have shown it to you if it hadn't been mended so quickly. The wood wasn't rotten at all. There was no reason for it to break so easily."

"Tampered with?" Letty's hands went on with their work, and she did not look at Camilla. "For what purpose? By whom?"

"I think it was intended that I should be badly hurt on that step. But I don't think you planned such a trap, Aunt Letty. Nor do I think Aunt Hortense did. It's the sort of thing a man would execute."

Letty whirled to look at her and there were high spots of color in her cheeks. "You're making a dangerous accusation. And without proof."

"The proof is gone," Camilla said. "But I know what I saw."

"I don't believe it," Letty said, her lips quivering as she spoke.

"What about the riding crop then? I know that worried you when you saw that Booth had painted it into his picture. And I think I know why. You were wondering why he saw it there in his mind's eye—just as I was wondering. That's why you brought it in and showed it to him, isn't it?"

Letty shook her head a little wildly. There was no serenity in her now. "I won't listen to such insinuations, Camilla. Ever since Booth came to this house, everyone has been against him. No one has understood him or loved him but me. I didn't expect you to turn against him too. Of course he is—different—and perhaps a little eccentric. But that is often true of the highly gifted."

"Then you don't believe, Aunt Letty, that Booth would ever make an attempt on my life? Or even, perhaps, on my mother's?"

There was a long moment of silence in the room. Letty seemed to be struggling with too strong an indignation for words. In the end she merely shook her head fervently in answer.

"Very well," Camilla said. "I just wanted to know where you stand in all this, Aunt Letty. I'll go out for my ride now."

As she went upstairs, she felt torn and saddened. If it came to a choice between her safety and Booth's, she suspected that there would be only one decision Letty could make. She was no more to be trusted then Hortense or Booth himself. At Thunder Heights every hand was against her, and that was as it would always be. And for such emptiness she must give up her love.

She let herself out the heavy front door and started down the steps. Behind her Letty's voice called out and Camilla turned around. Letty stood on the steps, breathless from running upstairs.

"Don't go riding, dear," she said. "There's going to be a storm."

Camilla looked up at the sky. It was blue and hot and still. What clouds there were still hung motionless on the horizon as they had seemed to do all day. Not a breath of air stirred the leaves in the park before the house.

"There's not a sign of a storm anywhere," Camilla said.

She would have walked on toward the stable, but Letty came after her and caught at her arm in entreaty.

"Please, dear. You must believe me. I have a feeling that something terrible will happen if you go riding today."

"A few moments ago you were encouraging me to ride," Camilla said. "What made you change your mind?"

"I—I don't know." Letty looked as if she were about to crumple in upon herself. "I never understand these feelings or how they come. I just know they must be listened to. It's a feeling I have about that horse. You know I was against your buying the mare from the first. Just as Ross Granger was against it."

"And I've proved you both wrong," Camilla said. "Firefly and I understand each other. I feel safer with her than I do—in this house."

Letty drew back as if Camilla had slapped her. Then she turned and went up the steps, a drooping, pitiful little figure, her crooked arm held against her body. With a mingling of impatience and sympathy, Camilla walked away toward the stable. There was nothing more she could say to Letty, and it was just as well to leave her with that last thought.

CHAPTER 23

SHE had not sent word to have Firefly saddled, so she had to wait for it to be done after she reached the stable. More than once she scanned the sky to see if there was any evidence of Letty's threatened storm, but it burned blue and empty and no hint of a breeze stirred the breathless air. She wondered if Ross were upstairs in the rooms over the coach house, but she could find no reason for calling to him.

Firefly was restless and eager for a run. She stood impatiently, while Billy helped Camilla into the saddle. Out upon the road Camilla gave the mare an easy run as far as the place where the winding trail led up Thunder Mountain. With the horse moving like a dancer beneath her, full of spirit and life, something of the joy of riding returned and Camilla could put Thunder Heights away from her for a little while. For her there would always be both a physical and an emotional release about riding.

They climbed the trail up Thunder Mountain, but this time Camilla did not dismount at the top. Firefly was behaving skittishly, sidestepping, and swinging her hind quarters about in a balkish way. She was like a lady in a state of sulks because no one had paid attention to her for several days. She would be sweet enough after a while, but first she would make clear her displeasure and refuse to forgive the neglect. Camilla coaxed her, teased her, spoke to her lovingly, but Firefly tossed her pretty head and would not relent.

"All right," Camilla told her, "I'll let you have your fun, but first let's get over to the next hill. There's more room there for your tricks. I don't care for them at the top of a cliff."

Rising on the far hill were the "ruins" of Castle Dunder. From this distance the gray heap of stones looked convincingly like an ancient castle, and rather grim and forbidding.

With her hand firm upon the reins, Camilla urged the mare through the woods that hid a trail winding around the inner curve of hill. They walked now, due to low-hanging branches and the very narrowness of the path. When they merged upon an open slope of hillside, they were just below the ruins, and the clustered stones rose ahead on the crest of the hill. Approached from the rear, the place looked an empty shell and far less picturesque than it seemed from a distance. However, the main tower appeared solidly built, for all that the crumbling walls which fell away behind embraced only an empty expanse of weeds and grass.

There seemed to be a shed built at the rear of the structure, and Camilla let Firefly prance up the slope. Clearly the mare distrusted the gray pile of stones, but Camilla insisted and she gave in, though still displeased. A low wall offered an easy foothold for dismounting, and Camilla stepped down to it, jumped to the ground and tethered Firefly in the shelter of the stable-like shed.

As she started across the grassy field toward the main tower of the castle, a spate of rain struck her head and shoulders. She looked up in surprise and saw that the wind had risen so that trees on the hillside were thrashing their branches. Letty's threatened storm clouds had puffed their sails with wind and were moving up the sky.

She hurried toward the tower entrance where a few stone steps led to an oblong opening and stepped gingerly into the dark lower room. In the dim light she could make out a circling of stone stairs marching to the top of the tower. The room smelled of damp left over from old storms, and the stone walls had the authentic chill of a castle. She had no desire to linger here in the dim light that came through the door.

The circling stone steps drew her, and she followed their spiralling wedges upward in a dizzy climb until she emerged in a bare room at the top. Here several archers' windows, deep and narrow, slit the circular stone walls, letting in slivers of gray light. A rusty iron ladder led upward to still another level and what appeared to be a trap door to the roof.

Now she wanted to reach the very battlements and watch the storm clouds rise. Testing the rungs to make sure they would hold her weight, she climbed up beneath the trap door. At first it refused to give as she pushed with her shoulder, but when she persisted, it creaked open, sending shivers of dust and rotting wood down upon her head.

Up here the air smelled sweet and clean. She stepped out upon the flat, open top of a tower, and stood beside the circling parapet. The spurt of rain was over for the moment, but wind rushed at her jubilantly and tore at her veil and hat. The distant mountains of New England were obscured by mists, and even the nearer Catskills had been hidden from sight, but the rolling panoply of the storm gave in itself a tremendous view. Far below the Hudson was whipped with curling threads of foam, and the entire scene was like one of Booth's wild Hudson valley paintings.

So lost was she in watching the swiftly rising clouds that she had almost forgotten Firefly when the mare neighed. She must go down at once, she thought, and start for home. Letty had been right after all, and it would be raining hard before long. As she hesitated for a last long look, she heard the answering neigh of another horse.

At once she walked to the land side of the tower and looked toward the shed. Firefly was there, and tethered near her was a second horse, a man's saddle upon its back. No rider was visible, and she was puzzled and a little uneasy. This was not one of the horses from Blue Beeches, and she wondered what passerby might have discovered her presence. At the foot of the tower a step sounded, and she leaned over the steep parapet to look straight down.

She was just in time to see a man enter the narrow doorway below. It was Booth Hendricks. A shiver ran through her as she shrank back from the parapet. He must have hired a horse in the village and ridden out here deliberately. She could hear him walking about below and wondered helplessly what she must do.

He came to the foot of the spiralling stairs and called up to her. "Camilla! Are you there, Camilla?"

If she did not answer, perhaps he would not come up to search for her. Perhaps he would think she was elsewhere and go away. But almost at once she heard his footfall on the echoing stone of the steps and knew he was coming up the stairs. She was trapped with no means of saving herself and only the riding crop in her hands to fight him with.

With deadly certainty she knew what his purpose would be. There would be no need for indirection this time in his attempt on her life. A fall from the tower could be easily explained later, and Booth's ends would have been met.

In a moment he would emerge in the room at the top of the tower and then it was only a few steps to the roof beside her. As she trembled there, her mind turning this way and that like a hunted thing, a course of possible action came to her mind. Foolish, perhaps, and hopeless. But the only chance she had.

She pulled the gray hat from her head and tossed it to the far side of the tower. Then she dropped to her hands and knees and crouched in the one hiding place the roof offered—the niche made by the trap door where it lay propped against the parapet. The door itself shielded her and he could not see her as he climbed the stairs. He would need only to turn around for her to be visible, but for an instant when he stepped from the top of the ladder to the roof, he would have his back to her hiding place.

Her breathing seemed almost as noisy as the rising wind. Her throat was tight with fear. She pulled herself small in the cramped space as he came up, his feet ringing on the iron rungs.

"Camilla?" he called again—and was out upon the roof.

He saw her hat at once and went toward it. In that instant Camilla flung herself from her hiding place and down the ladder. She had no time to feel for her footing, but used her hands as well as her feet to swing herself down. Caution was impossible. There was no time to be quiet, and she set the echoes ringing. She was on the stone steps now, slipping, stumbling, catching herself before she pitched headlong. Above her she could hear him following— and he was unhampered by a heavy riding skirt.

At the tower door, she did not trouble with the few steps down, but sprang to the ground and fled across the grass to the shed. Fire-fly heard her coming and pawed the earth, neighing in nervous excitement. But Booth could move more swiftly than Camilla and his hand caught her arm, whirling her about. She saw his face in the gray light. He knew she had guessed the truth. There was danger in his eyes—exultant danger. And death.

She struck at him with the silver head of the riding crop, lashing it across his face. For an instant he was taken by surprise. Pain blinded him and he drew back. She twisted free of his grasp and sped the few yards to the low stone wall beside the shed. In a second she was up on the wall, from there into the saddle, and the reins were free in her hand.

She swerved Firefly about and made her rear, her front feet striking out in Booth's direction. Again he fell back, and Camilla turned the mare toward the woods trail and was away, with Firefly's hoofs pounding the turf. Crouching low over the saddle she gave the mare her head along the narrow trail. Caught up in Camilla's own fear, Firefly hurled herself into breakneck speed, seeking only to flee the unknown terror. At least the curve around the hill was steady and gentle, so no sharp turns need be taken. Camilla could not hear the other horse behind, and she dared not look back, but Booth would be in the saddle by now and after her.

"Hurry, hurry!" she moaned to Firefly. "Hurry!"

Suddenly they were in the open, and she knew they had reached the top of Thunder Mountain. Before she could turn the mare, Firefly was out upon the bare top of the mountain, with cliffs falling away on three sides, and the downward path behind them. Camilla fought her to a halt and turned her about. She could hear hoofbeats now, as Booth ran his horse through the woods, and despair swept over her. Thunder Mountain, with the way down cut off, would be as bad a trap as the top of the tower.

And then, without warning, Ross Granger rode out from the lower path and was between her and Booth. She jerked Firefly about and urged her toward him.

"It's Booth!" she gasped, pointing.

Ross understood at once. He leaned over and slapped Firefly's flank with the flat of his hand.

"Go home!" he shouted. "Ride for home!" With a violent jerk, Ross wheeled his own horse across the path to intercept Booth.

She had no need to urge the mare now. Firefly was tearing down the lower path. But now there was something new and frightening about her gait. She lunged against a tree in passing, and Camilla felt a crushing pain in her left leg. The mare was fighting to get the bit between her teeth, and she was trying as well to rid herself of a rider she now feared.

Camilla ducked low beneath the next branch before it swept her from the saddle, and clamped the toe of her right boot behind her left calf. It was clear what Firefly was trying to do. This was no pretty sulking spell. She meant to dash her rider against a tree, or scrape her off beneath a branch, and she was wickedly intent on her purpose. Camilla could only flatten herself over the pommel, ducking as well as she could the thrashing branches. The pungent taste of pine was in her mouth, and her hands ached with their effort to bring the mare under control.

The trail was steepening and danger lay in a misstep, lest the mare stumble and roll on her. Pinned beneath her mount, she might readily be killed. But the fight was hard on Firefly too, and with Camilla clinging like a burr to the saddle, and never relinquishing her struggle to get the mare's head up and under control, the horse was tiring too. When the road suddenly opened on a level before them and the trees fell away, the fight drained out of the mare and she cantered to a halt a little way down the road. Camilla had won.

The quiet, the absence of buffeting and wild motion was almost shocking. Firefly stood still on the dirt road, and both girl and horse were trembling. Camilla pushed her tumbled hair from her forehead and spoke in a low, soothing voice to the mare. She was docile enough now, her wild fright drained away, and Camilla turned her toward Thunder Heights.

Only then did she have time to think of what might be happening back there in the woods. Ross, she knew, would stop Booth and engage his attention. But what would happen between the two men? Both had been spoiling for trouble for a long while. If it came to a fight, Camilla knew Ross would handle himself well. But she did not trust Booth. He would stop at nothing if he were pressed, and she was suddenly fearful of the outcome. But there was nothing she could do now but wait. More than once, she drew the mare in and listened for the sound of a horse's passage on the hillside above. Thunder rumbled in the distance and lightning flashed far away. There was wind in the trees, but no other sound. And still it did not rain.

At the gate of Thunder Heights Hortense stood waiting. When Camilla turned off the road, she called for the stableboy, and came forward herself to take Firefly's bridle.

"Get off," she said curtly to Camilla. "If you can. You look beaten."

Camilla's body felt sore from the lashings and her left leg was bruised, but she took her foot from the stirrup and slipped down into the stableboy's grasp. When he set her on her feet, she swayed for an instant, and Hortense gave the boy the bridle and took her arm.

"That mare has a vicious streak, hasn't she?" Hortense said. "I've been waiting for it to come out. I expect she's killed a rider or two somewhere along the line. That's why Booth had her brought here to Berton's. That's why he told me to—'find' her for you in the village. You didn't know that, did you?"

Camilla shook her head wearily. "It was my own fault. I was frightened and I frightened the mare."

"I've been a fool," Hortense said. "I believed that he only wanted to make you afraid—so you'd give everything up and leave. I wanted that myself. I thought if I made you sick with that tea . . . but the cat drank it. Letty knew I'd been down in the larder that day . . . she could have told you."

Camilla could only stare at her numbly. Hortense looked faintly bedraggled, for all her old-fashioned elegance. The lace at her throat was worn, and pins were visible at her belt line. Yet in spite of this outward disintegration, she was more convincing and forceful than Camilla had ever seen her. She was a woman to be heeded.

"He means to kill you, Camilla. You must know that now. He tricked me on the matter of sending you down to the cellar on a trumped-up errand. I'd never have been a knowing party to that broken step. I've never meant you serious harm. But Booth will stop at nothing."

"Yes, I know." Camilla's lips barely formed the words. All this was something she must come to later. Now the only part of her mind that still functioned focused entirely on what might be happening on Thunder Mountain. For herself, she wanted only Letty's ministering hands and ointments and a bed to lie upon.

"Where is Aunt Letty?" she asked.

There was a strained note in Hortense's voice. "She's locked herself in her room. She's waiting for them to bring your body to her. Down from Thunder Mountain. The way they did Althea's."

CHAPTER 24

The driveway seemed endlessly long as Camilla followed it, leaning on Hortense's arm. She limped a little as she walked, but bruises were nothing compared to the pressure of anxiety in her mind.

"Who sent Ross after me?" she asked.

"I did," Hortense said. "When I learned that Booth had hired a horse from the village and was riding up the mountain, I knew he meant you harm. So I told Ross. He got a horse from Blue Beeches and went out at once."

"Aunt Letty didn't want me to ride," Camilla said. "She tried to stop me from going."

Hortense tossed her head scornfully. "You mean that nonsense about a storm? It must have surprised her as much as anyone else to have one really blow up. She was afraid to tell you the truth—about that horse. Though she knew, because that's what I went to her room to tell her. She said she didn't believe me. Perhaps she didn't want to believe me. Booth has always been the center of her existence. Or—perhaps she knew all along."

"Letty never wanted to harm anyone," Camilla said. "I know that."

Hortense clutched her arm and Camilla winced. "Look—there on the steps!"

The afternoon was growing dark, and a few lamps had been lit inside the house. Against the light a man stood before the front door of Thunder Heights—a tall, lean, elegant figure. It was Booth, and he stood as if braced, with his legs apart, his arms akimbo. His eyes were alive with a grim mirth as he waited for them.

Hortense ran toward him. "How did you get here? Where is your horse?"

Camilla followed, and as she drew near she saw the jagged tear in his jacket. His tie was gone, his hair disheveled. A cut from the riding crop marked his forehead, and a bruise had begun to swell the cheekbone under one eye.

He gestured carelessly in answer to Hortense. "I left my horse and came down the cliff by way of the short cut."

"Where is Ross?" Camilla demanded—that one question uppermost in her mind.

"We met—if that's what you're wondering." He regarded her almost airily. "Granger managed to interfere with my seeing you home, Cousin. But where he is now I don't know or care."

"What did you do to him?"

"A better question might concern what he did to me. I've never taken to rude physical brawling. But I know the mountain better than he does. I knew it as a boy."

"You went up the cliff the night Althea died, didn't you?" Hortense said. "I always thought you were up there."

"But since you doted on me, my dear mother, you kept your suspicion to yourself? That was kind of you."

A deep, tearing anger began to stir in Camilla. "What happened that night? What did you do to my mother?"

He stepped back from the fury in her face in mock alarm. "You've proved yourself a dangerous woman, Cousin. But I did nothing. Nothing at all. I knew she would go up there, and I tethered my horse at the foot of the cliff while I was supposed to be out searching the river path. I could get to the top easily by the cliff path, while Orrin was taking the long way around by the hill. But I assure you she was already dead when I came upon her body, and she couldn't laugh at me, or taunt me any more."

"Is that when you found the crop?"

"Yes. I'll admit picking it up was a foolish impulse. I wanted to make sure no one would ever strike me with it again. So I carried it down the mountain without thinking. You can understand that I was in a state of some excitement. When I found it in my hand,

I carried it out to the lawn and flung it into the river. Or so I thought. I didn't dream it would turn up years later to be used against me in the hands of Althea's daughter."

The bitter light in his eyes was frightening, but Camilla stood her ground. The only thing that mattered now was what had happened to Ross. Before she could speak, a voice called from the upstairs sitting room in the house. The three on the driveway looked up to see Letty at the open window.

"Booth?" she called. "So you're back, dear." Her eyes flicked briefly over Camilla, and the look was without emotion. "Please come up here, Booth. I want to see you."

Booth shrugged. "I'll go see what she wants," he said.

Camilla followed him slowly into the house. The candles in the antehall had been lit, and so had the lamp that hung above the staircase. She moved toward the marble arch opening upon the stairwell, her worried thoughts on Ross, even as she watched Booth start up the stairs.

Part way up the third octagon turn, he paused, one hand on the banister, and looked upward. Apparently Letty had come to the rail above, for Camilla heard her speaking to him softly. Booth cried out in sudden warning.

"No—no, Aunt Letty! Don't!"

There was alarm in his voice and Camilla stopped, with Hortense just behind her. Even as they stared, a sheet of flaming oil streamed down from the great lamp above as Letty's hand must have tipped it. The fall of flame spilled over the wooden steps, encased the octagon railing, and dripped to the floor below. It was caught at once in the strong draft of the stairwell and in a flash the entire wooden structure was a roaring chimney of flame. Letty could escape, above, if she chose, but Booth, part way up the stairs, was trapped.

To her horror Camilla saw that Letty had not moved back from the fire, but was coming down the stairs toward Booth, toward the very heart of the blaze. In the same instant Booth tore off his jacket and leaped up the stairway, to fling it over Letty's head. He picked her up in his arms and came down through the flames, his own clothes on fire, his very hair burning.

Hortense had rushed wildly outside, screaming "Fire!" and a

man dashed through the door past Camilla. It was Ross, and he took Letty from Booth's arms, beating out the streak of flame in her skirt. Then he caught up a small rug, wrapped it around Booth and rolled him across the floor to the door. In a moment Ross had him outside on the grass, and Camilla drew Letty down the steps, where she crumpled to her knees on the driveway.

The servants had rushed out of their quarters at the side of the house, and one of them ran off toward the village to summon help. Hortense kept up her screaming until Camilla took her by the arm and shook her.

"Stop it!" she cried. "You can't help anything by screaming." Then she turned to kneel beside Letty.

A patch of Letty's gray skirt fell to ashes when Camilla touched her, but her aunt sat up dazedly and leaned against Camilla's arm. Beyond them the heart of the house was burning like an enormous torch, and the fire was spreading into both wings, even as they watched.

"Booth!" Letty cried. "Where is he?"

She flung off Camilla's restraining arm and sprang up to run to Booth where he lay upon the grass, with Ross bending over him.

"Don't touch him," Ross warned. "He's unconscious. You'd better leave him for the doctor to tend."

Letty stood quietly, looking down at the man who lay at her feet. The extent of his burns were frightful, and Camilla turned away, faint and shaken. No matter what he had been, she would not wish this for him. But Letty did not wince.

"He won't live." She spoke softly, but her voice did not quaver. "It's better that way."

She leaned sadly upon the arm Camilla put around her, and they walked a short distance away beneath the trees.

"He saved my life," Letty said. "He came up through the flames and brought me down. I didn't mean it to be like that. I didn't want him to live, but I meant to go with him."

"Hush," Camilla said. "Hush! You mustn't say such terrible things."

Hortense had come to stand beside them, and she was past her hysteria now. "Let her be," she said. "She means them. Let her say what she pleases."

Against the stormy darkness of the sky the great tinderbox of a house flamed with a wild brilliance. Sparks showered as a center turret collapsed, and Camilla felt the touch of ash upon her face. Suddenly there seemed to be many people thronging the grounds, some shouting and moving about, some watching helplessly.

"Let it burn," Letty said. "Let it burn to the last ember." Tears had begun to stream down her cheeks and she made no effort to stop them. "I knew when I saw the riding crop that he'd painted into the picture. Even then I wouldn't believe such evil of him. I wouldn't accept my own thoughts, or the things you tried to tell me, Camilla. I'd always remember him as a little boy. Such a sad, handsome, unloved little boy. But when I saw the riding crop in the picture I knew that he'd gone up Thunder Mountain the night Althea died, and later I had to face the truth."

"He told us she was dead when he found her," Camilla said quickly. "Perhaps that was the truth."

Letty shook her head. "Only part of the truth. He sent her to her death. I made him tell me today. He taunted her and made fun of her courage until she was so angry she struck him with the crop. But he knew she would ride Folly if he made her angry enough, tormented her long enough. When the time came he saddled the horse for her and he left the girth only partly buckled, knowing it would give if Folly acted up in the storm as she was sure to do. Althea was too angry to check the saddle when she mounted. I think she could have handled Folly in spite of anything if her saddle had been safe. She must have been thrown violently when it began to slip. Folly came home dragging the saddle, and Booth went out to catch her."

The volunteer firemen were here now, with the horse-drawn engine from the village. The play of the hoses made a weak hissing against the tornado of flame. At least they could wet down the trees nearby so the woods wouldn't go.

"Afterward," Letty said, "Booth went up the mountain by the short cut to see what had happened to Althea. I—I don't know what he might have done if she had been alive then. But I believed him when he said she was dead." She looked up in entreaty at

Camilla and Hortense. "You see why I had to act? He couldn't be allowed to go on like that. There would be no end to it as long as he lived. Yet in spite of everything, he saved my life."

Dr. Wheeler came, and when he had examined Booth, he shook his head gravely. "It will be only a little while now," he said.

Letty knelt on the grass beside Booth, her eyes tearless, her gaze never moving from his burned and blackened face. Camilla stood with Hortense, waiting. Ross had gone away to work with the firemen. There was nothing to be done. Nothing at all to be done.

Only once did Booth open his eyes, and for an instant the spark of life burned bright with its old intensity. His look moved from Hortense to Camilla, and there was recognition in it, and the old sardonic amusement. Then his gaze was all for Letty.

"Thank you," he said strangely. "We'll all be free now."

His eyelids closed. This time he had stepped across the knife edge of danger.

Toby brought a blanket from the coach house to put over the figure on the grass.

The fire was past its fiercest burning now, though one tower was still in flames and the ruins would smoulder for a long while. Ross had left the futile struggle. He came to draw Camilla away into the deep cool shadow of the trees, and she realized that her face burned from the heat of the fire.

"You're safe," she said. "I worried so. What happened between you and Booth?"

"We fought." Ross was short. "I think I was getting the best of it, when he broke away. I don't know how he got back, and I didn't much care. The fight was out of him for the moment. I had to take the long way back with the horses. But don't think about that now."

Camilla looked up between high branches and saw the stars in a night blue sky. The storm had rumbled away in the distance, and the rain had never come. She turned in the shelter of Ross's arms and looked into his face.

"Booth spoke the truth," she said softly. "We're all free now. There's nothing to tie any of us here."

He held her closely, and she put her cheek against his. "Will you take me with you, Ross? Wherever you go?"

His kiss answered her, his arm was her support.

The last burning tower crumbled and fell with a great roar and a rush of high-flung sparks. The sound echoed against the mountain above and clapped back and forth across the river. The quiet afterwards was intense. Far below the quiet Hudson waters flowed as they had always done. But Thunder Heights was gone forever.

Window on the Square

by *Phyllis A. Whitney*

CHAPTER 1

MY FIRST summons to the house in Washington Square came to me inscribed in an imperious feminine hand on rich cream note-paper. Apparently a friend had recommended me as dressmaker to Mrs. Brandon Reid. The note stated that Mrs. Reid would be pleased to receive me on Saturday, if I would come to her residence at eleven o'clock in the morning.

The name of Leslie Reid had a familiar ring to my ear. Had there not been some scandal a year or two before? Something to do with the death of her first husband and her eventual remarriage to his older brother? The details escaped me. In any event, they had no bearing on this work I needed so badly.

How anxiously I went to my appointment with Mrs. Reid that Saturday. The business of dressmaking was my mother's, built up painstakingly in the ten years and more since my father had died in the fighting at Shiloh. Now, with the sudden, shocking death of my mother and young brother beneath the hoofs of a runaway horse only six months before, I was left to continue my mother's work. I lacked her skill and interest in dressmaking, however. A fact that was all too evident to the ladies who had come to her for so long and were now reluctant to trust their wardrobes to a girl of twenty-two. I had a single order to complete and then I would not know which way to turn for my sustenance.

Autumn leaves were drifting from the trees in Washington Square and lay in golden swirls on every walk, crackling beneath my feet with the crisp sound that spells October. With increasing doubts of myself, I approached the row of red brick houses that faced the square, their tiny garden plots fenced in fancifully with wrought iron. The Reid House had marble steps and balustrades mounting to a columned doorway of the Greek revival period. I had often admired these handsome homes.

As I waited for an answer to my ring, I lifted my face to the hazy sunlight, letting its mild warmth flow through me. Grief had left me cold for so long, it seemed. The butler who opened the door did not warm me with his manner. He was high of nose and stiff of neck, and a glance at the unfashionable cut of my mourning must have told him that I was beneath his notice. He ushered me into a small, elegant sitting room and went away to announce my presence.

I had always enjoyed glimpses into the homes of the wealthy. Thanks to my mother's reminders and my memories of our own home, these surroundings neither abashed me nor made me envious. If my father had lived, I would have grown up in our big, rambling house in New Jersey, where he had been a professor of history.

Thus I looked about me at the teardrop chandelier, the French gilt furniture, and fine paintings, and found interest in them. I was fond of such evidence of good taste and elegance, and there was nothing about that bright small room to warn me of the blight that lay upon the rest of the house. Over the mantel of Italian marble hung a large oval mirror, gilt-framed, and I suppressed a feminine impulse to leave my chair and look at myself. After all, I did not want to be caught primping and I knew well enough how I looked.

Mourning did not become me. My coloring was too dark, my hair too black. Only the blue of my eyes must have lent contrast to the unhappy picture of sorrow I offered. My dress I had made hurriedly, with no time for the pains I must give to the gowns of my mother's clients. While it was drawn into a bustle at the back, it lacked the fussiness of present styles—a fussiness I decried and would not put upon my own person. The basque bodice fitted my figure well, with neckline that ended in a touch of white ruching at my throat—since I could not resign myself to unrelieved black. The skirt was the current overdrape, with plain black showing beneath. In my ears I wore tiny gold earrings, and my hat was an old one of my mother's, small and rather flat, tilted forward over my bangs. Its black veiling I had put back upon entering the house.

So lost was I in this inventory of my appearance—sans mirror—that I heard no step in the doorway. I was staring at black-gloved hands clasped about my black reticule when a voice startled me.

"You are Miss Megan Kincaid?"

I rose at once, being here for purposes of serving, and faced the man who watched me from the doorway. Having once gazed, I could not look away. Seldom had I seen eyes so coldly gray and appraising. They were set in a face leanly handsome, somber, the brows dark and winged beneath high brushed dark hair. The nose was strong and faintly crooked, with a marked hump of bone at the bridge, the mouth full-lipped, or it would have been were it not pressed into so straight a line. He was a man in his early thirties perhaps, though he might have been older. I felt unaccountably drawn and yet a little repelled at the same time. Later I was to know that Brandon Reid often had this effect upon those who met him for the first time. Particularly when they were women.

"Yes, I am Megan Kincaid," I managed and wondered why I should feel suddenly nervous in this man's presence. After all, I had come here to see Mrs. Reid and no one else.

"I'm sorry," he said, coolly courteous. "My wife is indisposed this morning and unable to keep her appointment with you."

My face must have betrayed my disappointment, though I tried to hide it at once. I straightened my shoulders proudly, having discovered that it is often by the set of one's shoulders that inner despair is revealed.

"I am sorry Mrs. Reid isn't well," I said. "Perhaps I may see her another day?" With that I moved toward the door to indicate that I meant to take nothing of his time.

He did not, however, move out of my way, and I was forced to come to an awkward halt a foot or two from him. His gray eyes had never left my face except for the moment in which they flicked over my person, as if still measuring, still weighing. Then he stepped abruptly out of the doorway.

"If you will come with me, please," he said and turned toward the stairs.

What this meant I did not know, but his manner of authority was not to be disregarded. I followed as he led the way, aware of his distinguished height and carriage.

The houses of Washington Square are apt to be narrow and fairly deep, but this house seemed of greater width than most. The staircase was graceful in its upward curve around a central oval. My hand on the black walnut banister, I glanced up and saw the oval glass skylight three stories above. There was no landing, but a continuation of wedge-shaped steps around the graceful turn, mounting to the second floor. The wallpaper was a dark figuring of raspberry upon cream, with the darkness predominating. The gas fixture on the wall lighted our way with a greenish-yellow, faintly hissing glow. Above, the hall was as gloomy as the stairs.

The man who conducted me led the way to closed double doors at the front of the house, flung them open, and stepped back to permit me to enter. Still commanded by his manner, I went past him into a great square library. Here there was brightness again, for the dark green draperies had been drawn back from windows that made up one wall of the room. Pale sunlight set the glass aglow and lessened the dark severity of the room.

On each side of the double door, on each side of the mantel and chimney, and covering the remaining wall were shelves of books. My heart quickened a little at the sight. I could remember such a library from my childhood and I could remember my pain when from time to time since his death my mother had sold my father's books. But this room had some foreignness of ornament that I did not look at closely just then, my attention being mainly for the man who had brought me here.

Mr. Reid drew a chair before the handsomely carved mahogany desk and seated me. Then he took his place in a larger chair behind the desk, still watching me in his curiously intent manner.

"Tell me about yourself," he said, and I heard the rich, deep timbre of his voice, warmer and more winning than his cold, grave manner. Again my face must have betrayed bewilderment, for he added quickly, "I have good reason for asking."

By now I had lost much of my earlier poise. I felt younger than I wanted to feel and I did not like to be measured and studied as this man seemed to be studying me. I had come here to offer myself as a dressmaker to his wife. Why should he question me?

Nevertheless, I began somewhat stiffly to tell him how I had taken over my mother's work and mentioned the name of a client who had stood by me and found satisfaction in my efforts. I did not get far with this recital because he stopped me with an impatient wave of his hand.

"No, no—I know all that. What I want to hear about is you. Tell me about your background, about your family life."

More bewildered than ever, I managed a brief account of where we had lived when I was a child. Of my father's death in battle during the war, and of the way I had learned to help my mother.

"Your education?" he asked curtly.

I mentioned the well-approved seminary for young ladies which I had attended at home, and explained that my parents had tutored me besides.

All these things he listened to with the same slight air of impatience, so that I wondered why he bothered to ask. When I fell silent with nothing more to tell, he picked up a carved ivory paperweight from his desk and weighed it from palm to palm.

"Have you any special interests?" he asked. "Is there any subject that particularly absorbs you?"

"I used to be fond of history and geography," I said. "My father helped me to cultivate an interest in foreign lands and antiquity."

I fancied a flicker of attention and surprise in his face, but his next question had nothing to do with my education.

"You had a brother, did you not?"

I didn't want to talk about Richard. He had been so young to die—just before his twelfth birthday. And yet, although I missed him with all my heart and had not yet been able to face the task of putting away his toys and small possessions, I knew death had been a release from a burden too heavy for one so young to bear.

With more self-possession than I had shown before, I managed to return Mr. Reid's measuring look.

"My brother died in the same accident that took my mother," I told him quietly.

Perhaps his manner toward me softened a little, but his words remained remote, objective. "I can understand your pain in this recent bereavement, Miss Kincaid. A mutual friend has told me of how good you were with your brother, of how he improved to the fullest of his capacities because of your interest and care."

"My brother was injured at birth. Mentally he would never have been more than a child," I said with dignity and then was silent, not understanding what this interrogation signified.

The man behind the desk set down the paperweight, and I followed the movement, noting his long, thin hands and strong, flexible fingers. He rose abruptly and stepped to the windows behind the desk, staring through them, not looking at me now. With the removal of his gaze, I stirred in my chair, feeling as though I had been released from a spell.

"Why are you asking me these things?" I inquired.

His gaze was fixed upon the street and the square, and he spoke over his shoulder without turning.

"It was at my suggestion that my wife wrote asking you to come here today. Neither of us is interested in your dressmaking skill. She has a son—the son of my brother who is dead. He is a difficult, unbalanced boy. Neither his mother nor I, neither his tutor nor governess, has been able to handle him. He responds to no one. We have reached a point of desperation with him. Would you, Miss Kincaid, consider coming here to devote yourself to this boy?"

The suggestion was so startling that I could only stare at him. My reply when it came was faltering.

"But I have no training as a teacher. Caring for my brother was a simple matter. A matter of loving him dearly. I doubt that it would be wise for me to let my mother's business go while I attempted something for which I am unprepared."

"I've taken that into consideration," Mr. Reid said, and mentioned a monthly salary that made me gasp inwardly. It was more than I could hope to gain in months of dressmaking. Yet something held me back and I could not give my assent readily.

"I cannot see that what I have to offer is sufficient to justify this experiment," I told him.

He swung away from the window. "It may be that you will make a frock or two for my wife while you are under this roof. If you wish at any time to withdraw from this . . . arrangement, Mrs. Reid will see to it that you do not want for dressmaking orders from her friends. Is that not enough of a guarantee?"

It was more than enough, yet still I hesitated, unprepared to the core of my being for this sudden turn of events. There was an air about this house, about the somber, handsome man before me that set up an uneasiness in my spirit. There was more here, I sensed, than was to be easily fathomed or quickly explained, and however much I might need employment, I must now move with caution.

"This boy is unbalanced in his mind, like my brother?" I asked.

"Unbalanced, yes. Not in the same way as your brother, however. We believe that his mental growth is not impaired. But he is unpredictable, moody, with a violent, dangerous temper. There is nothing easy, I warn you, about this assignment, Miss Kincaid."

I did not want him to think I was afraid of the difficult. "May I see the boy?"

Brandon Reid seemed to hesitate for a moment. Then he gave a flick of his fingers that indicated decision. With a long stride he crossed the room to a braided rope of dark red silk and jerked it. A bell sounded in the depths of the house.

"I will send you up," he said. "It will be better if I do not go with you. Perhaps a little dissembling is necessary for the moment. There is another child—Jeremy's younger sister, Selina. The boy is nine, the girl eight. They are together in the nursery at the moment with their governess, Miss Garth. Let us say you are here in the role of dressmaker—to make a frock for Selina. It is she you wish to meet. Perhaps you can take her measurements—something of the sort?"

I had brought with me the equipment of my trade in a small basket and I nodded. When the maid appeared, Mr. Reid gave her directions and I was led into the hall and up a second flight of stairs to the top of the house.

On this floor the somber gloom of dark wood and wallpaper continued to prevail, and again the hall area was lit by a single gas globe. There were closed doors all around and from beyond one at the front of the house I could hear voices raised as if in anger or excitement. The pert young maid gave me a sidelong glance and rolled her eyes skyward as she tapped on the panel. From her look I gathered that this sort of thing was not uncommon in the nursery.

A feminine voice bade us enter, and the door was opened upon a room of moderate size in which a roaring fire blazed and the atmosphere was stifling for the bright, mild weather outside. I was to learn that Thora Garth was always cold to her very marrow and no room could be too warm for her.

The maid bobbed a curtsy, murmured that the master had sent me to measure Miss Selina for a dress, and fled as if she could not wait to get away. With the door closed, facing the angry scene in that hot room, I did not blame her. The turkey-red carpet on the floor seemed to add its own burning heat to a room busily crowded with furniture—sofas, chairs, tables, cabinets, all set in an array that made them seem as quarrelsome as the persons in the room.

The governess, a tall, full-figured woman in a severe dress of brown merino, must have been in her late forties. She wore her thick, ungrayed brown hair in fashionable waves and puffs that revealed a certain vanity in its arrangement. Her face, with dark, deep-set eyes beneath the forehead puff, was handsome if forbidding. She wasted hardly a glance on me. All her attention was for the slight, brown-haired boy who sat at a round table near the fire, his head bent intently over the pages of a book.

About them danced a sprite of a little girl with long fair hair floating about her shoulders, her face screwed up in a mischievous grimace.

"He took it, Garthy, he took it!" the little girl shrilled. "Make him give it back to me at once!"

Miss Garth held out her hand to the boy. "Whatever you have taken of your sister's, give it to me immediately."

The boy might have existed in a world of his own. Indifferently he turned a page and continued to read, ignoring her. While the girl was probably pretty when she wasn't grimacing, I found the boy had about him the look of an angel—a dark and sullen angel.

I stepped hastily to the table to present myself to the governess and interrupt this unpleasant scene. "You are Miss Garth, I believe? I am Megan Kincaid. I'm to make a frock for this young lady and I would like to take her measurements if I may."

The little girl whirled across the room to me, petticoats flying beneath her pink pinafore, offering herself readily to my tape measure.

"There!" she cried in triumph. "Mama is going to let me have a length of the new China silk after all. I knew she would if I cried for it hard enough."

For all Selina's effort to capture the center of the stage, it was the boy I watched as I unrolled my tape measure. For the first time he raised wide dark eyes from the page to stare at me, and a strange interest came alive in his face.

"Someone has died in your family," he said. It was a statement, not a question.

I realized that he was staring at my black dress and I answered him quietly. "You're very observant. It's quite true that I'm wearing mourning."

"Don't make impertinent remarks, Jeremy," Miss Garth chided. "You are a wicked boy for taking your sister's things. Pay attention to me and give whatever you have back, or I shall have to smack you."

The long, deadly look he gave her before returning his attention to the book was not reassuring. Her words echoed through my mind. *Wicked boy*, I thought, and something stirred, tugging at my memory. I gave my attention to Selina, measuring and jotting down figures, turning her about.

"Tell me what sort of dress it is to be," Selina beseeched. "Is it really the green China silk?"

It was hard to resist her coaxing ways, and I smiled. "I won't know until I've had a chance to talk to your mother. Then I'll tell you all about it and we can plan it together."

She started to clap her hands and fumbled because of one closed fist. Suddenly suspicious, I took her delicate wrist between my fingers and turned her hand over. The child did not resist me, but only laughed as I opened the fingers to reveal a small red emery strawberry. I held it up for the boy to see.

"Your sister was teasing you, I think. See—here's what she thought she had lost. You didn't have it after all."

"Of course I didn't have it," the boy said scornfully and went on with his reading.

Miss Garth glanced at him impatiently and then turned a fond look upon the little girl. "You mustn't tease us like that, dear," she said and came to watch my measuring with a critical air. There was an aura of violet scent about her that I found a little oppressive in the stuffy room.

Everything I observed here increased my feeling that what Mr. Reid had asked of me was impossible. No matter what the boy's need might be, he would welcome no further supervision, and Miss Garth would clearly resent any filching away of her authority. I would make this dress for Selina and end the matter there, I told myself firmly.

"Who was it in your family that died?" the boy asked, fixing me again with his queerly avid gaze.

I made no attempt to evade his question, but answered him simply before the governess could interfere. "My mother and my brother were killed in an accident a few months ago. By a runaway horse."

The child's eyes were dark and fixed, the iris almost as black as the pupils, and I sensed in him a thirst for horror that troubled me. In a moment he would ask for details, and I changed the subject quickly.

"Your face seems familiar to me, Jeremy. Perhaps I've seen you playing when I've walked through Washington Square."

The dark eyes flickered and excitement came into them. "I never play in the square," he said. "But my picture was in all the papers a couple of years ago—drawings of me. That's where you must have seen me."

"That is quite enough, Jeremy," Miss Garth snapped. "If you are through, Miss Kincaid, you had better go. The boy is becoming unduly excited. I can't think why you were brought to this room in the first place. Selina could have come to you in the schoolroom."

I put my things away in silence. There was nothing to be said to this woman, but my heart went out to the sullen, morbidly excited boy. His trouble was very different from Richard's, and I felt myself untutored for so disturbing an assignment. In spite of my pity, it was impossible for me to accept this post.

As I went into the gloomy hall, closing behind me the door to that overheated, tension-filled room, I had a sense of escape and at the same time the feeling that I was abandoning someone in dire need. If I did not try to help that boy, who would?

266

At the top of the stairway leading down to the second floor, where Mr. Reid awaited my decision in the library, I hesitated, torn and uncertain. The words Miss Garth had spoken flashed through my mind again—that phrase no one should use to a child, no matter what the provocation—"wicked boy." And suddenly I remembered. Jeremy had been right. The papers, spilling sensation across their pages, had first shown me his face. I recalled his father's name and identity now. Dwight Reid, the younger brother, had enjoyed a brief and brilliant career as District Attorney in New York, a career ended by a tragic accident with a gun—at the hands of this very boy. Yet, remembering, I found my sorrow mainly for the child, who must carry so terrible a guilt through the rest of his life.

Further indignation against Miss Garth for terming him wicked stirred in me. She would be a formidable woman to oppose, and I had no desire to enter a life of tumult and emotional conflict. Jeremy Reid had no suspicion that he had sent my way a plea for help. Indeed, if I offered him the slightest assistance, he would undoubtedly reject me at once. And yet . . . I had no choice. I'd had none since my first glance fell upon that face of a very young angel, dark and lost.

Resolutely I put doubt and reason behind me and followed my heart down the stairs to the library where Mr. Reid sat behind his desk, looking as though he had not stirred since I had left him there.

He rose when I entered the room, waiting in silence as I came toward him.

"I don't know whether there is anything I can do," I told him, "but I see the need. I would like to try—for a time at least. I will stay if I find myself failing."

He came round from behind the desk and held out his hand. His smile did not light his eyes. "Thank you, Miss Kincaid. All I have learned about you indicates courage. This acceptance most of all."

It was disconcerting to realize that I must have been covertly observed, that questions must have been asked about me, and all the small details of my life looked into.

I put my hand into the one he proffered, and his fingers closed over mine. There was a strange instant in which I sensed through his clasp something of the stormy force of this man, and it alarmed me. I drew my hand away too hurriedly and was aware that he noted the fact.

"I must tell you," I said, "that I have remembered the story the papers printed—though I don't know how much of it was true. I believe it was through an accident that your nephew shot and killed his father two years ago when he was seven."

A stiffening seemed to run through Brandon Reid. "Very little of what was printed during that unfortunate time was true," he assured me, his tone bitter.

I asked no questions then. Eventually I would have to know the full story. I would need to learn all I could about Jeremy Reid. If his uncle imagined that I would respect a natural reticence regarding the past, he would have to discard that notion. But this, I knew, was not the moment to press for information. There would be time later on.

"When would you like me to come, Mr. Reid?" I asked.

"As soon as possible. When may we expect you?"

There was nothing to keep me longer in the two rooms my young brother, my mother, and I had occupied in a boarding-house. It would be possible, I said, to come by the middle of next week. But if I were to approach the boy gradually and win his trust, I would prefer to come as a resident seamstress and appear to be working on frocks for Selina.

Mr. Reid thought this an excellent plan. There was a room I might have on the third floor next to Jeremy's. He would see that it was made ready. And he would send a carriage for me whenever I wished.

There was one point about which I felt uneasy. "I wonder," I began, "would it be wise to return for an interview with Mrs. Reid before . . ."

He broke in upon my words decisively. "The matter is settled, Miss Kincaid. We will expect you next Wednesday in the afternoon, if you can be ready by then."

He saw me to the door himself and added a last word before I left. "Would you mind very much if I request that you give up your mourning dress before you come here? The women in this house avoid black. It is better for Jeremy not to be reminded of death."

"Of course," I said. "I understand."

I did not mind. Black was something one wore in order to conform to custom. Grief for those who had gone was not based on the color of a dress, or the wearing of a black veil.

He opened the door for me and said a polite "Good day," but he did not offer his hand again. I went down the steep flight of marble steps and walked toward Broadway, where I could find transportation home. With every step away from the house, I could feel his eyes upon me and it was an effort not to look back.

CHAPTER 2

THERE WAS pain for me in the next few days. Once the dress order was completed I could give myself to packing my few possessions and to disposing of what it would not be wise to keep. My brother Richard's things were the hardest for me to touch. I gave away his toys except for a small music box carrousel he had loved. This I packed along with a few pieces of my mother's jewelry and my own trinkets and clothing.

By Wednesday afternoon, when Fuller, the Reid coachman, came to carry a portmanteau and small trunk to the carriage, I was ready. It was pleasant to travel in a victoria instead of by horsecar, and I tried not to look back, or to think of the ties with the past I was breaking.

This time the haughty butler was busy elsewhere and the little maid, who said her name was Kate, came cheerfully to let me in. She would not allow me to carry my portmanteau upstairs but took it herself. Mr. Reid was not in evidence, and I was led at once to the small room that had been prepared for me at the third-floor rear.

Kate set down my bag, murmured doubtfully that she hoped I would be comfortable, and hurried away. As before, she seemed eager to escape the third floor.

The small room had a bare, unwelcoming look, as though it had been prepared hastily with necessities rather than comforts. There was a narrow brass bedstead, with one of its brass head knobs missing, and a worn rag rug on the floor beside it. A plain, square table, its surface scarred and without covering, had been set before the window at the rear, a single straight chair drawn up to it. The bureau was tall and severe, topped by a somewhat watery mirror. The washstand needed varnishing, but the basin and pitcher upon its marble top were flowered and not unattractive. At least the room had a fireplace and a narrow mantel, and there was a good drop-front secretary, though paper had been folded under one leg to prevent its wobbling.

I told myself resolutely that the plain little room could be made attractive and I did not mind being given what came to hand. Nevertheless, the lack of tempering touches to indicate that someone thought kindly of my coming, left me, in my present mood, a little depressed. I took off my hat and hung my cloak on one of the bare hooks provided for my clothes. Today I wore a dress of gray-blue, serviceable, but not by any means the color of mourning.

I was about to approach the window and look out when a tap on the open door behind me made me turn. Miss Garth stood there, impressive in dark green, with an elaborate, bow-trimmed bustle, her heavy hair as fancifully combed as I had seen it before. She greeted me formally and without a smile. As I had sensed, I would find no welcome here.

"Mrs. Reid wishes to see you," she said curtly. "If you will come at once, please, since she is going out."

I nodded agreeably and followed her to the floor below. It had disturbed me that I had not seen Jeremy's mother on my previous visit and I was glad to have this matter remedied without delay.

As she walked ahead of me, I could not help but observe Miss Garth's high, proud carriage of shoulders and head. Again I would have found her handsome had she been less formidable.

She opened a door off the middle of the hall and showed me into a small, very feminine boudoir in which a lamp burned on a table and a fire was dying to red coals. A cushioned chaise longue of brocade and gilt, brocaded chairs, and a small marble-topped table, bearing a vase of flowers, made up its attractive furnishings. The single window looked out upon an air shaft shared with the next house and introducing gray-filtered daylight into the room. On my left hung long draperies of light-green velvet, perhaps hiding a door. On the right were similar draperies, half parted to reveal the adjoining bedroom.

Miss Garth stepped to this opening to announce my presence, and a woman came through to greet me. I could see at once that she was a great beauty, and she looked amazingly young to be the mother of two children. She was dressed for the street and her high-piled red hair gleamed beneath iridescent brown feathers on her hat. Her skin was pale and clear—the fair skin that went so delicately with that shade of hair. Her eyes, wide beneath dark lashes, had an amber tinge. Her gown was of a rich, deep violet, and over one arm she carried a sealskin cape. A muff of the same fur dangled from one slender hand. A knot of hothouse violets had been pinned to the fur, and there was a faint, delicious scent of violets about her. The odor made me wonder if Miss Garth had borrowed her perfume the other day when she had worn it so copiously.

In spite of the governess' urgent summons and the fact that Mrs. Reid was about to go out, there was no haste in her movements. She seemed rather languid and lacking in vitality. Her amber eyes were indifferent as she turned them upon me, and she brushed a hand across her forehead, as if troubled by pain. Nevertheless, when she spoke, her words recalled the imperious handwriting of the note she had sent me and I realized that this woman was not likely to condescend to friendliness.

"I must tell you, Miss Kincaid, that I do not approve of this experiment of my husband's. If Miss Garth is unable to help Jeremy, it is unlikely that a stranger can do any better. Naturally I will not oppose my husband's wishes, but I think it wise for you to understand my own feelings in the matter."

I was dazzled by her beauty and would have liked to win her respect and liking. I repeated what I had told Mr. Reid—that I would not stay if I found there was nothing I could do for the boy. But first I would like to try. Miss Garth sniffed audibly, and her mistress' eyes flicked her way, then back to my face.

"I am late for tea at Sherry's," Mrs. Reid said. "If you will excuse me . . ."

But I would not let her go as quickly as that. "Will you tell me when I may see you?" I said hurriedly. "There are matters I would like to consult you about as soon as possible."

She seemed surprised and reluctant, but she set the time of ten o'clock the following morning. Then she went gracefully past me to the door and Miss Garth and I stood looking after her.

The governess spoke aloud, though more to herself than to me. "A good thing it is for Miss Leslie to get out of this house and see her friends now and then. These days she stays too close to home."

"Isn't she well?" I asked.

Miss Garth remembered my presence with an impatient glance, but before she could answer there was a sound on the stairs and I turned to watch the encounter that took place. Mr. Reid was mounting from the lower floor, momentarily blocking his wife's descent.

My first glimpse of Brandon and Leslie Reid together was a picture I was to carry in my mind for a long while. How handsomely they were matched, those two! How right that his sort of man should have so beautiful a wife. Mr. Reid took his wife's hand affectionately, and the look he turned upon her was hardly less than ardent.

"You're off for tea, aren't you? Have a pleasant afternoon, darling," he said.

She turned her head languidly so that his kiss just grazed her cheek, and drew her slim, ringed hand from his touch. She did not answer him and a moment later she had moved out of sight down the stairs. Mr. Reid glanced at Miss Garth and me standing in the doorway of his wife's boudoir. He nodded to us casually and went by before I could so much as say, "Good afternoon." His look in my direction carried with it no recognition, and I must confess to a certain annoyance. After all, I had come here at his request. Yet apparently he had forgotten my face, or was now indifferent to my presence in this house.

Miss Garth flicked her handkerchief beneath her nose as if in disdain, and I caught a scent of lavender that was less lavish than the violet she had used the other day.

"Come," she said to me. "I'll show you where you can do your sewing on our floor upstairs. This is not a large house, you understand. It will be necessary to arrange some sharing."

Again we climbed the stairs, and she led me into a room at the back that was being used for lessons. A tutor came in to instruct the children five days a week, she explained. Naturally, she taught them French, deportment, and other graces. Since lessons were held only in the morning, the room was empty now. It could be used for my sewing as well as lessons, Miss Garth said, and pointed out the long table suitable for spreading materials, and the sewing machine that had been placed in a corner. It was a bare room, with an odor of books and chalk about it that was not unpleasant. To me it seemed a more comfortable place than the hot, crowded nursery at the front of the house. Nevertheless, there was a bleakness here that I regretted. It had always seemed to me that children respond best to cheerful surroundings and work better in them. At least it was so with my young brother Richard.

Well, we should see. I would have to move slowly, I knew. My mere presence was apparently a revolution in this house, and if Mr. Reid had not even recognized me at our second meeting, I might find myself with less backing than I had hoped for.

Miss Garth left me, and I returned to my own small room. This time I went at once to see what view I might have from the window. Its curtains were fresh and crisply white, and I looked out between their folds upon the mews behind our row of buildings. Across an alleyway were the stables and coach houses that serviced this block. There was brick paving and little in the way of vegetation, except for a hardy ailanthus tree that reached its branches toward my window. The long leaves were turning brown, and clusters of them had drifted on the bare ground beneath. Looking through the branches I could see Fuller the coachman rubbing down one of the horses. Beyond were nearby rooftops, but no great expanse of view. At least there would be human activity within sight, and the coming and going of domestics. The thought made me feel less alone.

Now I must unpack and begin to make something of this desolate little room. There was an insistent voice in my mind all too ready to ask how I had dared to give up a life that was at least familiar for the uncertain task that faced me in this house. My meeting with Mrs. Reid, her admission that she did not want me here, the indifference Mr. Reid had shown on our second encounter were far from reassuring. But I thrust these thoughts aside and went to work.

I could almost hear my mother's voice after the news of Father's death had reached us. "We must work, dearest—keep busy. It's the only way to lessen pain."

My first move was to light the coal fire, ready laid in the grate. The kindling caught at once, and lizard tongues of flame licked upward through the coals. No room could remain completely cheerless with a fire burning. Now that I had its gentle humming for company, I opened my portmanteau and began to hang up my clothes, set out a few of my possessions.

I found an embroidered table scarf and brought out my mother's blue Lowestoft tea set. I could never touch the pieces of that set without remembering her hands moving graciously from teapot to cups, without remembering how much she had enjoyed a pause in her afternoon's work for tea with Richard and me. The pang of loneliness was there again, and I fought it down.

There was no reason to feel sorry for myself. In a week I would have made this room my own, and I had an absorbing challenge ahead of me in the person of Jeremy Reid. How to approach him was my first concern, how to win his trust and then his liking. These were the things I must think about. I took out Richard's little musicbox carrousel that had cost me more than I should have spent one Christmas. Though I was glad now, for it had given him much pleasure. I wound the key and set it upon the mantel, where it made a gay touch of bright color. Small red and green and yellow figures on horses, a little sleigh with miniature children, turned merrily about and the old nursery favorite, "Frère Jacques," tinkled through the room.

A somewhat demanding knock summoned me to the door. I blinked away a stray tear and went to open it. On my threshold stood Selina Reid, her eyes dancing and soft folds of green China silk spilling through her hands.

"I have it!" she cried in triumph, holding up the material. "So when will you make my dress?"

Here, I thought, was my first approach to Jeremy, to learning all I could know about him. I stepped aside and invited her into my room. The carrousel still turned and the music played.

She walked directly to the mantel. "I like this," she said. "May I have it to play with?"

I shook my head gently. "It belonged to my brother, who is dead.

275

Sometimes when you visit me, I will wind it for you, but I don't let anyone else touch it."

She looked at me in no little surprise, and I gathered that few requests of Miss Selina's were refused in this house. All the more reason it was wise to have an understanding between us at once. She seemed to think better of sulking as I took the silk from her hands and examined it in admiration. What thin, soft stuff it was—like gossamer, yet strong and finely woven. The color was pale—the new green of leaves in the springtime. It would suit her coloring beautifully.

"We'll start your dress tomorrow," I assured her. "This is lovely silk. It will make up beautifully, though it's more suited to spring and summer than to chilly fall. I have some fashion books to help us. Perhaps we can design it together."

That pleased her, and she gave me a charming, sunny smile. "What am I to call you?" she asked. "I don't remember the name Garthy said when you came here before."

"Would you like to call me Miss Megan?" I suggested. "It seems more friendly than to use Kincaid."

She tried the name over softly to herself and then spoke it out loud as though she had decided to favor it. The music-box tune came to an end, and Selina suddenly remembered that she had been sent here with a message.

"Oh dear, I forgot! I'm to ask you to come downstairs at once for high tea. That's what we have at five-thirty in the dining room. It's an early supper really, but Miss Garth has been to England and she likes English ways. You are to eat your meals with us, Miss Megan."

Though it was early for supper, I could accommodate my habits, and I was happy to have this opportunity to join the others. This would enable me to see more of Jeremy.

We folded the China silk carefully and put it in a drawer of my bureau. Then, while Selina waited for me, I washed my hands in the blue-flowered basin. The Reids' house was extremely up-to-date in having a bathroom, but it was downstairs on the second floor. When I had poured the water into the slop jar hidden below and dried my hands, we went downstairs together.

For this dark and somber house, the dining room on the first floor was surprisingly bright. The dark paneling of the wall reached only halfway up, and above it a light wallpaper sprigged in delicate green gave the room a bright and airy appearance. The furnishings were elegant, as they were throughout the house, and a handsome chandelier hung from the center of a plaster medallion in the high ceiling. Through the glass doors of an enormous cabinet I could see an array of fine china and crystal.

At the front of the house French doors opened upon a small iron balcony overlooking the square. Though they were closed, the light of late afternoon poured in from the street.

Miss Garth and Jeremy were already seated at the long table, with a coal fire murmuring cheerfully beside them. Miss Garth's chair was, as always, closest to the blaze, but this was a large room and not easily made stuffy. Somewhat curtly she indicated my place at the table and remarked that promptness at mealtime was a virtue.

I found myself opposite Jeremy, who did not look at me at all. Through most of the meal he remained silent and remote, indifferent to those about him. He ate listlessly and without appetite, and more than once Miss Garth chided him, criticized his table manners, or urged him to finish what was on his plate.

Selina went her own charmingly impertinent way, often addressing her remarks to her brother, whether he paid any attention or not. She told him delightedly about the carrousel music box in my room and warned him not to touch it. She boasted about the new clothes she was to have, speaking as though "Miss Megan" were her private acquisition.

I remarked casually that when I had time I would perhaps make a new suit for Jeremy. Still he did not look at me, but he spoke in a rough, ill-mannered way.

"I don't want any new clothes. And I won't be measured or fitted."

"As you like," I told him. "I'll be quite busy as it is."

"You will have new clothes if your uncle wishes it," Miss Garth insisted.

For once the boy raised his eyes and threw her a quick, resentful look. "Why should my Uncle Brandon wish it? You know he hates me. You know he wishes I were dead."

I thought this a terrible and shocking thing for a little boy to say with such conviction and I wondered if Mr. Reid knew of this notion. But for the moment there was no way in which I could contradict it. I was still feeling my way toward an understanding of the relationships in this house. Until I knew the meaning behind the emotional undercurrents I sensed, I could not tread with safety on what might well be unstable ground.

When the long, wearing meal was over, I returned to my room and sat down in the single straight chair to think about the problems which rose like a series of mountain ranges ahead of me. It was clear that Jeremy wore a prickly armor all about him—armor without a visible chink. Yet he was a child and he had needs of which he could not be wholly aware. Needs perhaps that he had suppressed after the tragic accident in which his father had died. Somewhere there would be a way through his defenses, and I must find it. I must have the patience to wait and the wisdom to recognize the way when it presented itself. This seemed a very large order, and I did not dare allow myself to be frightened by it.

The evening, after so early a supper, stretched endlessly ahead, and I found myself restless. I knew that ladies did not walk alone after dark in New York streets. The assaults of footpads and thugs, the accosting of lone women, and even unarmed men, were commonplace in these dreadful times. But to sit here for hours when I did not feel like reading or sewing seemed a greater danger to my spirits than was possible outward danger to my person.

I put on the gray dolman mantle with its capelike top that my mother had made me in a new and fashionable style, and tied gray bonnet ribbons under my chin. When I left my room I found the upper floor quiet and I heard and saw no one on my way downstairs. But as I descended the lower flight, I came upon a scene so magical, so warmly felicitous, that I paused with my hand on the rail and stared without conscience.

The double doors to the dining room had been left open, and I could look down upon the long table where the children and I had so recently sat through that unhappy meal with Miss Garth. Now the table was bright with fine linen and silver. Lavish chrysanthemums made a centerpiece, and candles burned in branched candelabra. At each end of the table sat the master and mistress of this strange household.

Again Leslie Reid's beauty caught at my breath. What is it a woman feels when she beholds such perfection in another woman? There is envy perhaps—but I think curiosity as well. We look and marvel and try to see this vision as a man must see her, and thus gain some knowledge of what it is we ourselves should emulate.

Mrs. Reid had dressed for dinner in a yellow brocade gown that set off her red hair—more beautiful than ever now that she wore no hat. Diamonds shone at her ear lobes and on her fingers. Candlelight enhanced and softened the amber of her eyes.

When I had studied his wife, seeking an answer to a tantalizing enigma, I looked at Mr. Reid to observe his response. Henry, the haughty butler, was serving, and as Henry helped him from a silver dish, Brandon Reid bent the same ardent attention upon his wife that I had noted earlier in the day. He was asking her about her afternoon, as a husband might, and she was answering him, seemingly less remote and cool now, telling him of someone she had seen at Sherry's. There was a vivacity in her manner that had been lacking before.

I believe I am not more envious than others. Yet in that moment I ached with loneliness and—let us call it longing, rather than envy, since that is a kinder word. How fortunate Leslie Reid was —there at her own attractive table, with a husband so attentive, so loving and admiring.

Mrs. Reid remarked on a draft just then, and the butler came toward the doors to close them. I blinked the vision from my eyes and fled down the stairs and out through the heavy front door to Washington Square. I would walk until I was weary and drink in great draughts of fresh air and forget those who dined graciously by candlelight.

Only a few years before, the old Washington Parade Grounds had undergone a transformation, turning the square into one of the most beautiful parks in the city. Flower beds had been set out and shade trees planted. The sidewalks were of concrete, the roadways of new wood paving—all centering about a huge fountain basin and converging into Fifth Avenue.

I had read in the papers that some political chicanery had resulted in the building of more lamp posts than was necessary in the square. At least it was the best lighted park in the city. The lamplighter had already gone his rounds and in such a brilliance of gaslight there seemed little danger that any of the city's criminal element would be abroad. I walked along the paths and around the broad basin of the fountain, my feet scattering crisp leaves at every step.

The scene at the dining table still haunted me. I hoped that Mrs. Reid was kind to so obviously loving a husband, and that he was gentle and loving with her. From my observation he had not seemed a particularly gentle person, but perhaps he reserved this quality for his beautiful wife.

Her coolness earlier had perhaps been due to some small marital spat. My mind skipped and speculated. What had Dwight Reid been like? Had the younger brother been as fascinating as the older? Fascinating? Now where had I come upon such a word for a man who repelled me no little?

I could recall only a smattering of information about Dwight Reid. He had been something of a Galahad in city politics, fighting crime, helping those in need, and doing a great deal of good during his time in office. The papers had seemed to attack him less than they did other men in our venal public life, and his death had been a blow to the honest element of the entire city. Since Leslie had married him first, he must have been the better man. How dreadfully the whole household must have suffered over his death. Yet in a year's time she had married the older brother. Now how had that come about?

So my thoughts ran in the manner of a mind which lacks sufficient life of its own to feed upon.

I walked briskly around the square, glad to see others out on this pleasant autumn evening. I put my speculations aside and by the time I returned to the house, I had cleared my head of cobwebby doubts and foolish envy. Tomorrow I must be up early, ready to approach my new duties.

As I reached the steps I glanced up and saw that the dining room was still radiantly lighted and that Mr. Reid had come to stand in one long window, open now upon the square. I lowered my eyes and hurried across the sidewalk, thinking he would not observe me, or would ignore me if he did.

But he called out to me suddenly. "Catch!" he cried, and I looked up in surprise to see him toss out something that resembled a yellow ball. I moved instinctively, without thinking. Often I had played ball with young neighbors, and even a bit with Richard, who could not throw or catch very well. I reached up with both hands and caught the sphere of yellow as it fell toward me. The man in the window above laughed out loud as he closed the shutters. I stood there foolishly, holding in my hands the orange I had caught in so unexpected a manner.

I couldn't help smiling as I let myself into the house with the latchkey Kate had given me. Mr. Reid was nowhere in sight as I went upstairs, but now I knew something I had not known before. It seemed that the dark and somber Brandon Reid could also be a man of light impulse. He knew perfectly well who I was, and though this was an odd way of showing it, I felt somehow reassured.

My steps were soft on the carpeted stairs. The second floor was as usual dimly lighted by its single globe-encased gas jet. The small figure bending before a closed door next to Mrs. Reid's boudoir did not hear me until I was directly behind him. Then he whipped around to face me with one hand hidden behind his back. But not quickly enough, for I had glimpsed the key in Jeremy's fingers. We stared at each other, equally surprised, and it was the boy who spoke first.

"You'd better not tell Garth," he whispered, and there was a threatening note in the words.

I answered him calmly. "I really don't know anything to tell."

He gave me a long look, guarded and enigmatic, before he dashed ahead of me up the stairs. By the time I reached the floor above, all doors were closed and I went to my own room, feeling more pity for the child than anything else. What secretive life went on behind that darkly handsome young face? To what room had he a hidden key, and why?

Before I went to bed I peeled and ate the orange Mr. Reid had tossed me. Its tangy aroma scented the air and clung to my fingers. Somehow, in spite of the strange happenings of the day I felt more determined than ever to help Jeremy Reid. And I did not feel nearly so discouraged.

CHAPTER 3

THE NEXT morning I was up early. As Kate had explained to me, all of us on the third floor—myself, Miss Garth, and the two children—were expected to breakfast in the nursery and stay out of the dining room mornings. In the crowded nursery I found a pot of hot coffee on the table and a covered dish of scrambled eggs, cold toast, butter, and marmalade. It was pleasant to eat alone and then get to work in the schoolroom, setting my things out at one end of the long table. Perhaps I could make a start before the tutor came for lessons.

I was deep in fashion books, searching for a style that would become the flyaway sprite that was Selina, when Miss Garth came to summon me to Mrs. Reid's room. Jeremy's mother would see me now instead of later. She had slept badly and was having an early breakfast in bed. I was to come downstairs at once. Again the summons seemed imperious, though perhaps that was due to Miss Garth's delivery.

This time I was taken directly into the front bedroom adjoining the green and gold boudoir. It was a room of satin and lace, of furbelows and mirrors. But in spite of the fact that bright morning pressed at the windows, the gold brocade draperies were drawn and the light that lay upon the room was cast wholly by flickering candles. Set upon the highboy was a branched candelabrum of silver, its six candles burning tall. Small candleholders of painted china lighted each side of the dressing-table mirror, and beside the hearth stood a giant brass candlestick awash with golden light.

There was no denying that this soft illumination flattered and enhanced the beauty of the woman in the bed.

She sat up with lacy pillows behind her, a small lap table across her knees. Her red hair, tied youthfully with a green ribbon at the top of her head, fell about her shoulders, and its warmth held my eyes. Once more I caught the whisper of a light violet scent pervading the room.

Miss Garth left me there, and I was glad to see her go. I might accomplish more with Mrs. Reid without the presence of the governess.

This morning I was prepared with specific questions and a few suggestions, but Mrs. Reid, sipping coffee, and playing delicately with a bowl of fruit, took the interview from my hands. She invited me to draw a chair beside the bed and began to speak of my duties and hours with the somewhat haughty air of mistress to servant.

"Perhaps," she said, "it will be possible for you to help with the children on Sundays when Garthy goes to visit her father. Perhaps you can also free her on an occasional evening when I need her, or when she wishes an hour or so away from the house. She is more than a governess, you know. Much of the management of this house rests in her hands, since I am not strong enough to cope with it. I am not always well, and, as a result, Miss Garth has been overworked."

I would be happy to comply, I agreed, but I did not mean to have this interview entirely one-sided and when she had paused and turned to her tray as if she were done with me, I began my questions.

"I've been wondering about the children's activities," I said. "What sort of things do they like to do? What are Jeremy's main interests? When I understand these matters I will be in a better position to make friends. Not that this will be difficult with Selina. We already have a bond between us because of the dress I'm making for her."

Leslie Reid looked slightly bored. "Oh, yes—the China silk. I had planned to use it myself, but my husband believes this is more important."

She yawned, tapping her fingers to her mouth, and seemed to forget me and my questions.

"You were going to tell me about the children's interests, Mrs. Reid," I prodded gently.

"Was I? But what is there to tell? I suppose they like the usual things. Dolls, toys, games—what else?"

"A boy of nine often has some special fancy that absorbs him," I pointed out.

The woman in the bed gave me her sudden, full attention, and there was a note of distress in her voice as she spoke. "He has become such a difficult child—not at all like other boys. He seems to enjoy destructive things. Miss Garth and I, and even his tutor, Mr. Beach, are at our wits' end to deal with him. My husband feels that you may have something new to offer the boy. We will be more than grateful if you can turn him from his present course of moody wildness, but as I've told you, I have little hope of this, Miss Kincaid."

"Perhaps that's the one thing we must never let him sense," I said. "That we have lost hope would be too discouraging. Perhaps he needs a belief in his ability to grow. Has he no special pastimes? No hobbies?"

Leslie Reid's long lashes fluttered for an instant upon pale cheeks, and a shiver seemed to run through her.

"My son is fond of guns," she said. "Dwight—his father—had a collection of fine pistols with which Jeremy was obsessed. I warned my husband long ago that such an interest was not wise for a child. But no one would heed me."

This, I sensed, was dangerous ground, and it would not help me in my search for Jeremy's interests. I spoke again of the dress I would make for Selina, asking whether Mrs. Reid wished to instruct me as to the style. Again she seemed listless and ready to leave the matter in my hands, eager only to have our interview come to an end. I asked if there were any particular hours she liked to spend with the children, any time that should be saved for her visits with them.

She pushed the tray from her with a small gesture of distaste and tugged at a bell rope beside her bed.

"Selina comes to see me here whenever she likes. Often I take her with me when I go for a drive. But when it comes to Jeremy,

I can find no pleasure in his company. This is not an easy matter for me, Miss Kincaid."

She reached toward the table beside her bed and picked up a double miniature in twin silver frames. Wordlessly she handed it to me, and I saw that it contained the portraits of two men. From one side Brandon Reid's dark countenance looked out at me, his mouth unsmiling, his eyes upon faraway things. The other man was totally different in appearance, though I knew this must be Dwight Reid. The younger brother had a bright, sunny look about him. Except for his fair coloring he resembled his son amazingly. He was younger and far handsomer in a boyish way than was Brandon Reid. I returned the miniature, wondering why she had shown it to me.

"You may have heard of my first husband," she said. "There were many who blessed his name. Since his death, New York citizens have been building a memorial to honor him—the Dwight Reid Memorial Home, which will be opened before long and will care for homeless children. Dwight had a great future ahead of him. It's possible that he might have been governor, or gone on to the national legislature."

I waited, troubled by the sudden flash of feeling I saw in her face. The amber eyes were no longer cold, but misted with tears when she turned them upon me.

"It was all destroyed—everything! Do you understand? Do you see why it may be painful for me to have Jeremy in my company?"

For the first time my sympathy went out to her, and yet I could not accept her attitude. Jeremy was a child, whatever he might have done.

"I can understand," I told her. "Yet even something so dreadful must be forgiven when the boy's life and sanity hang in the balance. Perhaps your son blames himself more than anyone else can possibly blame him. Perhaps he is in desperate need of love and help."

Diamonds flashed on Leslie Reid's hand as she brushed it across her face. Listlessness had fallen upon her again.

"Do as you wish," she said. "I am not an unnatural mother, but he is an unnatural son."

Kate tapped on the door and came in to remove the lap table

and tray. The interview was over, and I followed the maid soberly from the room. At least I knew now that there was little I could hope for from Jeremy's mother. Undoubtedly her wounds had been as deep and as shocking as the boy's. In spite of her marriage to Dwight's brother, it was clear that she had not entirely recovered from the experience. It was not for me to judge her, but my sympathy still lay with her son.

In the hall I spoke to Kate as we passed the door in front of which I had found Jeremy the night before.

"What room is this?" I asked.

Kate gave the door a quick, fearful look and paused at the head of the back-stairs flight. "It's no one's room now, miss. But it used to belong to him that—that died. Cook says it was right in there it happened. They keep it locked now. And a good thing it is I'm no believer in haunting."

She hurried downstairs, and I returned thoughtfully to the third floor. How strange that Jeremy should have a key to his father's locked room.

When I reached the schoolroom, I found that someone was there ahead of me. A man stood before the table where I had left the folds of China silk, and he seemed to be surveying the room with an air of wry dismay. This, of course, was the tutor, and I could not blame him for regarding my intrusion with something less than enthusiasm.

"Good morning," I said. "I'm Megan Kincaid. They've put me here to work on a frock for Selina. I hope I won't be too much in your way."

He turned his attention from the table to me, and I faced Andrew Beach for the first time. I could not know then the role he was to play in my life and I saw before me only a young man of rather nondescript appearance. He was of medium height, stocky, and rugged of feature. Like Mr. Reid he was clean-shaven in this day when mustaches were the fashion. His brown hair fell over a high forehead and his eyes, regarding me from beneath sandy lashes, were a bright blue and sharply perceptive. There was a twist to his smile as he returned my greeting and introduced himself. I suspected that he might be as ready to laugh at Andrew Beach as at the rest of the world.

"I'll admit," he said, "that I was prepared to object strongly to having my schoolroom invaded by your pins-and-needles brigade. But now that I've met the dressmaker, I withdraw my opposition." He made me a mocking bow, his look impertinently flattering.

Somehow I could not take offense or resent his words. Even when the day came that he became critical of me and outspoken in his disapproval, I could never be angry for long with Andrew Beach. There was a quality in him that disarmed one at the very moment when his words cut deepest.

"I know my presence will make it difficult for you with the children," I told him, "but I'll do my best to distract them as little as possible. My work at the sewing machine can be postponed till afternoon and—"

"Don't worry," he said. "If I can't make my lessons interesting enough to hold my pupils in spite of your competition, then I'm not much of a teacher, am I?"

Relieved, I began to clear everything to the far end of the school table. And as Mr. Beach set out his books and papers, I studied him covertly. Here, I suspected, was my road to the understanding of Jeremy's interests and problems that Mrs. Reid had not given me. But I did not want to launch outright into questions. For all this young man knew, I was merely the hired seamstress with nothing more on my mind than the making of frocks for Selina.

It was he who disabused me of this notion and opened a door between us before the children came in for their lessons.

"You might as well know," he said over his shoulder as he wrote something on a small blackboard, "that I've been told why you are here. And I might as well add that I don't envy you the task you've taken on."

"You mean—Jeremy?" I said. "But isn't he your task too?"

"Not in the same way, I'm relieved to say."

I asked my questions hurriedly then, no longer dissembling. "Perhaps you can help me more than anyone else. There are surely subjects which interest Jeremy. If I am to make friends with him, I must find an approach. His mother would tell me nothing."

For all his wry mockery, there could be a gentleness in Andrew Beach, as I saw for the first time.

"How could she?" he asked. "Mrs. Reid has her own suffering

to live through. I can only tell you that the boy has withdrawn inside himself. Those of us who are with him constantly know this. His uncle won't face it. Perhaps Mr. Reid's conscience troubles him. Who knows?"

I did not understand what Brandon Reid's conscience had to do with the matter, but I had another question to put to this young man while I had the opportunity.

"How long have you been tutoring the Reid children?" I inquired.

He put down the chalk and dusted his fingers. "Nearly two years. A very long time, it seems to me, when I consider it."

Two years? It had been two years ago that Dwight Reid had died. Had Andrew Beach been here during that time? I wondered.

He seemed to guess my thoughts. "I was not here when the tragedy occurred," he told me. "Though I had occasion to come to the house very soon after. Later it was decided that Jeremy needed a man to take him in hand, and I was offered the task. To little good effect, I'm afraid. But if you don't mind, Miss Kincaid, there are some things I don't particularly want to talk about."

I flushed at his implication. "I've no intention of prying and I am not a gossip," I said with spirit.

His good nature returned, and he grinned at me in impudent mockery as if he did not believe my words.

I returned to my main quest, caring little what he thought. "If you've held this position for so long, Mr. Beach, then you must know something of Jeremy. You must have learned what interested him before the accident. I don't mean his father's pistol collection. Mrs. Reid has already mentioned that."

Andrew Beach seemed to muse over my question. "I believe the seeds of trouble have always been evident in the boy. His nature is high-strung, even violent at times. It's likely that he would have been in serious difficulty sooner or later. And it's likely that he will be again. Do you understand that, Miss Kincaid?"

I nodded impatiently. Jeremy was a child and in grave need of help. "I want to know everything about him I can learn," I persisted.

"There's little I can tell you," he said. "I believe he was devoted to his uncle in the past and fascinated by Mr. Brandon Reid's travels to distant places. Miss Garth has mentioned that he used to enjoy stories about Egypt and the work his uncle has conducted in expeditions there."

Egypt? Expeditions? I recalled a certain strangeness about Brandon Reid. Perhaps there was a quality in those who had beheld far horizons that set them apart from the rest of us, who merely dreamed. My interest quickened.

"I didn't know that Mr. Reid had worked in such expeditions," I said.

"It was the Reid money that worked," Andrew Beach assured me sardonically. "Brandon's mother died when he was young, and she left him wealthy in his own right. For all that his father wished him to join the firm of attorneys headed by his name, Master Brandon chose another course. It's probable that he lacked his younger brother's flare and brilliance. His taste was for adventure, and he had an interest in Egyptology. He had the money as well to call in experts to take charge of the actual work. So he has been off in Egypt and India and other distant places much of the time for a good many years. That is, until his brother died and he settled down in this house to become a tamely married man."

There was a scornful undercurrent here telling me clearly that Andrew Beach did not like his employer. None of which mattered to me.

"If the boy was interested in Egypt once, then perhaps he can be interested again," I said. "My father was a history teacher, and I've always been fascinated by the subject."

The tutor regarded me in quiet appraisal. "You are very young, Miss Kincaid. You have a good deal to learn. But don't say I haven't warned you."

I did not care to be weighed and dismissed as if I were a child. "Warned me of what? Will you tell me clearly what you mean?"

"The boy is not interested in Egypt or anything else. He has gone outside our reach. Do you think I haven't tried? Do you think I've not seen the road he was taking and attempted to bring him back? His uncle is too much occupied elsewhere to see what has happened. Or he's afraid to see it. I'm not certain which. You've been given a thankless task, Miss Kincaid. An older, wiser woman would have refused it. I can only hope that you've given up nothing else of consequence to come here."

This young man was probably not yet thirty, and I found his patronizing attitude toward my youth ridiculous and infuriating.

"I have given up nothing of consequence," I said stiffly. "If experience means the facing of difficult problems, then I'm not so young as you think."

With that I turned to my sewing materials, ignoring the faintly pitying amusement with which he regarded me. I had no intention of accepting his word as final, no matter how well he thought he knew Jeremy. If I gave up, the boy's future might be dark indeed. So far I had yet to take my first steps in his direction and I did not discourage easily. If no one in this house would help me, then I must manage to help myself.

CHAPTER 4

In the days that followed, the children grew accustomed to my presence in the schoolroom, in the house. Selina, at least, accepted me in a friendly, though slightly superior, manner. Since Jeremy seemed to move in some remote world of his own with little recognition of those about him, I could not tell, much of the time, whether he knew I was there.

As I sat sewing during lessons, I had considerable opportunity to observe him. He did not seem to dislike Andrew Beach as he did Miss Garth, but so neutral an attitude could hardly be called liking. He did what he was told, and I found his obvious skill in mathematics and in answering questions on paper an encouraging sign. Mr. Beach let me look at his written work, and while it now and again indicated a mind that followed tortuous routes, there was obvious intelligence revealed. Yet he would not recite aloud at all. While Selina chattered away, giving wrong answers blithely, Jeremy froze into sullen resistance whenever he was asked to recite. Only by an occasional scornful glance was it possible to see that he thought his sister foolish and could easily have corrected her answers.

Nevertheless, for all her teasing and her spoiled ways, he did not seem to dislike his sister. She could approach him as no one else dared, and I noted more than once that both Miss Garth and Mr. Beach reached him through her when they could get his attention in no other way.

Mealtime was always an unhappy period, though more bearable at midday because it was the custom for Andrew Beach to be with us then. He stood in no awe of Miss Garth and often teased her mercilessly, paying her exaggerated compliments, pretending to flirt with her. That she had no love for him was evident, and there were times when she would plead a headache and retire, merely to avoid him.

During this period I came to know a little more about the children's tutor. I discovered that he had a talent for sketching and a flare for caricature. Occasionally his lampoons on city officials appeared in James Gordon Bennett's *New York Herald,* and in his spare time he often visited courtrooms and drew sketches of those on trial. Tutoring had given him this steady position in the Reid household and provided him with a living. From some of his drawings I had cause to think that he might do well if he applied himself seriously to his talent.

Of the Reids I saw little in those early days. Now and then I passed Mrs. Reid in the halls and she nodded absently, offering me no opportunity to speak to her. As Miss Garth had intimated that first day, she seldom left the house, seldom entertained, and seemed content to nurse her precarious health in the candlelit twilight of her green and gold rooms. For all her imperious ways, she seemed a strangely shadowy figure in the house.

Mr. Reid was often away at one museum or another during this time, delving into matters concerning the excavation of historic ruins, in which he was still interested. Sometimes, I learned, he visited his invalid father, who lived with a sister in a New Jersey seacoast town. These visits seemed to give him both pleasure and concern, and he often came home from them in a saddened mood.

Kate was my cheerful informant on all these affairs, volunteering information without being questioned. I was eager to know all I could, for only through knowledge could I help Jeremy, and I made no effort to still her chatter.

I soon came to note how quiet the house seemed without my employer's vigorous and somewhat disquieting presence. He too, now that he had installed me here, showed no further interest in what I might or might not be accomplishing. I told myself that I did not care. The only thing that mattered was how I moved ahead in my relationship with Jeremy.

As far as the boy was concerned, I still bided my time, allowing him to accustom himself to my presence, learning perhaps that he could trust me a little. After all, he must realize that I had not betrayed my knowledge of the key in his possession.

During this time I became increasingly aware of the favoritism shown to Selina. Miss Garth clearly doted on her, and the child even wound Andrew Beach around her small fingers. When things went wrong with Selina's studies—a common enough matter—the tutor was summoned at once to confer with Mrs. Reid. But no one bothered to consult about Jeremy and I found myself growing jealous for the boy, indifferent though he was to my presence.

All too quickly October's mild days slipped away and it was mid-November. The green silk dress was finished to my lady Selina's pleasure, though not to that of Miss Garth, who remarked that she could have done better herself. While I did not admit it, I felt she was probably right, and the next frock I began to work on was of a less ambitious pattern.

One morning I put my work aside and slipped out of the schoolroom for a walk through the neighborhood. It was time, I felt, for a definite move in Jeremy's direction. On my wanderings through Greenwich Village I had noted a basement bookshop and it was to this I went that morning. I had seen maps in the window, and it was a map I wanted.

"Of Egypt," I told the bespectacled bookseller. "And I'd also like a book about recent expeditions and excavations in that country."

Fortunately he had both a large map and a recent book by a well-known authority on Egyptology. Pleased with my finds, I started home, my parcels under my arm. The first step had been made in purchasing the bait. Now it must be tactfully placed in the hope of attracting a nibble.

As I walked toward the square I passed a billboard advertising a lighthearted comedy in which Cicely Mansfield had recently opened. I paused to read every word while a new idea came into my mind. I had always loved the theater and with my present fine salary I should be able to attend an occasional performance. But this notice appealed to me because it was the sort of play children might enjoy. I would consult Mr. Reid about taking them both to a matinee. What child could reject or resist the magic of the theater? It was the sort of thing Jeremy needed.

While Selina had friends whom she visited, and who came to play with her, Jeremy seemed to have no one. There was no gaiety in his life, no playtime. Sometimes he read the novels of Dickens, of the French author Victor Hugo, the romances of Sir Walter Scott, or other such light reading. But often when he was not at lessons he would sit staring at nothing with a blind, vacant look that I felt was a mask for some frightening tumult that went on within. A matinee would be good for him, if Mr. Reid approved. It did not occur to me to ask his mother.

I returned to the schoolroom during the recess that Andrew wisely ordained in mid-morning. The young should frequently stretch their legs, he said, and have their stomachs filled. So he would send them off to the nursery for milk or hot chocolate, and do some very wide stretching and yawning himself, oblivious of my presence.

Miss Garth was with him when I stepped into the room, stiffly consulting over some problem of Selina's unsatisfactory lessons. I paid no attention to either of them, but unrolled my map upon the table to admire the brightly colored area where fabled Cairo, the Pyramids, and the Nile had their being. I could not read these names without a tingle of excitement running through me. Surely they would bring a response from Jeremy.

"What have we here?" Andrew asked and came to stand beside me.

Miss Garth glanced at the map and sniffed in disdain.

I was not discouraged. "It's time for action," I said. "Perhaps the map will interest the boy. And if it doesn't, I have a book—" I patted my brown paper package. "Furthermore, I mean to ask Mr. Reid if he will permit me to take Selina and Jeremy to see Cicely Mansfield in her new play. A Saturday matinee, of course, so there'll be no interfering with lessons, or staying up too late at night."

I was so pleased with myself that I did not at once note the silence that greeted this announcement. When I looked up from the map I saw incredulity in Miss Garth's eyes. She was struggling for speech, while Andrew clearly stifled an impulse to laugh out loud.

"What is it?" I asked in bewilderment. "What have I said?"

Miss Garth answered me coldly. "Miss Mansfield is a person of low reputation. Mrs. Reid will certainly not approve of your taking the children to see her. The idea is outrageous."

As if she could scarcely contain her indignation, Miss Garth flicked a lavender-scented handkerchief to her nose and swept regally from the room. I could only turn to Andrew in bewilderment.

"You've shocked the lady to her very toes," he told me, chuckling. "You're going too fast for her, I'm afraid. But I'm with you on this, Megan. Go ahead and beard Reid in his den. Tell him to get you those tickets. A little excitement will be good for this mausoleum of a house."

It was odd how easily Andrew and I had fallen into the use of first names. There was an informality about him that dispensed with anything stuffy. I did not feel that I knew him well—indeed, I kept glimpsing facets to his character that surprised and puzzled me—yet I felt quite comfortable in calling him Andrew. It was good to have him behind me on this, and I told him so. A little to my surprise his amusement vanished.

"Don't count on me," he said. "Never count on anything when it comes to a man, Megan. Stay safe and doubt us all."

This sudden shift puzzled me. "Then you don't think this matinee—"

He slapped one square hand down on the map of Egypt. "Put this away for now. And listen to me, Megan. No one in this house has been fair to you—including myself. But Mr. Reid is to blame most of all. There is a conspiracy to keep the truth from you. However, no one has asked me to be silent and I think you must know."

His words alarmed me. "What must I know?"

Once more an odd, rare gentleness of tone wiped away the mockery. "It was no accident in which Dwight Reid was killed. His son shot him to death deliberately, monstrously. The boy planned exactly what he meant to do and he carried out the plan. All this was kept from the papers. Brandon Reid would do almost anything to keep the family name unsullied—mainly for his father's sake, I think. There was scandal, of course, but not as bad as it might have been. Between them, he and Leslie convinced the police that it was an accident. Those who knew better were silent. I can sympathize with the purpose behind this action. The truth would have been far worse for everyone, and particularly for the unfortunate boy."

I heard him through in growing dismay, but I was not yet ready to accept his words as fact.

"How do you know these things?" I asked. "If you came here afterwards . . . ?"

He answered me almost curtly. "Jeremy was taken into court. I was there for my paper to do sketches of those concerned. I couldn't help feeling sorry for the boy, and the drawing I did of him was kinder than others that appeared in the papers. Because of that drawing, I came to Brandon Reid's attention and he learned that I did odd tutoring work when I had the chance. He called me in for an interview, since Mrs. Reid was leaning heavily on him for assistance at that time. I seemed to suit them, and they gave me the task of coming here mornings to instruct the children."

"They told you the truth when you were employed?" I asked.

Andrew shook his head. "Not immediately. They couldn't be sure of my discretion at first. When they were convinced that I wouldn't run to my paper with the story, Mrs. Reid told me exactly what had happened. She felt that I must know that Jeremy was capable of dangerous, deliberate violence. Just as I feel you must know now, Megan. They've let it go too long."

My sense of horror and shock were not because of any fear for myself, but because I could now realize the weight that lay on Jeremy's shoulders. How could a young, unformed mind deal with so dark a crime? The problem seemed larger now, more appalling, but this new knowledge did not deter me.

"You are not afraid of the boy," I said to Andrew. "Why should I be?"

"I am a man. And I don't live in this house. Did you know that Miss Garth sleeps with her door locked at night? She has said so."

"I would expect that of her in any case," I said. I felt disturbed and angry without recognizing as yet the true direction of my anger.

We could hear the children leaving the nursery down the hall, and Andrew spoke to me hurriedly. "You are a generous person, Megan. Don't let your generosity be given in so wasteful an effort."

I did not answer. There was no time, for the children were in the room. Besides, I already knew that Andrew considered Jeremy beyond recall. He considered my hiring a foolish last effort on the part of Brandon Reid to save his brother's son. But I have always been of an independent frame of mind. Too much so at times, as my father used to tell me. At any rate, I was far from ready to give up without trying. My campaign with the boy had only just begun.

I found myself looking at him compassionately, wondering what torturing, confused thoughts went on behind that handsome young brow. He sensed my regard and for once he looked at me uneasily as if he could not altogether dismiss me as he dismissed Miss Garth. That was fine, I thought. Let him come out of his apathy and puzzle about me a little.

Selina had begun to babble about the return of her Uncle Brandon from his latest trip. He had brought her a new doll, and she could not wait to go and play with it. How dull to do sums on such a morning!

"He brought Jeremy a game," she added. "But Jeremy will only break it up or throw it away. I don't know why Uncle Brandon bothers."

"The games he brings me are childish," Jeremy said.

But you are a child, I thought to myself. You are not an elderly, world-weary criminal, poor little boy.

The news that Mr. Reid was home gave a sudden focus to my rising indignation. Now I had an object for my anger. Andrew was perfectly right. I should have been told the truth when I was brought into this house. How did they think I could be useful when my whole conception of what had happened was incorrect?

Gathering up my rolled map and the book on Egypt, I took them to my room and summoned Kate. When she came upstairs I requested her to ask Mr. Reid if he would grant me some time at his earliest convenience. She was back in a few moments to say that if I would wait for him in the library Mr. Reid would see me in ten minutes.

I wasted not a second but flew downstairs to await his coming. A fire had been newly started, but the day was dark and the common gloom of the house penetrated to the library this morning. A jet globe burned high on one wall, and an oil lamp had been lighted on the great mahogany desk. I did not sit down, but stood looking about me. It was the first time I had really studied the room. When I had been here before, my employer's presence had held my full attention and I had scarcely noted my surroundings.

Now I observed the portrait of a distinguished, bewhiskered gentleman over the mantel. He had Mr. Reid's strong nose and firm jaw line, and he was extremely sober of expression. Mr. Reid's father, undoubtedly—Rufus Reid, whose reputation had once been without peer in the courts of law.

I noted too the indications of wide travel on every hand. An elephant tusk rose in an ivory column at one end of the mantel, and dwarfed beside it was a little jade Buddha. In a nearby glass case were amulets, seals, and tiny figurines that I learned later were made of diorite, quartzite, and the fragile blue faïence that dated back to the Eighteenth Dynasty in Egypt.

Then as I turned, I saw the object that dominated the entire room. Once the eyes rested upon it, it was difficult to look away. The life-sized head and shoulders of a man had been sculptured in some whitish stone and polished to a cool sheen. The head stood on a pedestal before a tier of bookshelves and it was recognizable at once as Egyptian. The tall headdress, almost like a bishop's miter, but decorated with the rippling body of a snake, its head raised above the human forehead, was clearly Egyptian. The stylized beard, the elongated eyes, were those I had seen in drawings of Egyptian art.

So strongly did the stone face hold my attention that it made me forget for a moment why I had come to this room. It seemed a narrower face than that of most Egyptian statues and ageless in its expression, with maturity of wisdom in the brow and in the all-seeing eyes. The nose was proudly aristocratic, while the mouth betrayed a trace of tolerant humor in its curves. This man had been a king, I was sure, and no mere princeling or nobleman. Yet, for all the stylization, a living man had surely been its model. One sensed in the eyes, the brow, the mouth, those same tribulations and emotions which burden men who walk the earth today, and who in turn must belong to antiquity.

I didn't hear Brandon Reid's step on the soft carpet, did not know he stood behind me till he spoke.

"I see you've made the acquaintance of Osiris. You know who he is, I presume?"

I knew of the cult of Osiris. "Lord of the dead and judge of all souls in the hereafter," I said softly. "Yet I think he must have been a man first. A man who learned wisdom through suffering."

My employer's eyes, so cool and gray, regarded me with a certain surprise, as though he had not expected my comment on the statue.

"This came from a tomb in Egypt," he said. "I couldn't resist keeping it for the time being, though eventually it must go to a museum."

"You found it yourself?" I asked.

His smile was disparaging. "I was permitted to brush the earth away from the surface when the discovery was made. I am not regarded as a trained archaeologist. But I'm sure, Miss Kincaid, that you didn't come here to talk about Egypt."

"Oh, but I did!" I told him and almost smiled at his increasing surprise.

He waved me toward a chair beside the fire, but today he did not retreat behind the great expanse of the desk. Instead, he seated himself on a corner of it, with one leg swinging, and regarded me intently.

"You have a report for me about Jeremy?" he prompted, since I did not at once follow up my remark about Egypt.

I was marshaling both my thoughts and my indignation and I straightened in my chair. "I have no report as yet. I've been giving the boy time to grow accustomed to my presence. Now I'm ready to make certain moves in his direction. But I've just been told the truth about his father's death, Mr. Reid, and I find myself astonished that this information was not given me when you first interviewed me for this position."

Absently, he fingered the carving of the ivory paperweight on his desk. His gaze, however, did not waver from my face. Behind him lamplight etched the outline of his fine, vigorous head, touched to a gleam the thick dark hair. I turned my eyes upon the fire.

"And if I had told you, would you have taken this assignment?" he asked.

I was not sure. Truthfully, I did not know. I could see his reason for silence, and yet it was a silence that should have been broken before this.

"Now that you have been—informed—are you afraid?" he persisted.

I shook my head vehemently. "No matter what he has done, Jeremy is a child. He needs help, not condemnation."

"And you think you have found some way to help him?"

I waved my hand at the head of Osiris. "Perhaps that is the way. I've been told he once had a great interest in Egypt and in your travels. I've bought a map of Egypt and a recent book about discoveries there. If I could touch off a spark of attention, perhaps I can fan it to life."

I hesitated, wondering if I dared go farther. Then I steadied my resolve and looked directly into those remote, chill eyes.

"I would like your help in this," I told him.

There was an almost visible withdrawing about him. "Whatever you please, Miss Kincaid. Help yourself to my books as you choose. Or if you have specific questions, I will try to answer them."

"That isn't what I meant," I said. "The boy has almost no contact in this house with his mother or with you. Surely this isn't wise?"

For once his gaze shifted and did not meet mine. He stared across the room at the proud, calm face of Osiris as if he would gain wisdom from it. Then he shrugged and turned back to me.

"I'll make you no promises. It may be that you will ask more of me than I can give. The boy must have his chance. After that—there are human limits to patience and forebearing."

He flicked the air with strong fingers, and I sensed that if he made a final decision against Jeremy it would be immutable. I would have to move as cautiously with the uncle as I did with the child.

"Have you anything else to tell me?" he inquired.

I was not ready to conclude. This man was busy and difficult to see. I would say what I had come to say while the opportunity offered.

"The boy shows an unusual interest in the room that used to be his father's," I said, and related my experience the night I had come upon Jeremy outside the door of the locked room. I did not, however, betray the fact that Jeremy possessed a key to that room.

Brandon Reid's dark, winged brows drew down in a scowl. "I've been told about this obsession of his. So morbid a preoccupation with the room in which his father died must be stopped. We can't allow it to continue."

"And how," I asked, "do you propose to stop it?"

He threw me a quick, impatient look. "You have some plan?"

My heart was thumping at my own audacity. I did not like to admit that I found my employer a little overwhelming in his force and somber vitality. I did not know what would happen if I openly opposed him in his wishes. Yet I had to follow my aim no matter how angry I might make him.

Deliberately I kept my voice low and even. "I would like to take Jeremy openly into his father's room and let him tell me about what happened there—if he wants to talk about it."

The anger I feared exploded about my hapless head. Mr. Reid took a quick turn around the room as if he sought to control himself, and then came back to face me.

"The idea is ridiculous and probably dangerous," he said. "I forbid you to do this. The boy is not to go near that room again. He is not to be encouraged in this morbidity. I would have expected greater wisdom from you, Miss Kincaid."

I was not accustomed to being spoken to in so arrogant a manner and I could feel the blood flame into my cheeks. I reminded myself that I must not be so foolish as to lose my temper with this man. Yet I was not entirely in control of myself as I rose from my chair to confront him.

"You won't help your nephew yourself, but bring a stranger into the house to do what you are unable to do. Yet now you want to tie my hands, revoke my plans, tell me what I may or may not do. If that is the way I am to work I might as well leave now, Mr. Reid."

If he had told me to pack my bag and go at once, I would not have been surprised. I had said more than I intended and now I could only stand there with my eyes snapping and my cheeks flaming, waiting for my dismissal.

Strangely, it did not come. Mr. Reid returned from another wheeling about the room and stood staring at me as if I were some doubtful object he had just unearthed on one of his expeditions. Something he might properly throw back. We eyed each other, bristling with antagonism. Then he threw up his hands.

"Have the matter your own way!" he flung at me. "But don't come weeping to me if you make the boy worse."

"I will not come weeping to you under any circumstances," I told him evenly. "And now there is another matter about which I must consult you."

His exasperation was clear, but before he could protest, I hurried on. "Jeremy goes nowhere, has no friends, no pleasures. I would like to take both children to a Saturday matinee performance of Cicely Mansfield's new play."

He gaped at me in blank astonishment, and dark blood flushed into his own cheekbones. What an angry-looking, red-faced pair we must have seemed to anyone passing the door.

"You would do *what?*" he demanded.

I could not understand why so mild a request should result in this reaction but I repeated my words. By this time my voice was no longer steady and it broke into a squeak that annoyed me no little. His manner changed with startling suddenness. Without warning he put his head back and allowed hearty laughter to ring through the room. He laughed as he had laughed the time he had flung the orange out a window at me. I waited in amazement until he recovered himself enough to speak.

"A capital idea, Miss Kincaid," he said. "You shall have your wish. I'll get the tickets for you myself as soon as possible."

Before I could thank him there was a sound at the door and I turned to see Leslie Reid coming into the room. Clearly she had heard him laughing and there was a question in her eyes.

"May I see you for a moment?" she asked.

I said, "Good morning, Mrs. Reid," and would have gone past her from the room in order to leave them alone, but Mr. Reid touched my elbow, holding me there.

"Wait—we must tell my wife your plans. Leslie my love, Miss Kincaid feels that it will have an excellent effect on Jeremy and Selina to take them to a Cicely Mansfield matinee. Can I persuade you, my dear, to make one of the party?"

Mrs. Reid gazed into her husband's face for a long cool moment.

Then she turned without a word and went from the room, not stopping to tell him whatever it was she had intended.

The smile he turned upon me as she swept away was not altogether mirthful. "You are small to be such a hurricane," he said. "You have all the devastating results a storm carries with it. Perhaps like a storm you'll sweep away dry brush, sweep the air clear in this house. Or perhaps you will simply bring the whole structure down about our ears. Which, remains to be seen."

I did not know what he was talking about and I asked no questions. I had achieved my aims and was ready to leave. But he spoke to me again, his voice as casual as though he had never raised it toward me.

"I've observed that you sometimes walk alone in the square of an evening. May I advise you not to, Miss Kincaid. The streets of New York are far from safe for an unescorted woman after dark. Even I never go abroad at night without a loaded pistol in my pocket."

I could afford not to oppose him on this. "Thank you for the warning," I said meekly. "I'll try to heed it."

As I went away, I carried with me a picture of Brandon Reid staring again at the Osiris head as if he sought to gain from it some answer that eluded him.

CHAPTER 5

THE NEXT morning, when I saw Jeremy at breakfast, I asked him to come and help me in the schoolroom before lessons started. He obeyed indifferently and informed me without interest where I could get a hammer and tacks when I asked for them.

In the schoolroom I had him help me hold the map in place above the mantel and keep it steady while I stood on a chair and tapped in the first tacks. When I glanced at him carelessly, I saw that he was reading some of the names on the map. However, he remained indifferent when I turned hammer and tacks over to him and he worked with them so awkwardly that I had to take them back and finish the task myself. It had been my hope that he might ask questions, or show some curiosity, as any other child would have done. But he did not, and I had to make my own opening.

"I've seen that wonderful head of Osiris in your uncle's library," I said, "and it has renewed an interest I've always had in Egypt. This room is too plain anyway, and I thought it might be ornamental to put this map on the wall. While I'm working I can look at it occasionally and learn more about its cities and rivers."

My speech sounded unconvincing in my own ears and I was not surprised by Jeremy's continued apathy. At least I had placed Egypt in view. If there was any latent interest in the boy, the map might renew it. If there was not, then I must try some other course.

During the morning Mrs. Reid made one of her rare visits to the schoolroom. She excused herself pleasantly to Andrew and asked if she might have a word with me. I put down my work and went to the door. She was going out this afternoon, she told me, and

Miss Garth was coming with her. It was her wish to take Selina as well, and she wondered if I would look after Jeremy for two or three hours while they were gone.

Her manner was less that of mistress to servant than it had been and she seemed truly grateful when I agreed to take charge of the boy. Nothing could have pleased me more. For the first time Jeremy and I would be left alone and I would have an opportunity to talk to him without interruption.

In the beginning, however, the chance seemed to promise little. When Selina, gay in her new green frock, had gone off with her mother and governess, we had the upper floors of the house to ourselves. Mr. Reid was out, Andrew had finished with his lessons and gone, and the servants were in their own quarters below stairs. Jeremy settled down to read in the nursery, ignoring me.

From my room I had brought the book on Egypt and in what I tried to make a cheerful, companionable atmosphere, I too settled down to read. Once I laughed out loud over an amusing paragraph and then read on without explanation. Jeremy gave no sign that he had heard me. At another point I said, "Listen to this!" and read aloud a passage that mentioned the splendid discoveries of an expedition a few years ago, made possible by Mr. Brandon Reid of New York City.

Jeremy looked up from his book, and I suspected a normal curiosity. But he suppressed it at once and returned to his own reading. Now, however, his book did not seem to hold him as it had. He seemed to be attending to something outside this room. It was as if he listened for some special sound. The house was still and though I listened too, I heard not even a footfall from the floors below.

Finally he put his book aside and went softly to the door, opened it, and looked out into the hall, his slight body tensed with listening. Still he heard nothing and he came back to his chair without looking at me. I began to feel uneasy and Andrew Beach's warning about the boy returned to my mind. My uneasiness, however, was not fear. It was more like the feeling one might have with an unsettled companion who listened for—ghosts. Was that what he listened for?

His restlessness was growing, and he began to roam the room. He poked among Selina's dolls and dishes, grunting scornfully to himself. He picked up tin soldiers and tops and jacks; he went to a shelf and pulled out a large thin geography from beneath a stack of books. This he brought to the table, placing it before me. Without explanation he flipped open the pages as though he knew exactly where to look and drew out a square of drawing paper. He gave the paper a quick, intent look and then held it out to me, still without speaking.

As I took it from his hand, I saw that it bore a pen-and-ink sketch of Jeremy's face. The likeness was excellent, though this was a younger Jeremy. The artist had caught shock and tragedy in the eyes and a mouth that was clenched to suppress emotion. Yet there was nothing here of viciousness or violence. I remembered my own first impression of a dark young angel and found that the artist had seen the resemblance too. In a corner of the paper were the initials, "A.B."

"This is very good," I said. "Mr. Beach drew it, didn't he?"

Jeremy nodded. "Uncle Brandon liked it, so he kept it. I took it out of his desk after he married my mother and came here to live. He has forgotten about it by now. It's not a good picture though. It's a lie, and Mr. Beach knows it is a lie. He's painting a portrait of Selina and my mother now, but he doesn't want me to be in it."

I felt my way warily. "I don't understand what you mean. This seems a wonderful likeness to me. Though of course you're older than you were then."

The boy took the picture abruptly and replaced it in the geography. I had a feeling that I had disappointed him in some way. Had he wanted me to deny the likeness, to tell him he did not look like that?

When the book had been returned to its shelf, he went to the door and opened it once more upon the hall. The air of listening was upon him again, and I knew he was deliberately challenging my attention. This was the opportunity I had waited for. I spoke to him quietly, almost carelessly.

"Jeremy, would you like to show me your father's room downstairs?"

This time I had his full attention as I had never had it before. He turned from peering into the hall and faced me, dark-browed as his uncle, but with a child's startled fear in his eyes.

"What are you up to?" he asked rudely.

"You have a key to the room," I reminded him. "Though I've never told anyone that you have. The other night you wanted to go into your father's room and you ran away when I surprised you in the hall. Who is to stop you now if you show the room to me?"

Distrust was visible in every line of his body. When I rose and touched his shoulder I found him as stiff as one of his own tin soldiers.

"Get the key and come along," I said as lightly as though I had suggested a stroll in the park.

His shoulder rejected my fingers. Stirred to sudden action, he darted down the hall to his room and returned a moment later with the key in his hand. When he held it out to me, I reached for it, but he snatched it back at once.

"You'll be afraid," he said. "Everyone's afraid of that room. Everyone but me."

He, I suspected, was the most frightened of all, but I did not say so.

"Try me," I told him, and started ahead down the stairs.

He slipped past me, and in the lower hall we both stopped in mute accord and listened for sounds from the floor below. All was quiet. Yet now irresolution seized him and he stared at the key in his hand as though he did not know where it had come from, or how to use it.

I spoke to him gently. "I've heard what a fine person your father was, and of how generously he gave his help to those who were in trouble or in need. I would like to see the room where he lived. I think it must be a pleasant, friendly place. If you can't manage the key, I'll do it for you."

"Miss Garth will give you the very dickens," he said, as though he half hoped I would draw back. "My mother will cry if she knows, and my uncle will be in a rage."

I smiled at him. "Your uncle has said I may take you into the room any time you like."

He grimaced like a street urchin. "You're lying to me. Everyone lies to me. But I don't care. I'm not afraid of my uncle."

Gathering up his resolve he attacked the door with the key. That was the very word for the rough, angry way he went about inserting it in the lock and turning it. Then he pushed the door ajar upon the cold stuffiness of a place long unused and unaired.

Shutters had been closed and draperies drawn so that a thick darkness lay upon the room, scarcely penetrated by thin light from the hall. I will confess to a faint prickling at the back of my neck as if the supernatural had touched me. But I would have none of that.

"I'll open the shutters," I said and started resolutely across the room.

Jeremy flew after me and caught me by the arm. "No!" he cried. "No!" and there was terror in the syllable.

I wanted to force nothing upon him that he did not wish. "Would you rather we went back upstairs?"

That was not what he wanted either. It seemed that it was bright daylight he feared. He went to the place where matches lay upon a bureau and held one out to me in silence. As silently I struck a light and reached upward to a gas jet, turning the cock. With a puff the gas caught and the illumination of evening lay upon the room.

While Dwight Reid's personal effects had been put away, it appeared that nothing else had been touched in the room and I looked about it, seeking to know what manner of man Jeremy's father—Brandon Reid's brother—had been. There was no austerity here. Two or three small, bright rugs, figured in a mixture of brown, yellow, and green, lay upon the over-all gray carpet. A four-poster bed of walnut boasted a valance of dark gold and a spread of gold-green. The fine old highboy had brass handles to every drawer. A painting hung above the mantel—a hunting scene that picked up the gold and greens of the room, and added a warm splash of red. While Leslie Reid's room had seemed to indicate a love of ornate luxury, Dwight's room showed true elegance of taste without severity.

But it was the boy who interested me more than the room. He was moving almost systematically, opening a drawer here, the doors of a commode there, touching, searching. What it was he looked for I could not guess and I did not ask. I waited quietly for this fever of reacquaintance with the room to wear off. There seemed some purpose behind his actions and if this search gave him ease, I did not mean to obstruct it.

There was a long carved box on the bureau, and he removed the cover, looked into it, found emptiness, and went on. He even touched the pillows on the bed and groped beneath them. I half expected him to get down on his hands and knees and look under the bed, but he did not. When he had searched beneath the coverlet along one length, he rounded the foot of the bed to the side nearest the door to the adjoining boudoir. Dark draperies of heavy green brocade hid the door, and he thrust them apart and examined the bolt that locked the door from inside the room.

"They always keep it locked now," he said over his shoulder. "But my father used to leave it open. I had only to come through the curtains that day. He was standing right there by the bed."

He turned and gave me a long, searching look.

"I can show you something," he said. There was a gleam of excitement in his eyes, and his usual apathy had vanished. He seemed a different boy—a more frightening one.

I knew he was measuring me in some way, testing me, perhaps, and I steeled myself against any betrayal of emotion.

"Very well," I said. "Show me whatever you like."

He bent swiftly and caught up a corner of the small rug on the floor beside the bed. With the air of a magician producing something sure to confound me, he jerked it away. I stared at the faint brownish stain on the gray carpet and felt the finger of horror touch the back of my neck again.

"I'll bet you don't know what that is!" Jeremy cried, his voice chill with an eerie triumph. "You'll be afraid when I tell you. You'll be sick!"

It took all the self-control I could summon to keep from running off to the safety of my small room upstairs. Away from this place of tragedy, from the stain on the carpet, and the suddenly evil child. For the sake of Jeremy's sanity I fought for control.

"Of course I know what it is," I said as calmly as I was able. "It's a bloodstain, obviously."

A little of his wild elation subsided. More than anything else he seemed puzzled by my response. I went on quickly before he could speak again.

"When a person is shot there is always blood," I told him in matter-of-fact tones. "It was in this room that your father died, wasn't it? So this must be a bloodstain."

"So much blood," Jeremy whispered. Then he spoke more loudly, defiantly. "Now you see why it is that you can't like me. You needn't try to fool me by pretending to be friends. No one likes me. Mr. Beach knows that picture he drew was a lie, and Uncle Brandon hates me. So does my mother and Garth. And you will too. Only Selina doesn't because she's too young and silly to understand what I did."

I thought of the bloodstain no longer, but only of the desolation I saw in the eyes of the child before me. I too needed the wisdom of Osiris to deal with this matter, and I possessed so little sagacity. I could only follow my instinct and hope it was sound.

"How can I know so soon whether I like you or not?" I asked him. "I never make up my mind about people that quickly. When I do decide, it's because of how a person is with me and not because of what may have happened long ago. Or because of what other people say about him."

Jeremy looked at me without trust, but as though I continued to puzzle him. His next words surprised me.

"Would you like to see the pistol collection? It's downstairs in the drawing room. I'll show it to you if you like."

Was I wrong? I wondered. Was I letting him excite himself unwisely? Should I put a stop to this as I knew anyone else in the house would have done? Against reason, I once more gave him the lead. I turned out the gas and he relocked the room, pocketing the key. Together we started downstairs. There was no one about, and he opened the door of the drawing room softly.

Again there was gilt and damask elegance, and underfoot the rich soft colors of Persia. Though the room was reserved for special occasions and the shutters closed, the shadows here were not so dense. Enough light to see by seeped in. Jeremy went directly to the rear of the room, where a tall glass cabinet stood on spindly carved legs. Upon its shelves lay spread an array of small arms from all over the world.

Now Jeremy seemed more like a small boy showing off his knowledge. For the moment the horror of the room upstairs had faded into the background. This was a dueling pistol, he pointed out, and there was its mate. That one with the silver fittings had been carried in Napoleon's army, while this plain one with the bone handle came from our own West. Here was a revolver, there a clumsy, old-fashioned double-barreled pistol. He had learned his father's hobby well and forgotten nothing. But he could not touch the pistols or take them out, for the cabinet was securely locked.

"They always keep it locked now and the key hidden," he said. And added with a meaning that turned my mouth dry, "That's because of me."

As I watched, he counted the guns carefully, then counted them again, and yet a third time.

"It's always the same," he assured me. "They never put it back. I keep looking and looking for it, but I don't know where they've hidden it."

I knew what he meant. The missing gun must be the pistol he had used that terrible day.

"Why do you want it?" I asked him.

He held out his hand, the forefinger curling as though he pulled a trigger. "I like guns," he said. "I like to feel them in my hand. But I can't get these out without breaking the glass. Maybe I will break it someday. When I want to shoot someone."

The entire eerie experience was beginning to wear on my nerves, and something of what I felt must have revealed itself in my face. Jeremy pounced upon my reaction with malice.

"You're afraid of me, aren't you?" he demanded, looking pleased with himself. "You know what I'm like now, and you're afraid!"

I rallied my last resources against him. "Yes, I know what you are like," I said, sounding cross. "You are a little boy showing off, and people who show off rather bore me. I believe I will go upstairs and read my book about Egypt."

I did not wait to see what he made of that, but went briskly to the door of the drawing room. I heard him follow me and I turned toward the stairs. Just behind me he paused.

"I'd like to go outside for a while," he said. "I'm tired of the house."

So normal a suggestion pleased me. "That's a fine idea. Let's get into our coats and go out for a walk."

For the first time I heard him laugh, but the sound was far from reassuring.

"I'll race you upstairs!" he shouted and tore past me.

I lifted my skirts and went after him, but he had a head start and beat me soundly. I was out of breath, but laughing when I joined him at the head of the stairs.

"I can beat a girl any day!" he announced, triumphant again and overly excited. "You can't catch me going down either."

He turned and ran down again before I could move to stop him, and as I watched he opened the front door and disappeared outside, slamming it shut behind him.

That alarmed me, and I hurried down and stepped out into the cold brisk air. He was already out of sight. Perhaps he was hiding nearby, playing a trick as any boy might. It was too cold to be out without a coat, so he wouldn't stay long. I called him, but had no answer. When I turned shivering to the door I found the latch had caught and I had to disturb the butler in order to get in.

With little effort Henry managed to imply that he did not regard me as gentry. He stared in disapproval at my disheveled and un-cloaked appearance. I did not stand on ceremony, but told him at once that Jeremy had run outside and I didn't know where he had gone. Undoubtedly he would return as soon as he got cold, but perhaps someone should look for him.

"If you've let him get out, he's off and gone by now," the man said, his disapproval of me increasing. "He has run away in his nightshirt—that one. We didn't find him till morning one time."

I was truly frightened now. I sent Fuller and Kate to search for him, put on my wraps, and stood outside for a while, calling. Kate went to the nearest police station, but there had been no sign of Jeremy. At last I returned indoors to pace the hall. It was there Brandon Reid found me when he came home. I could only tell him at once that the boy was gone.

His cold look let me know that he placed the blame upon me—where, after all, it belonged. But I wanted no time wasted on reproach or questions.

"What can we do?" I cried. "Where can he have gone? He will be cold without his coat!"

"Don't chatter," Mr. Reid said. "Or if you must, go upstairs. I dislike excitable females."

He strode toward the rear of the hall, and I heard him giving orders for the carriage to be made ready at once. For all that his words angered me, they steadied me as well. At least the problem was now in sure hands and I could hold my anxiety for the child in abeyance. I stood where I was until my employer returned to the front hall.

"I have an idea where he may have gone," he said curtly. "I'll drive out in search of him as soon as the carriage is ready."

"Let me come with you," I pleaded. I could not bear the thought of waiting here, inactive. And besides, if the boy were found I wanted to be there to take some of the blame from him. I did not trust the bright anger that had replaced the chill in Brandon Reid's eyes.

He stared as if he found everything about me distasteful, and I could see refusal coming.

"I'll promise not to chatter," I said meekly. "I know what has happened is my fault. But please let me come and help you, Mr. Reid."

"Help me?" The dark brows drew down in a scowl.

I faced him with increasing determination. "It may be better if I am there. I think the boy doesn't altogether dislike me."

"This is a fine way of showing his liking," Mr. Reid said. Then to my relief, he said, "Come if you like. This is not a life-or-death matter, I fancy. We're not unaccustomed to dealing with such crises. Though they disturb his mother. Is she home as yet?"

I told him she was not. We waited in silence until the carriage was brought around and Mr. Reid and I went down the steps together.

CHAPTER 6

In the carriage I sat stiffly beside my employer, sensing his continued anger, though I did not know whether it was directed against the boy or against me.

Without looking at me, he spoke. "Please tell me exactly what happened that led up to this running away."

I told him all that we had done, keeping nothing back. He listened in chill silence to my account of the visit to Dwight's room and of how Jeremy had revealed the stain upon the carpet, of how he had shown me the pistol collection downstairs. When I was through he made a single, devastating comment.

"You are very young, Miss Kincaid, to have been given so difficult a charge. The fault may be more mine than yours."

It distressed me to realize that he thought my judgment immature, my actions lacking in wisdom. For all I knew, he might be right, yet a spark of stubborn conviction within me insisted that I would behave again in just the way I had, and that in spite of Jeremy's running away, I was not yet proved wrong. The most important thing now was to have my chance. I could sense the promise of dismissal in the very stiffness of Mr. Reid's posture and in the tone of his voice when he spoke. Somehow I must find the way to forestall him.

The carriage had turned off Fifth Avenue and was moving among the heavier, less elegant traffic of the West Side. Drays and carts shouldered us wheel to wheel, there were single riders on horseback, and the citizenry on the sidewalks seemed a rougher lot, both in clothing and manner.

"I'd better tell you where we're going," my employer said abruptly. "Jeremy has had some sort of compulsion about this place ever since its conception, and he has run away to it twice. You've heard, perhaps, of the Dwight Reid Memorial Home that has been built through donations given by admirers of my brother?"

His tone had hardened, almost as if he resented such honor being paid to the name of his dead brother. I glanced at him in surprise.

"I've heard of it," I said. "Its purpose is to serve homeless children in New York, I believe? But why should Jeremy go there?"

"You ask me riddles I've no answer for," he said. "I suppose it's the same sort of thing as going to his father's room—a wallowing in horror."

Fuller pulled the horses over to the curb, and I saw that we had stopped before a large building of brownstone, still marked by scaffolding across its face. The arched doorway stood open, and workmen were tramping in and out. My companion called one of them to the carriage and asked if he had seen a small boy, but the man shook his head and went back to his work.

When Mr. Reid got out of the carriage, I followed him before he could tell me to stay where I was. We started up the wide steps and just as we reached the door someone called his name from the sidewalk. We turned, and I saw a police captain dismounting from his horse. He secured the reins to a hitching post and ran up the steps to join us.

"Good morning, Captain Mathews," Mr. Reid said. "This is Miss Kincaid, Jeremy's—history instructor."

The captain touched his cap and smiled at me. "Good morning, miss. Kate came over to the station a while ago to learn if we'd seen anything of the boy. Said you were frantic with worry. So I thought I'd ride over here and see if he was up to his old tricks. But you've made it ahead of me."

He seemed a kindly man, with a smile nearly as wide as his shoulders. But as the three of us went into the building, I noted a jaw line that might well have been cast in metal. This, I suspected, was a man who could hold his own in the rough and dangerous life of a policeman in New York.

Painters and wallpaperers were still at work on the interior of the building, and bare floors echoed to our steps. Captain Mathews took over the task of inquiring for Jeremy, but no one had seen him. We went through a long hall with tall windows down one side— a dining hall, in all probability—and then across to other rooms, and at length upstairs to a large dormitory.

Here the work had been finished, and iron bed frames were already installed. Here our search ended. In a far, shadowy corner of the room Jeremy sat on the floor, still and huddled, with his knees drawn up and his forehead against them. I saw him first—a small, touching figure in the long dim room—and I put a hand on Mr. Reid's arm.

"Let me, please," I whispered, but neither man paid any attention to my plea.

"Ho there, boy!" Captain Mathews called out cheerfully while Jeremy's uncle started down the room toward him with long strides I could scarcely keep up with.

At the first shout, Jeremy uncurled and jumped to his feet. I saw terror in his face and a frantic desire to run. But he was cornered, and there could be no escaping the two who bore down upon him.

"It's all right, Jeremy," I said and ran past them to hold out my hand to him.

Jeremy seemed not to see me. He stared at Captain Mathews, and the same horror looked out of his eyes that I had seen in evidence in his father's room earlier that day. He said nothing, but stood as if frozen, watching the police officer in a strange agony.

"Come now, boy, don't look like that," Captain Mathews said. "We're old friends, aren't we? I'm here just like your uncle is, to see you safely home again. You're a big boy now; you oughtn't to go frightening your family with this running away."

"He knows that," Mr. Reid said quietly. He took Jeremy by the arm, not unmindful of the boy's upset state, and led him out of the room and down the stairs. Once outside, he assisted him into the carriage seat. Then he turned and held out a hand to the officer.

"Thank you, Captain. We're sorry to have troubled you. We shouldn't be taking up your time like this."

The look Captain Mathews turned upon Jeremy in the carriage was both stern and kindly.

"I remember him from that bad time you had at the house, sir," he told Brandon Reid. "I've taken what you might call a personal interest in him ever since."

"You understand that, Jeremy?" Mr. Reid asked. "If you don't want to be in wrong with the police, you'll have to stop running away."

With that he handed me into the carriage. Captain Mathews mounted his horse and rode away.

Jeremy said darkly, "If he knew—if he really knew—he'd arrest me, wouldn't he, Uncle Brandon?"

His uncle did not answer, but gave Fuller the signal to drive us home.

I felt Jeremy's shivering as he huddled between us, and pulled the lap robe over him.

"How cold you are," I said. "Here, tuck your hands under this. It was foolish to go off without your coat. We could have come outside comfortably, if you'd waited."

He stared straight ahead without answering. Only when the carriage turned back into the brisk stream of Fifth Avenue, did he speak again.

"Are you going to punish me, Uncle Brandon?" he asked in a voice that was far from steady.

"You've done what you know is forbidden and you deserve punishment," his uncle said. "I'll think about the matter and decide upon a proper course."

Beside me Jeremy still shivered, and I rebelled inwardly against his uncle. When we reached home Mr. Reid did not release his hold on the culprit, but took him up the steps and into the house, leaving me to follow as I pleased.

Miss Garth was home, though Leslie Reid was not, and Mr. Reid turned the boy over to her at once.

"Give him some hot milk and put him to bed," he ordered. "Get him warm, if you can."

I longed to offer Jeremy some comforting word as he was led upstairs in Miss Garth's undisputed grasp, but there was nothing I could say, no assurance I could offer. I too was a culprit and I went despondently upstairs and into the deserted schoolroom. The fire had gone out, and there is little more dispiriting than a cold hearth, gray with the ashes of a dead fire. I was cold now and shivering like Jeremy. Cold and not a little despairing.

Had I taken on a task that was too big for me? It was quite likely. The future did not look bright at that moment. I was not likely to get a recommendation from Brandon Reid that would serve me in finding another position as either seamstress or governess. Yet it was not my own probable predicament that troubled me most. I could recall Jeremy's white face as he sat so stiffly between his uncle and me in the carriage, hear the quiver in his voice as he asked about punishment. With all my heart I longed to help him, to be allowed to help him. Yet by tomorrow I might very likely be sent packing.

"May I come in?" It was Mr. Reid at the door behind me.

I whirled to face him, and my chin came up. I would not have him guess my discouragement.

"I'd like to apologize for any unconsidered words I may have spoken," he said stiffly.

I was too astonished to do anything but stare at him.

"The fault was not entirely yours," he went on. "If you were to be left in full charge of the boy, you should have been warned about his propensity for running away."

I sensed that apology did not come easily to Brandon Reid and knew I should accept his words with gratitude and humility. But while I was trying to don the proper manner, he spoke again.

"I'd hoped, Miss Kincaid, from what I'd learned about the excellent results with your young brother, that you would be able to exert a gentling influence upon Jeremy. I realize that it's too soon for definite results, but I must admit that I'm disappointed in your choice of action this afternoon."

How quickly I forgot to be grateful and humble! My temper began to rise at once.

"Why do you think the boy behaves in this way?" I demanded. "Why shouldn't he run away from the unloving atmosphere of this house? He told me this afternoon that no one can ever like him, and that is a horrifying belief for a child to hold. He even believes that you wish him dead."

A somewhat exasperated sigh escaped my employer, but at least he did not accuse me now of "chattering." When he spoke his impatience was well contained, his tone even.

"Love, Miss Kincaid, is not easily simulated."

"I know that," I said. "I know how hard it must be for you, considering what happened. But your brother is dead, and his son's very life is at stake."

Mr. Reid closed the door upon the hall so that our voices would not carry and motioned me to a chair near the cold hearth. He seemed in that moment a sadder man than I had seen before. He did not sit down but went to stand at a rear window, looking out upon the ailanthus tree.

Quietly, without emotion, he began to tell me of his brother. Their mother had died when the two sons were young, and he, being the elder, had taken to looking after Dwight a good part of the time. Their father had been older than his wife—a severe, proud, brilliant man, with a deep love for his sons, but often preoccupied with his work in the firm of attorneys he headed.

"He hasn't been well for some years," Brandon Reid said heavily. "Dwight's death was a crushing blow, and the full truth of what happened was kept from him. He lives in southern New Jersey now with a younger sister. My aunt is devoted to him, though he is still strong-willed enough to give her trouble at times. We all feel it best that he live away from New York. He forgets his triumphs when he comes here and remembers only the disappointments and hurt the city has held for him."

As he spoke, I sensed the affection in which Brandon Reid held his father, and I sensed something more—perhaps a lacing of deep regret or pain.

"To lose his favorite son and have left only the one who disappointed him . . ." He moved his hands in an expressive gesture and smiled at me wryly. "The least I can do is see that his last years are peaceful."

"What was so remarkable about your brother Dwight?" I found myself asking.

"He had the flashing brilliance of a comet," Brandon said. "And sometimes as little forethought. I pulled him out of more than one scrape in his younger years. Jeremy resembles him a great deal. Looking at him, I can almost see Dwight again. Believe me, for Dwight's sake, for the boy's own sake, I want to give him every possible chance. But don't ask me to love him, Miss Kincaid. Love is not something I give easily. Unfortunately that is my nature and there is nothing I can do about it."

I thought of Leslie Reid and the ardent attention he seemed to pay her. There, at least, he had given his love, and I wondered irrelevantly what it must be like to be loved by such a man. Nevertheless, though I was reassured by the fact that he had wanted me to understand, I could not be merciful.

"You could at least pretend," I told him. "Even a pretense of affection and interest would help. How do you think the boy feels when he senses revulsion in all those about him?"

Brandon Reid shook his head. "He would not be fooled by pretense. He is not stupid."

I gathered my courage and put the question this conversation gave me a chance to ask.

"How did it happen? Would you mind telling me?"

He paid me the compliment of answering without hesitation, though his telling was brief. In swift, sure words he made me see what had occurred that night when Dwight Reid had been killed by his own son. Earlier on the day of the tragedy the boy had misbehaved in some way. All the Reids, it seemed, had quick tempers, even the gentler Dwight. That afternoon Dwight Reid had lost patience with his son and had shaken him soundly. Jeremy's own temper had flared. He had always resented physical chastisement and he struck his father's hand away, uttering threatening words. His father recovered at once and laughed at him. No one took the boy seriously.

But that night while Dwight Reid was getting ready for bed, the boy got a pistol from the collection downstairs. He knew where bullets were to be found and he knew all about the loading and shooting of guns. On trips to the country, Dwight had indulged him in his own hobby, believing that every boy should be trained to handle guns safely and shoot like a gentleman.

"By odd chance I was in the house that night," Brandon Reid said. "I had been abroad for more than a year on my last trip to Egypt and had returned only that morning. Late in the evening I went to Dwight's room to talk with him. I had just stepped to the hall door when Jeremy came through the curtains from what was then his father's dressing room and is now Leslie's boudoir. Before

I could realize what he was about, he pointed the gun at his father and fired. I dashed the pistol from the boy's hand and rushed to my brother. There was nothing to be done. At that range Jeremy could hardly have missed."

His voice had grown hard in the telling, and I listened unhappily.

After a moment's silence, he went on. "Perhaps now you'll better understand what you refer to as the unloving atmosphere of this house. Afterwards the boy showed a bold, unrepentant attitude. Captain Mathews, as you may have gathered today, worked on the investigation. He never learned the whole truth and he gave the boy every consideration and kindness within reason. But it was as though Jeremy was proud of what he had done. We can't trust him or rest easily with him in the same house. Yet no school would take him under such circumstances, and in any case it would not be fair to submit other children to his company and influence. The only person he seems to like is Selina, and my wife is afraid he may harm her in some violent rage."

My eyes were swimming with tears, yet it was still the child my heart ached for. I could not rid myself of the conviction that, in spite of everything, it was he who suffered now, concealing his suffering as no child should have to conceal so terrible a self-blame. Concealing it behind a guard of pretense and antagonistic behavior.

My employer was regarding me almost kindly, and it seemed strange to see those gray eyes warm a little and lose something of their condemnation.

"Truly," he said, "I'm grateful for your interest and your sincerity in dealing with Jeremy. What I fear is that your youth and your own feminine instinct to forgive a child will blind you to sensible action. I don't dismiss the possibility that you may still help the boy. But too much softness will not be good for him either."

"What softness has he had?" I asked quickly. "Must you punish him for running away today?"

"The boy wants to be punished," he told me. "He is constantly asking for punishment."

"That in itself should be a warning to you," I said. But I didn't want to oppose him further. Events had moved in my direction, and I was to have my chance to help the boy if I could.

For the first time Mr. Reid glanced about the room and noted the map of Egypt I had tacked up over the mantel.

He nodded toward it. "What, exactly, do you hope to gain by that?"

"All I ask for is a show of interest," I said. "The boy isn't as indifferent as he pretends. I'm sure of that. For one thing—he admires you tremendously."

Mr. Reid looked shocked. "It's possible that he did in the past. His imagination was caught by my adventures in distant places, as any child's might have been. But now he looks at me sometimes with hatred in his eyes. Don't count too heavily on his devotion to me or you'll only delude yourself. At least you've brought a quality of mercy into this house, Miss Kincaid, and I'll grant you that has been lacking. Perhaps it will reach the boy. I hope you'll continue to forgive what isn't always to your pleasure and do your best."

I rose and held out my hand in frank acceptance of so fair a request. He took my fingers in his and held them for a moment. Again I felt the vigor and strength of this man as it flowed to his very fingertips, but this time I did not flinch away as I had before.

"I haven't forgotten about the matinee tickets," he told me. "I hope to have them for you early in December. I want a box, not the lesser seats. Perhaps the children would enjoy a box."

I assured him that they would, hoping it was true, and he went away, leaving me more reassured than at any time since I had come to this house.

When I returned to the hall, I met Miss Garth coming out of Jeremy's room.

"He's warm at last, and asleep," she told me. "What did you do this afternoon to excite him into running away?"

I had no intention of giving Miss Garth fuel for her already smoldering resentment, and I countered with a question of my own.

"Why didn't you warn me that he was given to running away? Then I could have been on guard against what happened."

She drew herself up, regarding me out of those dark, deeply set eyes—a handsome and redoubtable woman. "We expect you to exert extreme caution with this boy at all times, Miss Kincaid. Specific instruction hardly seemed necessary." She swept off down the hall, her full brown skirts rustling, wafting behind her a strange mixture of scents—lavender blended today with just a whiff of violet.

I went gladly to my own room. My nerves had been strained more than once today, and I wanted to rest and speak to no one. Beneath my door I found a folded sheet of paper of the sort on which Jeremy did his sums. Spreading it out, I discovered that Andrew Beach had written me a note.

Would I, he requested, have a modest supper with him tonight? He had returned to the house to leave some books this afternoon and had learned of Jeremy's running away. He hoped all was well by now, but I undoubtedly needed a change from gloom and the company of a half-mad little boy. He would call for me at six.

I read the note through with pleasure. Andrew's astringent company would be good for me tonight. I did indeed need a change from the depressing atmosphere of this house.

CHAPTER 7

KATE, MY one friend among the Reid servants, came at six to tell
me that Mr. Beach awaited me in the sitting room downstairs. I
had already let Miss Garth know that I would be dining out and I
went down to greet him.

It had been fun to dress up for once. My wardrobe was not ex-
tensive, but my mother had insisted that I own at least two good
dresses and she had put hours of loving work into making them.
Tonight I had chosen a long-sleeved gown of garnet satin with a
loose-falling skirt draped up at the back in a slight bustle. It was not
overtrimmed, but had a touch of black lace running from my throat
down the front of the tight-fitting bodice. I had fluffed my bangs
and pinned my hair in loose curls at the nape of my neck, finding
in such frivolous gestures the sort of release only a woman under-
stands.

I went downstairs rather slowly, not wholly admitting to myself
that I wished Brandon Reid would appear in the hallway, not wholly
admitting that I would like him to see me in my finery, instead of
as the gray dove of a seamstress I had become. Mr. Reid did not
appear, however, and when I went into the sitting room I found
it empty. This time I did not resist the pull of the mirror and I was
standing before it studying myself when Andrew entered behind
me.

"I'm sorry to keep you waiting, Megan. Mrs. Reid summoned
me upstairs to reprove me for disciplining Selina this morning.
They're a difficult pair to please at times—both master and mistress.

But let's forget all that. Turn around and let me see your fine feathers."

I turned and saw the half-amused lighting of his eyes.

"You're a bit elegant for the little place where I'm taking you. But I'm flattered and I'll make the best of looking at you. You're a very pretty girl, Megan."

He helped me into my mantle and we walked the few blocks to the Italian restaurant he had chosen.

"As a matter of fact," he explained as we strolled along, "I have my lodgings upstairs at Mama Santini's, so I know her fare is hearty and good, if not as fancy as Delmonico's."

The November night was growing sharp after the cold day, and there was almost a feeling of snow in the air. I have a liking for the winter months and find them enlivening, invigorating. My earlier nervous shivering had vanished, and this entire change was already doing me good.

The small restaurant seemed a cheerful, unpretentious place, with bare table tops scrubbed to the bone, and an appetizing odor of tomatoes and onions and peppers perfuming the air. There were no soft lights here, but bright gas globes everywhere and a cheery clatter of voices and laughter from diners already eating.

Mama Santini came to greet me herself and eyed my garnet gown with approval. I did her place honor, she stated, implying cheerfully that the place deserved it. Did she not, after all, serve the best Italian cooking in New York?

Because Andrew was clearly a favorite, a corner table had been saved for us, and we were shown to it with as much flourish as any headwaiter could have managed. Mama Santini clearly enjoyed her own cooking and she shook with good-natured laughter that seemed to start with her cheeks and ripple downward over generous bosom and a stomach no whaleboning could restrict.

I took my chair in the corner and pulled off my gloves, smiling at Andrew. "What a lovely place! Thank you for thinking of this."

His faint cynicism did not disturb me tonight. Andrew might entertain a mocking attitude toward the world and the people about him, but even when he stated unflattering truths, he never cut me to the quick as Brandon Reid could do.

By now a desire to talk was bubbling up in me, and, while we ate the delectable antipasto and sipped red wine, I began to tell him of all that had happened that day. He stopped me short almost at once.

"None of that!" he ordered. "Your unhappy adventures will keep for another time. We'll not spoil good food with them. Tell me about yourself instead, Megan. Where do you come from, where are you going?"

The first was easy to answer, and I told him of Princeton, New Jersey, the town in which I had grown up and where my father had taught. I didn't mind that a certain nostalgia crept into my words, although I knew that Andrew was wholly city-bred and would regard a small university town with amusement. I told him briefly of my father's death during the war and of my mother's struggle to earn us a livelihood here in New York.

"Unfortunately," I confessed, "I lack her skill with a needle. Indeed, I was doing so badly that I was at my wit's end when Mr. Reid offered me this position."

"And what will happen," Andrew asked, "when your position ends?"

"It's not necessary to worry about that now," I objected. "Indeed, Mr. Reid gave me a reprieve this afternoon. I'm to have more time to work with Jeremy and try to help him. After all, I've scarcely begun."

Andrew broke off a thick crust of Italian bread. He did not look at me, but I heard again the bitter note that sometimes came into his voice when he spoke of Brandon Reid.

"If I were you, I would not count on staying too long in Reid's good graces. When he's through using you, he'll make short shrift of letting you go. And he'll trouble himself not at all as to what happens to you once you are out of the house. Take care of yourself first, Megan. A bit more self-interest would serve you well."

I had no answer for him and I did not attempt one. Our steaming plates of spaghetti came and I found myself eating more hungrily than I had in days. Andrew watched me knowingly.

"Even your eating improves when you're out of that house. Don't think I haven't seen you pick at your food with Garth presiding. Not that she wouldn't ruin anyone's appetite if you let her. I turn the tables and interfere with hers. Have you noticed how fond she is of me?"

I laughed, glad to get away from the subject of Brandon Reid and my position in his house.

"It's your turn now," I said. "Tell me about your own ambitions. I know what skill you have in capturing likenesses on paper. Jeremy showed me the drawing you did of him during the investigation of his father's death. I thought it sensitive and penetrating. You saw past the ugliness of what had happened to a shocked and frightened child."

"I doubt that," Andrew said dryly. "I merely gave the public the sentimentality it wanted. Most adults would rather weep over a child than believe him a monster."

I hated to see Andrew so harsh when it came to Jeremy, but when I would have protested, he changed the subject.

"I'm more interested now in the oil portrait I'm doing of Selina and her mother. The child is an ideal model, the mother more difficult to catch. Unfortunately, sittings aren't as regular as I'd like."

I knew Andrew sometimes stayed after lessons, or returned in the afternoon to work on the portrait Mrs. Reid had commissioned, but so far he had not shown it to me.

"I'd like to see what you're doing," I told him.

"I'm not sure you'll approve," he said cryptically, and went on to speak of his free-lance work for the newspapers.

Often, it seemed, he was called in on assignment and had developed a faculty for doing quick sketches of those in the public eye. I had seen some of his fearsome drawings of convicted criminals and could realize by comparison how gentle he had been with Jeremy.

He spoke now with matter-of-fact good cheer of pickpockets and thugs, of political spoils and sanctioned law-breaking as if they were everyday matters to the newspaper world. As indeed, they must have been.

I brought up the subject of Dwight Reid and his work in fighting crime and mentioned that we had pursued Jeremy that afternoon to the Memorial Home being built in Dwight's honor.

Andrew seemed unimpressed. "Dwight tried hard enough, I suppose. But Sir Galahad himself would have been lost in New York

327

City today, what with our corrupt judiciary and the selling of justice."

"Even with Jim Fisk behind bars?" I asked.

"Only a start has been made. Dwight Reid made scarcely a dent. More's the pity, since he had captured the public eye." He changed the subject abruptly. "Are you still planning to take the children to the matinee of Cecily Mansfield's play?"

I told him that Mr. Reid had mentioned getting us a box only that afternoon, and Andrew whistled softly.

"A box! The man must be out of his mind. Doesn't he know that Selina and the boy are likely to be recognized, even if you are not?"

"What of it?" I asked in exasperation. "Must everyone go on behaving as though a tragedy that happened in the past must blight these children's lives forever?"

Andrew pushed a lock of hair back from his forehead as if he puzzled over something.

"What is it?" I asked. "What is the matter with this play that everyone behaves in an odd way the moment I mention it?"

"You might as well be told," he said. "Though I don't know why I must always be your informant. At least I have no sense of delicacy about Reid's reputation. It's not a savory reputation, you know. His name has been coupled with the Mansfield woman's for some time. His infatuation with her is public knowledge."

My silence was filled with dismay. I disliked gossip and never cared for such columns in the papers. Yet if what Andrew had just told me was true, it explained much that had puzzled me. It gave me the answer to Mr. Reid's own reaction—first of anger, then of amusement when I had made the suggestion. He had decided easily enough to play this outrageous joke upon me. It explained Miss Garth's dismay, too, and the way Leslie Reid had walked out of the library that day when her husband had suggested that she join the party.

Andrew was watching me, aware of my groping bewilderment, even a little amused by it. "Now you are in difficulties, aren't you? What is a genteel young woman to do under such circumstances? Are you going to tell Master Brandon off and refuse to go?"

"Stop looking at me as if I were someone you meant to sketch for your paper," I said indignantly, still struggling with my confusion.

"Perhaps that's just what you are," he said, laughing out loud. "You'd make a charming heroine for a news story, though perhaps you're full of more contradictions than most of the ladies I sketch. Perhaps that's part of your attraction, Megan. You don't always do exactly what I would expect of a young woman in your proper position. It's entertaining to watch you. But you haven't answered my question, you know."

I made up my mind abruptly, dismissing his nonsense. "If what you've told me is true, then Mr. Reid is playing an inexcusable trick on me, amusing himself at my expense and the expense of his wife. But how am I to know what the truth is? You've repeated gossip, and gossip is not my affair. I'll take the children to the performance when the time comes. Their enjoyment is more important than what people think."

With that, I hoped I had settled Andrew, Brandon Reid, and my own conscience in one swoop.

"Bravo!" Andrew cried and reached across the table to cover my hand with his own. A mustachioed Italian gentleman at the next table smiled in approval and toasted us gallantly with his glass of wine.

"To be perfectly fair," Andrew said, "Brandon Reid is not wholly to blame. What else is a man to do when he's married to a woman who loves only his dead brother?"

So that was it? No wonder Mr. Reid so often seemed chill and remote and unhappy. I remembered the warm looks I had seen him turn upon the beautiful Leslie and the cool way in which she seemed to slip away from him. That felicitous scene at the dinner table my first night in the house must have been make-believe after all. And that was sad to contemplate.

"Come now," Andrew said. "Don't feel too sorry for him. He's not the man to suffer long from unrequited love. He has an appeal for silly women. Don't let it touch you, Megan."

I could feel myself flushing. "Touch me? You're being ridiculous. The boy is my only concern."

"You're an obstinate girl," he said. "And you're also rather a darling. I wish I could believe in a favorable outcome for your hopes.

But I don't. I continue to feel lucky to be out of that house when darkness falls."

Like the silly sort of woman Andrew deplored, I fastened my attention on the word "darling" and forgot the rest. While Andrew was not, I told myself, the type of man who appealed to me romantically, I liked him and I could not help feeling pleased to have him call me a darling. Even though I knew he used the word lightly, I gave him a smile and he blew me a mocking kiss. We were friends again.

It was past nine by the time Andrew squired me back to Washington Square. I'd had a pleasantly gay evening and I told him so. He held my hand a moment longer and more warmly than he should have.

"Be careful, Megan," he warned me again. "Do take care."

The words meant little to me. Already I had forgotten my uneasiness in Jeremy's company that afternoon. I let myself in with my latchkey and went upstairs, humming softly to myself because for once I felt young and irresponsible and not unattractive. There would be time enough tomorrow to become again my workaday self.

When I had taken off my outdoor things, I went to the door of Jeremy's room next to mine and asked if I might come in.

He was sitting up in bed reading a book and he stared at me in bright defiance. I noted the title with surprise. It was the book on Egypt that I had left in the schoolroom.

"I see you've been out of bed," I said.

His manner dared me to scold him. "I'm reading about Osiris."

I was more than pleased, but I did not betray that fact. "A most interesting subject."

"My father is an Osiris now," he announced, the defiance still in evidence.

"What do you mean?" I asked.

He seemed to sense that I was not going to scold him for getting out of bed, and he seemed to relax a little. Most intelligently he explained what he had read in the book. The Egyptians had believed during the period of the Osiris cult that when a man died he became "an Osiris," accountable to the god for his sins on earth.

"Some day," Jeremy said, "I will stand in the Judgment Hall of Osiris and be punished for everything I've done on earth."

My heart went out to him in pity. I sat in a chair beside his bed and spoke quietly of the sort of God in whom I believed. A forgiving, understanding God.

"Not even the modern Egyptians believe in Osiris any more," I said.

"But I've *seen* Osiris," Jeremy insisted. "He's there in Uncle Brandon's library, wearing the White Crown with the plumes. And I'm not afraid of him. He's beautiful and stern and wise. If he wants to punish me, it will be right."

His words distressed me. It didn't seem wise to identify the head in his uncle's library with some supernatural force, and I tried to persuade him from the notion.

"Perhaps all the old gods add up to one God in the end," I said. "Osiris is part of a very big pattern."

He looked at me with something strangely like hope in his eyes, but I lacked the wisdom to know exactly what I had said or done that had helped him. Before I could tell him good night and leave him, Miss Garth came to the door and saw him sitting up in bed with the book on his knees.

"You should be asleep," she said and took the volume from him so quickly that he had no time to hold it from her. When she saw the title she frowned her disapproval.

"What sort of heathenish trash are you reading?" she demanded, and then looked at me. "I believe this belongs to you, Miss Kincaid?"

Even as I nodded, I found myself wondering how this handsome woman, with her fine carriage and beautiful dark hair, could be so invariably unpleasant. For the dozenth time she was making me feel myself a culprit who could do nothing but harm to Jeremy. I supposed that was her purpose—to be so unpleasant that I would eventually leave this house in defeat and her jealously guarded prerogatives would be again unchallenged. I would not play into her hands. I took the book from her and set it on the table next to Jeremy's bed.

"Mr. Reid approves of our interest in Egypt," I told her. "It's perfectly all right for Jeremy to borrow my book if he likes."

I glanced at the boy and found him watching me in a curiously intent way. He ignored Miss Garth and spoke directly to me.

"Sometime will you let me play with your carrousel?" he asked. "Selina talks about it all the time. She says you won't let her touch it."

"Perhaps I'll let you play with it sometime," I said and smiled at him.

CHAPTER 8

BACK IN my own room I found myself restless and disturbed. The words Jeremy had spoken about the Osiris head had touched me with a now familiar chill. His identifying the head with his own destiny was somehow frightening. When he said, "My father is an Osiris now," he touched on something deeper and more menacing.

It was too late to light my fire anew, and I got ready for bed quickly. Yet when I had bound my hair in plaits and put on my warm flannel nightgown with the feather-stitched collar that spoke of my mother's patient fingers, I sat absently on the edge of the bed, lost in thought.

It was encouraging, I told myself, that Jeremy had shown interest in the book about Egypt and in the carrousel. Perhaps both these things could be used to draw him into further interest, even if his notions about Osiris followed a strange road. If only I could prevail upon his uncle to talk to him as he used to about Egypt and his experience there, his own interest might help to counteract Jeremy's apathy.

The thought of Jeremy's uncle led me down another road. If Leslie Reid was still in love with her first husband, as Andrew said, who could blame Brandon for finding solace elsewhere? How must he feel when his brother had won Leslie as he had not been able to do? A pattern had begun to reveal itself concerning Brandon's relationship with his brother. Dwight had been the gifted, handsome, successful younger son. Or so everyone seemed to claim, though it was hard for me to imagine Brandon in a lesser light when it came to comparison with any man. Yet it seemed that

Dwight had stood in his older brother's way at almost every point. He had been favored by a father Brandon loved devotedly. He had carved out a successful political career, and his star had been brightly on the rise at the time of his death. He had married the beautiful Leslie, who had loved him and still did.

All this was clear. Yet still I could not understand how it happened that a year after Dwight's death his grieving, loving widow had married the brother she could not love. The more I puzzled, the more confusing the maze became. Somewhere there must lie a key, but so far I had not found it. It was even possible that an effort was being made to keep it out of my hands. Even, perhaps, by Brandon himself?

The room's chill penetrated my preoccupation at last and I turned out the gas and got under the covers, pulling the quilts over me to my very nose. Now that I lay in bed and tried to sleep I began to hear the wind. It had risen without my noticing and it rattled the branches of the ailanthus against my window pane, and set a distant shutter banging. What a wild dance it must be enjoying through Washington Square with all those trees to play among and all that space in which to wheel about.

I fancied the wind as a dark, hooded figure, stormy-browed and bitter, stripping the last dead leaves from the trees, hurling winter upon us before it was time. In this fanciful state it was easy to confuse the dark and hooded figure of my imaginings with Brandon Reid. He too was stormy and bitter, strewing bleakness about him, offering little of warmth or reassurance. And yet . . . and yet . . .

I suppose I dozed, for I know that time passed and I occasionally waked from some uneasy dream. Then the wind held its breath and the very lull wakened me so that I lay listening to the sudden quiet. In the hush it seemed that the stairs creaked with the weight of feet upon them. Was Garth up? I wondered. It was unlikely that either Mr. Reid or Jeremy's mother would come to the third floor at this hour. There was another creak, and, thinking of Jeremy, I knew I must investigate.

Slipping out of bed, I threw my blue flannel wrapper over my gown and lighted a candle. Then I opened my door and stepped into the hall. The gas was always turned off at night and shadows stirred and wavered as chill drafts touched my candle flame. The dark wind capered over the rooftops and pressed at every cranny, puffing its breath the length of the hallway. Jeremy's door stood open and when I stepped into his room I found that he was indeed gone from his bed.

I had no doubt as to his goal and I ran down the stairs, shielding my candle from drafts, hoping its feeble flicker would not forsake me on this windy night. Beneath the library door there was an edging of light which told me that Brandon Reid was working late.

Dwight Reid's door stood closed, but the knob turned beneath my fingers and I went softly into the room. Here heavy draperies drawn across shuttered windows muffled the wild sounds outdoors, and only the sobbing of the boy on the bed filled the room. Here my candle flame burned straight, and the shadows were quiet. Jeremy lay face down upon his father's bed, weeping his heart out. I did not touch him, but stood close by.

"I'm here, Jeremy," I whispered. "Cry all you like. I'll wait for you until you feel better."

After one startled instant when he turned his head to look at me, he paid no further attention, but gave full vent to a grief so terrible that it wrenched my heart. I put the candle upon the high bureau and sat in a chair to wait. The boy's sobs grew stormier, and I wondered if I had better try to calm him.

In the distance the library door opened, and I knew that Brandon Reid had heard. His footsteps sounded firmly as he strode down the hall. I rose to face the door and was sharply aware of the picture he made, impressively, darkly handsome in the deep burgundy of his dressing gown, his thick hair touched to brightness by candlelight.

I put a finger to my lips and went swiftly to him. He blocked my path in the doorway as he had done once before when I had first met him. But this time I stood upon no ceremony. I put a hand to the smooth satin facing across the chest of his gown and pushed him back into the hall in no uncertain manner.

He was clearly displeased, and his dark brows drew into a frown. "What is wrong?" he demanded. "How did Jeremy get into that room?"

"Don't let him hear you," I pleaded. "He needs to cry, as he needed to run away today. Perhaps when he has released all this pent-up emotion he'll be quieter, happier."

I could sense a stirring of high impatience in Brandon Reid, as though he too had borne more than enough for one day and was moving toward some explosion.

"There has been too much of coddling," he said angrily. "The boy must be stopped at once."

He moved again toward Dwight's room, but at that moment Leslie's door opened and she came into the hall, her red hair in soft disarray about her shoulders, a lacy, silken gown caught half-revealing over the full curves of her bosom, her amber eyes wide with alarm. In both hands she held the tall brass candlestick I had noted beside the hearth in her room, and its flame dipped and bowed in the drafty hall.

"What is it?" she cried. "What has happened?"

For once her husband seemed to look in cold distaste upon her tremulous beauty. "Your son is in Dwight's room," he told her curtly.

Leslie's gaze flew toward the source of those wrenching sobs and then back to her husband's face. "But that's dreadful! He must be brought out at once!" She put the great candlestick down upon the hall table and flung out her hands in entreaty to her husband.

"Go in and comfort him, then," Brandon Reid challenged. "Go in yourself and bring him out."

She shrank before the whiplash of his tone, and I saw tears in her eyes, saw the wide searching look she turned upon him, as if she beseeched him for something without speaking a word.

He looked into the white face, lifted so pleadingly to his own, and a derisive smile touched his mouth. "Always so beautiful," he said. "There's no disarray that doesn't become you, my dear. Dwight was a fortunate man."

What his words meant to her I did not know, but she turned from him and fled back to her room, leaving her candle to add to the guttering shadows. From the open doorway Jeremy's sobs had lessened a little, though they still wracked his small body. His uncle wasted no further time on me. He strode to the door and went into the room. At least his encounter with Leslie had taken the edge from his anger, for now his tone was more restrained.

"Listen to me, Jeremy," he said. "I have decided on your punishment. Sit up and take it like a soldier."

To my surprise, Jeremy gave a long, strangling gulp and then sat up on the bed, his face puffy and streaked with weeping. Brandon Reid took a large white handkerchief from the breast pocket of his gown and gave it to the boy, waiting sternly until Jeremy had wiped his face and blown his nose. Then he spoke with the air of a judge pronouncing sentence.

"Because you willfully disobeyed my rules this afternoon and ran away, causing much grief to Miss Kincaid and worry to me, I have decided that you will not be permitted to attend the matinee for which I now have tickets."

Jeremy, of course, had known about the planned outing, but he had never given any sign as to whether it pleased him or not. Now his eyes widened and I saw his lips quiver.

"Yes, sir," he said, swallowing hard, and I knew he had been stricken with a dreadful disappointment.

His uncle gave him a curt good night and went out of the room. But while he was done with the boy, he was not done with me. I flew into the hall after him.

"How could you be so cruel?" I demanded, forgetting that I was hardly more than a servant in this house. "Your punishment is too severe; it's the wrong one. He needs the pleasure of that matinee. I won't have him cheated of it!"

He looked at me impatiently and without liking, and the chill in his gray eyes cut through my every defense. Clearly he did not like importunate women.

"Have it your own way," he said coldly, "but get the boy back to his own room."

As he turned from me his look fell on the oversized candlestick. He gestured toward it as carelessly as though there had been no clash between us.

"My wife has forgotten her favorite illumination," he said. He picked up the huge ornamental stick and held it high, smiling without amusement. "It is not inappropriate that this once graced a seraglio in the days of the Ottoman Empire. If you'll excuse me, Miss Kincaid, I'll put this where it belongs." He carried it toward

Leslie's door, and from the tail of my eye I saw the door open, as though she had been watching.

I had no interest in candlesticks, seraglios, or the Reids' marriage and I returned to Jeremy at once. He still sat on the edge of the bed, with his uncle's large white handkerchief clutched in his fingers.

"Come," I said, and held out my hand to him gently.

He let me take his hand as if he were a very small child, and came with me docilely. Back in his own room I tucked him into bed. With all my heart I longed to put my arms about him, to offer the unspoken comfort of a caress, but I did not dare more than a light pat on his shoulder.

"Don't worry," I said. "Everything's going to be fine. You'll sleep well now. And you needn't worry about the matinee. I've spoken to your uncle, and he has relented. The punishment is withdrawn and you'll have a lovely time at the play."

I waited for some sign of pleasure, but he lay back quietly on his pillow, staring at me as though I had offered him a gift of ashes. With a flash of understanding I knew that Brandon Reid had been right and I wrong. Jeremy had *wanted* to be punished and he had wanted a punishment that was real and would deprive him of pleasure. In the same flash I knew that I must undo the harm I might have wrought in canceling his uncle's edict.

Conversationally, as though I had noticed nothing, I began to talk to him. "I've never liked the word 'punishment.' It's true that when we do wrong things, we must pay for them. That goes for grown-ups as well as children. So I'm going to choose a payment for you to make. You've asked me to let you play with my brother's carrousel. But now I will not, after all, allow you to touch it. And that is final."

For a moment longer he stared at me. Then he closed his eyes heavily as though he could stay awake no longer. I knew he had accepted my authority and was not dissatisfied. He was still a little boy who wanted very much to go to a play.

I stood looking down at him, so quickly and peacefully asleep, and wondered how I had ever felt a moment's fear of Jeremy Reid.

CHAPTER 9

THE FOLLOWING days were surprisingly quiet. As I had hoped, Jeremy had spent himself completely and it had done him good. He was not markedly different in his general attitude or behavior, but he was not so wound up with tension within himself. As a result, I felt more secure in my position. My employer would have to admit, if he troubled to observe Jeremy at all, that I had not been wholly wrong.

One December morning when Miss Garth and I were having breakfast with the children in the nursery, Selina brought up the subject of Christmas and the presents she wanted to make for her mother and her Uncle Brandon. She bubbled with her usual enthusiasm, and I saw Jeremy watching her with something like speculation in his eyes.

"What are you going to make for your uncle?" I asked the boy.

Selina, always swift as a hummingbird, answered before he could find words in his more thoughtful way.

"Last year he never made a thing for anyone!" she cried. "He was a very selfish boy."

Jeremy retreated into his shell of indifference and would not be coaxed out. I could have spanked Selina for quenching the look I had seen in his eyes.

However, after breakfast, when I went into the schoolroom to start my work on a set of pinafores I was making for his sister, Jeremy followed me there, a thoughtful expression on his face. I did not press him and paid no attention as he roamed about the room, poking into things as he liked to do. He paused before a basket of assorted trimmings I had stored on a shelf, and after a moment's searching he brought out a small box of tubular, cut-steel beads and held them up to me.

"What do you do with these?" he asked.

I told him they were used for embroidering a pattern on a lady's gown.

He rolled a few of the shiny beads out upon the table and studied them for some time in silence. This way and that he pushed them, as if he were attempting some design. I waited for him to tell me what he was about.

"Have you any wire?" he asked me finally.

I shook my head. "I can let you have some strong thread, but I have no wire."

"Mr. Beach will get me some if I ask him," Jeremy said. "Miss Megan, may I have these beads?"

"Of course you may have them, Jeremy. Take them all, if you like. And if you want more, I can get them easily."

"Thank you," he said with unwonted courtesy. "I have an idea for a Christmas gift I may make for Uncle Brandon."

"That's fine," I approved. "Let me know if there's any way in which I can help you."

He nodded absently and did not explain. He took the box of beads away to his room and later I heard him asking Andrew to bring him a few lengths of fine wire.

Curious and interested though I was, I asked no questions. It was enough that Jeremy seemed more cheerful, that he had some private absorption. Several times he asked me about the play we were going to see and appeared to be looking forward to the occasion.

On the Saturday morning of the matinee, Mr. Reid appeared in the nursery—there were no lessons that day—to astonish us with an announcement. He had decided, he said, to come with us to the play. It was a fine day, and he expected that we would all enjoy ourselves. He mentioned the time when the carriage would be ready, warned us not to be late, and went out of the room. I could have sworn that he gave me a swift look in which amusement was evident, but he was gone so quickly that I could not be sure.

The news had a varied effect upon us. Selina clapped her hands in delight and said she would wear her new green dress. Jeremy said nothing, yet there was a glow of pleasure in his eyes that touched me. I only hoped that his uncle would not disappoint him and that this unusual good cheer on the part of Brandon Reid would last through the afternoon.

My own reaction was curiously mixed. I did not in the least like the quickening of my spirits at the thought of being in his company under more pleasurable circumstances than were usually the case. I told myself several times that morning that his was a violent nature and that this light mood would not last. Surely the man repelled me far more than he attracted me. Besides, in spite of my determination to ignore gossip, Andrew's words about Cicely Mansfield returned to prick me further with distaste for the children's uncle. Must he sit with us and dote upon this actress as she coquetted with him from the stage? No—having Brandon Reid with us was an altogether unfortunate turn of events, and his presence would undoubtedly set a blight upon the occasion, regardless of the children's pleasure.

So I guided my thoughts and warned myself. At the same time I took great pains when I dressed in my garnet satin, even to the final touch of fastening on my mother's garnet earrings and sunburst brooch. After all, this was a more suitable occasion for dressing up than the evening of the dinner I'd enjoyed with Andrew Beach. Andrew, I knew very well, would not approve of Mr. Reid's accompanying presence and I was just as glad he was not about on Saturday to scowl at me and make biting remarks.

Miss Garth's reaction was one of outraged indignation. At the moment of Mr. Reid's announcement she merely smoldered, then looked her disapproval when he had gone out of the room. She released her feelings by telling Selina she had spotted her green dress and could not wear it and she lectured Jeremy on all that his uncle would expect of him by way of good conduct. She did not, however, speak her mind openly until a few moments before we were ready to leave.

There was a long mirror at the head of the third-floor stairs and I had gone out to examine myself from head to toe. By this time I had thrust back all doubts, shut Andrew out of my mind, and felt as ridiculously gay as though I had been Selina's age. Or as though a man were taking me alone to the theater. Miss Garth caught me before I could pretend I was only passing the mirror, and she took time to speak her mind in a low, deadly voice.

"What a little fool you are," she said. "Don't think it isn't clear for whom you're preening. Do you think he'll really look at you? It's hardly likely, when all his attention will be for his inamorata there on the stage."

Her words left me shocked and nearly speechless with fury. Before I could manage an indignant retort, or she could continue in this outrageous vein, Selina popped out of her room in a whirl of green silk, spots and all, and hurled herself upon me.

"Do let's go downstairs, Miss Megan! It would be dreadful to be late." Then she saw my dress and circled me in delight. Mischievous and teasing, she might be, but there was a warmth in Selina as well. "Why, you look beautiful!" she cried. "That's a lovely, lovely red. And you've combed your hair in such a pretty way, so it shows under your hat. Uncle Brandon will approve of you . . . he likes pretty things."

Miss Garth fairly snorted, but she said no more. She went off to rout Jeremy from his room, and I tried to put out of my mind the sharp things she had said. I would not listen to gossip. If she thought I was primping for Brandon Reid, then the rest of what she had said was as likely to be untrue. I gave Selina a hug for her compliments and tied her sash a little higher to hide the more prominent spottiness. The frock, quite aside from spots, was not as great a success as it should have been, but I was glad it gave Selina pleasure.

Miss Garth returned in a moment with Jeremy and now she was doing her best to make him uncomfortable.

"This is altogether too much excitement," she said. "The boy will be sick at his stomach, you'll see. Probably disgrace you all right there in the box. And that will teach his uncle to take him out in public."

She made me so angry that if the children hadn't been present I would have given her a piece of my mind. The sooner I persuaded Mr. Reid to put the boy wholly into my hands, the better. There was at least a quiet acceptance between Jeremy and me by now, and the pretense of being a seamstress alone need not be continued.

Having given us the worst possible send-off, Miss Garth flounced away to her room and I held out a hand to each child so that we could walk downstairs together in a gay and friendly fashion.

"Don't you worry," I told Jeremy. "You've eaten nothing to make you ill. And besides, happiness never upsets anyone. This is going to be a lovely day."

Brandon Reid was waiting for us at the foot of the stairs. He had an approving word because we were a good two minutes ahead of time, and he admired our dressed-up state collectively, with no special compliments for anyone. As he helped me into my dolman, I noted how very fine he looked. Though that was not unusual. Under the black Inverness cape that he wore with such aplomb, his suit was a fine weave of broadcloth in pearl gray, and when he had settled us in the carriage he put on his pearl-gray topper. We could not, I thought, have found a more distinguished-looking, more striking escort in all New York.

As Fuller flapped the reins and the carriage drew away from the curb, something made me glance up at the front of the house we were leaving. A woman stood at a window on the second floor, and, with a start, I saw that it was Leslie Reid. Until now she had not appeared to say good-by to either her husband or the children, and the glimpse of her at the window disturbed me. So often Mrs. Reid seemed hardly more than a shadowy background figure in the house. Her frequent headaches, the spells of illness that made her languid and given to remaining in bed for days at a time, removed her from the rest of us so that we almost forgot her presence. Now it was as though I had glimpsed a melancholy ghost watching us from an unreal world of candlelight and violets.

No one else saw her, and, as we drove away, I did not look back. Yet the memory of her standing there was not something I could easily shake off.

The children's uncle was in an extraordinarily light mood, and I suspected that he had made a pact with himself to give Selina, and particularly Jeremy, a pleasant afternoon.

The theater was just off Union Square, and carriages were already drawing up before the doors when we arrived. By the time Mr. Reid had handed us into the blue, white, and gold auditorium, and had settled us in the best seats of our box, we were all atingle with excitement. Jeremy was quiet, but there was a shine in his eyes that delighted me and he missed nothing as the house filled up. From the vantage point of our lower box, we could look out over the entire sweep of the theater. I could not help but note, however, that Brandon Reid remained in the shadows at the rear of the box and made no attempt to join us in our scrutiny of the house.

Once he leaned forward to speak to me. "Do you like the seats?"

I could only nod raptly. I had never sat in so fine a place before and I didn't dare try to tell him how I felt, lest I sound as young and enraptured as Selina. At last the house lights went down, the rustling of programs quieted, and the gas-jet footlights came on in all their brilliance against the lowered curtain.

Cicely Mansfield did not appear until near the end of the first scene, and the play moved with an amusing sparkle toward the moment of her entrance. Then she whirled onstage with the gaiety that was so essentially hers and from that moment on took possession of the audience.

I edged a little forward in my seat because I wanted to see exactly what sort of woman she was. Certainly she was not beautiful—not in the sense that Leslie Reid was a beauty. Pretty—yes, and with a warmth about her that reached across the footlights to embrace the audience. "Of course you love me," she seemed to be saying. "You love me because I love you!"

The play was light froth. The children loved it, and I laughed aloud with them. Once, when I glanced back at Mr. Reid, seated in the shadowy rear, I saw that he was not even watching the stage. Indeed, he looked as though he might be dozing. Of course he must have seen the play before—perhaps several times. Yet I would have expected him to feast his eyes upon Miss Mansfield at every opportunity and this display of indifference gave me a sudden hope that the gossip, after all, was untrue. Or, if there had ever been any truth in it, perhaps the affair was well in the past. Even as the thought came to mind, my own readiness to be pleased, to hope that the gossip was untrue, dismayed me as something shameful. There in the darkened theater I could feel the burning of my cheeks, the unwelcome quickening of my heartbeat. Why should I care? Why should I be concerned one way or another with Brandon Reid's past or present infidelities?

When the curtain came down on the first act, I tried to applaud with as much eagerness as the children. Perhaps they had not understood every line, but the pace was fast and I felt I had chosen well for their pleasure.

During the interval I watched the rustling theater with interest. In the box directly across from us several women had gathered for this matinee, and I realized that opera glasses were being turned upon us and that the ladies were whispering to each other. Did this mean that Selina and Jeremy had been recognized?

Mr. Reid spoke from the shadows. "The twittering has begun. The ladies in the opposite box are puzzled about your identity."

"Why should they be puzzled?" I asked, not turning my head. "I'm obviously here with the children."

His voice went on softly, mockingly. "Since you scarcely look like a governess, they're wondering who it can be who is so new and fashionable in town and has escaped their attention."

For the first time I realized the impropriety of my dress. As the children had dressed up for theatergoing, so had I, and my gown was quite suitable for a matinee had I been here in a social position. As it was, I should have clung to my dove gray or wren brown.

"We might as well give them something to twitter about," Mr. Reid went on, and before I knew what he was about, he left the dark recesses of the box and stepped to the rail beside me, holding out a program, bending over my shoulder as though he pointed something out.

"Please don't," I said. "You're quite right that I shouldn't have dressed like this. I'm sorry, Mr. Reid."

"Don't be ridiculous," he told me, impatient again. "You're more bearable to look at the way you are this afternoon than in those drab things you wear at home."

A retort was rising indignantly to my lips when the curtains at the rear of the box parted and an usher appeared with a note for Mr. Reid. He took it, frowning, and read it through.

"It appears," he said, "that I will have to go backstage for a moment."

He bowed to us and was gone so quickly that I could only stare at the blue velvet curtains swaying gently from the briskness of his passing. He had gone backstage to see Miss Mansfield—that was evident. He had not even troubled to dissemble. And he had not minded in the least if I knew what he was about. I began to fume inwardly, though I kept my feelings from the children.

So I was more "bearable" to look at today and he did not care for the way I dressed at home! He behaved as though I had no feelings, no pride. Andrew was right, and Brandon Reid was an insufferable person. He had the arrogance and lack of consideration that was sometimes typical of the wealthy—particularly when wealth was inherited instead of earned. I bit my lips and kept my gaze from the interest of that opposite box. By the time the curtain rose on the second act, I had studied its slightly rippling scene until I knew every painted line by heart.

Mr. Reid was late in returning and he uttered no apology as he slipped into his chair. I did not look at him, but kept my attention fixed upon the play. Though the second act was even more lively than the first, my pleasure in the production had faded. Once or twice it seemed to me that Cicely Mansfield glanced directly at our box and that her famous smile was flung rather challengingly in our direction.

During the second-act intermission Mr. Reid seemed restless and increasingly bored. Once or twice he pulled out his handsome gold watch and studied the time, toying with the long chain that looped across his waistcoat. He had dropped all pretense of playing the role of benevolent uncle and he made no further effort to keep the children happy. It was at this worst possible moment that Selina asked the question she had been saving up for hours.

"Uncle Brandon," she said, "what is an inamorata? At home Garthy and Miss Megan were talking about your having one."

In spite of the voices and rustling all through the theater, there seemed an area of deadly quiet about our box. I felt cold perspiration dampen the palms of my hands, but my mind was blank of any possible response. There was, after all, nothing I could say, no defense I could offer.

After a moment of endless silence, Mr. Reid addressed Selina coldly. "I suggest, my dear, that you ask Miss Kincaid for the answer to that question. I suspect that by now she is an authority on the subject."

His words shocked and angered me, yet still I could not answer

346

him. My position was one I could not readily defend, however indignant I might be, however unfair his attack.

He rose and made us an elaborate bow that must have been quite visible to anyone in the theater who happened to be looking.

"I hope you will excuse me from remaining for the rest of the play. I confess that it bores me and I am never willingly bored for long. I'm sure you can get the children home, Miss Kincaid. I will not need the carriage."

I said nothing at all, and in a moment he was gone, completely spoiling our afternoon.

I knew it was spoiled even before Selina's wail of protest. I saw the withdrawal in Jeremy's eyes and knew that he was blaming himself, however mistakenly, for this sudden departure. He had been quietly enjoying both the play and his uncle's company. I had sensed this in the way he hung on Brandon Reid's every word and gave him all his attention. I tried to find some lame excuse for his uncle's going, but I think not even Selina believed me. Both knew that he had lost interest in our company and taken himself away because he did not care to be with us any longer.

Through the final act any last trace of embarrassment I might have felt died away as my anger increased. Neither the children nor I had deserved such treatment. His lack of consideration, his indifference to the feelings of others was insufferable. When the opportunity arose I would tell him so—and let him dismiss me if he liked.

Andrew was right, and I should have listened to him!

We were far from gay on the drive home down Fifth Avenue. When we should have been full of talk about the play and still under the spell of the theater, no one had any desire to talk.

Just before we reached Washington Square, the first snow of the winter began to fall, drifting down lightly, thickly, with every promise of going on forever.

At least Jeremy waited until he was home before fulfilling Miss Garth's prophecy and being dreadfully ill. We were busy with him all evening long.

When it was that my employer came home that night, or if he came home at all, I did not know. And I certainly did not care. What I had to say to him would not lose its strength by waiting.

347

CHAPTER 10

CHURCH BELLS wakened me the next morning, and I heard the whisper of snow against the pane. I left my bed with the eagerness one feels to view the unsullied beauty of winter's first snowfall.

White fringe clung to the branches of the ailanthus, and a quilting lay thick upon my window sill. Drab rooftops were padded with white coverlets, and the chimneys wore little caps of snow. Even the dreary alley of the mews had been touched with beauty. Fuller was already up and busily shoveling a path from carriage house to back door. The hush of a snowstorm lay upon the city.

I pulled on my wrapper and went to light the fire. Usually on Sundays I traveled some distance by horsecar to the church my mother and I had attended, but I did not want to battle snowdrifts and slowed traffic this morning. I had noticed a church nearby on Fifth Avenue that I might attend. The Reids—Mrs. Reid, at least —went farther uptown to one more fashionable, and the children often accompanied her. What Mr. Reid did I had no idea. One hardly saw him of a Sunday.

Remembering my anger, I fed it anew to make sure the coals remained hot until my opportunity came to confront him and speak my mind. Yet even as I stirred my indignation with reminding, I was troubled by a contrary yearning for peace and quieter thoughts.

Sunday had one rather pleasant aspect, for it was the day when Miss Garth went home to visit her elderly father. She waited till after churchtime and midday Sunday dinner, then took herself off, and was gone for the afternoon and most of the evening. Thus for part of the day I had both children to myself unless Mrs. Reid went calling and took Selina with her.

That morning Jeremy did not rise for breakfast, and when I looked in on him, I found him listless and interested in nothing. There was no more to look forward to now, and the reality of the matinee had disappointed him. Not even my inquiry as to how the gift for his uncle progressed roused him from apathy. He had kept the secret of what he was making, working on it only when he was alone. This morning that interest too had forsaken him.

I needed my escape to church. Apparently the snow had changed Mrs. Reid's plans and Selina was not going out with her, so both children were left in Miss Garth's charge until I returned.

Our front steps had been swept of one layer of snow, but already they had filmed over as the thick fall continued. At least the fall lacked the biting sting of a blizzard. The flakes fell, slow and thick, without wind to set them whirling. Washington Square was a great white field, its dull browns hidden and every bush and tree wearing puffs of white. Snow lay thick upon the fountain, and a few sparrows hopped about its rim, seeking the crumbs some kindly citizen had sprinkled there.

My skirts brushed the snow, and I lifted them high so that I would not sit indoors with their wet hems against me. The effort of tramping through snow that had not yet crusted to offer solid footing, set my blood tingling by the time I reached my destination three blocks away. There was the usual traffic on the Avenue, with a few sleighs adding their melodic jingling of bells to the sounds of this snowy Sunday.

The church was small and built of the same brownstone that was quarried across the Hudson at Weehawken, furnishing a favored building material for so many New York homes and buildings. In contrast the steeple wore a frosting of white and the doors and windows were bright with welcome. I entered the enclosure of a little iron fence and went up the steps along with others who had not been kept home by the storm.

The organist was playing, and the deep full tones sounded through the quiet place and added to the feeling of light and warmth and peace that met me as I stepped inside. I sought a long bench near the rear and took a seat near the wall aisle where I might be alone and quiet with my thoughts. This moment before the service began was always one I prized. I could make my own prayers best and did not need a minister to tell me how to pray.

Quietly, avoiding the banked fires of my anger, I went over in my mind the disturbing problem of Jeremy Reid. More than anything else I needed strength and guidance to help him. A beginning had been made. He must not be allowed to slip back into the old way that was so filled with darkness for him. It was for these things I asked in my heart that quiet Sunday morning.

The little church was filling up, and before long the choir began to sing. The congregation rose to join in a hymn, and at length the minister took the pulpit to give his sermon. By now my disquiet was stilled and I felt hushed and strengthened. I knew that when the time came I would fight for Jeremy with renewed courage and vigor.

I will confess that I did not at first follow every word the minister spoke. I prefer a quiet preacher, and this man was breathing fire. Nevertheless, when he launched into an attack upon the wave of crime which held New York in a fearsome grip, I began to listen. Vice and corruption were the sins of man, the minister admonished us, but with the help of men of good will, they could be opposed and stamped out.

Not long ago there had been a man in New York, he reminded the congregation, who had fought against these things with courage and selflessness. This good fight had been led to a great extent by Dwight Reid, and the good he had begun was now being carried on by others. We must remember that early in January the Dwight Reid Memorial Home for children was to be opened with a ceremony which he hoped many of us would attend, and he advised us to contribute to the cause. The building itself was virtually completed, but its running must be assured for years to come.

A collection was taken for this cause, and, as I made my contribution, I thought of the day when Jeremy had run away to this very building of which the minister spoke. In the boy's mind the place must seem to offer refuge to the son of the man it honored.

When the service was over and the congregation began to file out, I sat on for a few moments, waiting for the church to empty. Then I left my seat and stepped into the uncrowded wall aisle, turning toward the back of the church. Two rows behind me another woman had waited for the crowd to thin before leaving her seat. She sat with her head bent, her furs drawn closely about her, as though she were cold in this stove-heated interior. With a start I recognized the brown feathered hat with glossy wings of red hair showing beneath, and in the moment of my recognition, Leslie Reid looked up and met my eyes. For an instant I thought she would look away purposely, not choosing to see me. Then she seemed to reconsider and nodded in my direction. She rose, edging along the row. I waited, and, when she reached me, she indicated a side door that offered an easy exit.

Outside the snow was deep in the churchyard, and we clasped hands in order to help each other through it to a side gate. We did not speak until we were on the sidewalk, moving toward the Avenue. Then Mrs. Reid threw me a quick melancholy look.

"I did not want to be recognized," she explained softly. "There would have been a great to-do if someone had seen me there. But I knew this sermon was to be preached and I wanted to hear it."

She appeared gently sad this morning and not so far removed as she had sometimes seemed before. As always, I beheld her beauty with wonder that a woman could be so lovely. Her skin at close range seemed flawless, the lashes that shadowed her eyes were thick and upward-curling, her brows neatly drawn in a line of perfection. This was the woman Brandon Reid had married. How could he look at Cicely Mansfield?

I was surprised when she began to speak to me, not as if I were a semi-servant in her house, but a woman in whom she could confide. The imperious manner had vanished.

"Nothing must happen to keep the Memorial Home from opening," she said, speaking from behind the shelter of the muff she held to her cheek. "The good my husband began must live on. It must not be wasted."

"Is there any danger that it won't open?" I asked, a little startled by her outburst.

"There must not be!" she cried vehemently. "Though from the first my husband has set himself against the entire project."

It seemed strange that Brandon Reid should oppose what was done to honor his brother, and I said as much, with something less than tact.

Mrs. Reid threw me a quick, tragic look. "Brandon has always been envious of Dwight. From the time they were children, it was Dwight who did everything well, Brandon whose aims were futile. The older brother has never forgiven the younger for being all he was not."

It did not seem that such a word as "futile" could be used in regard to Brandon Reid, but it was not for me to defend him to his wife. I offered no comment, and for nearly a block she was silent. When she spoke again it was in a lost, sad tone.

"Dwight died in January and my father in March. Within two months of each other. This time of the year, as we move toward January, always seems unhappy to me."

I felt a little impatient with her. I could sympathize with suffering such as she had endured. I had known suffering too, and great loss. But it seemed to me that she had every resource within her grasp for renewed happiness.

"Most of my family is gone now," she went on. "My father, Hobart Rolfe, built a house on the Hudson River to please my mother. When the financial crash ruined him, that was all that remained. Our home on Bleecker Street was merely loaned us by a friend. Now my mother lives alone up the Hudson. Perhaps I'll visit her soon, if I can persuade my husband to take me up there. Perhaps it would do me good to get away from New York for a little while."

There was a plaintive note in her voice, as though she had been dwelling too long in solitude on old grievances.

"I'm sure you'll enjoy a trip up the Hudson," I said cheerfully.

She sighed. "How wonderful to have such robust good health as you enjoy, Miss Kincaid. You seem not to know what it is like to have a day's illness."

I suppressed a desire to tell her that I was too busy to afford time for illness. It was clear, I think, to everyone in the house that Leslie Reid's poor health had its basis more in her mind than in her body. Doctors kept her plied with nostrums but seemed unable to do anything for her.

"What of the children while you are away?" I asked.

"We plan to take Selina with us," Mrs. Reid said. "Miss Garth will remain here with Jeremy. The boy doesn't travel well, and it's wiser not to take him."

Besides, you can't endure him, I thought rebelliously. Perhaps she sensed my unspoken criticism, for she gave me a wistful smile.

"I know you think I am ungrateful, Miss Kincaid, and that isn't wholly true. I believe you are trying very hard to help Jeremy and I hope with all my heart that something can be done for him. In the meantime the thing that concerns me most is his continued association with Selina."

"He likes his sister," I said in quick defense. "He never minds her teasing, and I think he has a real affection for her." Then, since I had gone this far, I decided to go farther. "I feel, however, that Miss Garth is often too severe with the boy. He's still recovering from a serious shock and should be dealt with more gently."

"I'll speak to her," Mrs. Reid promised. "I know she believes in bringing up children very strictly. After all, she was my governess when I was a young girl. Undoubtedly she feels privileged in my family. I trust her judgment completely, but I'll try to persuade her to be more lenient with Jeremy, if you think that is wise."

Such a concession surprised and pleased me, though I doubted that it would have much effect on Thora Garth. At least Mrs. Reid seemed more human this Sunday morning, less remote, less chilly and superior. I wondered if she were perhaps a rather shy person, since shyness can often make one seem unfriendly.

As we neared Washington Square we found the sidewalks fairly well shoveled and the walking became easier. Mrs. Reid, however, did not quicken her pace. Indeed, she seemed to slow her steps even more.

"You enjoyed the play yesterday?" she asked suddenly, and I saw the rising color in her pale cheeks.

"It was quite amusing," I answered carefully. "The children enjoyed it very much."

"And this actress—this Cicely Mansfield? I've never seen her. What is she like?"

I could not meet the entreaty in her eyes. "She seems a gifted comedienne," I admitted.

"Is she—is she very beautiful?"

Mrs. Reid had forgotten to shield her cheeks with her muff and white flakes fell upon her uplifted face unheeded, or were caught and held for an instant in those breathlessly long lashes. I warmed toward her more than I ever had before, and my resentment against Brandon Reid deepened.

"Miss Mansfield isn't beautiful at all," I assured her quickly. "She's rather pretty and she has a certain charm and good humor. Nothing more."

Mrs. Reid seemed to take a pitiful comfort from my words, and I felt both touched and distressed by this revelation. It seemed likely that Andrew was wrong about her love for the younger brother and that Leslie Reid had far more of an interest in the husband she treated so coolly than he suspected.

Yet even as I considered this, she spoke of Dwight again, repeating without self-consciousness some compliment he had paid her. Perhaps she wanted to show me that she had once been placed very high in the estimation of a man she had loved.

My feelings were a mingling of embarrassment and pity, so that it was a relief when we reached the house. I was no little disturbed by this glimpse behind the mask of Leslie Reid's cool, untouchable beauty. There was an indication of hidden fire here, and it troubled me. Jeremy's mother was not indifferent after all, but driven in contrary directions by her own unhappy memories.

When we entered the house, I went at once to the third floor. I could hear voices in the nursery, and knew Miss Garth was there with the children. As I turned toward the rear, the door of the schoolroom opened and to my surprise Andrew Beach looked out at me. Ordinarily he did not come to the house during the weekend.

"How did the matinee go?" he asked without preliminary greeting.

I was deliberately casual. "Well enough. The children seemed to enjoy the play."

"And the master?" Andrew persisted, quirking a disbelieving eyebrow.

"Perhaps you'd better ask him," I said firmly. "Why are you here today?"

"I'm to be given an extra sitting for the portrait." He gestured toward the room behind him. "Come and see what I'm doing."

It was the first time he had offered to show me the portrait, and I followed him into the schoolroom, where an easel stood near a window. On it rested a small canvas—the unfinished portrait of a woman and a child. I studied it with interest.

Andrew had captured the sauciness of Selina's expression, the flyaway quality of her fair hair, the suggestion of ready laughter around her mouth. Work on the child's face was well along toward completion. The mother was still no more than a hazy suggestion—the oval of a face with an ethereal beauty about it and more than a hint of sadness. So it was the ghostly Leslie he meant to paint—though apparently without the plaintive, self-pitying quality so often evident.

"She's very hard to catch," he said. "I'm still groping for the right approach."

I thought of the several Leslie Reids I had seen—the imperious mistress, the all-but-forgotten sick woman in a candlelit room, and in contrast the emotion-torn wife I had met just now in the church.

"I'm not sure you've found it," I said thoughtfully. "First you will have to decide which Mrs. Reid you will paint."

Andrew smiled. "I suspected that you'd not approve. Don't underestimate her, Megan. There may be more there than meets the indifferent eye. But at least our little seamstress has got the master out of the way long enough to notice the mistress."

The anger that flared in me was out of proportion to the cause, and it was as well that I was saved an answer by Kate's sudden appearance in the doorway.

"Mrs. Reid is ready if you'll come for the sitting now," she said to Andrew, and then spoke breathlessly to me. "Mr. Reid has been asking for you all morning, miss. Will you please go to the library at once."

I nodded to her and went to my room without another look at Andrew or his portrait. Once there, I did not hurry. As I took off my mantle and bonnet and combed the black bangs over my forehead, my reflection in the glass startled me. With the mere mention of Brandon Reid's name an angry light had come into my eyes. I might be dressed as a brown wren, but an indignation, further aroused by Andrew, had given me life. It was not displeasing to find that I looked ready for battle.

When I went down, I found the library door open and my employer standing before the pedestal on which rested the Osiris head.

355

He seemed to be studying it in complete concentration, though he sensed my presence and spoke to me without looking around.

"Come in, Miss Kincaid, and close the door behind you, please."

My movements were decisive, my step firm. There was no banking of angry fires now. I walked straight toward him, meaning to speak my mind quickly and have it over with. Unfortunately this determination went unnoted and he spoke first.

"I never tire of the artistry of such sculpture," he said and drew an admiring finger along the proud Egyptian nose. "How well it reveals the man behind the god. Look at those elongated eyes. They aren't wholly the eyes of a stylized pattern. There's thought and intelligence there. But what I like best is the humor of the mouth."

His finger moved, touching the wide, full lips that were strangely like his own—though it seemed to me that the mouth of the man lacked the humor he admired in the statue. However, I had not come here to discuss an Egyptian head. I braced my shoulders and spoke before he could stop me again.

"I don't wish to remain in this house under a false pretense, Mr. Reid. I must express myself concerning your conduct yesterday."

This opening remark, stiff-sounding to my own ears, at least arrested his attention. He gave me a quick, startled look and pulled a chair toward the comfortable fire.

"You needn't stand up like a schoolmistress while you lecture me. Come and sit here. You can be just as indignant with me sitting as standing."

I did not mean to be disarmed and made fun of. I stayed where I was.

"In the first place," I continued, "it was not necessary for you to accompany the children to the play. But since you chose to do so, it was your obligation to carry the afternoon off cheerfully. Since you started out with a pose of good humor, you should have continued it, whatever the effort cost you. You had no right to vent your own displeasures and private resentments upon two children. Particularly upon Jeremy. He was ill last night. This morning he didn't want to get up and he has lost the progress he has been making in the last few weeks. I feel that the blame is yours."

I paused, a little astonished at my own outburst, but not in the least regretting it. His face was expressionless, guarded. He stood at ease before me, listening—and I could not tell at all what my words meant to him, or what their effect might be. When he stepped toward me suddenly and put his thin, strong hands upon my shoulders, I gasped. I could feel their warmth and strength through the goods of my dress.

"Whether you like it or not, you will sit down," he commanded. "I'm quite sure that you enjoy making me uncomfortable, but I don't enjoy it myself and I don't propose to endure it. You will sit here by the fire and relax a little."

Without an unladylike struggle I could not move except in the direction he wished. Into the seat before the fire he plumped me in a far from gentle manner. Then he took the opposite chair and gave me his brilliant, startling smile.

"What else have you to scold me about, Miss Megan?" he said.

How very cunning he was! How clever. His smile, even his use of the children's name for me was intended to dispell my anger, to dispose me more gently toward him. And I did not mean to be so disposed. I sat upright in the cushioned chair and stared at him even more angrily than before.

"I do have something else to say. I would like to tell you that while I have heard gossip, I have not indulged in gossip. I have no knowledge as to whether any of the things I've heard are true or untrue, and it's not for me to judge you. However, your behavior in the theater box yesterday was indecorous and without consideration for the children or for me."

There—I had said all that I had come to say. The words were out, and I sat stiffly on the edge of my chair, waiting for the skies to fall.

Mr. Reid was no longer smiling. He did not look at me now, but away from my face into the fire.

"I asked you here to offer you an apology," he told me, after what seemed a struggle for composure. "As you say, I behaved badly yesterday. And even before—when I used your suggestion to take the children to this play as an instrument for humiliating others. Since it's quite true that Miss Mansfield's name and mine have been coupled in the newspapers, I had no business encouraging you to attend that particular play, or to take the children to it. I didn't know I would feel so deeply ashamed of my action, Miss Megan. This has been a chastening revelation."

I did not altogether trust him, and I could not tell whether he was wholly serious. Prepared as I was to meet anything but this, I could not immediately retreat from high indignation and respond with grace.

"I accept your apology," I said stiffly. "But the damage has been done, and it cannot be easily remedied."

There seemed no trace of mockery in him now, but an acceptance of my words in almost sorrowful regret. How strange a man he was. How filled with contradictions and driven by who could know what inner demons. Often he seemed misplaced in his present role. With him I had always an awareness of a man who had lived in far places, whose eyes had beheld incredible sights, whose thoughts were concerned with worlds far removed from my own.

"I've wanted to tell you how much I appreciate the effect you are having on Jeremy," he said when the silence grew too long between us. "His improvement has been visible even to me, though I see him so seldom. Let's hope this setback won't be permanent."

This was a subject I could warm to. "He's making you something for Christmas," I told him. "I don't know what it is, but I know he wants to please you and gain your approval. Whatever the gift may be, I hope you'll accept it warmly when the time comes."

The somber look touched his eyes again. "I'll accept it with a proper expression of appreciation, I hope. But warmly—no. That's too much to ask of me."

"But it's not!" I cried. "So much has already been withheld from the boy. It must be made up for. You are an adult. You have the strength he lacks."

I could sense that I had touched him on the raw. He gazed up at the portrait of his father over the mantel, and I was once more aware of the affection in his look. Had it pained him as a young man, I wondered, to disappoint his father, to be less in his father's eyes than his brother Dwight had been?

"Jeremy destroyed a great deal," he said quietly. "There is a point past which you cannot push me."

I did not speak, and he changed the subject.

"Mrs. Reid has been pressing me to take her up the Hudson to visit her mother. She feels such a trip will improve her health. While I'm not convinced this will be the case, I intend to do as she wishes. Selina will come with us, but I want to leave Jeremy in your charge while we are gone."

"What of Miss Garth?" I asked.

"Miss Garth may be free to visit her father, or attend lectures, or do whatever she pleases. I'm not sure how long we'll be gone, but I have every confidence in you, Miss Megan. I know you won't let the boy run away again and I'll feel better if he is in your . . . in your gentle hands." He smiled, and I saw there could be humor in the curve of his lips after all.

For the space of a moment I regretted the fact that he did not find me altogether gentle. But what he thought did not matter, so long as he left Jeremy in my care. This was the step I wanted, and I felt elated at the new trust placed in me.

In spite of myself, during the course of this interview certain of my views about Brandon Reid were being softened and revised. Because I wanted to show that my rancor was gone, I spoke to him pleasantly, assuring him that I would do my best for Jeremy. Then, thinking little of it, I mentioned the church I had visited that morning—though I did not mention seeing Leslie there.

"The minister said wonderful things about your brother," I told him. "He spoke glowingly of the Dwight Reid Memorial Home and its opening in January."

My employer stiffened, and I recalled too late what Mrs. Reid had said about her husband's opposition to the Home, and her claim that Brandon had been envious of his brother. Now I saw his eyes return to his father's portrait with an almost passionate pride. Pride in what? Did he really oppose the opening of the memorial? And why?

He turned back to me without comment, his manner indicating clearly that our interview had come to an end. I was not expected to sit here chatting in a sociable manner. I rose at once and took my departure with far less indignation than had ridden me when I came in.

Not until I was out of his company did I realize how thoroughly the wind had been taken from my sails. I had not retreated from any stand I had made, yet I had the feeling that I no longer blamed or condemned him as I had when I entered the room. How this change had been brought about, I was not altogether sure. Nor was I entirely sure that it pleased me. I did not want to be won over against my better judgment. On the other hand, what *was* my better judgment? It was so difficult to know.

CHAPTER 11

THE FOLLOWING day, on the very heels of the snowstorm, New York was enveloped in an unusually early freeze. Before the snow had time to melt, the temperature plummeted and a sharper foretaste of winter was upon us. A jingling of sleigh bells could be heard along the Avenue, and the panes of every window were etched in patterns of frost.

The sub-freezing weather held for several days, and on the afternoon before Brandon Reid was to take his wife upriver to visit her mother he paid an unexpected call upon us in the nursery.

I had scarcely seen him since our interview in the library, but evidence of his plan to put Jeremy into my hands had been made clear. Miss Garth was sulking and casting dark looks in my direction. She was crosser than ever with Jeremy, yet, until the signal was given to put me in full charge, I did not want to stir her to further opposition by the objections I longed to express.

While I bided my time, I planned the history lessons we would do together, Jeremy and I. Andrew, I'd found, was good enough when it came to American history, but he had little interest or knowledge in the ancient world. So I intended to open to Jeremy's bright mind more of the subject of Egyptian civilization and what it entailed for the world of that day. So far his state of apathy had not lessened and he would sit for hours huddled over the pages of a book he did not read—just as he had done when I first came to the house.

That afternoon when his uncle strode into the nursery, the boy was lost in his own troubled thoughts and did not look up. The rest of us—Garth, Selina, and I—stared in surprise, for I had never seen him set foot in the nursery before.

He left the door open so that drafts from the hall cut through the warm stuffiness and Miss Garth shivered pointedly, edging a shade closer to a fire that must nearly scorch her as it was.

"Good Lord, how can you breathe in a place like this?" he demanded. I half expected him to stride to a window and fling it open and I would have welcomed a cold blast of fresh air.

Jeremy glanced at him briefly and then stared at his book again, his face expressionless.

"This is a day to be outdoors," Mr. Reid said, his eyes on the boy. "How would you like to go skating in Central Park, Jeremy?"

Selina squealed at the suggestion and demanded to go too, but Jeremy did not look up or answer. I sat in silence, waiting uncertainly for whatever was to come.

"What of the ice?" Miss Garth asked, ready as always to oppose any plan that was not her own. "There has scarcely been time for it to freeze, Mr. Reid."

"I've checked, of course," Brandon Reid said impatiently. "The flags are showing on streetcars running uptown—white flags with a red ball. Which means the red ball is up on the Arsenal and the ice is firm. Get the children into their warm wraps, Miss Garth. We'll leave as soon as they're ready."

I believe the governess would have liked to refuse, but the master of the house was in no mood to brook opposition. He had made this sudden plan and he would do as he chose. When I glanced again at Jeremy, I was ready to bless his uncle. A faint stirring of interest had come into the boy's eyes, and he had pushed the unread book away. When Brandon pointed a finger at him and said, "Hurry up, boy!" Jeremy followed Selina and Miss Garth willingly from the room.

Once they had gone, Brandon Reid stared at me with a light of challenge in his eyes.

"I shall need you to help me with the children, Miss Megan. Garth is too old for skating, if she ever learned. You are able to skate, I presume?"

I felt a sudden eagerness in me, though I tried to answer sedately. "I learned to skate when I was very young, sir."

"Then into your things at once," he ordered. "You've been look-ing pale lately. We'll get you out in the cold and whip some color into your cheeks."

"This will be good for Jeremy," I said. But though I ignored the reference to my own appearance, as I left my chair I felt suddenly as young as Selina and as eager for exciting action. If any warning voice whispered in my mind, I shut it away and hurried to get ready.

I still had the skates I had used as a girl and I had sturdy high shoes to fasten them to. I put on my warmest dress and wrap, tied my bonnet ribbons firmly, and wrapped a green muffler about my neck. Then I went downstairs to find the others waiting.

They were prepared for the cold, with Brandon Reid wearing a turtle-necked jersey under his tweed hunting jacket and a red stocking cap on his head. Jeremy's cap was blue and white stripes, with a long tassel down the back. Selina looked like a miniature of her mother, with her hands clasped in a small sealskin muff.

Miss Garth waited downstairs with the children, and I saw that her mouth was set in tight disapproval. When Mr. Reid went out the front door to see if the carriage was ready, the children hurried in his wake, Selina calling to me to come along. Before I could obey, there was a moment in which Miss Garth and I were alone. The governess raised the heavy lids of her eyes and looked at me without evasion.

I will never forget the sense of shock I experienced as she turned her dark gaze upon me. Her look was one of pure malevolence. I had seen her angry and disapproving and resentful before. But I had seen nothing like this. Thora Garth did not merely dislike me. She hated me and I knew in that moment that if the opportunity ever came she would do me harm. Yet no word was spoken between us. She simply stared at me with that ill-intentioned gaze. Then she turned and went upstairs.

I ran down the steps to join the others in the carriage, shaken more than I wanted to admit. Quite suddenly I did not like the prospect of being left alone in that house with only the children and Thora Garth for company.

This time as we drove away, I did not glance up to see if Leslie watched us from her window. If she did, I did not want to know. I was disturbed enough and I desired only to shed the spell of threatening evil Miss Garth had seemed to promise me.

Overhead that day the sky was the color of wet ashes, but the air was clear and cold. The first horsecar we passed on Fifth Avenue displayed the skating flag, and our anticipation quickened. Gradually, with the house behind us and Brandon Reid's electric mood growing contagious, I began to throw off my somber misgivings and regain the earlier sense of excitement that had filled me over this outing.

Even Jeremy began to enjoy himself. His uncle was making up for the disaster of the matinee, and I knew I would have a happier boy to work with when the Reids left on their journey tomorrow.

Certainly we could not have asked for a more thoughtful escort that afternoon, nor one more amiable. On the drive uptown Jeremy's uncle entertained the children with stories of winters when he was a boy, and he drew out of me an account of one New Jersey holiday I liked to remember.

In Central Park he chose his favorite pond, and we found that a long wooden building had been erected to offer accommodation for skaters. There was a restaurant inside, counters where skates could be rented, and a room with benches all around where we could sit while putting on our skates. Two potbellied stoves offered rosy warmth to the cold-nipped fingers and toes of skaters.

While Jeremy and Selina put on their skates, Brandon Reid knelt to fasten mine to my shoes. His touch was surprisingly gentle, and I sensed in him an eagerness to please me that I would never have expected him to show. It seemed likely that speaking my mind the other day had accomplished more than I had hoped for. We were dealing today with a man almost boyishly intent on giving us pleasure.

The ice had been newly opened for skating, and its gleaming surface spread smooth and cloud-white from shore to shore. The four of us teetered down a plank walk that led to the pond, and in the beginning we set off with Mr. Reid skating hand-in-hand with Selina, and Jeremy with me. But Selina's efforts required a slow patience that Brandon lacked and before long we had changed partners. Jeremy, who had been taught to skate by his father and had considerable skill, seemed willing to take Selina in hand and set his speed to her capability. Before I knew it Brandon Reid had drawn me away from the shelter where the crowd was thick and we were striking out for the far curve of the pond, our hands crossed, our glides well matched so that we moved smoothly as one.

For this little while I was content. I looked neither backward nor forward, but gave myself into his sure hands and let him guide me as he would. For this one afternoon I would exist in a world of snow and ice, suspended away from all the problems of my life. Or so I foolishly thought.

There was a change in Brandon Reid that I did not attempt to weigh too closely. I knew only that he was not the mocking, impatient man who had taken us to the matinee as a joke. It was as if he too had shed the smothering atmosphere of candlelight and violets that pervaded the house and had become at once a more natural and a kinder person.

When we reached the far curve of the pond, I could have wished for an endless horizon that would never require us to turn back. Though that wasn't possible, I held to my dreaming state, my hands secure in his as we rounded the curve and started toward the place where we had left Jeremy and Selina. Before we had skated far, he slowed our glides and drew me toward the bank. I sensed that he too was reluctant to return and that to Brandon Reid, as well as to me, these moments were ones of blessed escape.

"Here's a place where we can stop and catch our breath," he said.

Up the nearby bank a few skaters had gathered about a chestnut vendor. His cart—a converted baby carriage—had a basket of burning charcoal for a stove set into one end. There was warmth and good cheer around the cart and the delicious odor of roasting chestnuts. We climbed the bank, and Brandon Reid bought a sack of chestnuts that warmed our hands as we shelled and ate them. The group around the vendor changed constantly and paid little attention to us. Standing somewhat apart from the others, our skates balancing us in deep snow, we felt as if we were quite alone.

As I watched the skaters on the pond below, gliding past in the thickening gray light, I became aware that my companion was not watching the crowd or the chestnut vendor. His attention was upon me, and there was no unkindness, no criticism in his look. I had the feeling that in some strange way we had become friends this afternoon, as we had not been before. A curious thought for a woman in my position, yet it was there and it was true.

"Don't think I'm unaware of all you're doing for us, Megan," he said quietly. "You've brought something into that house that is making itself felt. We've had little of kindness for one another, and I'm sure Jeremy has suffered for it. Perhaps this day of skating will get you off to a better start with him. Has he forgiven me, do you think?"

"Oh, yes," I told him quickly. "He would forgive you almost anything. It was good of you to think of an outing. Good for both children."

"And for you, Megan? Good for you—as it has been for me?"

He held my eyes with his own, and yet I could not read his full meaning. Or perhaps I did not want to. I looked away, suddenly perturbed. He thrust the sack of chestnuts into his pocket and took my mittened hands in his. In spite of the sharp, cold wind that blew upon us, I felt the warmth of his hands through wool and longed to let my own hands clasp his as warmly. Some strange chemistry stirred between us, and in the very instant of awareness I knew that we must not be drawn toward ice that cracked treacherously at our very feet. To linger meant danger.

I stepped back quickly and nearly lost my balance. My companion laughed and steadied me. The moment was past, and I did not know whether I felt relief or regret.

"We'd better return," he said, and we went down the steep bank together and started toward the far end of the pond and the shelter. Our steps matched less perfectly now, and I knew my glides were often ragged. When we rejoined the children, we found that Selina was growing cold and ready to start home, though I think Jeremy could have skated till dark.

In the carriage Brandon gave them the bag of chestnuts and they occupied themselves with shelling and munching on the long drive downtown from the park. It had begun to snow again, and once I saw Brandon glance up at the filmed sky with a look so unhappy that it stabbed me to a pity I had never expected to feel toward Brandon Reid.

CHAPTER 12

THE NEXT morning I wakened to the realization that this was the day when I must meet my new responsibilities.

I tried to put from my mind the insistent memory of that moment near the chestnut vendor when Brandon Reid had held my hands and I'd heard the first faint cracking of the ice. I tried to dismiss the look Miss Garth had given me as something I must have exaggerated. Detest me, the woman might, but there was nothing she could do to injure me and I must not let such imaginings possess me. Malevolence was far too strong a word.

Mr. and Mrs. Reid left early that morning, with Selina sitting between them in the carriage. They would drive to the pier to take passage on one of the river boats that ran between New York and Albany. Miss Garth, having been informed that all control of Jeremy was to be relinquished to me for these few days, slept late and arose sullen. But there was nothing so alarming as malevolence in her. She was pleased, she told me tartly, to have Jeremy off her hands, and she wished me well with him in a tone which implied her true wish that everything possible would go wrong.

Jeremy was up and restored again, and I began to devise ways in which to keep him busy. There were, of course, the lessons with Andrew in the morning, and I sat through them, not sewing, but taking part in the discussions, and often working out the wrong answers to arithmetic problems, much to Jeremy's superior amusement. Andrew took his cue from me, and we were more frivolous than usual about lessons. I believe we all enjoyed the change and that it was good for Jeremy, even though studies did not progress as well as they might.

Miss Garth did not appear at lunchtime—Kate said she was having a cup of tea in her room—so the meal went well. By the time Andrew left the house, Jeremy was cheerfully ready to interest himself once more in the gift he planned to make for his uncle. I had never asked him what it was, but now he told me about it voluntarily.

When we were again in the schoolroom, which for all its bareness, I preferred to the stuffy nursery, he brought me the book I had purchased on Egypt and showed me the picture of a statue. The figure wore a wide, flat collar of the type so often seen in Egyptian paintings and sculpture.

"I'm making a collar for the Osiris head," he told me, his eyes ashine with pride. "I'll need more of those steel beads you gave me, and I'd like some other beads of the same shape and size. Perhaps in green, and a few red ones too. Mr. Beach brought me the wire, and it's just right for making the collar stiff."

He showed me the plan he had drawn with colored crayons on paper and the work he had painstakingly commenced. The design was attractive, and its execution revealed the boy's creative gift. I was happy to give him my unstinting approval and promise him the beads.

This seemed a good time to urge upon him an interest in making gifts for his mother and Selina as well, but this suggestion left him indifferent.

"Selina likes silly things," he said. "And my mother has everything she wants. When she wishes something new, she buys it. So there's no use trying to give her anything."

I sensed that his resistance was due to more than the difficulties he named and I insisted quietly that some sort of gift for his mother must be thought of. I made various suggestions, but he shrugged them all aside.

Later, when we were engaged in a game of chess, with Jeremy beating me badly, he made one of his unexpected capitulations.

"All right—I'll make a gift for my mother if I can think of something," he offered.

I suspected that his change of mind was due to a desire to please me and I took pains to show my approval. Any positive steps he might make were in the right direction.

"Perhaps if I went to her room and looked around," he suggested, "I would get an idea of what to make. Will you come with me, Miss Megan?"

The notion did not appeal to me, but he had already slipped from his place at the table.

"Do come along," he said, sounding as impatient as his uncle.

The important thing was to encourage him in any sort of generous gesture toward his mother, I told myself. There could be little harm if he looked about her room for inspiration. I would not enter, but would stand in the doorway and watch to see that he touched nothing, performed no mischief.

We went downstairs together, and Jeremy led the way first into his mother's small boudoir. The heavy green velvet draperies that hid the door to her bedroom were drawn across the opening, and before we could approach them, a sound reached us from the room beyond. I realized with a start that someone was moving about in Leslie's room.

Jeremy put a finger to his lips. "Hush," he warned. "I know who it is. She does this sometimes when my mother is away. Come and look."

Before I could stop him, he went to the doorway and parted the velvet curtains to a narrow slit. Puzzled, I stood behind him and looked through upon an astonishing scene.

Miss Garth had her back to us and she was dressed in one of Leslie Reid's beautiful gowns. It was a green satin that went dramatically with Leslie's red hair, and it was too tight for Miss Garth to hook all the way up. The flesh of her upper back showed pinched above the hooking, and, as she moved before us, I caught the scent of the violet spray she had used lavishly upon her person.

For a moment I stood shocked and frozen, watching her in something like horror, unable to draw myself away from the sight. As I stared, she picked up the full pleated skirt of the underdrape, turning and dipping before the long mirror until her heavy dark hair, loosened from its puffs, trembled on the verge of dishevelment. She gave her head a quick toss that sent the tortoise-shell pins flying, and her hair came down in thick profusion about her face and shoulders.

I did not like the glow in her eyes or the smile on her lips as she watched her own image. But when I put a hand on Jeremy's arm to draw him away, I could feel his resistance. I did not want to betray our presence by a struggle, and, as I hesitated, the woman in the green gown swooped toward the bed table and picked something up in her hands. As she turned toward the lamp that burned on Mrs. Reid's dressing table, I saw that she held the double miniature Leslie had shown me on my first visit to this room.

Miss Garth's back was still toward us, and I could not at first see her face, though I knew she was studying the twin portraits— or one of them. Slowly she turned with the framed miniatures in her hand, and now I could catch her expression. It was the warm, glowing look of a woman in love, and my sense of shock and horror increased. This time I bent warningly to Jeremy and put pressure behind my grip on his shoulder. Somehow I managed to get him quietly away, and we did not speak until we had returned upstairs.

The thought came to me that in Jeremy's hands, if he were indiscreet, lay a frightening power to wound and humiliate Thora Garth. For all my distress at what I had seen, an uneasy pity toward the woman moved me. She had gone too far along the road of daydreaming, and sure disaster lay in the course she followed.

Back in the schoolroom Jeremy returned calmly to the chess game and began to study the board as though nothing untoward had occurred. A lecture on the evils of spying would have little effect, I knew, but at least I must express an attitude.

"I don't think it's fair to watch anyone who doesn't know she is being watched," I told him gently.

Jeremy shrugged and began a triumphant move across the board with his red queen. "Garth is crazy," he said. "Crazy as a witch."

I pushed a black bishop absently into a castle's path, unable to concentrate.

"She certainly isn't crazy," I insisted. "You must never say such a thing about anyone."

"Why not?" His dark eyes met mine almost insolently. "It's what they say about me. But Garth is a lot crazier than I am."

I leaned toward him across the board. "Listen to me, Jeremy. Miss Garth must be a very lonely woman. Especially now when your mother and Selina are away. I expect she feels at home with your mother's things because she took care of her when she was a young girl. Since children like to dress up in older people's clothes, why shouldn't older people enjoy dressing up like someone younger?"

"You don't know what she's like," Jeremy said carelessly, unconvinced by my feeble logic. His main attention was still for the game. Deliberately he moved his queen and said, "Checkmate," ending the contest. "You're too easy to beat, Miss Megan," he added.

I sensed that further argument would not reach him just now and cast around in my mind for something cheerful to do with the rest of the afternoon. It was then an inspiration came to me.

"Let's have a tea party in my room, Jeremy. I can heat water on the hearth in my little kettle, and I've some biscuits I've been saving for a special occasion. I've even a new rocking chair to show you—and my new lamp. Come and keep me company."

He seemed to like the idea, perhaps because I had never before invited him into my room. He helped me with the fire, and we soon had smoke and flames writhing up the chimney. In a little while there would be bright warmth. I lighted the lamp I had recently purchased. A plump china globe sprigged with pink rosebuds circled the chimney and added a touch of cheer to the small plain room. I spread a cloth of Irish linen over the table and set Jeremy to work putting out the blue Lowestoft tea set. When I opened the tin of Huntley and Palmer biscuits, Jeremy took pleasure in arranging small pink and white frosted cakes on a blue plate.

While we made our preparations, I told him of the morning I had gone to church and of the fine things the minister had said about Dwight Reid. Everyone else avoided any mention of his father's name to Jeremy, and I felt this to be unwise. It could only add to the burden of unspoken guilt the boy carried. He listened somewhat warily to my account and I sensed his inner bracing.

"Miss Megan," he said when I finished, "if there's an opening ceremony for the Home, do you think Uncle Brandon would permit me to go?"

"I don't see why you shouldn't go," I told him recklessly, since I had no knowledge of how his uncle might react to this suggestion. "Anyway, it's a month or more away, so we needn't worry about it now."

Absently, he put the cover back on the oblong biscuit tin. "I *must* go," he said, and I wondered what expiation such an act might signify to the boy.

We did not mention the matter again that day, however. To distract him, I went to the mantel where Richard's carrousel sat and while the water heated in a kettle hung over coals, I wound the toy and set the tiny horses and sleigh to whirling as the music box played. Jeremy's eyes brightened as he watched and I sang the old nursery tune for him in French.

> "Frère Jacques,
> Frère Jacques,
> Dormez-vous?
> Dormez-vous?
> Sonnez les matines,
> Sonnez les matines,
> Ding! Dang! Dong!
> Ding! Dang! Dong!"

He was clearly fascinated, but when I would have taken the toy from the mantel to let him see it more closely, he put his hands behind his back, remembering what I had forgotten.

"I'm still being pun—that is, I'm still paying a penalty, Miss Megan," he said. "I mustn't touch it."

I set it back on the mantel and wound it again, deciding then and there that this toy would be my Christmas gift to Jeremy.

When the kettle had bubbled and the tea was steeped, we enjoyed our little party to the full. Jeremy looked so contented that I wished his mother and uncle had been there to see him. There was nothing wrong with this child that new interests, patience, and a little loving kindness would not cure.

When our cups were empty and a sufficient number of biscuits had been consumed, I told him something about Richard, who had owned the carrousel, and there was an easing in my own heart for the telling. Finally I drew out a book of fairy tales that had belonged to me when I was little, and from which I used to read to Richard. Jeremy seemed delighted at the prospect of being read to, and I realized with a pang that he knew nothing of the companionable experience of reading aloud. He took a cushion from a chair and sat upon it cross-legged before the fire, studying the flames as all children love to do, while I began the story.

I had found a favorite of Richard's, though I was not quite sure how Jeremy would receive it. He did not look at me as I read, but there was a rapt expression in his eyes and a faint smile curled his lips.

The tale was the one of the ugly little toad whom no one could love until the kindness of a beautiful maiden freed him from enchantment and he became again a handsome, shining prince. Jeremy made not a sound until the last word was done and silence lay upon the room. Then he turned toward me and I saw a mist in his eyes.

"Even while he was a toad," Jeremy said, lost in wonder, "he found someone to love him. Someone who didn't mind how ugly and warty he was."

It cost me an effort to speak in the matter-of-fact manner I knew I must adopt. I wanted to kneel on the hearth beside him and put my arms about him, but the gesture must not come too soon or it would be suspect and thus rejected.

"I think that was quite natural," I told him. "The girl in the story was kind and she could see past the toad disguise to the fine prince he really was inside."

Jeremy nodded. "But first there had to be something fine for her to see. What if there hadn't been anything at all? What if he were wicked clear through?"

The lump in my throat was unbearable, and while I sought words to reassure and comfort him, a sharp rapping sounded on the door.

I went to open it and found Miss Garth on the threshold. She was dressed once more in her brown merino, though the breath of violets still clung to her person. Color rode high in her cheeks, and she was furiously angry.

CHAPTER 13

THE WARMTH and gentle happiness of the little room was gone in an instant. The moment I opened the door Miss Garth saw the boy and she pushed past me, entering without a by-your-leave.

"What did you do with them?" she cried, pouncing on him. "Where did you hide them?"

Jeremy went white and sullen beneath the angry pressure of her hand upon his shoulder. He stared at her with contempt rising in his eyes and said nothing at all.

"What is it?" I asked. "What is it you think he has taken? Surely you can ask him more kindly!"

My earlier sympathy for the woman had vanished, and I was ready to oppose her for the boy's sake.

"He knows very well," Miss Garth snapped. "He has taken the gold scissors and thimble that were my mother's. He has played with them before and now he has stolen them from the sewing basket in my room. What have you done with them, you wicked boy?"

He shrugged her hand aside and rose to his full height before her, clearly unafraid of the anger that burned in the woman.

"Why do you try to pretend that you're my mother?" he asked coolly. "Why do you dress up in her clothes and make believe that you're young and pretty when you're really so very old and ugly?"

Every vestige of color went out of Miss Garth's face. While I stood helpless and alarmed, she gasped as if she could not draw her breath without pain. Then she reached out and caught Jeremy by the arm with fingers turned as vicious as claws. He lacked

374

the strength to resist her, and she pulled him with her out of my room and to his own, next door.

I followed them, my anxiety rising. I had no intention of abandoning Jeremy, but the woman was in so demented a state that coping with her would be difficult.

In his own room she flung the boy from her. "Are you going to tell me what you've done with my things?" she demanded. "Or must I search your room for myself?"

He recovered his balance and would have hurled himself upon her if I had not put my arms about him, holding him back. "Wait," I whispered. "Let her be, Jeremy. You shouldn't have said what you did."

For a moment he struggled, then went limp in my arms. Together we watched as she moved about the room, pulling open drawers, looking into boxes. When she reached the bed she lifted the pillow and pointed dramatically. There beneath it lay the gold scissors and thimble. She snatched them up and held them out accusingly to Jeremy.

"So now you are a thief as well!" she cried. "Don't expect to escape without punishment this time. Your uncle shall hear of this when he returns. A thrashing is what you have coming to you, and a thrashing you will get!"

"My uncle will not thrash me," the boy said tensely. "He wouldn't dare. Nor will you."

Her eyes, glazed by rage, searched the room as if to find some means of punishing him. Her eyes fell upon the collar Jeremy was making for his uncle's Christmas gift, with loose beads and wire strewn around it. With a spiteful, slashing gesture, she dashed the collar from the table, scattering beads over the carpet.

"Trash!" she cried. "Worthless trash!"

Jeremy escaped my arms and flung himself to his knees where he could pick up the collar. Over the shimmering circlet he stared up at Miss Garth.

"When I find the gun," he said in a low, deadly voice, "I will kill you too."

The woman looked at him, and the crazed fury went out of her, replaced by sudden fear.

"I'll not stay in this house tonight!" she gasped. With the scissors and thimble clutched in one hand, she fled from the room without looking back, and I knew she was truly frightened.

Silently I knelt beside Jeremy, helping him pick up the scattered beads. They were small, and the loose ones had scattered widely. I held to my silence until his harried breathing quieted and some of the trembling went out of him.

"I think the collar hasn't been damaged," I said. "And we've found most of the beads. I'll get you more tomorrow."

He emptied his own handful into the empty candy box that served to hold them and did not answer me at all.

While Miss Garth had behaved in an outrageous fashion, the boy was at fault too, and I could not let his threatening words pass without comment.

"Why did you borrow her things?" I asked softly.

He gave me a troubled look from wide, dark eyes. "I don't know," he said. "Do you think it's because I am what they say I am—mad?"

I couldn't endure his white, solemn expression and I made a move to put my arms about him. He stepped back at once, rejecting the gesture.

"Of course you're not mad," I went on as reasonably as possible. "All of us do foolish things we're sorry for afterwards. The next time you feel like doing something you know is wrong come and tell me first. If we talk it over together, perhaps you won't want to do it after all."

"How can I tell you when I'm going to do something like that when I don't know ahead of time myself? How can I not say dreadful things when I don't know I'm going to say them? Like what I said about killing her."

"You didn't mean that threat," I assured him. "She upset you, and you wanted to pay her back. Though paying people back doesn't serve us very well most of the time."

He looked straight at me, his eyes cloudy with emotion. "Once I made a threat like that and I meant it," he said.

So unsettled was the look in his eyes that I shivered involuntarily. At once he noticed this evidence of weakness.

"You're afraid of me, aren't you?" he said, dark triumph in his voice. "You're afraid of me too!"

I suppressed the shiver and shook my head firmly. "Of course I'm not afraid of you, Jeremy. I'm never afraid of someone I trust."

For a moment longer he stared at me; then his thoughts seemed to turn inward and his stare lost its focus. I knew he was slipping away and out of my reach, yet I could not bring him back.

We had supper alone in the downstairs dining room that night, for, true to her word, Miss Garth had left the house. We dined in loneliness at one end of the long table, and it was a somber meal, with no conversation between us. Jeremy scarcely ate, and I did not urge him. I had little taste for food myself, and it was a relief to leave the big room and the watchful eyes of Henry and return upstairs.

How empty the house seemed that night. Not only because Jeremy and I were alone in the upper story, but also because Brandon Reid was away. The vigor of his presence always filled the house and gave it life. When he was not indoors, the house seemed to wait for his coming. When he was home, the noises of everyday living were present and a voice that spoke out with no fear of raising the echoes. When he was away altogether, the house whispered and creaked and murmured, but it did not speak aloud reassuringly.

That evening was long to get through. Jeremy retreated behind the book on Egyptian archaeology, yet he turned the pages so seldom that I sensed how active his mind must be beneath the pretense of reading. There was no way to draw him out, no reassurance I could offer. I sewed on a frock for Selina until my eyes wearied and then I too sat in silence, staring at the plaid wool in my lap.

When bedtime came, Jeremy startled me. He put his book aside and stood beside my chair.

"Miss Megan," he said, "will you please lock me in my room tonight?"

I considered the suggestion soberly and felt the quick beating of my heart beneath my calm reception. It seemed a dreadful thing he suggested. Why should he need forcible restraint when Garth, with whom he was angry, was not in the house tonight? Or did he fear a return to his father's room and a repetition of the wild hysteria of sobbing he had indulged in once before? I knew he still had the key to the room, for I'd seen it in a box on his bureau, though he had not used it again.

Quickly I sought for a counter suggestion. "I've a better plan than that," I told him. "Come and help me and I'll show you."

He followed me doubtfully into his own room and watched while I stripped his bed.

"Now then," I said when the covers were off, "you can help me with the mattress. It's too heavy for me to manage alone."

"What are you going to do with it?" he asked.

"Help me and you'll see," I said with as lighthearted a smile as I could manage.

He took one end of the mattress, and I led the way, backing, as we carried it into my room. With a little rearranging of the furniture, we were able to spread it out on the floor near my bed.

"There!" I said. "This is where you may sleep tonight. We'll keep each other company, since there's no one else upstairs in the house."

He did not answer or come with me when I ran back for the bedclothes, but stayed where he was, staring at the mattress.

"You won't mind sleeping on the floor, will you?" I asked. "It will be like something from a story—like camping out. We'll put an extra quilt over you to keep away the drafts, and you'll be cozy warm."

I glanced at him and saw that he was watching me in a queer, tense way.

"What if I try to hurt you in the night?" he said.

I was on my knees beside the bedding and I could look into his eyes more nearly at his own level. I took his hands and held them lightly in my own. Somehow I even managed what sounded like a laugh.

"Jeremy, you are only a little boy. I'm much stronger and bigger than you are. I won't let you hurt me, and I won't let you hurt yourself. There now—that's a promise!"

For once I had found the right words. The heavy load of anxiety seemed to slip away from him. He gave me a smile that was strangely sweet, and I knew that for the moment he had given me his complete trust. Again I held back an impulse to catch him to me and let him know the feeling of arms that loved and protected. But I could go so far and no farther until he was ready to come to me.

Though Jeremy slept quickly, I could not fall asleep at once. I lay listening to his light, even breathing and thought about the incidents of the last few days. Of Brandon Reid and his apology to me, his change of attitude. Of yesterday, when we had skated in Central Park and everything between us had been strange and different. Beguilingly, dangerously different. My hands knew again the pressure of his, warm despite the cold, and I grew warm again remembering. Such thoughts frightened me because of my very willingness to indulge them. I pulled my imaginings up short and chose another course.

With Mr. Reid on my side, wonders might now be achieved with Jeremy. If only we could weather such setbacks as occurred, real progress might be possible. Miss Garth, of course, should be kept away from the boy. He must be left wholly to Andrew and me.

When my thoughts turned to Thora Garth, it was with sick distaste. Yet I could not entirely condemn her. If Jeremy was caught in a web of circumstances he could not overcome, she too was similarly trapped. Behind all that was unpleasant hid a woman whom life had cheated. Or was it possible for life to cheat us? Did we not do the cheating ourselves when we could not meet with wisdom and courage and joy what befell us? Had Thora Garth allowed herself to indulge too long a fantasy that would now destroy her? Which of those two miniature portraits had attracted the fervent expression I had seen on her face? To what extent did her dressing up in Leslie Reid's gowns mean an identification with Leslie so that she might share vicariously experiences her mistress had known?

These thoughts were not conducive to sleep, and again I tried to change their course. It was of Andrew I must think. He was the one person in this house I could count on, whether I always agreed with him or not. At least he spoke the truth as he saw it, even though his words might sometimes sting and bite. He was fooled by no one. He could find good in a pickpocket and be disdainful of those in high position. There was a sharpness to his view that cut through to the secret self a man might hide beneath pretenses. Or a woman.

I knew he disliked Brandon intensely. I knew he pitied Leslie. Garth he simply detested and tormented. Yet I suspected that he would understand very well if I told him what Jeremy and I had seen today.

Thinking about Andrew did not, after all, help me to fall asleep. I knew Andrew would have been horrified by the fact that Jeremy lay asleep on the floor beside me. I would be in for a lecture tomorrow if I told him. Yet nothing anyone could say would stop me in my course. Some of the love I had given my brother was turning toward young Jeremy. It was there within me to be given, and I must have something human to turn it upon.

So I lay and watched the red coals turn black in the grate and heard the sifting of ashes. I watched the bright glow of the snowy night at my window and listened to Jeremy's breathing as he slept.

It must have been long past midnight when I too slept, dreamed, wakened fitfully, and then slept again. When a clock somewhere in the house struck three I came wide awake, listening for more than a striking clock. I could no longer hear the rhythm of Jeremy's sleep and I turned quietly in the bed so that I could look out upon the cold, still room. Between me and the window something moved, and my breath caught in my throat. The boy was up, silhouetted dark against the snowy light beyond. Softly, almost stealthily, he was moving toward my bed. A thrill of unreasoning terror left me weak and breathless. Fear that this was not the harmless child I had claimed. This was a boy who was given to violent angers and who had once deliberately killed.

"Jeremy?" I managed his name between stiff lips.

The relief in his own voice was very great. "Oh, you're awake? I'm sorry if I wakened you. I was so cold—I couldn't sleep."

I flung back my quilts and carried one of them to his pallet. "Lie down quickly and let me put an extra cover over you. You'll be warm soon. There's nothing to fear."

My voice soothed him, and he slipped beneath the covers, snuggling down into warmth with the sigh of a very young child. I knelt beside him, holding his hand until his shivering ceased, and I sang once more the music box song in French. Drowsily he began to repeat the words and fell asleep murmuring, *"Dormez-vous?"*

There was only peace in this room, the snow gently falling beyond my window, and no fear anywhere in the Reid household.

CHAPTER 14

THE FOLLOWING days were blissfully uneventful. Miss Garth stayed away, and there was no word from upriver. Jeremy went back to sleeping in his own room, again willing to be nine years old and scornful of babyish ways. I did not, after all, tell Andrew of the things that had happened on that very disturbing night.

Lessons progressed well during Selina's absence, and Jeremy seemed to work with a will that surprised Andrew. Once or twice I found the tutor looking at me in a speculative manner as though he were almost ready to give ground a little when it came to Jeremy.

After Andrew had gone, the afternoon hours belonged to us, and Jeremy and I started our studies of ancient Egypt. The boy's mind was eager and intelligent, often ready to leap ahead and leave me, who posed as a teacher, far behind. At least I could open the door for him and that was worth doing. Sometimes we forgot about books and walked in the square or explored the nearby Village, but I saw to it that the boy had time for his private concerns as well. I knew he was working once more on the gift for his uncle.

Something occurred during this period that encouraged me more than anything else. One afternoon Jeremy came to me in the schoolroom where I was reading and dropped something into my lap. I put my book down and saw that it was the green silk I had made for his sister. He spoke to me almost fiercely.

"I felt like cutting it up! See, I put the scissors in my pocket and went into Selina's room to get the dress and cut it up."

"But you didn't," I said.

382

He shook his head violently. "No! I remembered what you said about coming to tell you when I felt like doing something wrong. So I brought it to you instead. And here are the scissors too."

"That's fine," I assured him. "Now we can talk about what made you want to hurt Selina. You're fond of your sister. You wouldn't truly want to injure her, would you?"

"They took her with them when they went upriver," he said. "I like my grandmother and she likes me. But they left me at home."

I nodded my understanding of his feelings. "It's true they took Selina with them, but that isn't her fault. Besides, you enjoy being with me, don't you?"

"Uncle Brandon never wants me around," he said, putting his finger on the true source of his brooding.

There was nothing I could do about the actions of Brandon Reid. Indeed, I tried to think about Jeremy's uncle as little as possible. I had discovered in myself a tendency to daydream, to recall too often the day we had gone skating, and this I distrusted in myself.

"I want you here," I told the boy. "I'd have been terribly lonely if you had gone away with the others."

When I returned Selina's dress to him with complete trust, he took it proudly to her room, having vanquished temptation. I was pleased with him and told him so.

Once or twice the subject of the Dwight Reid Memorial Home came up. During lessons one morning Jeremy asked whether the date of its opening had been set, and Andrew knew more about the matter than I. There was some dispute, he said, about the setting of the exact date, due to the continued opposition of Brandon Reid. At once Jeremy wanted to know why his uncle did not like the idea of a Home that would take care of some of New York's homeless children. Andrew told him curtly to work at his lessons and leave grown-up affairs to others. I sensed that the tutor was holding something back, and I wanted to know more about the matter.

When Kate served Jeremy's ten-o'clock chocolate and biscuits in the nursery and the boy left us for his recess, I brought the subject up again.

"Is there something wrong about this memorial for Jeremy's

father?" I asked. "I keep hearing about Mr. Reid's opposition and the obstacles he seems to be putting in the path of the opening. What does it mean?"

Andrew shrugged. "Preserve me from a curious woman, Megan. Why should I know any more about it than you do?"

"I think you do know more," I countered, and did not deny his accusation of being curious.

"If you want me to guess," he said, "it could be that he's afraid of further publicity. Afraid of having the papers rehash the old scandal. The slightest mention in the papers has a tendency to make Master Brandon nervous. There's been cause enough in the past for him to be sensitive when it comes to the press."

"I suppose there's always the risk of involving Jeremy again," I agreed. "We can't blame him for wanting to avoid that."

Andrew left his books and went to the blackboard, where he stood tossing a piece of chalk in a familiar gesture. I had a feeling that he was concerned about something more, something I did not understand. When he turned to me again he had his impatience in hand and spoke to me more kindly.

"Like your friend Miss Garth, I've taken to feeling trouble in my bones," he said. "In fact, it's probably Garth's muttering that has started me off. She seldom opposes Mrs. Reid in anything, but she's as dead set against this memorial as Reid is himself. She and I have both been smelling disaster in the wind. And when it comes, Megan, I'd like to see you away from this house."

His words made little sense, and I remained unmoved by such unexplained warnings.

"Why aren't you trying to get away yourself?" I asked.

"I can take care of myself," he said.

There was a sudden harsh note in his voice that surprised me. He seemed deadly serious now, with no mockery in him. But if there was trouble in the offing, I had no notion from what quarter it might come. Nor had I any desire to flee from what I did not see or fear. Jeremy needed me. He was improving. That was all I would concern myself with at the moment. So I merely shook my head at Andrew's gloomy words.

On impulse, however, I asked another question, one that I had asked myself many times by now, though without finding an answer.

"What puzzles me most of all is how Leslie and Brandon Reid came to marry. They seem to have so little—"

He broke in without waiting for me to finish. "I should think her appeal for a man like Brandon Reid would be clear enough. Why shouldn't he have been caught by her beauty?"

"But if she still loved her first husband—then why would she marry his brother?"

"Perhaps she had her price," he said carelessly. "Or perhaps he had his. Who can tell?"

I thought his attitude callous and was sorry I had questioned him. He laughed at the look on my face with one of his sudden returns to good humor.

"What a prim expression you wear, Miss Megan! You want to hear criticism only in a direction you choose. When I suggest that the master is less than perfect, you turn your head. Is that it?"

The conversation was out of hand, and it was a relief when Jeremy returned, licking a smear of chocolate from his upper lip. I would know better, after this, than to ask Andrew Beach anything about the Reids and their affairs.

That afternoon, when Andrew had gone and we had done our lesson on Egypt, the idea came to me that before his mother and uncle returned, I ought to arrange some sort of festive occasion for Jeremy. Often I regretted his lack of friends, but there was nothing I could do about it for the time being. Miss Garth had indicated that mothers in this area did not want their sons to play with Jeremy Reid. What had happened, even though it was considered an accident, left them fearful about him as a playmate for their children. Thus he was left in the unnatural position of having no friends of his own age. I hoped the time might come when we could mend this. But for now I would have to serve as a playmate.

When we came into the downstairs hall after our walk, I made my announcement. "By the way," I said, elaborately polite, "I am giving a little dinner party this evening, Master Jeremy, and I would like the pleasure of your company. Though perhaps I shouldn't invite you formally, since you must be the host in your uncle's absence."

He looked at me in such amazement that I had to laugh in his face.

"I really mean it, Jeremy. Come along and let's see what can be managed."

We went into the dining room together, and I rang for Henry and braced myself against the butler's opposition. We would, I informed him, not daring to look straight into that haughty face, omit our early supper tonight. Instead we would dine at eight, with candlelight and the best linen and silver. And Jeremy should have the privilege of choosing the menu.

Henry surprised me. He did not so much as blink an eye. His haughty mien did not soften, but he made me a suitable bow of acquiescence.

"Yes, miss," he said. "I will see that everything is properly prepared. May I suggest that Master Jeremy consult with Cook concerning the menu?"

I agreed that this would be wise, and we stood on no ceremony with Cook. We ran down to the basement kitchen to find out what would be possible. Jeremy wanted fried chicken with giblet gravy and mashed potatoes. And an apple pie with thick slices of yellow cheese. There was no problem with Cook, in spite of this late warning, and Kate entered with relish into the make-believe, putting herself out to help both Cook and Henry.

Perhaps the servants, more than I realized, were sympathetic toward Jeremy. They were not, of course, fond of Miss Garth, and since the governess did not approve of me, I may have had a place in their estimation I'd not otherwise have held.

I warned Jeremy that he was to wear his best suit that evening, with the round, starched collar and soft tie, and I spent as much time with my own dressing as though I had been going to a real dinner party. This was one evening when I could indulge in such pretense without fear of disapproving eyes upon me, of Brandon Reid to criticize my appearance.

In my room I took out my second good dress, a gown I had seldom worn. It was not altogether in style, but Jeremy was hardly likely to notice. The faille was a soft wisteria color, with black velvet banding for a trim. The fitted bodice was cut with a square neck, and the sleeves came just above my elbows. The tight draping over the hips was edged with accordian pleating, repeated again at the hem and in the fullness that fell away in a small train.

Selina could not have outdone me in primping that evening. Or even Miss Garth, dipping and preening before her mistress' mirror. The latter image was not one I wanted to recall. I too was indulging in make-believe tonight, with only a little boy to admire me.

Since I had no fine necklace, I adapted a black velvet band to wear about my throat and pinned to it a gold brooch studded with tiny diamonds. Dangling jet earrings of my mother's matched the velvet band, and I pulled back the dark curls over my ears to reveal the fall of jet. I was both pleased with my image in the mirror and wistful at the same time. It seemed rather a waste that there would be only Jeremy to see how I looked in my finest of feathers.

I forgot such foolish thoughts, however, when I went to call him to come downstairs with me.

"This isn't our grand entrance," I said. "This time we'll just run down and check to see that everything is right. Then a little before eight you can knock at my door and escort me downstairs."

Jeremy scarcely listened, for staring at me. "You look different," he said. "You look beautiful. But I like you the other way too."

This was as fine a compliment as I had ever been paid, and I thanked him sincerely. We ran downstairs hand in hand to the dining room, to discover that Henry had put himself to the greatest of pains.

The silver gleamed, and the best crystal was in evidence, even to an array of wine glasses we were not likely to fill. Tall white candles were ready in every holder, still unlighted. Henry's one apology was for lack of a centerpiece of flowers at such short notice. Jeremy frowned over this as though we had been faced by a major crisis. Then he glanced at me shyly.

"Your brother's carrousel would make a lovely table decoration, Miss Megan. That is, if—"

"A wonderful idea!" I cried. "Run upstairs and get it, Jeremy. You may touch it tonight, since this is a special occasion."

When he had gone I tried to show Henry my gratitude for helping in our make-believe, but he was as stiffly remote as ever.

"Thank you, miss," he said and left me alone in the room.

I would light the candles myself, I thought. Tonight candlelight would not mean Leslie Reid and the scent of violets. I lit a taper in the fireplace and had reached toward the first candle when I heard a key turn in the lock of the front door. Had Leslie and Brandon returned? Or Miss Garth, perhaps? Whoever it was, we were caught in our innocent pretense, Jeremy and I.

I blew out the taper and remained where I was, looking across the glittering table toward the open door to the hall. Steps came in the direction of the dining room, and a moment later Brandon Reid appeared in the doorway. His eyes noted the elegant table, the silver candelabra, my own dressed-up person.

"I see you are expecting guests," my employer said gravely. Then, before I could offer the slightest explanation, he turned and went away.

I stood beside the table, fingering the taper in my hands, wondering whether Leslie had come home with him, wondering what course I must now take. After all, this was a small enough pleasure I had planned for Jeremy and there was no reason to cheat him of it just because the master of the house had returned.

As I pondered a course of action, Jeremy came into the room, the carrousel held carefully in both hands, and apprehension on his face.

"Uncle Brandon is home," he whispered. "He just went into the library. Does that mean we can't have our party?"

I made up my mind. "Of course it doesn't," I said. "You stay here and arrange the centerpiece, and I'll go upstairs and speak to him."

I caught up the wisteria silk of my skirt and flew up the stairs. As yet no fire had been lighted in the library and the door stood open. Across the room Brandon Reid leaned upon a window sill, staring out over Washington Square. I tapped upon the open door, and he called to me to enter.

The room was gray with the winter light of early evening, illumined only by a dim radiance from the hall and reflection from the lighted square. Nearing him, I saw that his gaze was fixed upon the scene outside as if he saw something that held him enthralled. There was a strangeness in his face, the look of faraway vision in his eyes.

388

I coughed gently to make him aware of my presence so that he started and looked at me.

"Oh, it's you, Megan," he said.

"I hope your trip went well," I began.

He seemed not to hear my words. "Do you know what I was imagining out there? Not snow in Washington Square, but sun on desert sands. That blinding, burning, golden light that's like nothing else on earth." He turned his back on the window. "How I hate bleak city streets in the wintertime. At night the desert can be bitterly cold and sand can be harsher than any blizzard. But there's always the return of the sun to look for. Here winter's just started and there are endless gray days, endless dreary cold to be endured before spring comes."

Ordinarily I enjoyed cold weather, but his words made me shiver in my light dress. "How marvelous to have seen those sun-drenched places," I said softly. "I've read of Egypt so often, and I've tried to imagine—but always my vision falls short."

He smiled at me and so quickly was the chill gone from my blood that I was reminded unguardedly of the very sun of which he spoke. It was as if I uncurled a little like some dry plant touched by life-giving warmth.

He seemed to catch the echo of my earlier question about the trip. "My wife has not weathered her travel well," he said, and I noted a hint of impatience in his voice. "Indeed, my presence seemed to make her worse, so I decided to return alone. How have things gone while I was away?"

"Everything has gone well," I assured him. "Though Miss Garth disapproved of my handling of Jeremy and left the house. She hasn't returned as yet."

"Good!" he said. "I shall relish her absence. But don't let me keep you from your dinner, Megan. I saw what you intended. Pretend you haven't seen me; go on with your plans."

"It was only make-believe," I confessed. "Jeremy and I are playing host and hostess. It's just a change in the routine for this one evening. Though of course if we'd known you were returning—"

"You'd have given up your party? What an unkind opinion you have of me. I'd be happier if you were willing to invite me as a guest."

He was smiling again, yet almost hesitant in his manner. My nagging anxiety fell away, and delight surged into its place. Now our dinner would no longer be make-believe. The festive occasion was genuine, and I knew Jeremy would be as pleased as I.

"Will you really come?" I said. "And not be too angry with the liberties I've taken?"

He crossed the room to give me his arm, and the gesture was my answer. We went down the stairs together and I was aware of the fabric of his coat beneath my fingers, of the clean odor of unperfumed soap and the male scent of tobacco. Downstairs the beautiful table awaited us. Tonight I would sit there as though I belonged, and the thought went through me as dizzily as champagne.

CHAPTER 15

JEREMY'S FACE glowed with pleasure at sight of his uncle, and he dispatched Henry at once to set a third place. The carrousel lent a touch of gay color in its place of honor in the center of the table and, as Brandon seated me and took his own place, it caught his eye.

"What have we here?" he asked, leaning forward to examine it.

Jeremy explained. "It's a music box that belonged to Miss Megan's brother. When it's wound it plays a tune and the little horses and sleigh go round and round."

"Wind it for us, Jeremy," I directed.

He picked up the toy as though it were made of glass and turned the key carefully. The gay little carrousel whirled, and the tune tinkled lightly through the room. Brandon laughed aloud and nodded his approval of so remarkable a centerpiece.

So it was that our soup was served to the tune of "Frère Jacques" and it seemed as fine a melody to my ears as though violins had played for us.

Our guest was on his best behavior, the cold mood that had been upon him when he entered the house had faded, and he was ready to join us in our pretense for the evening. He entertained us with stories of his travels, to Jeremy's delight and my own enjoyment. He told us of the Nile and the great temples of Egypt. He called up before us the Sphinx of Giza, that most mysterious of all Egyptian monuments, and described for us the awesome sight of that stone face, bathed in the brilliance of a desert sky. The Watcher in the Sands, they called it, he said, and made us know the terrible intensity of its gaze as small human figures approached across the vast desert.

"I always feel that the eyes are commanding me," he told us. "I go back again and again to find the meaning of that look, yet I never have an answer. Even today we don't know whether the Sphinx represents a god or an ancient king, or both. And I suppose we will never know what it is it asks of us."

"Like Osiris?" Jeremy said, and smiled a secret smile that made me know he was thinking of the surprise he had fashioned for his uncle's Christmas gift.

Brandon studied him for a moment. "No, not like Osiris. The Sphinx doesn't judge. It merely poses an unfathomable riddle. Perhaps the very riddle of life itself."

How strange an experience was that dinner—perhaps for all of us. At first I was merely happy and pleased and innocent, a little like Jeremy in my enjoyment of a party occasion. I was glad that I had dressed with care and that candlelight lay gently upon me, that the look in Brandon's eyes was flattering. I felt at ease with him, and no longer angry or resentful. No longer abashed, as I sometimes found myself in his company.

Yet how subtly my mood began to change, how inevitably my thoughts began to turn in a direction I did not want to contemplate. Perhaps it was Brandon's comment about my dress that brought everything into focus, so that what lay beneath the surface of my mind thrust itself suddenly forward.

"That gown you're wearing, Megan— What do you call the color?" he asked me.

Jeremy was eating like any hungry boy and he paid no attention to this talk of clothes.

"Wisteria," I said, and to my ears the word sounded unexpectedly like a sigh.

Brandon nodded. "Yes, there's blue in the lavender, quite pale and soft. The shade makes your hair seem as black as your earrings, yet it brightens the blue of your eyes as well. It becomes you, Megan."

I dropped my gaze, less sure of myself than I had been, sensing once more beneath my feet the faint cracking of ice. The fire hummed its own song of warmth and contentment beside us, the candlelight shimmered as softly on linen and silver, yet my moments of easy confidence were gone. There was a look in Brandon's eyes that told me more than the compliment he paid me, more than I dared read. There was an eagerness in me to respond, to meet his look openly and frankly with my own. But now, all too sharply, I was aware that I sat in another woman's place, that my hands moved among the silver pieces that were hers to touch, that the stemmed glass I drank from was her choice and her right to handle —not mine. But most of all I was painfully conscious of the fact that the man who faced me down the table's length was Leslie Reid's husband.

"You're a pretty thing, Megan," Brandon said. "But then—there are younger men than I to tell you that."

As if he were old at his age! I might not meet openly the admiration in his eyes, but I did not want him to think I would listen to younger men.

"I know very few men, Mr. Reid," I told him.

"Pretty women should have men to squire them about and admire them, tell them they are pretty. What do you say, Jeremy?"

Jeremy considered the matter soberly. "Miss Megan is beautiful," he said. "She's always beautiful."

"Wisdom from the young!" Brandon laughed. But to my relief and faint regret, he said no more about my appearance.

We came to the pie Jeremy had requested for dessert, and afterwards Brandon and I sipped our coffee. But now, though we talked together of small matters, the awareness in me had blighted my enjoyment of the evening and I no longer wanted it to go on and on. I had sensed danger again and I knew the pleasure and innocence would not return. I believe Brandon was aware of the change of mood as well, for though we kept up a pretense for Jeremy's sake, it was as though a faint and ghostly presence had entered to sit between us at the table, as though a scent of violets drifted through the room.

We were silent when we rose from the table, leaving Jeremy to pick up the carrousel and carry it upstairs. Brandon gave me his arm, and, as we climbed to the second floor, the bleak gray mood weighed heavily upon me.

But Jeremy did not know that something had happened to spoil our gay time. He wound the music box again, and the little tune tinkled out cheerily as he climbed the stairs behind us. Suddenly Brandon laughed and threw off the blight with a snap of his fingers.

"Quick!" he cried as we reached the second-floor hall. "Music like this must be danced to!"

I had not time to hesitate or draw back, even if I had wished to. He drew me into his light clasp, and we went down the hall in the quick steps of a polka. Jeremy held the whirling carrousel and watched with shining eyes while we danced breathlessly down the hall and back. When the tune ran to an end, Brandon did not release me but held me close to him with the fierce quick possessiveness of his arm about me. For an instant my body responded of its own volition, my head touched his shoulder and longed to rest there heedlessly. There was the sweet wildness of danger singing around us to the lilt of a nursery tune. Then, almost as quickly as it had happened, he let me go.

Jeremy had noted nothing, and I stopped him as he was about to wind the music box again. "No more for now," I called to him. "I'm quite out of breath."

I could not look at Brandon again, for now I was frightened. Frightened more of myself than of him. I gave him a somewhat uncertain good night, picked up my wisteria train, and started toward the third floor. As I mounted the stairs, I raised my eyes and saw in dismay the figure on the steps above me. The figure in brown merino of a woman with outrage in her eyes. Thora Garth had returned. She must have slipped into the house under the cover of our gay dinner party and we had not known she was there, watching from the stairway.

Telling myself that I had done no wrong, I forced my look to meet hers, but her eyes chilled me as I went past. I did not know whether Brandon had seen her, and she did not speak to me. All her malice focused upon Jeremy.

"It's well past your bedtime," she snapped, marching to the upper floor behind him. "Does Miss Kincaid know no better than to keep you up later than the hour you should be getting your rest? Now you will be ill tomorrow. Get yourself to bed at once, young man."

With an unexpected pride of manner, Jeremy handed me the carrousel and faced her sturdily.

"I have special permission to stay up tonight. And I will not be ill tomorrow. I am only ill when something has upset me."

In her anger she seemed to have forgotten the threat he'd made that had driven her from the house a few days before. I suspect that her glimpse of Brandon Reid whirling me down the hall had wiped everything else from her mind.

"You are a rude, naughty boy!" she said tensely. "Get to your room at once. I will deal with you there."

I could see Jeremy's new courage begin to crumble before her attack. But before I could come to his defense, steps sounded on the stairway and Brandon came running up to join us. He disposed of Miss Garth with swift, cruel words, and I listened, both in relief and distress.

"Miss Megan is to have full charge of the boy from now on," he told her coldly. "She has done very well in caring for him during this trial period. He is to take all his directions from her, and you are to give him no orders whatsoever. If my wife chooses to keep you on to care for Selina because of old regard, that is her affair. The boy is my affair now, and I prefer to leave him entirely in Miss Megan's hands."

She inclined her head stiffly and went down the hall toward her own room. Strangely, I felt almost sorry for her, perhaps because I knew how I would have suffered if he had spoken so to me.

Jeremy smiled shyly at his uncle and ran off to his room.

"Are you pleased with me now?" Brandon asked. "The boy is wholly in your charge."

I answered him carefully, not wanting him to guess that I was still shaken, and not only from what had just happened.

"Thank you, Mr. Reid. I will do what I can for him." My words sounded primly stiff to my own ears, and I could not help it.

"What a difficult young woman you are!" he cried in exasperation. "For an evening I permit myself to be managed on every score. I give you whatever you desire, and still you look at me in that grave, disapproving way that sends me off with a guilty conscience. What are you objecting to now, may I ask?"

Disapproving of him? I thought. Was that the way I looked? If it was, the fact was fortunate. I knew his words were a mockery. Brandon Reid would always behave as he pleased and manage his conscience as he saw fit.

I answered him with evasion. "When I hear you speak so cuttingly to another, I can only wonder when you will turn words equally sharp upon me."

Once more he surprised me. He put out a finger and tilted my reluctant chin so that the thin gaslight touched my face. "I would like never to hurt you, Megan. But you would never be fooled by light promises. When the whim moves me, I may very well deal you a blow that seems ruthless. You will be wise never to expect kindness from me for long. Other considerations, perhaps, but not always kindness."

"Only the boy matters," I told him swiftly. "If you will be kind to him, then I shan't so much as wince if you grow angry with me."

"The bargain is made," he said. "At least for now. It's not something I'll promise forever, but I'll try this experiment for as long as I can. Certainly you've effected a remarkable improvement in Jeremy. At this rate, I should be able to leave him in your hands when our next Egyptian expedition makes up early in the year."

Jeremy called to me, and I nodded silently and hurried to his room. I sat down on the bed beside him, and all my movements were calmly automatic. Jeremy reached up and put his arms about me. I held him close, yet even as I kissed his cheek and drew the covers over him, even as I moved to turn out the gas, something cold and heavy weighed within me.

When I returned to the hall, she was waiting for me. The brown figure stood in the shadows before my door and there could be no slipping past her without speaking. I had to brush close to reach the doorknob, and she put her cold fingers on my bare forearm, stopping me there. I winced, my flesh shrinking from her touch.

"I saw," she whispered. "But don't imagine that you can succeed in what you intend. Miss Leslie will be home soon, and then you'll not be allowed to stay in this house—no matter what *he* says." She flicked her head scornfully toward the stairs.

"I've done nothing that requires an accounting," I said. "I will be happy to tell Mrs. Reid every detail of this evening if she wishes it."

Miss Garth did not answer. She folded her hands across her body and turned away. So softly did she move that I heard scarcely a footfall as she returned to her room. Quickly I slipped through my door and closed it tightly behind me.

I lighted no lights, but stood there in the darkness, fighting off the spell of evil that seemed to emanate from the woman. She might well cause trouble. She might threaten my very presence in this house. Yet it was not of her I must think in this sharply lucid moment. It was of the possible truth of her accusation.

I stood before the window, heedless of the cold, looking out upon a clear and starry night. How many were the silent stars. How complete my mortal insignificance. Yet the hurt within me seemed as vast and engulfing as the universe. I turned from the window and began to undress, paying little heed to the movements of my fingers or to what I did with my clothes. My mind was wide awake, and my thoughts were merciless.

I, who had never been truly in love before, had fallen desperately, foolishly in love with Brandon Reid. When he frowned at me, I was ready to tremble; when he smiled, I yearned toward him like any mindless blossom to the sun. When he held me in his arms I wanted only to stay there for always. And when he told me he would soon be away on a trip to far places, I ached with knowledge of coming emptiness, of the loneliness that waited for me when he was gone. Yet all the while this man was married to another woman. Married to the mother of the boy whose presence held me here in this house.

I did not sleep easily or well that night, and there was much that I could not dismiss from my mind. I kept remembering Brandon's eyes upon me—not always in mockery. Remembering the moment when he had held me so fiercely close. And foolish though I might be, how could I wish *not* to be in love?

When I slept at last, it was because I had relinquished the struggle and was ready to hug to my heart the very things that wounded me most.

CHAPTER 16

IN THE morning I wakened to the soft and dreamy mood of a woman newly in love that no feeble effort of reason could dispel. A remembrance of all that was sweet and unhurtful held me in an unreasonable enchantment. I longed to see the face of my love and quickly found an excuse to run down to the library. But Brandon had gone—up earlier than I, and off on some business connected, Kate said, with the new expedition he was financing.

I was not entirely sorry. Some stern sentinel in me knew that my mood was far too gentle and yielding this morning. My awareness of love, too new to be submitted to Brandon's sardonic gaze. I had never felt like this before and so wonderful a thing was my yearning that I did not want the clear light of reality to touch it. The man was real and for all that I longed to see him, I was afraid.

It was a further relief when Miss Garth, instead of Jeremy, remained in bed, ministered to with smelling salts and physics and peppermint tea. This morning I would not think of the day when my own turn to be cruelly hurt might come. I was young and in love for the first time, and I gave myself up to the all-engulfing knowledge. For the moment I did not look ahead to a disastrous future. I merely gave myself over to being.

While Jeremy did his lessons that morning, I sat in the schoolroom, a book in my hands, making sure that I turned a page on occasion, though my imaginings were far more beguiling than the story I used to conceal them. Only now and then was I aware that Andrew and Jeremy occupied the same world with me. I noted absently that Andrew was busy with paper and pencil and that

Jeremy seemed restless and not at all attentive to his lessons. Yet I could not bring myself to chide the boy, or even pay much attention to such prosaic problems.

I came out of my dreamy state to some degree when I heard Andrew speak to him sternly.

"Take your book and go to your room, Jeremy. When you can do your lesson with your wits about you, come back and we'll go over it again."

Being sent from the classroom was a disgrace. Selina was often punished in this way, but Jeremy, oddly enough, almost never. I shook my head at him in mild reproach, though I could not help but sympathize. Jeremy too had enjoyed an exciting evening and was probably living in a fantasy world, just as I was.

When he had gone, I gave my attention determinedly to my book, not wanting the intrusion of conversation with Andrew. He made no effort to speak, but went on for several moments working with his pencil. Then he tore a sheet of paper from his pad and held it off at arm's length. The gesture caught my attention, and I saw that he was studying a sketch.

"How do you like it?" he said and pushed the paper toward me across the table.

To my surprise I saw that he had drawn my own face on the paper. The likeness was not a true one. I would not have expected such flattery from Andrew. He had drawn a girl who was far prettier than I, and a far softer, more yielding person as well. Yet I was pleased that he could see me in such a light, for if he saw me thus, perhaps another man would too.

"You've flattered me exceedingly," I told him.

He regarded me with an unfathomable expression. "Do you think so? I wouldn't call it flattery. The face I've drawn is not that of a particularly intelligent woman. Here, let me show you."

I sighed, resigned to an enumeration of my faults. Andrew came to stand beside my chair. As he bent above me, pointing with his pencil, I found myself comparing him with Brandon. How much shorter he was than the man with whom I had danced last night. How very nearly ugly he seemed at times. Especially when the saving grace of humor had gone out of him. Yet I suspected that he might be a better friend than Brandon would ever be, and perhaps more single-mindedly loyal, if his devotion were once given.

He tapped with his pencil the parted lips he had sketched in the picture. "Note the mouth," he said, as if he criticized objectively the work of a student. "There's too much softness there, too much of giving. This is not the mouth of a woman ready to make up her mind and do what must be done realistically. Again—take the eyes. Too dreamy, by far. There's a lack of sound thinking there, too much of a turning inward to some foolish dream."

I glanced up at him, dismayed, and he took the drawing from my hands and went back to his chair.

"In fact, my poor Megan, what I have shown you here is the face of a woman abjectly in love."

I started to answer him indignantly, to deny and dismiss, but he would not listen. The anger his wry expression had masked came through to astound me.

"Do you think I'm a fool? Do you think I haven't seen it happening? Do you think they don't talk about you in this house? Not that anything else could be expected of Brandon Reid, but I'd have expected better of you, Miss Megan Kincaid."

"Talk?" I repeated the one word blankly.

"Talk!" he mimicked. "Do you think I haven't heard about your dinner party last night, to say nothing of your dancing in the hall, and the way Garth was told off. I am far from being a fool, my girl, but I suspect that you are making a very thorough one of yourself."

I could find only anger with which to answer him. "None of this is your business! Whether you are a fool or not is your own affair and of no interest to me. I haven't asked your opinion of my actions—actions you know of only through gossip."

Andrew subsided as quickly as he had exploded. When he spoke again there was pity in his eyes and that was harder to accept than unreasonable anger.

"Poor Megan," he said. "How could you know about a man like that? Foolish you are, my dear. Perhaps not a fool, but foolish. What else can we think of a dressmaker who falls in love with the grand seigneur? He is to blame. And yet it will be you who will suffer."

"If you please"—I resorted to haughty chill—"I can manage my own affairs."

"Of course," he said. "And you have that right. I apologize. I've a temper like all blazes when it gets away from me. But it wasn't you I was angry with, Megan. It was Reid, who knows very well what he is doing, and has no conscience about it."

He held the drawing up, as if to study it to better advantage. Then he ripped it down the center, tearing it quite ruthlessly into pieces before my eyes. While I stared, he blew at the bits, letting them drift across the table and onto the floor.

"I've shocked you—and that's fine. Perhaps if you're shocked badly enough you'll reject this softness, crush it, no matter what the temporary hurt. You'll be happier in the long run."

I could not endure his lecturing. That he had been watching me more closely than I knew, that he held me in so little esteem that he was willing to show his contempt, left me more upset than I would have expected.

"If you'll excuse me—" I murmured, still haughty, and went to the door, only to meet Jeremy returning with his lesson book in hand. But I could not linger now, even for Jeremy, and I ran past him into the hall. I was just in time to see Miss Garth come out of her room dressed in bonnet and cloak, carrying a traveling bag in her hand.

She blocked my path, and for a moment we stood face to face, neither one giving way. My heart beat more quickly as I met the dark intensity of her look. She did not step aside, and she did not speak. She merely stood there staring at me with such dislike in her gaze that I was once more shaken and not a little frightened. The woman seemed hardly sane at times, and her hatred for me promised nothing but disaster in this house.

"You are—going away?" I faltered.

She drew her cloak more closely about her and turned toward the stairs. "I am going upriver to fetch Miss Leslie home," she said and swept past me down the stairs.

I went to my room and sat down in its quiet haven. Something of an early-morning fire still remained on the hearth, but I lacked the will to add coals to the embers. Indeed, I seemed washed of all power to move or act. The encounter with Garth had sapped me. I knew now what lay ahead. She could not harm me with looks, however malevolent, but she could injure me viciously with words. I knew such words would now be spoken in a torrent of abuse to Leslie Reid. I suspected, too, which one of us Mrs. Reid would believe.

Yet, from this sapped and directionless state into which I had fallen, I must now begin from the beginning and rebuild myself into a woman of purpose and will. I must build, not in the shape of a tremulous girl in love, nor in the guise of the monstrous creature Miss Garth would represent me to be. I must begin with the truth.

And what was the truth?

It was true that there had been nothing outwardly wrong last night when Brandon had joined Jeremy and me at the table. Nothing wrong, indeed, in the moments of our playful dance together down the hall. There had been only that instant when he had held me close and I had felt a fierce exultance in him and an answering response in myself. But was not such an instant enough to destroy my usefulness where Jeremy was concerned? Would it not be better for all of us if I recognized the fact that my work with Jeremy had come to an end, that I could not remain in this house hoping to aid him when my own heart had betrayed me into so senseless a love for his uncle?

Yet—if this was basic truth—I still could not accept it. All that really mattered was Jeremy, and there was still much I could do for him. It was for him that I must fight to remain in this house, and not for my fatal, foolish love. There must now be innocence in my thoughts as well as in my actions if I was to face the boy's mother with the clear conscience which could be my only weapon.

In those few quiet days that remained, I faced my problem alone and I believe I began to win. That I loved Brandon, I accepted. Perhaps I would always love him. But if I were to remain here and help Jeremy, neither Brandon nor anyone else must know my true feeling. When Jeremy's mother came home, she must find in me only Jeremy's instructor and loving friend. There was no other identity I could enjoy in this house.

So did I caution and counsel and steel myself. When Brandon returned in a day or two, I was at first anxious lest he put me to some strain or test. But he did not, and I relaxed one segment of my guard. Perhaps he too had thought better of the way we had both stepped close to a line of danger that must not be crossed. I had retreated in time. I would continue to do so. Or so I told myself.

By the end of the week when Mrs. Reid and Thora Garth returned from upriver, I had reached a state of near equanimity. If my actions had been somewhat less than innocent on the night of the dinner, my conscience was clear enough now. It was what happened from here on that mattered, and I could meet whatever Leslie Reid had to say with no sense of present guilt to trouble me.

That afternoon there was a bustle of activity about the house, with Selina flying up and downstairs, happy to be home, full of her visit to her grandmother, eager to share her experiences with her brother. Jeremy seemed glad to see her and not at all jealous of her trip, as he had been at first.

About Miss Garth there was an air of triumph I could not mistake, and I knew it did not augur well for me. Yet there was no immediate summons from Mrs. Reid. Nothing happened until the following afternoon. When Selina came to tell me that her mother wished to see me, I knew the moment had come.

I did not find Mrs. Reid alone in her boudoir. Miss Garth was there, standing watchfully behind her mistress' chair. Andrew Beach was present too, putting away his painting things. I saw that the portrait on the easel had progressed since he'd last shown it to me. Leslie's head had come more definitely into being, and I paused to look at the picture, seeking any delay that might further strengthen me in the ordeal ahead.

Andrew's portrayal surprised me, for he had chosen to paint a woman not only of great beauty, but of generous spirit. The eyes of the portrait regarded me with warm understanding as they read my heart and still forgave. I resisted a startled impulse to turn to the real Leslie for corroboration of what the portrait revealed. Instead, I glanced at Andrew. As he removed the canvas from the easel, our eyes met. His back was to Mrs. Reid and the governess, and his expression was derisively clear. It was as if he had said, "What else did you expect?" A man who painted on commission must please his subject if he wanted other work, he seemed to be telling me, even challenging me to condemn him if I dared.

But it was not Mrs. Reid's portrait that interested me most at that moment, and when Andrew had gone, I turned toward the woman who had posed for it.

Leslie Reid lay back in the chaise longue, her eyes closed, dark lashes fringed upon her cheeks. The room had been flooded with afternoon light for the sake of Andrew's painting, but now Miss Garth moved to draw the draperies and light the inevitable candles. From the bedroom she brought the tall brass candlestick and placed it on a nearby table, where it seemed to tower, its flame touching an answering light in Leslie's bright hair. I thought of Brandon's reference to a Turkish seraglio and wondered if that candlestick had ever shed light on greater beauty. I breathed the scent of violets and was faintly sickened, even as my resolve strengthened. This woman held Jeremy's future in her hands and I must not be defeated by whatever was to happen now.

So brave was I in the first moments of our interview.

"Close the door, please, Thora," Mrs. Reid said. She opened her eyes then and looked at me. What I had expected, I don't know, but it was not this gaze, brimming with tears, that she turned upon me. She motioned me to a chair beside her, and I sat down without speaking.

"You could have been my friend," she said softly. "You were doing a fine thing with Jeremy. I know that now. I must try to be grateful for your past effort." There was a break in her voice as though it weakened, and she was silent, her eyelids closed again.

Miss Garth slid the candlestick nearer her mistress with a faint scraping sound across the table. I looked up at her and saw her eyes, bright again with triumph.

At the sound of metal upon wood, Leslie opened her eyes and went on. "You are not wholly to blame, Miss Kincaid. My husband has been given to this sort of thing before. I can only feel sorry for the woman when it happens. I doubted the wisdom of bringing you here in the first place, but I could not prevent him from doing as he wished."

It was clear that Garth had done her worst. I answered, speaking earnestly, steadily.

"You are dreadfully mistaken in your conclusions, Mrs. Reid. My one purpose in this house is to help Jeremy. He is beginning to make some progress. It must continue. Nothing must happen to set him back."

"You should have thought of that before this," Garth put in. But Leslie was still mistress, and she raised a finger in warning, halting the governess' words.

"Can you remain in this house and live with your own conscience, Miss Kincaid?" Leslie demanded, and now her eyes held mine with more strength in them than before.

"My conscience is clear," I said, but I knew I was flushing.

Mrs. Reid sighed and lifted her hand in a gesture of dismissal.

"If you will not leave of your own accord, Miss Kincaid, there is no choice left for me but to ask you to go. Please be out of the house as soon as possible. I shall see that you have a month's additional salary and the necessary notes to help you obtain another position."

I stood my ground for a moment longer. "And if Mr. Reid does not choose to let me go?"

Miss Garth made a faint, choked sound, but again Leslie's raised hand stopped her. The amber eyes—so unlike the eyes of Andrew's painting—met mine without wavering. Her cheeks were pale and unflushed, her voice steadier than my own.

"I am afraid, Miss Kincaid, that life would become intolerable for you in this house if you remained. My husband will be leaving for Egypt soon after the first of the year. To whom would you turn for support when he had gone? Would it not be wiser for us all to accept the good you have done Jeremy and see that it is carried on in other hands? Hands, Miss Kincaid, of my own choosing this time."

Bitterly the truth of all she was saying came home to me. How could I fight for Jeremy against such odds and without Brandon standing firmly behind me? Was my conscience so clear after all? Had not this sad, quiet woman put her finger on the very truth I had told myself I was seeking? In that moment I knew defeat and knew I must accept the verdict of her judgment.

"I will be gone from the house as soon as I can pack," I told her and went out of the room without glancing again at Thora Garth.

As I passed the library on my way toward the stairs, I saw a light burning there and Brandon seated at his desk. There was nothing I could say to him now, but at that moment he looked up and glimpsed my face. He rose at once and came toward me.

"What has upset you, Megan?"

He might as well know now as later, even though I could make no plea for myself, and I stepped into the room to face him.

"I am leaving as soon as I can," I said. "Mrs. Reid has just dismissed me. My usefulness with Jeremy has come to an end, and there's nothing else for me to do."

I saw color rise darkly in his face. "Wait for me here," he ordered and strode past me out the door.

There was no time to stop him, to tell him that his wife was right and had I been in Leslie's place I would have made the same decision. The angry violence that drove him alarmed me. Beyond Leslie's door I could hear the sound of raised voices, the whiplash of Brandon's tone. Sickened, I went deep into the library so that I could not hear. I must wait until he returned. Then I must make my own position clear to him, and the fact that, under the circumstances, I would be blocked at every turn in my efforts with Jeremy.

So preoccupied was I that I did not know that Jeremy had come to the library door until he spoke to me.

"May I come in, Miss Megan?" he asked.

"Come in quickly and close the door after you," I said.

He obeyed me with obvious reluctance, closing it slowly upon the sound of angry voices.

"Uncle Brandon is furious," he said with relish. "I wonder if he'll break something this time. The last time he lost his temper with my mother, he smashed a vase to smithereens. Why is he angry now, Miss Megan?"

I had no answer for the boy, and when he saw that I would not discuss what was happening, he moved about the room, pausing to look behind a row of books on the shelf, to open the lid of a carved humidor, and put his hand into it. I remembered the time he had seemed to be searching for something in his father's room. The pattern was repeating itself.

"What are you looking for?" I asked.

He replaced the elephant's tusk on the mantel and answered me readily enough. "I'm looking for the pistol, Miss Megan. I don't know where they've hidden it. But if I keep searching, some day I'll find it."

One part of my mind recognized that the voices across the hall had quieted. The other part was caught by the boy's ominous words. Perhaps I could do one last thing for him.

"Forget about the past, Jeremy," I pleaded. "The gun would only bring everything back and make you suffer all the more."

"But I don't want to forget," he said. "I want to remember it all. Always."

Before I could press the matter further, his uncle pushed open the door with a bang and strode into the room, the air of fury still upon him. He saw Jeremy and flicked a finger toward the door. The boy gave me a quick, frightened look and went away at once.

Brandon dropped into the chair behind his desk and put his hands over his face while I stood waiting in silence, not knowing what was to come. After a moment his shoulders relaxed a little and he looked up at me darkly.

"Jeremy will remain in your care, Miss Kincaid," he said. "I will not hear of your leaving this house."

I answered him as firmly as I could. "I have no choice but to leave. Under the circumstances there's nothing more I can do here. Your wife has chosen the only wise course. Isn't it better to accept it?"

He threw up his head and stared at me. "Do you think I will listen to such nonsense? I'm still master here, and you are in my employ, Miss Kincaid. The matter is settled; there will be no further trouble."

This I did not believe, but while I sought for words with which to persuade him, he spoke to me more gently.

"Is it your real wish to leave Jeremy, Megan?"

I could only shake my head helplessly.

"Then you shall stay," he told me.

Once more he leaned his head upon his hands, and there was such despair in the gesture that for an instant I longed with all my heart to go to him, to comfort him with my love. But this I must not do. He spoke to me again without looking up.

"Sometimes I am afraid," he said. "Sometimes I am mortally afraid."

"Of—what?" I faltered.

"Of myself," he said quietly. "Of myself more than of any other."

CHAPTER 17

It is fortunate, perhaps, that we cannot live at a continued high pitch of emotion. The matters of everyday living intervene. The nerves, the very muscles that are braced for disaster inevitably relax their tension when the battle is not joined. The mind turns to lesser problems.

In spite of telling myself that this was only a respite I had been given and that sooner or later Mrs. Reid, with Garth behind her, would have her way—when nothing at all happened, I began to behave as though I would stay here forever, as though nothing had changed.

Christmas approached us swiftly, and, in spite of the dismal mood which lay upon master and mistress, a flurry of activity gripped the Reid household. The servants, at least, knew the proper course events should take at Christmastime and much was left in their hands. There were the children to be considered and plans to make for their delight.

If angry words had been shouted concerning my presence in the house, and an edict had been set down, then countermanded, everyone pretended an unawareness of the fact. Garth might look vindictively in my direction, but for the moment she said nothing more. Leslie behaved as though her dismissal of me had never been spoken, and to a great extent we avoided each other. Eventually I knew she must have her way, Brandon or no, but for the moment there was something like a Christmas truce.

If Andrew knew what had occurred after he left the house that day, he did not mention the fact, and though I was aware that he watched me openly, I held him at arm's length and encouraged no friendship between us. If I told myself I felt only scorn for the way he had sold his talent to Mrs. Reid, I did not speak my mind. Now and then I thought almost wistfully of the evening I had spent with Andrew when we'd dined at Mama Santini's. That memory too was something I must put from me. I must depend on no one but myself.

It was shortly after her return from the visit to her grandmother's that Selina began to annoy us all with a foolish little song.

"Selina's-got-a-secret! Selina's-got-a-secret!" she would chant in a singsong that soon began to get on my nerves.

"Of course you have a secret," I told her. "Christmas is coming and we all have secrets. But we don't have to brag about them."

She wrinkled her nose at me saucily. "It's not that kind of secret. I know something you don't know. And Jeremy doesn't know it either. But I won't tell you what it is because if I did someone would spank me."

I found it best to ignore her chanting and I did not encourage her with questions.

From below stairs these days the odors of baking drifted up to us, pervading all the house. The fragrance of mince and pumpkin pies mingled with the tart smell of pickles in the making. The familiar warm scent of freshly baked bread was laced with the odors of cinnamon and molasses cookies.

A huge Christmas tree had been brought home by Fuller and set up in the drawing room to be decorated later. The arrival of the tree was an occasion for excitement in itself, bringing to us as it did green life out of a dead brown winter world, adding the scent of pine needles to the Christmasy smells of the house.

Yet in spite of such normal preparations and a certain bustle of excitement both above and below stairs, I could not help but contrast the atmosphere of the Reid house with that of Christmases I remembered from my childhood. How warmly loving had been our approach to the Christmas season. It was a special and wondrous Birthday we celebrated and we never forgot the fact, even in our joyous anticipation of gifts to be given and received.

The mistress, it was true, roused herself and began a round of unusual social engagements and plans. I know Garth disapproved and felt these efforts taxed her strength, but Leslie seemed nervously keyed to activity, though without any true core of happiness in her busy coming and going. Brandon remained indifferent to all that went on about him, doing what was required of him, but holding himself remote and uninvolved.

I saw little of him and, however much it cost me, I held to my single purpose of teaching Jeremy, playing and working with him, giving him my friendship. This was enough, I told myself, to occupy my mind and time, and a good portion of my heart.

Between Jeremy and Selina and me there was a great play of secrecy during the days before Christmas. Perhaps I encouraged and abetted these exaggerated precautions because I felt the true emptiness of Christmas in the Reid house. We indulged in much scurrying from one room to another so that each might avoid the recipient of the gift he was wrapping. And it helped a little. In spite of pale gaslight and the brooding darkness of the halls, the house seemed to liven and reflect something of holiday excitement as it existed in the excitement of two children.

Two days before Christmas, Jeremy came to my room with a plea. Selina, he said, was snooping. He had caught her at it twice. She had no honor whatsoever when it came to other people's secrets, and something must be done.

"She snoops in your room too," he warned me. "I saw her coming out of it yesterday when you were downstairs. So let's fool her, Miss Megan. Let's hide our presents where she won't go."

I was more amused than disturbed and not in the least on guard. "Where do you suggest?" I asked.

Jeremy held out his hand and dropped something into my palm. I felt the cold touch of metal and knew what he intended. My first impulse was to reject the idea of hiding our gifts in his father's room. Yet I had a reason for not refusing at once.

If I'd had my way, I would long since have opened that room, swept everything out, furnished it anew, given it a character and being that would have nothing to do with the past. As it was, locked and secret, with all mention of it avoided and forbidden, it seemed to hold an unhealthy fascination for Jeremy. Silence and averted eyes only contributed to a lingering sense of horror that I felt was injurious to Jeremy. While the boy had not returned to the room alone, as far as I knew, its locked silence still drew his attention and this was something I wanted to lessen. I made a quick decision.

"Why not?" I said. "Bring your packages here and put them with mine. When no one is about we'll find a chance to hide them where Selina will never look."

Jeremy seemed pleased, but not overly excited and I congratulated myself on making the right decision. From time to time during the day he smuggled his small, but now numerous, gifts into my room and Selina did not discover what he was up to. We waited until evening, when she was safely in bed, before we carried out our plan. I will confess to feeling somewhat uneasy by that time. Our conspiracy had begun to seem less sensible than in my early rationalization.

Jeremy did not go to bed at his usual time, but slipped into my room to help me carry the gifts downstairs. It was then I suggested a change in plans.

"Why not leave your packages with mine for now, Jeremy? Selina won't come here again. Tomorrow night is Christmas Eve, and we can put them under the tree."

The boy shook his head reproachfully. "You promised, Miss Megan. Selina is sure to snoop a lot tomorrow."

I was tempted to ask the real reason behind his insistence, but I did not dare. If I went back on my agreement now, he might shut me out and not confide in me again. Surely there was nothing that could happen if I went with him to his father's room. We would leave our gifts hidden there and come out at once. The plan seemed simple enough and harmless, and I wished I could dismiss my inner misgivings.

"*Now* is the time," Jeremy persisted. "Do come along, Miss Megan. Mama and Uncle Brandon will be having dinner, and all the servants are downstairs. Miss Garth has a headache and she has gone to bed. Selina's asleep."

I emptied a sewing basket and let Jeremy pile his gifts into it. Then, with a few of my own larger packages in my hands, I started downstairs with Jeremy beside me. We moved softly, giving each other sidelong conspiratorial looks. It would take more than one trip, and Jeremy seemed pleased that it should. We must not be caught, he whispered, and threw a look of exaggerated apprehension behind him and over the stair rail.

In one sense his behavior reassured me. How little of normal young excitement, how little of make-believe he had in his life. He was starved for the sort of play most children indulge in endlessly without question. Tonight, as I began to realize, we were not merely hiding gifts from a curious little girl. We were playing the role of pirates and brigands. We were desperadoes and highwaymen. We would hide our smuggled treasure in the teeth of the law and likely be hung to yardarm or the nearest gallows tree if we were caught in our derring-do.

The horror of what had happened in Dwight's room had nothing to do with our present escapade, and I found myself less fearful for Jeremy than I had been.

When we reached the room, he opened the door with his key and pushed me hastily inside. Unexpectedly, I found myself abandoned there in the dark with my arms full and the contents of Jeremy's basket dumped upon the carpet at my feet. Before I could object, he had shut the door upon me and darted off, leaving me there in the gloom of that cold and haunted room, while he ran off to get the rest of our parcels.

My eyes could see nothing in the gloom, and I stumbled over one of Jeremy's packages as I tried to fumble my way toward the bureau and a candle I knew was there.

As I moved hesitantly, my hands outstretched, my direction became suddenly uncertain. Which way was I facing? Which way had I turned on entering the room? There is something unsettling about finding oneself in utter gloom with the realization that surroundings have shifted, that nothing stands in its known place.

I moved gropingly and, as my breathing quickened, I caught a scent that was not the usual chill mustiness of the room. The odor choked me into sudden awareness. I held my breath, not daring to stir as the perfume of violets closed in around me. In sharpened realization, I knew I was not alone. Indeed, now that I listened with utter attention, I could hear the sound of someone who breathed as lightly, as softly, and quickly as I. But someone who had the advantage of being here first, with eyes accustomed to the gloom.

Some sixth sense warned me not to speak, not to challenge, not to remain for a moment shut into this dreadful darkness with the woman whose faintest movement wafted a scent of violets through the air. But where was the door in this pitchy gloom? And where was Jeremy? The moment he returned and opened the door, I would be safe, the hider in the room exposed. But he did not come and I heard the faint rustle of silk as the woman moved nearby—perhaps interposing herself between me and the door.

I tried to tell myself that this rising panic was foolish. There were others in the house, and I had only to cry out to bring them to me. But the sense of a presence that meant me harm was so acute that I could not speak or move.

She was so close now that as I put up my hand in a quick gesture of defense, my fingers brushed her gown, and a voice whispered suddenly in my ear.

"Be still!" it warned me in a whisper so hoarse that all identity was lost. Fingers, chill and somehow deadly, touched my face, my throat. I put my hands up wildly to thrust them away, and twisted from her grasp. She fell back for an instant, perhaps startled by my sudden movement, and I felt the tearing of cloth in my hands. The deadly whisper came again, from behind me now.

"If you go away, you will be safe. If you stay in this house, you will suffer for it."

My eyes were growing used to the dark, and now I could make out a faint line of light along the doorsill. I had my direction at last. Kicking Jeremy's packages aside, I ran to the door, thrust it open, then shut it behind me with a ringing slam that must have echoed through the house.

Jeremy was mounting the stairs from the lower floor, coming toward me. I turned the key in the lock with a sense of triumph, feeling that I had trapped something evil and contained it in the room—something that must now betray itself in order to escape.

I ran toward Jeremy and turned him about. "Not now!" I whispered urgently. "Go upstairs at once!"

My manner brooked no argument, and he obeyed me. We did not speak until we reached my room again. Then he faced me anxiously.

"What's the matter, Miss Megan? You're white and shaking. What has happened?"

"Why didn't you come, Jeremy?" I gasped. "Why did you shut me in there and run away?"

He was clearly startled by my state of fright, but he explained quietly. "Uncle Brandon called me. He was coming out of the dining room and he heard me on the stairs. So I had to go down and tell him why I was not in bed."

The thumping of my heart began to quiet a little, and, when I sat in my rocker, the weakness in my knees ceased to betray me.

"What did you tell him?" I asked.

"Only that we were hiding Christmas presents and it was all a secret. So he let me off without a scolding. He was in a hurry to go out for the evening anyway. Are you afraid of that room after all, Miss Megan?"

It was better to tell the truth than to let him think me fearful of the supernatural.

"There was someone in there," I said. "Someone breathing in the darkness. Someone who—who meant me harm. I came out as fast as I could and locked her in there alone."

"With all our presents?" Jeremy asked, his dismay having little to do with my predicament.

"She won't hurt the presents," I said. "But sooner or later she will have to get out. And then we'll know who it is. I wish your uncle hadn't left the house."

Jeremy's snort of scorn did not flatter my intelligence. He went to my door and opened it. "Come along," he said, gathering up the remaining packages. "There's nobody there now, and we must hide the presents and see if the others are all right. Let's take the rest of them down."

When I still hesitated, he spoke to me with a forbearance that was strangely adult and might have made me laugh at another time.

"There are other keys to the room, Miss Megan," he pointed out. "And besides, the second door is locked with an inside bolt. If anyone wanted to get out, he could draw the bolt and go into my mother's boudoir. Let's go down right away. You can take a candle if you like," he added kindly.

In the face of Jeremy's logic, I began to feel foolish. Perhaps the fright I'd had was due mainly to my own vivid imagination. After all, I had given whoever was in the room a thorough chance to frighten me. And she had done it well.

I made no further objection, but accompanied Jeremy downstairs, this time carrying a candle.

When we opened the door and left it wide to the hall light and my candle, I saw that Jeremy was right. There was no one hiding in the room. The bolt to the second door had been drawn to leave it unlocked. Jeremy knelt to count his packages and did not speak until he was sure they were safe.

My attention wandered from him and came to rest on something across the room. There upon the polished surface of a highboy stood the tall Turkish candlestick I had seen so often in Leslie's room.

"Was your mother downstairs having dinner with your uncle just now?" I asked.

He shook his head absently, his main interest for the packages he was storing in the depths of a bureau drawer.

"I don't know—she may have been."

Then she could have been here, I thought. She could have left her candlestick behind as she fled. However, I said nothing to Jeremy. With hands that were far from steady, I helped him pack away our Christmas gifts. No one disturbed us. No one challenged our presence, or, so far as I knew, went past the door while we finished our work. But the scent of violets persisted and with it a hovering fear. There was a growing certainty in me that far more than mere resentment of my presence existed in this house.

Had Garth dressed once more in a garment of her mistress' and worn her perfume? I didn't know. I couldn't tell. It could have been either.

For my own safety, it would seem that I should overrule Brandon and leave this house while I could. But there was still Jeremy, and I knew I would never abandon him for so cowardly a reason. There were stronger causes which might eventually force me to leave him, but what had happened in this room was not one of them, however uneasy it might leave me.

CHAPTER 18

I HAD NO answer the next day to the question of who had left the candlestick in Dwight Reid's room, or who had warned me in that hoarse whisper. The sense of a threat hanging over my head persisted, yet I could do nothing but ignore it. I saw Brandon not at all, and in any event I did not want to tell him what had happened. The violent anger he had already shown toward Leslie had disturbed me. I did not want to rouse it again.

That my usefulness to Jeremy was drawing to a close was becoming increasingly clear. Before long I must face Brandon and make him understand the reality of the situation. Not because of what had happened in that room, but because once he had gone away, my position would be untenable. Perhaps I would wait until after Christmas and then tell him whatever plans I had decided upon by that time.

On Christmas morning the master and mistress would preside at the opening of the packages—as was the usual custom—but on Christmas Eve they were to attend a ball at the Fifth Avenue Hotel. Thus we would have the tree-decorating to ourselves.

It was a relief to know that Leslie would be absent, yet in spite of my stern control over my feelings, I could not help but wish for Brandon's presence. Perhaps the innocence of tree-trimming might have relaxed him a little, lessened his tension. And, at least, I could have been in the same room with him openly, with no sense of guilt. There would have been pain for me in his presence, yet I could have lived for that little time in his company. Away from him, as I was coming to recognize with despair, I merely existed.

416

I was going to have such a long while to exist away from him entirely, once I left the house.

In spite of this heaviness of heart, I tried to give myself to the decorating of the tree. As I told myself again and again, it was Jeremy alone I must think of now.

For days we had been popping corn energetically over the nursery fire and threading white kernels into long strands. We had strung cranberries until our fingers were stained and pricked. Now, on Christmas Eve, we were hanging these decorations on the ceiling-high tree. And not even Miss Garth was present to set a damper on the children's pleasure.

While we were so engaged, Leslie and Brandon looked into the drawing room on the way to their party. Leslie was brightly beautiful, as always, and Brandon made her a somberly elegant escort in top hat and Inverness cape. They stood in the doorway for a moment, looking in upon the long firelit drawing room. With strained gaiety, Leslie blew the children a kiss, and Brandon wished us a courteous "Good evening." Then they were gone to their carriage, leaving a silence behind them in the room. A hollow silence that stilled our noisy merriment.

I turned quickly back to the tree and asked Jeremy to bring me the stepladder so that I could place the decoration at the very top. Jeremy had cut a star from cardboard and covered it with silver paper saved from chocolate-cream wrappers. But now he did not hear my request, for he was studying the small heap of gifts he had piled upon a chair. Together we had brought them downstairs from Dwight's room, and without incident. Not heeding me, he picked up a green tissue-wrapped package and turned it about in his hands. I knew it was the Egyptian collar. For the hundredth time I wondered if Brandon would remember my plea to him concerning Jeremy's gift. Or would his present tension result in ungracious or indifferent behavior? I could not forgive him readily, I told myself, if he failed Jeremy on Christmas morning.

In the end I brought the stepladder from the hall myself and climbed on it while Selina gave me the star. Jeremy came out of his preoccupation in time to instruct me on its proper position. Then the two of them handed up colored wax candles in small tin holders and I clamped them to the upper branches.

417

As I worked in what should have been contentment, I could not suppress the picture that kept returning to my mind. A picture of Leslie in Brandon's arms as they danced together at the Christmas ball. Was his anger with her based on his own bewitchment with his wife and her rejection of him? She was so lovely, so obviously capable of exerting great appeal.

To my regret, Miss Garth eventually joined us to supervise the tree-trimming. I told myself that she must have felt lonely upstairs and I bowed to her suggestions and let her direct the children. Her dislike for me was in the open now, and she did not hide it. I gave her a quiet courtesy and ignored her rudeness, for this was Christmas Eve.

Some strangeness was in Selina that evening, so that she seemed as keyed-up and as nervous as her mother. She danced about the tree, dropped ornaments she was hanging, and frequently made secret little grimaces to herself. I supposed she was reacting in mimicry to the example set by Leslie. But when the tree was nearly done, she suddenly reverted to her maddening little sing-song. She turned from hanging up a paper angel and went skipping around us.

"I know something you don't know!" she chanted. "I've got a secret and I won't tell!"

Even Miss Garth was less tolerant of her darling than usual. "What has you so excited, Selina?" she demanded. "It's not good for you to be this way."

Again the child made her odd little grimace. "I won't tell. I'll never tell. It's more fun to have a secret."

Jeremy threw her a scornful look. "You're being a stupid, Selina. Give me that string of cranberries if you're not going to hang it."

Selina would give up nothing and went back to her decorating, but for the moment we heard no more about her secret.

We had just finished the tree when Andrew Beach rang the bell and was admitted to our midst, his arms full of small packages.

"No one invited me till tomorrow morning when the servitors appear," he said wryly. "So I've invited myself tonight. Do you mind if I put my parcels under your tree?"

The children were happy to see him, and if Miss Garth was not, she at least made her disapproval less obvious than usual. With the decorations done, we all placed our gifts on the white sheet spread around the foot of the tree. The Christmas effect was perfect now, and there remained only the lighting of the candles. This was a careful task for adults, and by way of extra precaution I had brought in a huge sponge in a bucket of water as the same safety measure we'd always used at home in case a branch caught fire.

One by one we lighted the candles with tapers until the whole tree glowed with warm, living fire. In the big drafty room air currents sent the pointed flames dipping and tilting so that all the branches shimmered.

Selina, still overly excited, began to crawl among the gifts, examining this one, then that, sometimes holding a package up so that she could shake it and try to guess the contents. It was thus that she unearthed the package I had wrapped for Jeremy.

"Who's this for?" she asked. "It says, 'For the Prince.' We don't have a prince in this house."

Jeremy glanced at me quickly, and I smiled. "That's a secret between Jeremy and me," I told her, and saw pleasure come to life in his eyes. Bit by bit, just as had happened to the prince in the fairy tale, the ugly disguise was being stripped away and Jeremy was changing. I prayed that all would go well with the gift for his uncle so his happiness might be complete.

When the last candle had been lighted, we stood back to admire the effect. The tree had been placed in a corner of the drawing room, and from the wall opposite, a huge mirror reflected the strands of white popcorn and red cranberries, the bright ornaments and myriad flames.

Andrew held out one hand to me and the other to Selina. Softly he began to sing, and I was surprised at the deep timbre of his voice. Jeremy and even Miss Garth came to hold hands with us as we stood before the tree, our voices raised in "O Tannenbaum." We sang the English words, and they rang out strongly in the quiet room.

> "O Evergreen, O Evergreen!
> How faithful are your branches . . ."

It was a strangely lovely and healing moment. I ceased to think of Leslie and Brandon dancing together at their party. I let the sadness, the loneliness, the fear of the last few days flow out through my very fingertips as Andrew clasped my hand and we sang together. I had the curious feeling that through the very clasp of his fingers Andrew was offering his own quiet strength to sustain me. Tonight he seemed less cynical and critical. I took something of comfort from the hand of a man clasping mine, even though it was the wrong hand.

When at length our voices died away, Miss Garth broke the circle first and went back to her chair. For an instant I caught the shine of tears in her eyes and the thought came to me that we were all rather a forlorn and lonely lot.

Suddenly I wanted to hold to the Christmas spell that had fallen so gently upon us.

"I know the main gifts are to be opened tomorrow when your mother and your uncle are here," I said to the children. "But perhaps we could make an exception with one or two of our own presents for each other. Then we could have a little more of Christmas tonight."

Miss Garth did not approve. It was not the custom, she said. She did not know what Mrs. Reid would think. I suspected that Leslie would not care one way or the other, though I did not say so. It was Selina who settled matters. She flew to the tree and brought out a package from among those scattered below it. Surprisingly, it was not a present for herself, but the one she had made for me.

I opened it while the others watched and found that she had given me a pomander ball. It was an apple, painstakingly, though unevenly, stuck with cloves and tied with a blue satin ribbon for hanging among my clothes. I exclaimed over it in pleasure, and the gift opening was on.

The present for the "prince" came next, and Jeremy gravely opened the package I had wrapped for him. I watched with a lump in my throat as he slipped off the ribbon and pressed back the paper from about the carrousel. While Selina cried out in wonder and envy, he simply stared at it for a moment. Then he looked at me with such delight, such gratitude in his eyes that I could hardly bear it. Yet still he could not believe that this gift was truly for him.

"It belonged to your brother—" he began.

I nodded. "You are my brother now, Jeremy."

He wound the toy and set the tune tinkling, the carrousel turning, while we all watched enchanted. Even Miss Garth offered no criticism and did not warn him not to break it. When I glanced at Andrew I saw his eyes upon me, his look unfathomable as it so often was these days. There was a sadness in the smile he bent upon me. I did not know why, but I smiled back, offering without words my thanks for the quiet support he had given me tonight.

It did not take us long to open the rest of the gifts we had for each other. There were the usual penwipers, pincushions, and darning eggs. Selina had made a charming strand of sealing-wax beads in red and gold for Miss Garth. And Jeremy had carved a small Egyptian head for me from a piece of wood. It appeared to be a replica of the Sphinx and I thanked him for it warmly. Andrew gave me a sketch of Washington Square in a snowstorm, and I sensed that it was something of a peace-offering to make up for the drawing of me he had destroyed.

That Christmas Eve was almost a happy time. Happier perhaps for the absence of Brandon Reid, though this I hated to admit. Before Andrew left we sang "Silent Night," and the words were still singing through my mind, *All is calm, all is bright,* as we extinguished the candles. The odor of evergreen and snuffed candles was a perfume Andrew said he would carry into his dreams that night. I believe it brought to each of the three adults in that room a nostalgic memory of days long past, happier days than those through which we now lived.

With Andrew gone and no more packages to open for the time being, Selina returned to her annoying chant about a secret. I suspected that she would never sleep after all this excitement unless she confided whatever it was she had on her mind.

"You might as well tell us," I said. "Your secret is likely to keep you awake all night unless you do."

"It isn't a secret to tell!" Selina cried. "If you want to come with me now, I'll show you what it is."

Miss Garth broke in abruptly. "All this is nonsense. It's your bedtime, Selina. Come along, and on the way upstairs you can tell me about your secret. You needn't make a performance of it. Say good night, dear."

I was almost pleased when Selina laughed at her instruction and turned to Jeremy and me.

"If I'm going to tell, I want to show it to everyone!" she cried and ran through the door ahead of us, her fair hair bouncing against her back.

Jeremy left his carrousel beneath the Christmas tree and came beside me up the stairs, while Miss Garth followed gloomily, once more preoccupied with her role of Cassandra. This was not a good idea, she insisted. The child was too excited. The whole thing must be stopped.

My first misgivings came when Selina went to the closed door of her mother's boudoir. When Miss Garth would have stopped her from entering, she laughed mischievously and slipped out of the governess' grasp, darting into the room ahead of her. In the thin light from the hall I saw her run to the velvet draperies that hid her mother's bedroom and push them aside.

"Do light the gas, Miss Megan," she called. "It's dark in here."

"You'll do nothing of the kind," Miss Garth told me sharply. "The child has no business in this room while her mother is absent and neither have you."

She was right, of course, but now, in spite of a certain uneasiness, I was curious to know what so excited Selina. I went to the mantel, found matches, and lighted the gas Leslie so seldom used in this room of scent and shadow.

Kate had apparently been in to put things to rights after her mistress had dressed for the ball, for there was no disarray in the room. The bedclothes were turned down neatly, and Leslie's nightgown lay across the coverlet. All was in its usual place, and any dusting of powder had been wiped from the top of her dressing table, her perfume bottles and silver-backed brushes set in order.

For a moment the four of us stood looking about. Then Miss Garth moved decisively toward the gas I had just lighted and turned it out. But in the instant before the light vanished, Selina cried out.

"It's gone!" she wailed. "It isn't here at all. So how can I show you?"

Miss Garth gave Selina no further chance to explain. She took her by the arm and whisked her off to bed in such high indignation that not even her charge protested. Jeremy and I found ourselves in the hall, looking at each other in bewilderment.

"What do you suppose all that was about?" I asked.

Jeremy shrugged. "Just Selina being silly," he said.

I was willing to leave it at that.

"Perhaps it's bedtime for us too, Jeremy," I said. "This has been a long, happy evening."

He came upstairs with me and went to bed without objection. But when I returned to my own room, I found I had no desire to go immediately to sleep. A restlessness possessed me. To amuse myself, I sorted out the small gifts I had brought up to my room—Jeremy's sphinx, Selina's pomander ball, Andrew's sketch. I'd felt a sense of friendly companionship tonight while Andrew was there. For a little while I had been able to shut Brandon Reid away in a hidden compartment of my mind. But now I remembered, and remembering, I knew what it was to be lonely on Christmas Eve.

As midnight neared, I could endure my gloomy thoughts no longer. I slipped my dolman about me and tied a woolen scarf over my head against the chill of the night. Then I went softly downstairs and out the front door, taking my latchkey, so I might return without disturbing the servants.

I stood on the high marble steps and lifted my face to a cool wind blowing from the harbor, as if its very touch would clear my troubled thoughts and brush away longings that frightened me. The square lay peaceful and bright beneath the quiet sky. Through recent snow diagonal paths ruled long brown lines. Here and there about the perimeter a lighted Christmas tree brightened a window, and friendly lamps burned where occupants were still up on Christmas Eve. Along one edge of the square the Gothic buildings of the University formed a gray border without illumination, though lights gleamed in the windows of the church next door.

From downtown I heard the clock bell of old Trinity begin to strike the midnight hour and I knew that Christmas Day was nearly upon me. One by one I counted the strokes, and, when they came to an end, a hush seemed to fall upon the air. It was as if a concerted breath were held, as if all the city waited. Into this breathless pause came a burst of rich, sweet sound as the bells of Trinity began to peal their joyful welcome to Christmas Day.

My heart lifted in spite of myself, and I looked up at heavens deep and blue and spangled with stars. The words of the song we had sung earlier returned to whisper softly through my consciousness: *All is calm, all is bright* . . . Something of the night's peace descended upon me, and I returned more calmly to the house and started upstairs to my room.

Gaslight still burned on the second floor, and, as I followed the hall to the upward turn of the stairs, I caught a slight movement in the shadows. For an instant I was startled and thought of Jeremy. Then I saw that it was Miss Garth who had placed a chair outside her mistress' door and sat there, alert and watchful. She saw me, but she did not speak, and I went up the stairs quickly, wanting no encounter with Thora Garth in that lonely hallway.

The sense of peace was suddenly gone. It was a long while before I fell asleep. Sometime during the early hours of Christmas morning I wakened to hear horses being stabled in the mews beneath my window and knew that Leslie and Brandon had come home.

CHAPTER 19

EARLY THE next morning, before I'd had breakfast, I went downstairs, meaning to go for a walk in the winter sunshine of Christmas Day. More and more the atmosphere of the house weighed upon me, oppressed me.

But though I moved quietly, someone else was up as early as I, and, as I passed the library, Brandon heard my step and called to me to come in. I paused just inside the door. Here was my opportunity to tell him that I could not remain in his employ much longer. I must form my own plans soon and act upon them.

As he came toward me, however, I saw his face, haggard in the early morning light, the eyes sunken in the sockets. It could not be the late hours of a ball that had done this to him. With his vitality he could have danced the dawn in with ease, had the occasion been a joyous one. I put my intent aside, knowing I could not add to whatever trouble had set this stamp of suffering upon him.

"Merry Christmas, Megan," he said, but there was no merriment in the words. He put a hand into the pocket of his burgundy dressing gown, then drew it out, extending it toward me. In his fingers he held a small blue box, a jeweler's box.

I stared at it blankly, taken aback.

"It's for you, Megan," he said. "Today is Christmas, and this is my gift to you."

I did not want him to give me anything. I did not want him to be thoughtful and kind. I kept my hands behind my back like a willful child.

"We're opening our gifts under the tree later this morning," I told him stiffly.

With a quick gesture, as though I exasperated him, he caught my hand and drew it from behind my back, pressing the little box into my fingers and holding them closed about it so that I might not refuse.

"Under the tree you will find a proper gift chosen by Leslie. This is my own gift to you, Megan. It is a very small way of thanking you for all you've done in this house. You can't deny me so trifling a pleasure. Open it; I want to know what you think."

With uncertain fingers I pressed the catch of the box, and the lid flew up. Pinned to the white satin inside was a pale green scarab set in a simple silver brooch.

"That wasn't bought in the streets of Cairo," he said. "It is from the tomb of Queen Hatshepsut. I thought it might please you, so I had it set in a brooch."

It pleased me so very much that I did not want him to guess the extent of my delight.

"It's beautiful," I said in a low voice.

He touched the scrollwork of the design with his forefinger. "The material is glazed steatite. The marks it bears spell the queen's name. I wish you could see Deir-el-Bahri at Thebes where this came from. All those rows upon rows of great steps leading to higher levels where the gigantic enthroned figures sit. Images of the queen on every hand—the same broad-cheeked beautiful face repeated again and again. The place is both temple and tomb."

As I listened, studying the tiny scarab, my mind conjured up a vast temple set against bare brown hills. He broke the spell of my vision abruptly.

"What did you do on Christmas Eve?"

"We trimmed the tree," I told him.

"And—afterwards?"

I told him of how I had been unable to sleep and had come downstairs to stand on the front steps. Of how I had heard the bells of Trinity on Christmas Eve.

"I wondered if you'd hear them," he said. "At midnight I found an open window where I could breathe fresh air and be alone. I thought of you then, Megan. While the bells were ringing."

I had come into this room meaning to tell him that I could stay no longer in this house, but I knew I could not speak at this time. There was a burning of tears behind my lids, and I dared not remain in his company. I turned from him quickly and fled the room.

I ran upstairs with his gift held tightly and in my room I cried over it a little. No matter what this house held for me in the way of pain, I would keep this small brooch always and remember that Brandon Reid had thought well enough of me to want me to have it.

When I went to breakfast that morning I could not resist pinning the delicate brooch at the collar of my dress.

Miss Garth, the children, and I breakfasted together in the nursery. Only Selina still seemed excited about Christmas. Miss Garth appeared morose and greeted me with the news that poor Miss Leslie had danced beyond her strength last night and was too ill this morning to join in the Christmas-tree festivities. Though the governess said nothing openly, I caught the implication that Brandon Reid was to blame.

During the meal Jeremy inquired about the date for the opening ceremonies at the Dwight Reid Memorial Home, and Miss Garth answered him impatiently.

"Why don't you ask your uncle? I know nothing at all about it. And care less!"

"I want to be there," Jeremy said with the same persistence he had shown before. "Do you think my mother will take me?"

Garth glowered at him. "I hope your mother will stay home. If your uncle has his way, there'll be no ceremony."

Jeremy sighed and did not question her further. He and Selina left the table ahead of us, both eager for the opening of presents. Ordinarily I would have followed, loathe to be left alone with Miss Garth. But now I found myself regarding her with open curiosity. It was so seldom that she sided against Leslie. Only in this matter did she oppose Mrs. Reid.

"Why don't you want to see a ceremony held at the opening of the memorial?" I asked.

She was angry enough to answer me. "Because the whole thing is a mockery—that's why! The boy's father wasn't always the hero they make him out to be. There was bad blood there, I can tell you.

The boy is like him. For once his uncle knows what's right and what isn't. But my poor Miss Leslie is completely deluded and won't listen to reason. If Master Brandon hadn't been away in Egypt—" She paused, and I pressed her quickly, wanting to hear more of this astonishing revelation.

"What brought the older brother home from abroad that last time?"

"He came because Master Dwight sent for him! He wanted his big, strong brother to rescue him from the results of his own weakness of character."

"What had he done?" I asked bluntly.

"Enough to put the Reid name under a black cloud and perhaps land himself in jail in the reform wave that was picking off those in high places. Enough to ruin all he had built, and undoubtedly kill his father with shock over the disgrace."

"But—what was it he did?"

I had pressed too hard. Miss Garth's dark gaze returned from a stormy distance to focus upon me. "None of this is your business, my girl. It's past history now, and the only thing that matters is not to revive it and stir things up all over again. If you had any sense, you'd not stay around to be mixed up in it. You'd not wait for your next dismissal—you'd leave this house to save your own reputation . . . and perhaps more!"

Animosity toward me marked every line of her face, but I stood my ground.

"I don't like to be threatened," I said. "Neither by daylight, nor in a dark room."

Miss Garth pushed back her chair and left the table without another glance in my direction.

I sat on, thinking of the surprising things she had said. That the brilliant, successful young Galahad, Dwight Reid, might have had feet of clay. That he had sent for Brandon to come home and rescue him from some scrape of his own making. What did all this portend? I sensed some significance here, some meaning that would make everything clear, but I could not put my finger upon it.

There had been spite in Garth's eyes, in her voice when she spoke of Dwight. A memory of that day when I had seen her in Leslie's room, wearing Leslie's gown, with the double miniature in her hands, returned to me. I had wondered which brother her look of adoration had been for. Now it appeared that, unlike her mistress, she had harbored only contempt for Dwight. Could it be that a secret infatuation for Brandon throbbed beneath the stiff façade she presented to the world?

Selina called to me then, and I put aside these new troubling thoughts as best I could in order to join the children in their opening of Christmas presents.

It was as well that we had enjoyed a taste of real Christmas last night, for nothing was the same this morning. The tree was gay and bright, the candles shone with a lovely radiance, and the air was scented with evergreen. But the warmth that made all this important was lacking.

Brandon Reid's mood was far from festive. He stood with his back to the mantel, above which we had draped a string of red tissue-paper bells purchased from Stewart's store. The gay bells, unfolded to plump accordian pleating, presented a somehow ludicrous contrast behind his somber head, seeming frivolous to an improper degree. When Miss Garth told him that his wife would not be down, he looked increasingly displeased.

As their gifts were doled out, the servants offered polite thanks to the master and went off with their unopened packages. Brandon was courteous enough, but clearly remote. I could not help wondering what had happened at the party last night to result in Leslie's illness and this dark, angry mood of her husband's. Miss Garth's excuse that too much dancing had brought such a result did not convince me.

Now and then I glanced uneasily at Jeremy and saw that his attention was fixed mainly on the gift he had wrapped so carefully for his uncle.

When it came to giving out the family presents and those for the governess, Andrew, and me, Miss Garth employed Selina to fetch packages to her from beneath the tree. She would read off the name, and Selina would take it to the recipient. Jeremy's package had still not been chosen, and I could sense the boy's anxiety whenever his sister went near the tree. If it had been possible, I believe he might have taken the gift away and hidden it upstairs, rather than face this chill, indifferent mood of his uncle's.

Except for Andrew's occasional efforts, Selina was the only one with any Christmas spirit that morning. She had forgotten about her "secret" and bubbled gayly along, with no awareness of the pall that lay upon the room.

When the child at last picked her own gift for her uncle and carried it to him down the long room, I saw Jeremy's interest quicken. Perhaps he thought the reception of this gift might be some indication of how his own might fare. Brandon, to do him credit, endeavored to play the game. He held up the bright fluff of varicolored embroidered felt that Selina intended as a penwiper, and remarked over it as he was supposed to do. But the effort rang false, and even Selina sensed that her gift had not been received with a proper Christmas enthusiasm.

"I made it very quickly, Uncle Brandon," she apologized. "I know it isn't very neat, but there was no time to make another."

Her uncle did his best. "It's very pretty, Selina. I'll keep it on my desk and think of you whenever I use it. Thank you, my dear."

She seemed satisfied and skipped back to the tree to find a gift for Miss Garth. Nervously I fingered the scarab pin at my throat and caught Andrew watching my fingers. The look he gave me was mocking, and I knew he guessed where the pin had come from. It had been a mistake to wear it, I thought, and let my hand fall to my lap.

My own gift from Mr. and Mrs. Reid was a muff of gray squirrel —a luxurious present. Yet this had been chosen by Leslie and it did not mean to me what the little scarab meant. It was merely a conventional gesture, since Mrs. Reid wanted me out of this house.

By that time I believe Jeremy thought that his sister might overlook his gift for Brandon altogether and leave it there among the unopened gifts for their mother. But she crawled among the remaining packages on her hands and knees and saw it at last.

"Oh, look!" she cried. "It's for you, Uncle Brandon. Jeremy made it for you, and I know what it is."

The room was oddly still as she ran to put the package into her uncle's hands. Perhaps we all sensed in one way or another how much hung in the balance with this particular gift. All, perhaps, except Brandon himself. Ever since she had dashed the beads to the floor in his room, Miss Garth had hated what Jeremy was making and undoubtedly wanted to see no good come of it. Andrew had admired the collar more than once and shown some surprise at Jeremy's workmanship. Selina had been proud and admiring from the beginning.

I watched as tensely as Jeremy did and wished that I might catch Brandon's eye and send him a pleading glance to remind him of his promise. But he did not look my way at all. With maddening deliberation he fumbled with ribbon and paper, perhaps postponing the moment when he would have to pretend a role he had no heart for just now.

Jeremy sat on a low footstool near the fire in utter stillness. Only his eyes were alive and anguished.

"Oh, do open it!" I cried, unable to contain myself.

Brandon threw me a look that told me he did not care for impatient women, and at last opened the cardboard box in which Jeremy had nested the gift in tissue. Silently, without expression, he drew it from the box and held it in his hand. I saw again the wide, flat collar with its rows of beads strung on thin wire. Further spokes of wire around the wheel held it flat. Here and there the dark pattern of cut steel was broken with touches of red and green and turquoise blue.

Brandon held it up to examine it more closely, and I saw his eyes light with an appreciation in which there was no pretense. He knew what it was at once, and his smile of approval for Jeremy was surprisingly warm.

"It's for the Osiris, isn't it?" he said. "A fine piece of work, Jeremy."

"I'm not sure when those collars were in fashion," Jeremy said worriedly. "I'm not sure this is right for Osiris."

"That won't matter," Brandon assured him. "Long after the broad collar went out of style it was used as a funerary ornament, and the dead were Osiris' business. I suppose you've tried it for fit?"

Jeremy nodded as though he found it difficult to speak. Since I felt a little lightheaded with relief myself, it was easy to guess how he must feel.

Selina danced about them in delight, clearly pleased that their uncle liked her brother's work.

"Jeremy let me go with him when he tried it on Osiris," she said.

"Since the beard sticks out from the chin, the collar goes right under it. It looks beautiful."

"Miss Megan helped me," Jeremy said, finding his voice again. "She wouldn't let me give up when I got discouraged."

Brandon looked at me across the room. His gaze flicked from my face to the pin at my throat and back again, and there was something as gentle as a caress in his eyes. It was almost as if he reached out to touch me as a lover might. The look was so unexpected that it disarmed me completely. For an instant my guard against him went down and I gave him look for look. By the time I recovered and steadied myself, Andrew was watching me. I knew he had seen the exchange and I could feel his disapproval almost as if it were a tangible thing. I could not have cared less.

When the last present had been opened, Brandon suggested to Jeremy that they take the collar to Osiris. Selina wanted to go with them, but Miss Garth called her back. She was attending a Christmas luncheon party today, and it was time for her to dress. Jeremy went eagerly with his uncle, and I was glad to see them go alone, without interference. Selina, remembering the party, was now impatient to be off and went away pulling Garth along with her.

Andrew and I were left with the debris of Christmas, and this was a tête-à-tête I had no taste for. I went to work as busily as possible.

CHAPTER 20

"Help me snuff out the candles, will you?" I said to Andrew. "Then I'll ring for Kate to clear up the trash."

I gave him a snuffer on a long handle, and he came to assist me. As we circled the tree he reached the place where Leslie Reid's packages were heaped unopened.

"They look a bit forlorn, don't they?" he said.

I was surprised to hear such sentimentality from Andrew and I glanced at him in surprise. He was regarding me with a look that was oddly intent and a little pitying. I wanted neither his pity nor his interest and I turned my back and reached for a high candle.

"Why don't you take her packages upstairs to Mrs. Reid?" Andrew asked.

Was he baiting me? I wondered. Didn't he know that Mrs. Reid had wanted to dismiss me? I turned from the tree to face him. "Miss Garth says she doesn't wish to be disturbed. It's not my place to take her presents to her."

The wry, familiar smile twisted Andrew's mouth. "You're a kind enough person ordinarily, Megan. You're thoughtful toward everyone in this house. Even toward me at times, and toward poor old Thora. Toward everyone but Mrs. Reid." He reached a finger toward the scarab brooch at the throat of my dress. "But of course you can't be generous to Brandon Reid's wife."

I moved from his touch. "I don't know what you're talking about. I seldom see Mrs. Reid. It would be ridiculous for me to carry her packages upstairs and disturb her while she's ill."

"Would it?" Andrew said.

I began to suspect what he was doing and why. Whether I wished it or not, he was intent on protecting me from Brandon. Deliberately, cunningly, he was turning me to face the possible suffering of Leslie Reid. What he could not know was that I had settled all this with myself in my own way. I did not need the effort he was making.

He must have sensed my resistance, for he changed his approach. "Will you come for a walk with me, Megan? I'd like to tell you what I mean. We can't talk here without interruption."

There was an earnest persistence in him, and I realized again how little I really knew Andrew Beach. When he roused himself to action, he could be thoroughly determined. Perhaps it would be best to go with him and hear him out. Only then could I defend my own position against his misconceptions. Besides, there were certain things I wanted to tell him, and a question I meant to ask.

"I'll get my cloak and bonnet," I said and went upstairs.

When I came down ready for the street, he was waiting for me near the door and his eyes brightened at the sight of me. I could not help but think that all might have been easier for me if I had felt some answering response.

As we went down the steps, he tucked my hand into the crook of his arm. "It's pleasant to walk with a pretty girl on Christmas morning," he said.

The mood I remembered from that night at Mama Santini's was upon him again, but now the spell of a darker, more desperate love held me in thrall and I had nothing to offer Andrew Beach.

After a bright early morning, the day had turned gray and there was once more the smell of snow in the air. All about us bare branches etched a delicate brown tracery against the snowy area of the square, and I studied it as I walked in silence at Andrew's side. It was he who wanted to talk, and I could only wait for what I feared would be a lecture.

He began, however, with ancient history—with the time when Leslie Rolfe had fallen in love with Dwight Reid.

"Not that I knew either family then," he said. "But I learned a great deal about them when Dwight Reid died. And more has come to light since. Dwight fought in the war, as you probably know. Brandon didn't. Though it wasn't Brandon's fault that he saw no action. He went as a civilian aide on a mission sent to England for the purpose of swinging British sympathy toward the North. From what I've heard, it was a post he served well. I've no quarrel with him on that score.

"While he was away the Rolfes, in trouble financially, moved next door to the Reid house on Bleecker Street, and Dwight, home on leave, fell in love with Leslie. Perhaps she had a special aura of romance around her then—at least in Galahad's eyes. Before the war began her father's fortune had been ruined. He was trying to recoup with war profits, but the family was still in straits. I fancy that old Rolfe must have been more than pleased with Dwight's interest in his daughter."

"Brandon Reid was still in England at the time?" I asked.

"He came home after Dwight had rejoined his company. Garth says he met Leslie at a party and didn't know who she was, or that she was all but engaged to his brother. He followed suit, falling in love with her too."

We had reached the Washington Square fountain, and Andrew stared absently at icicles dripping in spears from the low rim of the basin. His story had roused my interest. I wanted to learn all I could about Brandon Reid, no matter how much pain such knowledge might bring me. Only through knowledge could I understand him now.

"Go on," I urged. "What about Brandon?"

Andrew reached down to touch a dagger of ice, and it shattered with a glassy crackle. "Brandon learned the truth, of course, and he accepted the assignment of a mission to France and got out of the country. His background of experience in England was useful to the government. When the war was over he went to Egypt and managed to be away on one expedition or another after that for years at a stretch. Leslie married Dwight, and, I suppose, should have lived happily ever after, since he was the better man."

That I would not accept. "*Was* he the better man?" I challenged. "Or is Dwight Reid's reputation a myth? Is it something Leslie clings to and the public was fooled about?"

Andrew threw me a questioning look, and I told him what Garth had said that morning at breakfast. He did not speak until I concluded with the matter of the letter Garth claimed had brought

Brandon home from his last expedition. Then he nodded with no great surprise.

"I've wondered sometimes if too much perfection was claimed for Dwight. And I've heard an unpleasant rumor or two. About the letter, I wouldn't know. At any rate, the great traveler, who had once been in love with Leslie, came home to his brother's house. And by great coincidence the brother died and the young wife was left unprotected."

I heard the bite of scorn in his words and stiffened. "You've no right to make veiled accusations!"

"I'm making no accusation of any sort," Andrew said.

"Why did you bring this up?" I demanded. "What has any of it to do with me?"

Andrew smiled and again drew my fingers into the crook of his arm as we walked on, crossing a path that led over what had been the Washington Parade Ground, and before that Potter's Field.

"You know very well why I've brought it up," he said. "I don't want Reid to accomplish with you what he has accomplished with other women. There's time to turn back, Megan, if only you'll try to see him as he is. There's a ruthless quality about him that drives through to get what he wants, no matter what the cost, or how long it takes. I want to see you sorry for Mrs. Reid as well as distrustful of her husband. You can afford to be more generous and kind."

This was too much. "As you are being generous and kind in that portrait you're painting! Do you really believe that *she* is so gentle and generous?"

He answered me quietly enough. "No, I don't. But perhaps she needs to see herself in a more flattering light. Sometimes I think we tend to become what others believe we are."

Since he had an apparently low opinion of me, I grew still more annoyed. "Mrs. Reid is a woman who married her husband's brother a year after the man she loved died. A woman who, you say, has never loved anyone but the younger brother. Give me the answer to that, if you will, instead of condemning Mr. Reid."

"You ask me questions I can't answer," Andrew admitted. "Whatever either of them may have hoped for in this marriage, each appears to have suffered disappointment. But it's you I'm thinking of now, Megan."

I was still angry. "You take too much upon yourself! You're not the keeper of my conscience. I know very well what I should or should not do, but I have very little sympathy for Mrs. Reid."

"I suppose that's natural enough," Andrew said.

I saw once more the hint of pity in his eyes and flared out against it. "Do you know that she tried to dismiss me?" I asked. "That she told me to leave the house? She believed whatever Garth told her and would not listen to me. It's only because of Mr. Reid's intervention that I've stayed on."

"Garth saw to it that I was informed," he said shortly. "What else could you expect but dismissal under the circumstances?"

"Expect? I expect nothing! But I did hope that I would be allowed to help Jeremy in my own way. And without being blocked by his mother or Miss Garth. As it is, who could be more unwelcome than I, if I were to take those gifts upstairs to Mrs. Reid?"

Andrew's steps had slowed beside me. "Can you give her no reassurance at all, Megan? Have you no sympathy for the humiliation of her position?"

"Perhaps there's humiliation for me too," I said, "when I'm given no chance to do the right thing as I see it."

He swung me suddenly about, his hands upon my elbows so that I was forced to look into his eyes. There was an insistence in him that I had never seen before.

"What I'm suggesting is the right thing. You've known what loneliness is like. Go back and take Mrs. Reid's gifts upstairs to her. She needs a friend in that house—a woman nearer her own age than Garth. You can help her if you will."

I did not want to be swayed by him. "Why do you involve yourself in this?" I asked.

For a moment he hesitated, the wry smile lifting a corner of his mouth. Then he did an unexpected thing. He leaned toward me and kissed me in a light quick caress.

"Perhaps that's why," he said. "Perhaps because of how I feel about you, Megan. Though that is something you've been too busy otherwise to notice." He laughed and was himself again, setting me gently from him.

For a moment I could only stare—perhaps not so much in surprise as in dismay. Had I not sensed the direction in which he was moving and even wished at times that I could respond? The reassurance he sought was not so much for Leslie, I suspected, as for himself, and I wanted very much to be kind to him.

"If it will please you," I said, making the only small offer I could give him, "I'll do what you ask. I'll take the gifts to Leslie, if you believe this will help."

I did not fool him. We had been walking in the direction of the house, and, as we neared the front steps, he paused.

"I won't try to tell you what you must do, Megan," he said quietly. "It's true that I have no right to advise you. Or to condemn any course you choose to take, for that matter."

He turned my gloved hands palm up and held them for a moment. I think he meant to say something more, but instead he let me go. He waited there motionless while I ran up the steps and let myself in the door. When I glanced back, he was still there, staring up at the house.

I let myself in and went to the drawing room, where Kate was at work clearing up. Whether it was foolish or not, I must keep my promise to Andrew, and when I had gathered her presents into my arms, I started upstairs to Leslie's room.

CHAPTER 21

My ARMS were so well filled with packages that when I reached Mrs. Reid's door I had not a free finger with which to rap. I called to her softly, half hoping that she would be asleep and never hear me. Then I could return my armload to the tree, my conscience silenced, with nothing further for me to do. I had no belief that this action was right or would in any way be welcomed by Mrs. Reid. Yet if it would show Andrew that I did not mean to follow my love in Brandon's direction, then this was what I must do.

In a faint voice Mrs. Reid called to me to come in. The door was ajar, and I pushed it open and went into the darkened room.

"I've brought your Christmas gifts," I said. "I thought you might like them here where you can open them comfortably."

She looked at me so blankly that I felt impelled to offer something more.

"You were missed at the tree this morning," I added as I put my burden down on the foot of her bed. "I hope you're feeling better."

She remained listless, indifferent, offering no response. How dreary this dim room seemed in spite of its luxury. The lack of air and light must surely affect the woman in the bed.

"Do you mind if I open the draperies?" I asked.

"Do as you like," she told me without interest.

When I had let in the light of late morning, I poured her a fresh cup of tea from the cosy-covered pot beside her bed and helped her to sit up. She did not resist me, but sipped the tea and watched me gravely over the rim of the cup.

Dark circles showed beneath her eyes, and there was no dusting of powder, no blush of coloring in her cheeks. The merciless day-light made her look wan and tired, and I saw the beginnings of fine lines at the outward corners of her eyes, the first etching of permanent unhappiness about her mouth. It would be possible, I thought, to pity her, as Andrew did.

I moved the packages where they lay tumbled across her feet and spoke cheerfully. "Which one will you open first?"

After a moment's hesitation she reached across the satin quilt and made a selection. It was her gift from Brandon.

She read the card and dropped it aside. I could not help but see the first words of the bold handwriting: "To my adored wife . . ."

She held the package in her hands and looked up at me. "Why are you doing this, Miss Kincaid?"

I did not want to tell her that the task had been thrust upon me and that I had begun to feel a little sorry for her.

"The packages looked forlorn under the tree," I said. And that was true enough.

With little interest, she untied the ribbon about the package. The wrapping opened to reveal a large flat box with a Tiffany label, and as she touched the lid it sprang open.

I caught my breath. Against rich black velvet lay a parure in chased gold, rubies, and diamonds. The set consisted of necklace, pendant earrings, and a bracelet. I had never seen anything so handsome and I was astonished when Leslie pushed the box from her and burst into tears. In utter devastation she wept without concealment.

Dismayed, I searched her dressing table, found a lace-edged handkerchief, and gave it to her in some concern. She dabbed futilely at tear-drenched amber eyes.

"It's always like this!" she cried. "He thinks money can make up for emptiness! Once I knew what love was like. Once I had a husband who adored me. That's why I know now what emptiness is."

Her outburst shocked me, not only because of her meaning, but because it meant a relinquishing of all pride. If she lost her pride, she would have nothing.

"At the ball last night he humiliated me dreadfully," she choked. "He would not even pretend to be pleased with my company. It was no better than our trip up the Hudson, when he was constantly impatient with me."

I could well imagine how Brandon might humiliate a woman if he chose, and I could not help but pity his wife. Yet he was not a man who would willingly endure in a woman endless headaches, vapors, and self-pity.

She must have sensed my softening toward her, for she grasped at it. "Sit down, Miss Kincaid. Now that you're here, you must listen to me."

I seated myself on the edge of a chair beside her bed, wishing myself anywhere but in that room and blaming Andrew for placing me in this predicament.

Her words began to pour out in complete abandonment. "There was nothing to live for when Dwight died! Yet I had to go on living. Can you understand what such a loss might be like, Miss Kincaid?"

I thought I might very well understand and I nodded.

"In order to live, I snatched at anything that seemed to offer me sustenance. Brandon had been in love with me before I married Dwight. He was Dwight's brother. They had been devoted to each other. So why shouldn't I find in him something of what I had lost? Instead—" the life went out of her voice, leaving a heaviness of despair, "instead there is only this!" She flung a gesture of rejection at the jewels Brandon had given her. "This and a prison from which there is no escape."

Nevertheless, I thought, I would fight back if I were in her place. She was allowing herself to be submerged. Yet I did not know how to offer her strength in this moment of appalling weakness.

Perhaps my silence seemed to spell condemnation, for she began to speak again, a little wildly now.

"You know why I married Brandon, Miss Kincaid," she said. "But haven't you ever wondered why he married me?"

"That is none of my affair," I said evenly.

"While that is quite true, I shall tell you. And it will be something for you to think about in the night hours, something for you to ponder when his face comes to your mind. He married me to buy my silence. Because if he did not, I would have told the truth he is so terribly afraid of. And now that I am bound to him in this empty marriage, I cannot speak out as I might like to do."

441

I made no response to her words as I moved quickly to gather up packages that lay in bright mockery across her quilts. I said nothing at all as I carried them into the boudoir and left them on the chaise longue, where she might later do as she liked with them. Then I returned to her bedroom and drew the draperies to shut out gray daylight and leave her once more to darkness. All the while she lay very still, her eyes closed, the lashes dark upon her pale cheeks. She did not speak as I went silently from the room and closed the door behind me.

Where the truth lay in any of what she had said, I did not know. It would be best not to think of her words at all, or try to sift truth from self-delusion. She was ill, not only in body, but in mind as well.

As I moved toward the stairs, Jeremy came from his uncle's library, pouncing upon me eagerly the moment he saw me.

"Come see how the collar looks, Miss Megan," he invited.

I had no heart for his request and no desire to see Brandon at that moment, but Jeremy was insistent. In the library Brandon stood at the window, his back toward me, and I went no more than a step or two into the room.

The fanciful collar looked a little strange against the stone from which the head had been sculptured. The tall white crown with its stylized plumes at each side made the patterned beads seem too bright by contrast. Yet in the expression of carved lips and eyes I fancied an understanding of all that had gone into the making of the collar. Osiris wore the gift with dignity.

"It's very beautiful," I told Jeremy, and turned toward the stairs before Brandon could speak to me.

When I reached my room I removed the pin that bore Queen Hatshepsut's name and put it among other trinkets, not daring to look at it again. Now that I was alone, the words I had thrust away as being the ranting of a sick woman, returned to plague me. What silence could Brandon have bought? What truth could Leslie speak out against her husband?

These things had no meaning for me, and I must not think about them. I must profit by Andrew's warnings. I must seek recovery of my own pride.

It was not for me to weigh the truth or falsity of the matters she had touched upon. They were no concern of mine. Brandon was out of my reach and always would be. I must tell him that I was leaving. I would wait only until the New Year had begun. That seemed a logical time for decisive action.

Leslie, having flung herself into the depths, roused sufficiently to undertake a further social round that must have left her exhausted almost every night. Perhaps that was what she wanted—the oblivion of exhaustion. She seemed to alternate between coolness toward Brandon and a trembling appeal for his attention, if not his affection. I was relieved to see little of either of them. And ashamed of that relief.

Miss Garth and Selina were away with Leslie much of the time, and I had Jeremy to myself. His mood of exultant happiness over his uncle's acceptance of his gift relaxed into something resembling contentment, and I was glad to see him come down from the heights. For the time being, at least, his uncle's manner toward the boy had changed encouragingly and I wished I had not the sensation of waiting for the unforeseen to happen when it came to the master of the house.

During that week when all was outwardly peaceful, only one small incident ruffled our daily calm. It was no more than a child's quarrel and of little consequence, had it not pointed to trouble ahead. The incident came about because of the carrousel I had given Jeremy.

It was the custom of the house for the family to leave all gifts beneath the tree during the week between Christmas and New Year. If they were taken away to be worn or played with, they were put back when the owner was through. Thus it was that Jeremy somewhat reluctantly left the little music box among his other presents under the tree. He warned his sister not to touch it, and this of course increased its fascination for Selina.

One afternoon when I heard wails of anguish from the drawing room, I ran downstairs to find that Jeremy had slapped Selina for playing with the carrousel. Though Jeremy had the toy safely back in his own keeping, Selina was screeching as only she could screech, while Jeremy watched her in anger and disgust. Miss Garth too heard the uproar, and we both reached the drawing room from different doors at the same time.

443

There were an unpleasant few moments in which I had to stand up to Miss Garth for Jeremy's cause as being just, while still condemning him for slapping his sister.

"The toy is fragile," I said. "Jeremy had a right to say who may touch it and when. He is very careful with it, and it would be a shame if Selina or anyone else broke it. Selina isn't always careful with her things, as we all know."

If I had not been there, I think Miss Garth would have returned Jeremy's slap and upheld Selina. But she saw that I would not retreat from my stand, so she carried the weeping Selina away to distract and quiet her. The immediate result of the incident—which the children quickly forgot—was an increased tension between Thora Garth and myself. I had a feeling that the woman was merely biding her time, waiting for an opportunity to catch me in some ill-advised moment when I would be at a disadvantage. Then she would raise heaven and earth to get me dismissed. That I did not intend to have happen. When I left, I wanted it to be by my own will, not because I had been put out in disgrace.

As New Year's Day approached, the house itself lent weight to my forebodings of calamity ahead. The holidays had not dispelled its atmosphere of gloom and hidden tragedy. Except for Selina, who wore her feelings lightly on the surface, every member of the household seemed possessed by some dark blight of emotion, hidden or disguised, but ready to burst into the open at a touch.

Had it been like this, I wondered, in the days before Jeremy's father had died? I did not like to entertain such a thought, but it returned more than once to haunt me. New Year's Eve seemed especially hard to endure. Since this was a time of facing both past and future, my thoughts were far from cheerful.

Leslie had long been planning a party for New Year's Eve and she hurled herself into feverish preparation which I could only view with new alarm. She could not go on like this, yet Brandon made no effort to stop her. He seemed to regard her behavior with a cold amusement that had no kindness in it.

On New Year's Eve I sat in my room and tried not to hear the sounds of gaiety two stories below. I read until eleven o'clock, then braided my hair and went deliberately to bed, pulling the covers well over my ears. I did not want to know when the New Year began. I did not want to hear the bells and I determined fiercely to be well asleep by the time they sounded.

I did not sleep, and I heard the bells quite clearly.

Not only the bells and the tooting and whistling from a distance, but racket from the immediate neighborhood and from within the house as well. Downstairs fringed paper crackers were being pulled with a bang and paper hats undoubtedly donned. One rapping noise came very close, and I realized with a start that someone was knocking on my door.

It must be Jeremy, disturbed by the noise. I flung a wrapper about me and opened the door. Brandon, elegant in evening dress, his shirt front stiff above a white waistcoat, his tie faultless, stood there smiling at me. Beneath dark brows his eyes were alight with a reckless gleam and in each hand he held a glass of champagne. He seemed more vibrantly alive than I'd ever seen him, and I sensed danger in him as never before. In quick remembrance I recalled the first time I had seen Brandon Reid. Even then he had drawn and compelled me, and now I found myself stirred by an excitement I was helpless to resist.

"Happy New Year, Megan," he said. "I wanted to toast the New Year with no one but you. Will you do me the honor?"

All caution was lost to me. I took the glass and held it up by its slender stem, raising it to his.

"To a way out for us," he said and touched the rim of his glass to mine.

My eyes did not drop from his as I drank the sparkling wine. I could not think or weigh or question. I could only feel.

I took no second sip, however, for he removed the glass from my hand and set both aside on the table near my door. I knew what was to come and I had only one will, one desire. As simply as though no other course of action were possible, I went into his arms. Their clasp hurt me, his mouth bruised mine, yet I reveled in pain.

When he released me without warning, I was startled, for there was sudden anger in him and it alarmed me.

"I'll force her hand. I'll make a way!" he told me, and the roughening in his tone spoke again of violence scarcely restrained.

I drew away, shaken and no longer yielding. He saw that he had frightened me and spoke more gently.

"Give me time, Megan. A little more time to find a way out of this trap I'm caught in. But don't run away. That's one thing I will not have. Do you understand me, Megan?"

I could only nod in agreement. I was held by a compulsion I could not resist. He accepted the answer my eyes gave him, picked up the glasses, and strode toward the stairs. But when he had gone the sound of his voice continued to ring through my mind and I heard the echo of fury driving him.

Shivering, I turned back to my room. Yet my body was warm with fever heat. I went to my window and flung it open upon the cold dawning of the New Year. Though the outward chill did not touch me as I leaned my arms upon the sill, a trembling I understood very well went on and on within me, and part of it was fear.

Outdoors the bells had pealed their way to silence. The last horn blast died raucously. Down in the mews one of the servants banged a final derisive clatter upon a dishpan, as if mocking this arrival of a year in which hope could be so little justified.

The chill I felt lay deep within me. Fear had its roots in a sense of unknown danger. Danger and betrayal. "Don't run away," he had said. Yet even then I knew I had no other choice. Not only for my own sake and for Jeremy's, but for Brandon's as well. If I remained where he could see me, find me, the violence would erupt into some desperate act. I knew this as surely as though he had told me so. The ingredients for tragedy were building, and I must be well away before an explosion could result.

Chilled at last through all my body, I closed the window upon the New Year and went back to bed. Brandon's kiss had burned itself out on my lips, the memory of his arms no longer warmed me to life. For me this coming week must be one of decision and action. Unhappy decision, action that would cause me endless pain. Yet I knew now what must be done.

CHAPTER 22

THE COLD light of morning brought a strengthening of resolution. Brandon had no right to order me not to run away. Nor could I obey him. Last night I'd learned enough about myself and about him, about the inexorable force that drew us together, to warn me thoroughly. The very fact that deep within me was an ache of longing to speak my love, to acknowledge it and let it rule me, no matter what the consequences, made the need for action all the more urgent.

Fortunately, I had saved most of the salary I'd received in the Reid household and I would have enough to keep me until I could find another position. My first thought was to tell Mrs. Reid that I would heed her wishes, then slip away without seeing Brandon again, and give him no chance to stop me. But the more I considered such a course, the more cowardly it seemed. If my own courage were as strong as it must be, then nothing he might say could alter my decision. Today was the time.

The master of the house arose in a mood so stormy that it made itself heard up the stairs. I began to suspect that he had regretted his actions of the night before and was thus angry with himself and perhaps with me as well. All of which played into the hands of my intention. Tenderness, pleading would be harder to face than anger.

Jeremy, playing the endless tune of "Frère Jacques" on his music box, incurred his uncle's wrath early that morning, and I heard Brandon shouting at the boy to turn it off. I ran to the stairs, meaning to call Jeremy up to the quiet and safety of the third floor, but Brandon saw me there and stared as though I were another child to be reproved.

"Where is the pin I gave you for Christmas?" he demanded. "Why aren't you wearing it?"

So unreasonable a question was exactly what I needed to brace me against any faltering, even though this was not the time to ask for an interview.

"I will return the pin to you," I told him coolly. "Come, Jeremy. Bring the carrousel upstairs."

Brandon scowled at me, but at least it was to his credit that he noted Jeremy's face and apologized to the boy, if not to me.

"I'm sorry, Jeremy. I've a beastly headache. I didn't mean to snap at you like that. Just play your box upstairs for now, will you, my boy?"

Jeremy accepted his words with good grace and came cheerfully upstairs with me.

By custom New Year's Day was a time when ladies remained at home to receive, and the gentlemen of New York, young and old, went from house to house, often imbibing so freely and so often that it was wiser for women to remain indoors and avoid the public streets. Brandon, however, had shut himself early into the library and showed no sign of leaving for a series of calls.

With Selina beside her, Leslie had gone to the drawing room to receive, and, as the doorbell began its constant pealing, servants hurried back and forth, and the day went into its full social swing. Miss Garth busied herself supervising the activity, and, as a result, Jeremy and I had the long day to ourselves.

We passed some of the time watching visitors from the front windows and speculating about them. I tried not to remember that soon this little boy would no longer be a part of my everyday life. It was all I could do to hide my feelings when the thought of coming loneliness engulfed me. Whatever we did, I could not forget that it might be for the last time.

Not until late afternoon, when the calls had wound to an end, when Mrs. Reid had retired, and Garth and Selina were once more upstairs, did I leave Jeremy and seek the opportunity to speak to Brandon Reid.

At the library door the tormenting reminder returned. This, too, was for the last time. He invited me in pleasantly enough and offered me a chair. His manner seemed faintly apologetic, as though he regretted his early-morning temper. But I wanted no relenting from him. It would be better for us both if only I could detest him.

I had brought the pin with me and I laid it upon the desk before him. "I have come to a difficult decision," I said. "But a necessary one. The only course of action remaining to me is to leave your employ as soon as possible. As you know, there are reasons why I cannot remain in this house any longer. Tomorrow I will look for a room and move out as soon as I can."

It took only a moment for the apologetic manner to vanish and anger to take its place. He picked up the scarab brooch and held it out to me.

"You need not insult me into the bargain. This belongs to you."

I took it from him in silence, waiting.

"I might have known you would run away," he continued. "The woman doesn't live who has the courage to stand by when she's needed."

Since I was exerting all the courage in me at that moment, his words did not help my own temper. "I know where I am needed," I told him with some vehemence. "Jeremy needs me. But there are other matters to be considered first, and my decision will stand."

It was at this unfortunate moment that Jeremy came unwittingly into the room with the carrousel in his hands. Bent on his own concern, he did not sense the atmosphere of the room. With the growing trust he had in Brandon, he held the toy out to him.

"Something is wrong with it, Uncle Brandon," he said. "See— it will play only when I shake it."

He proved this by shaking the toy so that it began the tinkling, monotonous little air I had once found so merry. Brandon flung out a hand in a gesture of impatience. His fingers struck the carrousel, and it flew from Jeremy's grasp and fell with a clatter on the bare hearthstone. The tune whined on for a moment and then clicked to an abrupt stop. I stared in dismay at the crumpled sleigh, the dented canopy.

Jeremy cried out in anguish and rushed to pick up the toy. All his hard-won confidence in his uncle had vanished. The carrousel was the finest treasure he had ever owned, and it was he who was angry now. He turned furiously upon Brandon, pummeling him with his fists until I came to put quieting hands on the boy's shoulders.

Shocked by his own impatient, but unintentional act, Brandon apologized for the second time that day. "I didn't mean that to happen. Give it here and let's see what damage is done."

This time his retraction had no effect. Jeremy held the toy behind his back. "You *did* mean it to happen! You were angry about it this morning and now you're glad you've broken it!"

White and stricken, he clasped the toy tightly to him and rushed out of the room. I stepped to the door and called after him, but he ran unheeding up the stairs.

His shrill voice had brought his mother to the door of her bedroom and Miss Garth part way down the stairs. He moved as though he saw neither of them, and Garth stepped back against the wall to let the small furious figure rush by.

"Let him go," Brandon told me, impatient again. "I'm sorry this happened, but I've had more of that tune than I can stand. When he recovers, we'll see what can be done to mend the toy. Right now I want to talk to you."

I was very nearly as upset as Jeremy. The incident had shaken me, and I could not remain to be argued down by Brandon Reid. Without replying, I went into the hall to follow Jeremy upstairs.

Leslie had thrown a loose yellow gown about her shoulders and she looked pale and worn from the festivities of last night and today. I could not face her either just now and I ran up the stairs, brushing past the looming figure of Thora Garth.

Jeremy had closed his door and he did not answer when I tapped on the panel. I stood for a moment listening to the pounding of my own heart, trying to quiet my trepidation. Then I turned the knob and went in.

The boy sat on the edge of his bed with the broken toy in his hands, staring at it intently. I took it from him and tried to minimize the damage.

"I think it's not too serious," I said. "If your uncle can't mend it for you, perhaps we can find someone who can. Or I'll go back to the shop where this came from and try to get another for you."

"He smashed it." Jeremy spoke evenly, without emotion, without expression. "He smashed it because he hates me."

I put my hand on his forehead and found it burning hot. He did not resist when I helped him to undress and get into bed. At supper-time he would eat nothing, and I sat beside his bed until he fell asleep. Only then did I tiptoe away to my own room.

I lay down fully clothed, meaning to get up from time to time and make sure all was well. But I was bone-weary. The emotional turmoil I had been through, the hard decision I had come to, all had taken as great a toll as physical action. I fell so deeply asleep that only some deafening sound could have awakened me.

The sound came during the night hours, shattering the quiet of the house. I sat bolt upright in bed, attending with all my senses the echoing crash.

I knew what had wakened me, though I had never before heard such a sound inside a house. The air still trembled with vibration, though otherwise all was silent. I went to my door and opened it a crack upon the dark hallway, waiting for the outcry that must surely follow. But now there was no sound, no sound at all—and that increased my alarm. The silence seemed too intense until I heard a creaking on the stairs. Was someone coming up, or going down? I could see nothing in the blackness. A terror I had not known I could feel washed over me, and I closed my door and stood trembling with my back against it.

Nothing happened, and reason slowly returned to steady me. I must not cower here because I thought I had heard a pistol shot in the house. In his room next door Jeremy would be awake and in need of reassurance. I must look in on him, make sure of his safety. Then, if no one else stirred, I would go downstairs and investigate for myself. Perhaps the sound had come from outside after all. Perhaps a forgotten dream had magnified it.

Lighting a candle, I opened my door softly. At once I saw Jeremy. He stood halfway down the hallway in his nightshirt, and I could hear the chattering of his teeth.

"Go back to bed, dear," I said firmly. "Get in where it's warm and I'll go downstairs and see if anything is wrong. I promise to come back and tell you as soon as I can."

He did not seem to hear my words. He raised his hands and held them away from him, staring as if they did not belong to him, as if he had never seen them before.

"I've done something terrible," he said.

His tone chilled me far more than the icy air of the hallway. I pushed him toward his room.

"Quick now," I said. "In bed with you; you're dreadfully cold."

I left my candle on his bureau, lighted another, and started downstairs. Dread of what I might find slowed my steps, yet I must go down. Where was everyone else? Why hadn't the servants come upstairs? But then—would they? Once before there had been tragedy in this house following a shot at night. Might not the servants take the course of wisdom and remain below stairs unless they were summoned?

As I descended toward the second floor, my feeble candle flame pushed back the darkness a bit at a time. When I reached the lower steps I saw that the sound had, after all, aroused others in the house —others as frightened as I.

CHAPTER 23

IN THE door of Leslie's bedroom stood Miss Garth, an arm about the woman who had been her charge as a child. Leslie's face was washed of all color, her eyes enormous. Both women stared at me as I came down the stairs. Neither looked as though she would be of any help, and I had to bolster my own courage.

"Do you think that was a shot?" I asked.

Leslie clung weakly to the governess, and it was Miss Garth who answered me.

"Of course it was a shot and it came from the library. I rushed downstairs at once to make sure Miss Leslie was unharmed. Where is Jeremy?"

"In bed," I said, my lips barely forming the words. My fingers tightened around the candleholder lest I drop it. Where was Brandon? Why hadn't he come out of his bedroom?

I could not endure this new terror. The door of the library stood open, a blank oblong of darkness that gave way dimly before the pale thrust of candlelight. Shadows swayed across the room as I held my candle high. At first glance nothing seemed amiss. I moved toward Brandon's desk and stumbled over something that lay on the floor beside his chair.

It was all I could do to hold the candle nearer and look down at what lay at my feet. For a moment no sound came from my lips. Then I called to the two women in the hall.

"Come here and see what has happened!"

Leslie was still afraid and would not come, but Thora Garth stepped into the room and stood beside me. Together we stared at

453

the debris before us. Someone had shattered the Osiris head. Broken pieces of it lay strewn across the carpet, and I knew it must have been smashed by a shot from a pistol.

"Where is Mr. Reid?" I asked. "Why isn't he here?"

"He went out before dinner," Miss Garth said stiffly. "As far as I know he hasn't returned. And a good thing for him it is!"

A sick understanding of her meaning swept through me. She meant that Jeremy had come into this room with a pistol in his hands, perhaps seeking his uncle as he had once sought his father. Not finding him, he had vented his anger upon the stone head his uncle treasured. This was his retaliation, his revenge for the breaking of the carrousel.

Miss Garth turned back to her charge. "It's all right, Miss Leslie dear. It's only that heathenish head that's been broken. You can breathe again, lovey."

Leslie came hesitantly into the library, and it was then we heard the turning of a key in the front door downstairs. Brandon Reid had come home. We waited for him, as still and posed as the inanimate objects in the room. He climbed the stairs, saw the light in the library, and came through the door.

"What has happened?" he asked.

I held out my candle to him and gestured toward the floor. He took the holder from me, staring in disbelief at the shattered bits of stone.

"Light the gas, Megan," he said over his shoulder.

I hurried to do his bidding, and he searched the room swiftly, purposefully. Almost at once he found what he was looking for and picked it up from beneath the desk. When he held it out to us, Leslie gave a cry. It was the pistol from which the shot must have been fired. An ornate weapon with elaborate fittings.

"Wait here," he said to us. "I want to have a look downstairs."

When he had left the room, Miss Garth spoke, her tone deadly cold. "This has gone too far. Something must be done about the boy."

"Yes," Leslie said helplessly, "something must be done."

I thought of Jeremy, trembling upstairs, waiting for punishment to befall him—perhaps asking for it again? I had promised to return quickly, but now I must wait.

Brandon rejoined us in a few moments, carrying a towel filled with slivers of glass. "It's as I thought. Someone wrapped this towel about a fist so as to make no noise and smashed the glass front of the cabinet that holds the pistol collection."

Leslie began to weep softly. Perhaps the memory of that other, more dreadful, shooting had returned to devastate her. But Miss Garth made no move to comfort her now.

"The boy would have killed you if you'd been here," she told Brandon fiercely. "Now perhaps you'll listen to reason."

"Get her to bed." Brandon's words were curt.

Miss Garth made a despairing gesture and then took Leslie by the arm. "Come, lovey. You must get your rest."

When they had gone, Brandon turned to me. "I'll talk to the boy," he said and went out of the room.

As I followed him up the stairs, I tried to plead for Jeremy, but there was so little I could say. If Brandon had been home, would it have been the Osiris that Jeremy smashed? Garth's terrible accusation silenced me.

At the head of the stairs Brandon spoke to me. "I'm partly to blame for this. Because of the carrousel. But that doesn't excuse the boy. Such outbursts are too dangerous, too violent. What if I had been working in the library tonight?"

Whatever I might say would only make matters worse, and I was silent.

For all his chill, Jeremy had not returned to bed. He sat on the floor cross-legged, as if he were trying to make himself so small that no one would find him there. Bleak misery looked from his eyes, and I was reminded of the time when he had fled to the Memorial Home and hidden himself there.

Brandon spoke to him, not ungently. "Tell me exactly what happened, Jeremy."

The boy stood up to face his uncle. He wavered for a moment, then flung himself across the bed in the same wild fury of grief I had seen before.

"I didn't mean to!" he cried. "I never meant to do it! Never, never! I only meant to frighten him. Never to kill him. I was just going to wave the gun at him; I never meant to pull the trigger."

Brandon and I looked at each other. It was not of the Osiris head

Jeremy spoke. His mind had fled back in time to the killing of his father.

I sat beside him on the bed and tried to soothe him, but he would not let me touch him. He hurled himself wildly from me, staring in terror at his uncle.

"Listen to me, Jeremy." Brandon spoke quietly. "It's not what happened long ago that we're talking about. Someone broke into the pistol collection tonight. Someone went into the library with a loaded gun and shot a bullet through the Osiris head."

The terror in Jeremy's eyes did not subside, but he stopped crying and sat up, stricken to silence, unable to speak at all.

"Don't question him now," I said to Brandon. "You can see he's in no state to answer you sensibly. You can talk to him tomorrow."

For once he heeded me. He told Jeremy a grave good night and started toward the door. Jeremy found his voice and spoke up in a high, strained tone.

"You'll punish me now, won't you, Uncle Brandon? But you won't keep me from going to the memorial service for my father? You *will* let me go to that?"

We were both startled by this sudden turn Jeremy's thoughts had taken. I believe Brandon hesitated on the point of immediate refusal. Then he said, "We'll see," and went out of the room.

I followed him into the hall. "Be gentle with him tomorrow. He's going through a dreadful time."

Brandon shook his head. "There's no use in keeping on with this, Megan. Especially since you're going away. I've given the boy every chance, but this is beyond our handling. He must be placed where he can do no further harm."

This was more than I could bear. "Then put him in my charge! Let me take him away and care for him. If he could be given a new life in different surroundings—where no one knew anything about him, where such terrible things hadn't happened, he would improve. He has been better lately. I know he has!"

For a moment Brandon stared at me coldly. When he spoke there was no kindness in his voice. "You are thinking only of the boy. Do you believe it fair to turn this violence loose on others who cannot even expect it, or defend themselves?"

For a moment I was held by a doubting that his words awakened in me. Was he right? Was there too much danger to others involved in keeping the boy in normal society? After what he had done to-night, it would seem that Brandon was justified. Yet I knew I could not abandon Jeremy to be put out of the way in some dreadful institution.

I returned to his room where he still lay across the bed, and persuaded him to get under the covers. Then I sat beside him and talked to him for a little while. He was quiet enough now, with the emotion drained from him by the outburst of weeping.

"I think you are old enough to understand that what happened to the carrousel was an accident and not deliberate," I said. "An accident to be forgiven. It was wrong of you to try to pay him back by hurting what he treasured."

He nodded his agreement, wide-eyed.

"Would you like to tell me about it?" I asked gently.

His gaze did not move from mine. "I can't remember," he said, and I heard despair in his voice. "I don't remember anything about it. Miss Megan, I can remember when I shot my father. But I can't remember taking Garth's scissors and thimble, and I can't remember this. It frightens me that I do things I can't remember afterwards." He sat up and flung his arms about me. "Help me not to do them, Miss Megan! Help me not to!"

I remembered the comfort he had taken that time when I'd told him I would not let him hurt either himself or me, and I wished I could give him some similar assurance for the future. But how could he be guarded every moment when one never knew what he might do next?

"I know you love your uncle," I persisted. "Yet you tried to hurt him. You worked so hard to make the collar for the Osiris. How could you destroy the head?"

His eyes were dark with anguish. "How *could* I?" he echoed blankly. "How could I do such an awful thing?" And he looked at me fiercely. "I don't even remember leaving this room."

I held him close, comforting him as best I could, while a flicker of astonishing suspicion ran through me. Was there something here I had missed entirely? Something we were meant to believe that might not be true? What if Jeremy was not guilty of all the mis-chief attributed to him? He admitted quickly enough the deeds he

457

remembered. If he could not recall the others—had they been his doing?

Such suspicion opened frightening possibilities, and I dared not so much as hint my thoughts to the boy.

"You'll be able to sleep now," I assured him. "I'll sit by your bed. You're perfectly safe. Nothing can harm you."

He closed his eyes with such trust in my words that I was shaken. There was so little real assurance of safety I could give him.

The candle on the bureau dipped and guttered, burning low. I went to my room for a shawl and came back to continue my vigil beside Jeremy's bed. I knew I could not sleep if I tried.

What if some of Jeremy's supposed mischief had really been managed by a malignant adult? Someone who wanted the boy put away, who hated his presence here in this house. If the boy could be made to seem increasingly unstable and dangerous, then a purpose might be accomplished. If he went, I would go too—that could be a part of this purpose.

Such a suspicion was shocking to contemplate. Whoever in this household was willing to let a child be blamed for something he had not done, indeed to place evidence at the child's door, was a person driven by a malevolence that knew no bounds.

Jeremy stirred and opened his eyes. "Miss Megan, I do want to go to the ceremony when the Memorial Home is opened. It's to be soon—only about ten days now. Will you speak to Uncle Brandon so he won't choose that for punishment?"

"Why does this mean so much to you?" I asked.

For a moment he seemed at a loss to answer. Then he struggled to explain.

"Since the ceremony will be to honor my father, perhaps he will be close by that day. Perhaps I'll be able to feel him there, and then I can tell him I didn't mean what happened. I've tried to reach him in that room downstairs, but I think he is truly gone from there."

I wanted to put my arms about him and hold him tenderly, lovingly. But I sensed that it was wiser to be matter-of-fact.

"I'll speak to your uncle," I promised, though I had little confidence that Brandon would listen now to anything I said.

My soothing and Jeremy's own weariness took effect at last. I sat beside him as he slept, a new force of determination growing within me. All my plans must now be changed. I would not look for a room tomorrow. I could not possibly leave this house until Jeremy was safe. I would stay, and, if someone was using the boy for a hidden, iniquitous purpose, I would expose whoever it was once and for all.

CHAPTER 24

AFTER SPENDING the remaining hours of the night in the chair beside Jeremy's bed, I felt thoroughly bedraggled and weary by morning. Nevertheless, I caught Brandon in the library immediately after breakfast and confronted him with my new resolve. I dared not tell him of my vague suspicions, but I said that I would stay on at my post if only he would not send Jeremy away.

Brandon was a sober, troubled man that morning. He too looked as if he had slept little. The maid had not yet come in to clean the room, and the broken pieces of the stone head still lay upon the floor. The tall white crown had cracked through and broken away from the serene brow of Osiris. The head of the snake—that mark of royalty—clung to a broken fragment, still alert and eerily raised, as if it had life of its own.

I had made it clear that it was Jeremy's interest alone that had caused my change of mind, and Brandon was coolly formal. Perversely, there was an aching in me because he had moved far beyond my reach, but I told myself this was what I wished and I faced him with a manner equally impersonal.

"I'll grant you time," he said. "But not a great deal. I'll grant it only because I want to investigate possibilities more carefully than I've been able to so far. It would be better to put the boy in some private home where he could be assured of good treatment and care. The Bloomingdale Asylum is not to my taste. At least I'm relieved that you'll stay for the time being."

This was not a great deal of assurance, but I must live from moment to moment while I sought an answer to the questions in my mind.

I bent to pick up the flat collar where it lay in the midst of shattered stone and held it out to him.

"It's hard to believe that Jeremy would destroy something he admired so much," I said. "Not after all this work on the collar he made for the head."

"Exactly," Brandon agreed. "The very fact is further evidence of an irrational pattern. I respect your feeling for the boy, Megan, but you mustn't be blinded by your own emotions."

There was no defense I could offer. For all I knew, I might well be blinding myself. Yet there was no other course I could take until I was sure. As I prepared to leave, I remembered Jeremy's request and put it to his uncle.

"Will you allow the boy to attend the opening of the Memorial Home? His heart is set on being there. It seems a small favor to grant him."

As had happened before, Brandon seemed to freeze at mention of the memorial, his disapproval clearly evident.

"That is something I can't allow," he said. "Why should he want it?"

"Perhaps it's a—a penance he wants to make," I suggested not wishing to betray Jeremy's confidence. "Why must you punish him in this particular way?"

Brandon knelt to pick up portions of the shattered stone head. "I'm not punishing him. The boy's behavior is too emotional, too uncertain. We can't have a scene at this ceremony. The papers will be eager for any sensational tidbit they can feed upon. I don't want them raking up what happened in the past because of the boy's presence."

I could understand this, but I felt that the effect upon Jeremy was more important and I said so firmly. Brandon had found a portion of the stone profile—a large piece with part of the brow and cheek, most of the nose, and the entire mouth almost intact. He rose with the piece in hand, and it was strange to see the stone lips with their tolerant smile still untouched by destruction.

"A paper weight for my desk," he said wryly. Then he looked at me again. "The matter is closed. The boy cannot be allowed to attend. If you can't make that clear to him, I will."

"I'll try to make him understand," I said.

All seemed to be at an end between us, and I would have gone from the room, but he put a hand lightly upon my arm and I remembered with a pang the warm clasp of his hands on that cold happy day when I had skated with him in Central Park. How long ago that seemed to me now.

"When did you last have a full night's sleep, Megan?"

I managed a stiff smile. "Not last night. But I can sleep during lesson time this morning." I moved from his touch because I did not like the way a weakness I decried started through me.

He noted my withdrawal as he had noted it the first day I had come to this house.

"I've granted you time with Jeremy," he said. "So now you must grant me time as well, Megan. Believe in me for a little while. I am not without ingenuity. A way out must be found. Do you understand what I mean, Megan? A way out for us."

But there was no way out with honor and without harm to others. His words broke my heart a little, and I knew I dared not stay, dared not listen, lest I be in his arms again. I gave him a quick, governess' bow and would have hurried away, had it not been for a sudden interruption.

Henry came to the library to say that a telegram had come for Mr. Reid, and the messenger was waiting for an answer.

Brandon opened the wire and spoke quickly to Henry. "It's my father. He is gravely ill. Will you pack my bag at once and call the carriage. I'll take the first train I can catch."

I wanted to offer my sympathy, ask if there was anything I could do, but he had forgotten me and I slipped quietly away and went upstairs to the schoolroom, where lessons were about to begin.

Miss Garth was with Selina, and Andrew and Jeremy were seated at the long table, their books spread before them. I had not seen Andrew since our walk around Washington Square on Christmas Day.

I told them the news about Brandon's father, and Miss Garth dropped her embroidery and stood up.

"I must tell Miss Leslie," she said, and hurried from the room.

462

"It's a wonder the old man has held on as long as he has," Andrew said. But there was something that interested him more, and he cocked an eyebrow in my direction. "Garth has been giving me an account of your exciting night," he told me. "With possible embellishments. Sometime I'd like your version, Megan."

I knew by the way Jeremy bent over the pages of his book that Miss Garth had let vitriol flow and he had retreated from the flood.

"I'll be happy to give you an account of what happened," I said. "It may be different from other accounts you've received."

Jeremy looked at me, suddenly intent. "Have you asked my uncle about attending the memorial opening?"

In the face of his anxiety I made a sudden resolve. "Yes, I have," I admitted. "For reasons that have nothing to do with any punishment, neither you nor Selina may attend. However, I am going in your place, Jeremy. I know it won't accomplish the same purpose, but at least I will be there *for you* and I'll come home right after it's over and tell you everything that happened. And later I'll take you there on a special visit. Will that help a little?"

He was far from content. Disappointment lay upon him heavily, but he returned to his book without argument.

Andrew was openly displeased with my plan. "If Reid had any sense, he would see that the affair was canceled. It's no place for you, Megan, or for anyone else from this house. Let Reid be the one to make a target of himself if he wants scandal to break again. The rest of you should stay home."

"He doesn't want it," I said. "He is very much against the whole thing."

"Yet he allows it to go on. Even Garth is worried about the outcome."

What could happen other than further unpleasantness in the papers, I did not know, and I was not at that time particularly interested. I left them to their lessons and returned to my room, where I lay down to rest.

It was disturbing to realize that Brandon would now be away in New Jersey and I would be left alone with two women who hated me.

Nevertheless, the days passed quietly enough and nothing untoward happened. Word that his father had died came from Brandon.

He would return immediately after the funeral, and in time for the opening of the memorial.

I began to count the days.

During this period Jeremy was not well. The destruction of the Osiris head was taking its after-toll in his own concern about his actions. I longed to offer him reassurance, but I did not dare because I could not be sure. My belief was something that seemed reasonable to me, but I had no shred of evidence to support it. With Jeremy's curious trick of absenting himself from the world around him, it was still possible that he had destroyed the head in a moment of fierce anger against his uncle and then blanked the incident from his mind.

The fact that after the occurrence Leslie, too, was ill, offered me nothing in the way of proof. These days she seemed increasingly upset by the slightest thing, and I wondered that she insisted upon attending the opening of the memorial to her first husband.

Garth refused flatly to go. Not even for her beloved Leslie would she attend this affair. My own intention of going I meant to keep to myself until the time came.

Brandon returned home a day ahead of the affair, and while he expressed grief over the death of his father, there was something strange about him that had nothing to do with his loss. Something suppressed and restrained, as if he held himself back with difficulty. I know he was closeted with Leslie for some hours on the day of his return.

On the morning of the memorial ceremony I hurried through the house looking for him, to announce my plan. I found him alone in the dining room, finishing breakfast. He invited me to join him, and I sat down reluctantly. I knew he would regard my purpose as sheer obstinacy and I wanted to get through the announcement of what I meant to do as quickly as possible.

He gave me no immediate chance, but began to reminisce about his father, telling me more of the old man and his fierce family pride, of how he had worshiped his younger son and taken satisfaction in his every achievement.

"I kept that intact for him, at least," Brandon said. "I let nothing destroy it, no matter what the cost. And he never knew the cruel truth about—about what happened. He seemed content to have

464

me with him at the end, even though I've never taken the course he wanted me to follow."

Brandon fell silent and when I knew he did not mean to continue, I told him what I had come to tell him.

"I've made a bargain with Jeremy," I said.

He began to watch me with an odd intensity, and I saw that some elation kindled him this morning. When he made no comment, I hastened to explain my plan.

"Since Jeremy cannot go to the ceremony, I've promised that I will go in his place, and that later I will take him there on a visit. Naturally I will not join the family. I'll slip in quietly and sit somewhere at the back of the room."

"As you like," he said with surprising indifference, and I sensed the excitement in him, barely restrained.

Suddenly he leaned toward me across the table. "Megan, I've talked to Leslie. I've told her that she must release me from this impossible marriage. She has cause enough, and it's hopeless to go on living together under the same roof when we detest each other."

I sat very still, saying nothing.

"She took it rather well," he went on. "At least she indulged in no fits of temper or weeping. In fact, she said very little, one way or another. How she will react when she's had time to think my proposal over is a matter for speculation. There may easily be a scandal if she chooses to make one. Or there may be nothing at all. In any case, I've decided to leave this house as soon as I am able."

In spite of my own involvement with his plans, I had to think of Jeremy. "If you leave, what of the boy?"

He set his coffee cup down sharply. "If the boy were normal, I would consider him to a greater extent. He is not. There's no further doubt on that score. At least I promise you that he will be placed in better circumstances than he lives in under this roof."

"But he will be a prisoner?" I said. "An—an inmate?"

"What would you have? If I leave him to the tender consideration of his mother, he'll be packed off to Bloomingdale at once. And you will be dismissed the moment I am out of the house. I give you my word, Megan, that I'll see the boy well cared for before I take any step to work out my own freedom."

465

"What if you're doing Jeremy an injustice?" I asked. "What if it was not he who did that dreadful mischief the other night?"

"What are you talking about?" Brandon's disbelief was evident.

I made a helpless gesture. "I can give you no proof. But while he remembers other things he has done, he doesn't remember this. I think he would tell me if he did."

"Nonsense! The boy is too unbalanced to know what he has done after he does it. Who would play such a trick? And why?"

"The person who most wants to see the boy put away without further delay. The person who has now succeeded—or believes he has succeeded—in proving Jeremy too dangerous to remain in this household."

Brandon made a sharp, quick movement, and his hand struck the coffee cup, spilling brown liquid across the linen. I was reminded of the quick gesture that had broken the carrousel. How could I love so angry and irritable a man? Yet love him I did and I watched miserably as he rang for Henry. When the butler came to clear up, I made my escape. For the moment there was no more to be said between us.

At least I had planted my seeds of doubt. Let Brandon consider them and perhaps nurture them into growth.

I went upstairs to dress for this morning's affair, feeling myself in a strange state of suspension. I could not believe that Leslie would easily let Brandon go, whether she loved him or not. No matter what he had said to her, I did not dare to hope. And whichever way I turned, there was always Jeremy. Even though she might detest the sight of him, Leslie was his mother and in the long run she would decide his fate. Perhaps it was she to whom I must talk. Perhaps if I went to her outright and told her that I would make an accusation if she tried to put Jeremy into an asylum, I could frighten her into a change of attitude.

But though my thoughts were never still, I could fix upon no sound course of action. The moments slipped by, and I moved with them as though I were carried by some sea current that held me inactive for the moment, yet would inevitably hurl me upon a rocky and dangerous shore.

CHAPTER 25

DRESSED IN my wren's brown, I left the house ahead of the others, saying good-by only to Jeremy, and took a Broadway car to my destination. My few months of riding in the Reid carriage had given me a greater distaste than ever for the dirty, vermin-ridden horsecars. I held my reticule tightly, for pickpockets often rode the cars in this crime-infested city. It was a relief that I need not travel far.

At my stop I left the car and hurried across the street. The sidewalks were rimmed with soot-strewn snow, and there was gray mud everywhere in this mucky thawing. Already there were carriages drawing up before the new brownstone building and people were thronging inside. The scaffolding and workmen were gone, the home ready for occupancy. No one questioned me as I stepped into the wide main hallway and followed others toward a long room that had been set up for this occasion with rows of wooden chairs. A small platform had been placed at the head of the room, with a lectern and several chairs upon it. The front rows, except for a section saved for the Reid family and dignitaries in charge, were already filling up.

Speaking to no one, I found my way to the rear and sat down to wait, trying to make myself as inconspicuous as possible. I was here merely as a spectator, to report to Jeremy all that I saw. At least there seemed no cause for the foreboding Andrew Beach had entertained about this affair.

The long room, perhaps a dining room under ordinary circumstances, was almost full by the time Brandon Reid came in with

467

Leslie on his arm. I could not help but note once more what a deceptively fine-looking couple they made together. He, tall and impressive in appearance; she, so slight and lovely in the black that gave her pallor an ethereal look. Various persons came forward to greet them and show them to their seats in the front row. A buxom, motherly woman, perhaps the matron of the Home, stepped up to shake Mrs. Reid's hand.

After a slight delay the speeches began. There was an impassioned eulogy for Dwight Reid, given by the minister whom I had heard in the little church on Fifth Avenue. From where I sat I could see both Brandon and Leslie in profile and I watched them as the words rang out over the assemblage. Brandon looked grim and uncomfortable, as if he longed to be anywhere else than here. Leslie's profile looked as pure and cool as though it had been chiseled from ice. She was following every word that was spoken, with the intentness of a sorrowing widow, and the black plumes of her hat trembled when she bowed her head. An inappropriate role, surely, and inappropriate mourning, since she had been married for some time since Dwight's death.

When the minister completed his words of praise and sat down, a member of New York's judiciary stepped to the lectern and spread before him the papers of his speech. I had heard of this man, had read about him in the papers. I wondered that he had been selected for this occasion. There was so much scoundrelism in high places these days, for all that Tweed had been sent to prison, and there had been much buying and selling of justice. Someone farther removed from the breath of scandal might have seemed a wiser choice, even though this man had been introduced as a friend of Dwight Reid's.

So dull was his speech that the listeners began to stir restlessly and there was disrespectful whispering. My own attention had wandered when I heard someone murmur, "Oh, the poor lady!"

I whipped my gaze to the front of the room and saw that Leslie was on her feet, facing the audience. She had flung out her hands in entreaty, as if asking to speak, and the man at the lectern paused in astonishment, gaping at her. She swayed a little as she stood there, and her pallor was alarming. The interruption occupied no more than seconds, for Brandon was at her side at once. He caught her lightly up in his arms and spoke to the chairman as he hurried toward the door with his burden.

"Forgive us, please. My wife is ill. She has fainted."

I did not think she had fainted, but at least she did not struggle as he carried her through the quickly opened door. As the buxom matron hurried after them, the speaker sought his place in his notes once more and droned on above the rustle of the room. I left my seat unnoticed, and fled through a rear door. Ahead of me the matron led the way to a room across the hall, and I followed as Brandon carried Leslie into it and laid her upon a sofa. After a moment of hovering, the matron said she would go for aromatics and hurried away. I closed the door behind her, and Brandon noted my presence with a quick glance, though he did not speak.

Leslie needed no aromatics. Her cheeks were no longer pale, but flushed as if she were feverish. She sat up and pushed Brandon away from her.

"How dare you stop me!" she demanded, and I heard the rising hysteria in her voice. "Why didn't you let me tell them the truth? All of the truth—while everyone was there to hear!"

"You're out of your senses," Brandon said coldly. "This sort of behavior will merely get you into the scandal sheets." He glanced at me. "Let no one in, Megan, until she recovers enough so that I can take her home."

I opened the door a crack to the matron, took the bottle of smelling salts from her, and said that Mrs. Reid wished to be alone with her husband. She did not challenge my presence, and I was able to close the heavy door before Leslie's voice made itself heard beyond the room.

All the stored-up emotion in her was finally spewing out, and it was a dreadful thing to behold. Her beauty had vanished in this ravishment of her features; her voice was high with tension.

"It's time I spoke the truth! It's time I told the world that it was you who killed Dwight. You, who were so determined that nothing should smear your precious family name, that you shot your own brother to death and used the boy to hide your crime."

Her voice broke, and a dreadful silence lay upon us. Horror possessed me. For one shocked moment I almost believed her. Then denial and incredulity washed through me and I knew Brandon must be protected from such madness. I braced myself against the door, knowing that I must let no one into this room.

His face had gone deathly white, and a muscle twitched in his cheek. When his hands closed into fists I thought he would do her bodily harm. Then his fingers opened slowly and he did not touch her, even though her words ran on in a wild stream of accusation.

"The boy had a pistol in his hands, yes! But it was your gun that fired the shot, not the one he held. Have you forgotten that afterwards I helped you to get rid of the extra pistol so that it would never be found? I protected you! Because I was foolish enough to love you in spite of everything."

She would have struggled up from the sofa, but he took her by the shoulders in a grip that must have hurt and held her there. Now, surely, he would deny her words. He would laugh at this vicious nonsense that could have no basis in reality. In silent anguish my thoughts pleaded with him.

He said nothing. He held her in that crushing grip till her head fell back and she stared up at him with a dawning of realization in her eyes. I think she knew then how close she was to death. And knowing, she went limp in his hands. He let her fall back upon the sofa and stepped away from her. I longed to be anywhere but in that room. I had seen and heard more than I could bear to live with, if Brandon did not deny her words. Yet still he said nothing.

Released from momentary danger, Leslie sat up and again her voice took up the tenor of dreadful condemnation.

"Do you think you can silence me now? Do you think I'll let you escape me for one of your light-o'-loves? Never! You'll stay with me and suffer as you've made me suffer. If you take a step away, I'll tell the truth to the world, as I nearly told it today!"

Brandon's hand flashed out, and the slap of it across her cheek sounded sharply through the room. Leslie crumpled upon the sofa cushions, silenced at last. He stood looking down at her, and, if there had been hot anger in him before, it had now turned to icy disgust.

"Get her home," he said curtly to me. "I can't trust myself if I listen to her longer."

He opened the door and went past me without reassurance or denial, and I closed it behind him, turned the key in the lock. I was torn in a dozen ways. I wanted to leave Leslie there and escape the very sight of her. I wanted to run after Brandon and beseech him to tell me that none of what his wife had said was true. But there was in me as well a primitive impulse to force a denial of her words from this woman by sheer force. That I should be so shaken by an instinct to injure, shocked and steadied me. For a moment longer I stood with my back to the door, waiting for my breathing to quiet so that I could act. There was, of course, only one thing I could do.

A quick look about showed me that the room opened upon a small service area, with a cellar staircase leading down. If I could rouse Leslie, perhaps we might escape without being halted for questions or sympathy. This was the only purpose I could cling to with certainty in my state of sick shock.

I went to the sofa and took her hand, pulling her up without gentleness. To my relief, she offered no resistance, more like a rag doll in my grasp than a woman. I could not speak to her with any kindness, and the sound of my voice was harsh in my own ears.

"Come," I told her. "You are ill, and we must get you home at once."

She came with me blindly, as though she scarcely knew my identity. On the stairs she stumbled and might have fallen if I had not put an arm about her to steady her as we went down. My flesh crept at the touch. I could have no task more abhorrent to me than to give aid to Leslie Reid. Yet even as I shrank from contact with her, my wayward mind heard again the torrent of her words and began to question of its own volition.

Could there be the faintest truth in anything she had said? For if there was, who was I to shrink from Leslie Reid? I, who loved a man who might have committed a murder and allowed a child to shoulder the blame?

No! I thought. No—never! Not Brandon.

Once down the stairs, I found a rear door easily and in a moment we were out upon the sidewalk. The hall had been drafty and we had both retained our wraps, so we were ready for the street. I made no attempt to find the Reid carriage, but hailed a passing hansom cab and bundled my companion into it. In mutual silence we sat side by side in the leathery-smelling dimness. The weight of shock still lay upon me, and I was fearful of my own traitorous thoughts that would not give unquestioning belief in Brandon as I wished them to.

The cab jounced along over uneven pavement, and Leslie began to recover. She sat up and fastened her plumed hat more firmly upon her head with its long skewer of a hatpin, thrust her tumbled red hair into place beneath the brim. Her breathing had gone faint after Brandon had slapped her, but now it quickened and she seemed aware of me for the first time.

"How queer that it should be you who rescued me," she murmured. "Have you ever thought of how we've been drawn together under strange circumstances, you and I? If you had trusted me, I could have helped you, I could have saved you from the trouble you are in."

"I am in no trouble," I told her unsteadily. I wanted none of her deceptive gentleness.

She went on, her voice soft as a whisper, and I remembered that day when she had stood in the window of her room and watched us drive away, that day I'd gone to the play with Brandon and the children. I had thought of her then as a ghostly presence in the house. How wrong I had been.

"You are in very great trouble, Miss Kincaid," the soft voice insisted. "You are in the same trouble I was in from the moment I first saw him. You are in love with him, and any woman who loves him must suffer."

I ignored her reference to me. "How could it be from the first moment? You were going to marry Dwight."

She nodded, and the plumes on her hat ruffled gently with the movement. "Yes. And I married Dwight. Because he loved me and always would. And because my father was ruined and everything had crashed about my head. But I never stopped wanting Brandon. Afterwards—when Dwight was dead and there was no safety to cling to—what choice did I have? Even to becoming an accomplice after the fact. And what could he do but marry me and thus assure my silence? Believe me, Miss Kincaid, he was not above buying that protection. Otherwise he would never be tied to one woman. Once he has what he covets, he grows bored and there's an end to it. Perhaps an end to everything for the woman. Do you think that would not happen to you also?"

I wanted to put my hands over my ears to shut out her words. Instead, I tried to deflect them.

"It was you who wanted Jeremy out of the house," I said. "You, most of all."

She made no attempt to evade the accusation. "Naturally. Because sooner or later the boy would convince someone that a second pistol existed and Brandon would be convicted. I still loved him. I still wanted to save him from the results of his own act. There would be no injustice to Jeremy. He is unbalanced and violent."

It was safer to think of Jeremy.

"He is your son," I said. "Yet you have no love for him."

"Selina is the child I love. Jeremy has always frightened me. He was so much his father's son, and I could never love him. You've seen for yourself how dangerous he is."

"I've seen nothing of the kind," I said. "I've seen only the aftermath of his self-blame." I turned my head and looked at her there beside me in the dim interior of the cab. How pure her profile, how deceptively lovely. "It was you who smashed the Osiris head, wasn't it?"

Faint laughter brimmed to her lips. "How clever you are! Yes, of course it was I. Brandon would never believe in his own danger. His sense of guilt has caused him to be overly generous to the boy. Your presence and influence on Jeremy has made everything worse, and I had to prove that we could keep the child with us no longer."

I could feel only loathing for the woman beside me. "Then it was you who took Miss Garth's scissors and thimble and hid them beneath Jeremy's pillow." I did not question; I stated. "But now the truth must be told," I went on. "All of it. Jeremy must understand his own innocence."

Her eerie laughter bubbled again, and afterwards the silence between us was potent with meaning.

To think of Jeremy was no longer safe. Freeing him from the years' weight of guilt might mean to seal Brandon's fate. Yet Jeremy must be cleared. There was no other choice. My heart contracted at the thought of his long helpless suffering. Surely, surely Brandon would never have taken his own freedom at so great a cost to a child. I would never believe that of him. He might kill in hot anger, but this he would never do. And he must tell me so himself.

I had only one purpose now. As soon as it was possible I would see him and ask for the truth. He would tell me that Leslie was a liar, that she held nothing over his head. He *must* tell me that he was innocent of his brother's death, of this long torturing of Jeremy. I could live only for the moment of seeing him. Nothing else mattered.

When the ride ended, Leslie got out of the cab and went up the steps without my help. She rang the bell insistently while I paid the cabby. When Henry opened the door, I followed her into the house.

CHAPTER 26

THE MOMENT Leslie was inside, she turned limp and helpless again. Garth was summoned to take her upstairs, and the household was in a stir of concern over her state. Such histrionic ability no longer amazed me. This was the way she kept everyone jumping through her hoops.

When I found that Brandon was not yet home, I went directly upstairs. I hoped to avoid Jeremy for the moment, but he was watching for me on the third floor.

"Come and tell us everything that happened, Miss Megan," he invited eagerly.

There was no escaping him, and I went into the schoolroom, where morning lessons were coming to an end. Selina and Andrew sat at the table. Andrew saw my face and brought me a chair, but I would not sit down. I wanted only to satisfy Jeremy and make my escape.

"I'm sorry," I told the boy, "but I have little to report. Dr. Clarke, the minister, gave a fine talk about your father, and there was a great crowd of people there. But the strain was too much for your mother. She became ill, and I had to bring her home. So I've no idea of what went on at the ceremony after that."

"Why you?" Andrew asked. "Why didn't Reid bring her home himself?"

I could not stand there and quibble. Fear and anxiety were building up in me, and Andrew recognized the fact that something was wrong. He did not press his own questions and he checked Jeremy.

"No more now," he said. "Miss Megan is tired. I'll see her to her room."

Not even the reassuring pressure of Andrew's hand beneath my arm could save me from my frantic fears. I wanted only the solitude of my room, where I could wait until Brandon returned to the house.

Andrew opened my door for me, but he did not let me go at once. "Tell me what's troubling you, Megan," he pleaded.

I was near the breaking point and I looked at him a little wildly. "Mrs. Reid has accused Brandon of his brother Dwight's murder. She is out of her mind—completely mad. What happened was dreadful—dreadful and nearly disastrous."

"So it's come at last," he said. "The lid has blown off with a vengeance. You'd better tell me about it, Megan. Perhaps it will help you to talk."

Even in my distraught state, I saw his concern for me, but I could only shake my head. "I don't know the truth yet. Perhaps I can tell you later—when I know. Let me go, Andrew, please let me go."

He put a hand on my arm in a quick, comforting gesture and released me. I went into my room and flung off my wraps, letting them fall where they might. I could not lie on the bed, or settle myself in a chair. I could only pace the small room. I heard the summons to the midday meal, but I did not go down. Would anyone in this house ever again be able to eat a quiet meal? The thought of food sickened me.

Once I paused in my pacing and summoned Kate, to ask if Mr. Reid had yet returned to the house. She told me that he had come home and was now closeted with his wife. I could not refrain from questioning her. I no longer had any pride.

"Are their voices angry?" I asked. "Do you think they are quarreling?"

There was pity in her eyes, and I wondered how much of my "secret" was known to the servants.

"I couldn't hear a thing," she told me frankly. "Though I listened outside the door. Garth came out soon after the master went in and she nearly caught me there. But their voices were low, miss."

When she had gone, I left the shelter of my room. The children were in the nursery, and Garth was with them now, Andrew gone. Like Kate, I listened at the door to make sure. After that I paced the

476

third-floor hall instead of my room. Up and down, up and down, pausing occasionally at the stair rail to look down at the floor below, or to hold my breath and listen. Now and then a murmur of voices reached me, but they were not raised until the very end. When I heard the door of Leslie's bedroom open, I went a few steps down without care for being seen. Thus I heard his words and saw them both in that angry moment.

"You can do your worst!" he flung at her in a voice that was deadly to hear. "It doesn't matter any more."

In her yellow gown, Leslie seemed as stiff as a dressed-up doll. But her face, as I saw it before she closed the door of her room, was that of a woman who would stop at nothing.

I waited only until Brandon went into the library. Then I flew down the stairs and entered without knocking. Entered and shut the door behind me. I would not let him send me away.

He stood before the window, where I had seen him so often, and he did not know I was there until I spoke his name. Then he turned and looked at me down the length of the room. Again I was aware of the high sweep of dark hair above his forehead, the gray eyes, the nose with its faint hump of bone, the mouth that could be cruel as well as kind. I knew only that this was the face of my love and that I must suffer now as he so plainly was suffering. Yet when I took a step toward him with my hand outstretched, he left the window and put the desk between us.

"What are you here for?" he asked coolly.

"I want only to understand the truth," I told him. "I will believe whatever you tell me."

His short laugh was far from reassuring. "The truth? That is a very large term. Do you, for instance, know the truth behind every action of your own, Megan?"

I had often enough had doubts of my own motivation, but now I wanted concrete reassurance—not of motives, not of reasoning behind some troubled act, but the truth of the act itself. There were exonerating facts, I was sure, if only he would reveal them, if only he would deny.

"What did she mean about there being a second pistol?" I asked.

For an instant I thought he would dismiss me angrily from the room. But he seemed to think better of it. With an absent hand he picked up the jagged stone, all that remained of the Osiris head. He spoke without looking at me, his fingers moving down the nose, touching lips that still smiled serenely.

"Leslie has always been a skillful fabricator of lies," he said. "She will invent any fantasy that suits her need, or play any part her fancy dictates. There was no second pistol that night, Megan. I was there when Jeremy fired the shot, as I've told you before. I picked up the pistol he used and found it still warm. You can take no hope for the boy's sake in this fantasy of another gun. She will say anything she could to condemn me."

He seemed to recognize the object in his hands and set it down as though the face of a judging Osiris repelled him. I leaned forward to touch the broken piece of stone.

"Mrs. Reid told me it was she who smashed the head with a pistol shot. Not Jeremy."

My words seemed to break through the guard he had raised against me. He stared at me for a moment and then nodded.

"Yes, I suppose that's possible. There's no end to what she may try. But I'm done with her now. Done with this house and everything in it. I'll be away as soon as possible. I've told her she can do her worst."

"I know," I said. "I heard." Once more I stepped toward him, wanting only to offer him my belief and trust. "Brandon, take me with you!"

His look softened. Then he shook his head, not unkindly.

"No, Megan. You must leave the house too. But you must leave alone. I'll involve you no longer. What is coming will be desperately unpleasant for everyone. It may destroy me completely. I'm ready to face that now."

"I would stand beside you, if you'd let me," I said.

He came to me then and took me by the shoulders. He shook me with something of his old exasperation and yet gently, with great tenderness.

"You will do nothing of the kind. You will go out of this room and out of my life and you will never look back. You will go now, Megan, while there is still time."

I saw there could be no fighting him at this moment. I would not be put aside forever if he wanted me, but I could not oppose him now.

"Why did you marry her?" I murmured despairingly. *"Why?"*

His hands dropped from my shoulders, and there was a dark opaqueness in his eyes. "You've asked for an answer," he said, "and I'll give it to you. I married her to keep her silent. Are you satisfied now?"

I knew that he was speaking the truth. No matter what concealment he might have attempted earlier, what he had just told me was true. He had corroborated Leslie's words. I turned without speaking, suddenly empty of emotion, able to say nothing more.

He made no effort to stop me as I went out of the library and fled upstairs to my room. There I flung myself upon the bed, and, as feeling and painful realization began to return, I think I died a little.

The afternoon went by in a strange, breathless quiet. With so much of terror and hatred stirring under one roof, it would seem that it must surely explode into sound. But on through mid-afternoon the house was still.

I did not die entirely, for my lungs continued to draw breath and my body went on living. I could not lie there on the bed forever, rejecting life, even though that was what I willed. Responsibility remained, and I rose at length and went to seek the children. They were alone in the nursery, playing checkers. Selina said Miss Garth had gone to her room with a headache. I sat with them, distraught and absent-minded, and Jeremy watched me gravely. Once he sought to distract me.

"Selina has told me her secret," he announced.

Selina laughed slyly, but I had no interest in secrets just then.

Jeremy went on. "She has found where the other pistol was hidden, Miss Megan. She has known where it was for a long time."

My attention focused abruptly, and I began to listen.

"I kept the secret!" Selina cried. "I didn't tell!"

"I always knew there was another one," Jeremy said reproachfully. "I tried to tell Captain Mathews and Uncle Brandon that the pistol I brought from the collection *wasn't* loaded. I'd checked it to make sure. I only meant to frighten my father. But then there was a terrible explosion and he fell. Afterwards Uncle Brandon picked up the pistol that had been fired. But, Miss Megan, it wasn't the pistol I'd taken from the collection. It was the same size, but it was a different one. So I kept looking and looking—even though I began to believe I must have shot my father. Everyone else kept saying I had, and after a while I didn't know what was real and what wasn't. Now Selina has found the pistol."

I had not died at all, I found. Every nerve was exquisitely atune and ready to throb with pain. Leslie's words were being proved true once again. The pistol whose existence Brandon denied was real and within reach. For two long years it had lain in concealment while a child pitted his futile child's strength against the disbelief and cruel concealment of adults.

Jeremy was looking at me strangely. "You're very pale, Miss Megan. Are you ill?"

I rallied strength to ask a question and was astonished that my voice did not crack with strain.

"How did you know where the pistol was?" I asked Selina.

She pushed a checker absently with a finger. "I was watching Mama one time when she didn't know. I was peeking between the boudoir curtains. And I saw her take it out and hold it in her hands. She was behaving as though she didn't know what to do with it. She put it in the drawer of her dressing table. Then she changed her mind and hid it in the first place again."

"What place?" I said. "Where is it now?"

Jeremy answered. "It's in that big brass candlestick that always stands on the hearth in Mama's room."

"Let me tell!" Selina protested. "It's my secret. Miss Megan, the top part of the stick unscrews and there's a big hollow space down inside the base."

"The pistol I took upstairs that time had an ivory handle," Jeremy said. "It wasn't the one they found."

I shook my head from side to side dazedly. Not in disbelief, but in pain and confusion.

"Show it to Miss Megan, Jeremy!" Selina cried. "You said someone put the candlestick in Papa's room, didn't you? Get it then, and show her the pistol."

"It's not there any more," Jeremy said. "Miss Megan, after Selina told me this afternoon, I went to Papa's room to find out about the pistol. I didn't notice that the bolt on the boudoir door was off. While I was there the door started to open and I didn't want to be caught in that room. I went down on my stomach and slid under the bed. Someone came into the room, walking softly, and went over to the bureau. I could hear the steps pause and then go back to the door. I looked out from under the bed, and there was enough light coming from the boudoir so I could see. It was Miss Garth, and she was carrying that big candlestick in her hands. So now I suppose it's back in Mama's room. And I can't show it to you. But we must do something about that pistol soon, mustn't we, Miss Megan? We must make my mother tell."

"Yes, we must do something about it." I could barely manage the words. "But wait a little while, Jeremy. We must—we must find the best way to handle this."

He nodded solemnly. "Now someone else will be in trouble," he said. "We have to think about that."

He pushed away the game board and went to look out the nursery window. Watching him miserably, I was reminded of his uncle, staring out at the winter bleakness of Washington Square, longing for escape. There was no comfort I could offer Jeremy. Fear was growing in me. And profound despair.

By late afternoon the wind began to rise—that dark, cold wind that made the square its playground. Shutters rattled, and there was a whining at every window crack the gale could find. Beneath its oval skylight, the stairway was a funnel that sucked up the stormy flow of air.

We had an early supper—just the children and I. Garth did not join us, but remained locked in her room, as Leslie did in hers. For once, I gathered, Mrs. Reid had refused the ministrations of her former governess and sent word by Kate that she wanted to rest and be alone. I dared not think what dark plans Leslie Reid might even now be concocting.

Though the children could not know the full cause, the sense of foreboding, of waiting for disaster to fall, made itself felt in them as well. Selina was less than her usual exuberant self, and Jeremy was quietly watchful, with an air of waiting about him. Now and then I caught his eyes upon me and knew what he waited for. But I could not yet decide what action was to be taken about the pistol. More than once that afternoon I wished for Andrew's presence in the house. I was ready to confide in him now. There was justice in Andrew. He would know what to do with this knowledge of the pistol's existence and its hiding place. He would help me to do whatever was right.

Had Brandon left the house? I wondered, and listened for his step, for the sound of a door. When would I see him again? Even while my mind tried to cope with his possible guilt, my heart dismissed it and would not believe.

As I descended the stairs from the third to the second floor, I saw that Andrew had not, after all, left the house this afternoon. Leslie must have chosen to recover from her earlier theatrical efforts and sit for her portrait, because Andrew was ahead of me, approaching the door of her room, some of his painting materials in hand.

I hurried when I saw him, intending to ask for a chance to talk to him. But by the time I reached the foot of the stairs, he had gone into Leslie's room and I determined to catch him later, when the sitting was over. As I followed the second floor hallway toward the lower stairs, I met Kate carrying up a supper tray.

"For Miss Leslie," she said as I went past her down the stairs.

I did not reach the front door, however, for the crash of Kate's tray resounded through the house. Startled, I stood at the foot of the stairs, while above me, over the sound of the wind outdoors, I heard a scream, followed by an eerie, wailing cry of terror, a keening that chilled my very blood.

I whirled about and ran upstairs.

CHAPTER 27

THE KEENING ceased, but now I could hear the desperate, terrified sound of a woman sobbing.

Kate was on her knees outside Leslie's room, her overturned tray nearby, its broken china and spilled food on the floor beside her. It was she who was sobbing, rocking back and forth with her apron over her face.

I shook her by one shoulder, shook her hard. "What's the matter? What has happened?"

She raised a tearful, frightened face. "I was just bringing the tray to Miss Leslie, as Miss Garth told me to do. And—and—"

She broke off with such horror in her eyes that I did not wait for her to finish. I started toward the door to find out for myself what had happened. At once Kate reached out and caught me by the skirt, holding me back.

"No, miss! Don't go in there! I saw, God help me. And I'll remember it in my dreams forever. He's still there, miss. Perhaps he's gone mad and we should run away before he kills us all."

She started to her feet, but I held her by the arm and would not let her go. "Don't be foolish," I said. "I saw Mr. Beach go into Mrs. Reid's room only a moment ago. Wait a moment—wait!"

How fearfully sharp every detail of that scene will always be, stamped forever upon my memory. The long hallway, half lost in the gloom of faint gaslight, just as I had seen it on my first visit to this house, the very pattern of the wallpaper, raspberry repeated endlessly on cream. There was a moaning of the wind and an accompanying rattle of shutters, the cold, dusty smell of the unheated hallway.

I heard his steps before they reached the door of Leslie's room, and the sound of them told me how dreadfully something was wrong. Kate heard them too and she gave a little shriek and clutched me tightly as Andrew stepped into the doorway, pale and shaken and sick with shock.

A cry from the staircase above jarred me into life. I released myself from Kate's clutch, and the girl began to weep out loud again. I whirled to see that Garth had come halfway down the stairs. Her attention was fixed upon Andrew, and she must have read in his face that something terrible had happened. He shook his head at her, but she darted down the remaining steps and would have gone past him had he not caught her by one arm.

"Don't!" he said. "There's nothing you can do for her now."

The woman struck away his hand and went directly into the room. I heard her gasp as she saw whatever was to be seen and caught her breath. But she made no other sound and in a moment she returned to the door. All color had vanished from her face, and her dark eyes were sunken hollows, her lips bloodless. She fought to command herself, but she could not speak. Only her eyes spoke for her, staring accusingly at Andrew.

"No," he said. "No!" and made a faint movement of denial with his hands, as though warding off the accusation she did not speak. Then he swallowed hard and went on. "I stayed to complete the portrait. She said I might come in for the finishing touches. But when I went in just now—" He put his hands over his face as if to shut out the image of what he had seen in that room.

At our feet Kate sobbed aloud and Garth touched her with the toe of a shoe, recovering her power to act.

"Stop sniveling at once! Go downstairs and send Fuller for the doctor. Send Henry for the police. Move, now—hurry!"

Kate scuttled away, clearly glad to escape. I stood where I was, stunned and bewildered, while a new, dreadful fear set up a clamor within me.

Garth turned again to Andrew. "I've never had much use for you, it's true. I thought her kindness to you misplaced. But you loved her, and I believe you. You wouldn't have done this. I think we both know who did."

Andrew nodded numbly. "Yes, we know. Is he still in the house?"

Garth moved at once. She flung open the library door upon emptiness and then went into Brandon's bedroom. Her voice came back to us, stronger now, as she gained mastery over herself.

"He's gone, and his bag's gone. He had it packed this morning."

Through my daze and confusion two things began to come clear. Whatever crime had been done, both Andrew and Garth meant to accuse Brandon of committing it. And Garth had said to Andrew, *You loved her.*

"Tell me what has happened," I pleaded as Garth came out of Brandon's room.

She spoke without looking at me, and there was venom in her words. "Go and see for yourself what you've brought upon this house!"

Andrew put out a hand to me. "Don't go in there, Megan. She has been beaten to death. Beaten in violence and anger."

"With that heathenish brass candlestick," Garth said. "He must have used it in both hands—like a club. Oh, my poor pretty lady!" Her control broke for an instant, but weakness was not for Thora Garth and she recovered at once. "He will pay for what he's done. I'll see to that. The police will find him; he'll never get away!"

This was worse than anything that had gone before. Dwight's death and a hidden pistol had no meaning for me now. I had only one instinct, and no matter what my fear, I followed it.

"Brandon didn't kill her!" I cried. "You can't make such an accusation! What proof do you have?"

"Proof!" Garth echoed the word scornfully. "Do you think there's no proof? Do you think we haven't all known what was going on between you and my poor lady's husband? Do you think he hasn't wanted her out of the way?"

Andrew tried to come to my aid, tried to spare me something of Garth's wrath. "That's not the whole of it," he said. "Reid had a stronger motive than that. She knew he killed Dwight. That's why he married her—to keep her quiet. But he must have pushed her too far, so that she was ready to go to the police. And he killed her to save himself."

485

Miss Garth flicked his words aside impatiently. "That's nonsense. It was the boy who killed his father; we've never had any doubt of that. It's true the older brother married her to keep her quiet. But not for that reason."

"Then for what reason—what reason?" I demanded.

She seemed not to hear my question, following the trend of her own thoughts in a bitter reviling of Brandon. "She was so sure she could win him, once she had him for a husband. And with any man who was human she might have done so. But he never touched her after they were married. He was off chasing other women within the week. Oh, he was gallant enough to his wife in public. He overdid his ardent attention and laughed in her face when they were alone. I know. She told me many times the truth about their marriage." Her voice rose, shrill now with fury. "But he'll pay for all the wicked things he's done. Now he will pay."

There was no reason left in me, but only unreasoning fear and a determination to help Brandon, whatever the cost.

"He didn't do this thing," I repeated mindlessly. "He didn't, he didn't!"

Miss Garth ignored me and returned to the room where Leslie lay.

"Don't, Megan," Andrew said gently. "Get yourself in hand and start using your mind. You needn't believe everything Garth says. She was in love with him too. She has always identified herself with Leslie, and, as her mistress began to hate him, she did as well. But she's wrong about there being another reason why he married Leslie."

I cared about none of this. "It's not what happened in the past that matters now. You were always just, Andrew, even though you didn't like him. You can't turn against him like this."

Andrew put the heel of his hand against his forehead as if there were a throbbing there. When he spoke, his voice had turned to a monotone, devoid of emotion.

"What's past breeds the present. Who else do you think has done this thing, Megan?"

The frightening thought was in me that there was no one else, no other choice, and I could not answer him.

486

He pressed me in the same toneless voice. "Do you think it was Garth then? After all her years of devotion?"

I wished I could believe the governess guilty of this. But I could not. She might have killed Brandon, who had scored and hurt her mistress, but I did not think she would have raised a violent hand toward Leslie. It would have been like injuring herself.

"Was it you, perhaps?" Andrew said. "Or me? Do you think I killed her, Megan? Do you think I could have?"

Again I did not think so. Andrew was capable of strong purpose, perhaps of deep love. But there was nothing of violence in him. In my mind I could see Brandon raising that candlestick in fury to crush out something that maddened him, but not Andrew. My skin grew clammy with terror, and my throat closed as though I were the victim of nightmare.

Andrew went on in the same dull tone. "I've loved her for a long time. I loved her as she was. I asked of her only what she wanted to give. Her games and pretenses never fooled me. I knew I was no more than someone to whom she could turn for solace. I loved her anyway."

Through the nightmare that held me in its grip I stared at him, and he must have seen my look.

"Forgive me a little, if you can, Megan. I've been fonder of you perhaps than I was of her. What I felt for Leslie was something different. How many times I've thought how much simpler life would be if you and I had met each other before we knew Leslie and Brandon Reid."

Who was I to condemn him? There had been times when I'd turned to Andrew Beach in the same way, wishing I could love where my heart was not truly given. But none of this mattered now.

"Where are the children?" Andrew asked.

For the first time I remembered them, upstairs in the nursery, undoubtedly frightened by Kate's screaming.

"I'll go to them," I said. "Andrew, you'll stay in the house, won't you? Until—"

"I'll stay," he said grimly. "I want to see him caught as much as Garth does. Besides, I'm the one who found her. They'll want me here for questioning."

I turned from the tragic recollection in his eyes and ran upstairs

487

to the nursery. When I opened the door, I found a scene surprisingly peaceful. Selina lay on the red carpet before the fire, listening to the story of the Toad Prince that Jeremy was reading aloud. He paused as I came into the room and gave me the grave look of one adult questioning another. An adult who has taken on the responsibility of distracting a child in a time of trouble.

I tried to sound natural and bright. "It's bedtime, my dears. Let me see how quickly you can get into your night things."

"We heard Kate drop her tray of dishes," Jeremy said guardedly. "She sounded awfully upset about it."

I offered him my silent approval and agreed that was exactly what had happened.

Selina went to bed with a minimum of delay, and, when I had tucked her in, I hurried back to Jeremy. He was in his bedroom, the gaslight on, waiting for me.

"Something bad has happened, hasn't it?" he asked at once.

I would not dissemble to the extent that I had done with Selina, but I could not tell him the truth.

"It's your mother, Jeremy. There's been an—an accident."

The gravity of his look dismissed my words as an evasion. Jeremy was all too sensitive to the climate of disaster.

"She's dead, isn't she?" he said, and then went on calmly. "I knew by the way Kate screamed. She's a silly girl sometimes, but the screaming was real."

"Yes," I agreed, "the screaming was real. You were good about Selina—keeping her from being frightened. Will you help me now, Jeremy? Will you stay here quietly. I'll have to go downstairs and I don't want to worry about you."

All I wanted just then was to escape his grave, questioning gaze. There had not yet been time for me to face the full horror of what had happened. I was still too dazed to think clearly. Fear stood at my elbow, waiting, and my heart beat so thickly it was hard to breathe. Strangely enough, it was Jeremy who had a calming effect upon me as he went quietly on.

"When I was little I loved her as much as I loved my father. But she never liked me. She didn't really like my father, either. The way she acted about him was only pretending. Because I looked so much like him, she couldn't love me. Once she even told me so

488

when she was angry. When I grew older I didn't mind very much. That's why I don't feel now the same way I did after—after my father . . ." He broke off, his young face expressionless.

"I understand," I assured him, loving him all the more for this attempt to be honest with me.

He was not through. "I can remember when I was little. I used to like the way she smelled of violets. I could have loved her very much, if only she had liked me."

His words accomplished at last what my single-minded concern for Brandon had prevented until this moment. The full realization that Leslie Reid was dead, that her cool beauty was forever destroyed and all that was evil in her as well. I could almost catch the scent of violets as Jeremy spoke and I knew I would dread that odor for the rest of my life.

The boy was in bed now, and I drew the covers gently over him and moved toward the light. But before I could turn it out, he asked another question.

"Miss Megan, did someone shoot her? The way my father was shot?"

"I don't think she was shot," I said. "We'll know more about it tomorrow. A doctor will be coming soon. And—other people who will know what to do. Shall I leave a candle burning when I go downstairs, Jeremy? I can look in and blow it out after you're asleep."

"Not a candle," he said. "Nor the gas either. Gas is cold-looking, and sometimes it whispers. And a candle makes the shadows jump. Would you lend me the rosebud lamp from your room just for tonight, Miss Megan?"

"I'll fetch it right away," I promised and went quickly to my room.

How deceptively quiet and untouched by tragedy the small room seemed—as though no one had told it of death.

When the lamp was alight on Jeremy's bureau, I kissed him on the cheek and went downstairs.

Outside Leslie's room Kate was on her hands and knees, cleaning up the mess from the spilled tray, working as if by her very industry she would keep from flying into hysteria. Andrew paced the hall as I had done upstairs—up and down, not pausing when I appeared, though he spoke to me as he paced.

"The doctor's in there now. And Garth's with him."

"Have the police come yet?" I asked.

"Listen!" Andrew said and leaned upon the hall rail above the stairwell.

Below Henry was opening the front door and I heard a voice that seemed familiar. A moment later Captain Mathews mounted the stairs in Henry's wake, a police sergeant trailing behind him. I remembered him as the man who had met us at the Home that time we had gone in pursuit of Jeremy. He nodded gravely to Andrew and me.

"Is it the boy again?" he asked.

CHAPTER 28

THIS WAS one contingency I had not thought of, and I answered a little wildly.

"Oh, no! Not the boy, Captain. Jeremy has been upstairs all day long."

"Don't worry," he said kindly. "We're only here to find out exactly what has happened."

Miss Garth heard our voices and came to the door. Her tremendous control had not forsaken her, though her color by now was ghastly. She looked first at Kate, still working on her knees.

"Go downstairs," she said curtly, and once more Kate fled with all dispatch. "In here," she told the captain, and he and the sergeant went into Leslie's room.

Andrew stopped his pacing and sat down at the foot of the stairs, resting his head in his hands. I felt sorry for him, but there was nothing I could do or say.

The doctor and Captain Mathews came out of the bedroom together, and a few moments later the doctor took his leave. Miss Garth crossed the hall to Brandon's library and motioned to Captain Mathews.

"You may use this room, if you like," she said.

He thanked her and glanced at Andrew, still sitting at the foot of the stairs. "I understand you found her, Mr. Beach. Will you come in and tell me about it, please?"

Andrew went into the library and Garth followed them, not waiting to be asked. No one closed the door, and I could hear the voices within quite clearly. The questions were routine, and Andrew was explaining dully what his own role had been. I could not relax enough to sit on the stairs as Andrew had done. Alternately I walked the hall, or leaned upon the rail, listening for any sound from upstairs or down.

Thus I saw Henry as he started up from the floor below. The butler still carried himself with dignity, but I caught the concern in his eyes as he looked up and beckoned to me with a secretive gesture. I asked no questions, but ran down to meet him on the stairs.

"Please, miss," he said. "In the kitchen. If you'll come right away."

I did not hesitate, but ran down to the basement at once. Brandon waited for me in the big warm kitchen. He nodded his thanks to Henry, who went away at once, leaving us alone.

I said the first thing that came into my head. "Why did you come back? They'll be looking for you now. If they find you here, you'll be in dreadful danger."

He put his hands upon my arms, steadying me, stilling my outburst. "I came because Fuller had the good sense to try the club, looking for me, and found me there. Tell me exactly what has happened, Megan."

Impatient though I was over the delay, I told him of how I had come downstairs and heard Kate screaming, and of how Andrew had come out of Leslie's room.

"He was in love with her," I said. "He has admitted as much."

Brandon brushed the information aside. "Of course. She could never rest unless she subdued any young man who came her way. She had to play at love-making constantly, since there was so little love in her. What of Garth?"

I told him of how she had come downstairs and gone into Leslie's room. Of her iron self-control that sometimes cracked a little around the edges.

"They both mean to accuse you," I said. "Please, please get away while you can. Leave the city before Captain Mathews knows you are here."

"My loyal Megan," he said. "I think you would stand by and sacrifice yourself to help me, even in the face of murder."

I was growing frantic. "Don't stay; don't talk! There's no time!"

"There is the rest of my life," he said quietly. "However long, or however short that may be. I am not going to run away, Megan. Come, we'll go upstairs together. Don't look so frightened. They have no evidence against me. Let them look to Thora Garth. Or to Andrew—the jealous lover who found her! I'm not the only one the police will think of."

For all the mildness of his tone, I knew that granite lay beneath his resolve. There was nothing to do but go upstairs with him.

We could hear Miss Garth before we reached the library, and it seemed that her control was failing as her vituperation mounted.

"Let them both pay for this terrible crime! It's the girl's fault as much as it is his. But *he* is the one who did the act. You can't sit here and let him get away while you ask us foolish questions."

Brandon stepped through the doorway, and the captain looked up calmly, noting his presence without comment. Miss Garth rose from her chair, her face working, but Brandon spoke before she did.

"I left the house earlier and didn't know what had happened until Fuller came to the club to tell me. I'm at your service, Captain, to help you in any way I can."

The captain bowed courteously. "Please sit down, Mr. Reid. You too, Miss Kincaid. Some serious accusations have been made here this evening and—"

"He always wanted to kill her, and now he has!" Miss Garth cried in rising hysteria. "You have the proof in your hands— What more do you want?"

The captain frowned at her. "Will you please wait in the hall until I send for you. You too, Mr. Beach."

Andrew took the governess gently by the arm, and, after an angry moment in which I thought she would shake him off, she gave in and let him lead her from the room.

Captain Mathews nodded to me. "You may remain, Miss Kincaid. The accusations concern you as well. Possible motives have been claimed. Perhaps you may have information that will help us."

Brandon seemed alert now and caught up in a tide of excitement, as though he scented battle and was willing to meet it halfway.

"There are plenty of motives," he said. "I can give you any number myself. But I didn't touch her and you'll find no evidence that I did. Rather than waste time on me, why not explore the motives of others who may be involved."

493

"I'll do that in good time," the captain said with the air of a man who knew his business and did not intend to be deflected. "For the moment we will consider something which has just come to light. A search of your room has been made, Mr. Reid. Have you any explanation for this?"

He reached into a drawer beside him and drew out something which he spread upon the desk. I leaned forward, anxiously. The object was a white shirt of the type Brandon always wore, and, as the captain opened it before us, I saw the bright red stains upon it.

Captain Mathews' tone was even. "This shirt was found wrapped inside a clean one in a drawer in your room. There was also pinkish water in the slop jar, where it must have been poured after you washed your hands."

I stared in growing alarm at the thing upon his desk. Brandon was no murderer, but someone wanted desperately to make us think he was.

Brandon spoke my thought aloud. "The murderer is very anxious that I should be blamed, but I know nothing of how those stains come to be on my shirt. Do you think I would be so foolish as to hide such evidence in my room and leave it behind if I were really guilty?"

"Rational and coolheaded behavior is seldom achieved at such a time," the captain said gravely. "This is a serious situation, Mr. Reid. A claim has been made by Mr. Beach that there was a second pistol at the time of Mr. Dwight's death, and that the boy did not fire the shot that killed your brother. That, indeed, the fatal shot was fired by you."

Brandon snapped out his answer, but I saw his color change and knew he realized the growing danger of his position.

"That is a story Leslie developed recently," he said. "I've heard nothing about it before. She undoubtedly took Beach in with her rantings. There was no second pistol. After all, you solved the case to your own satisfaction at the time, Captain."

Captain Mathews studied him thoughtfully for a moment. "I remember that the boy made some seemingly wild claim concerning a second pistol. Perhaps we'd better talk to him. Miss Kincaid, will you bring Jeremy downstairs for a moment?"

I had no choice but to do as Captain Mathews requested.

In the hall a chair had been found for Miss Garth, and she sat bolt upright against its straight back, her hands clasped tightly in her lap. Andrew still sat at the foot of the stairs and he raised his head from his hands as I came out of the room.

At the sight of those two, anger flowed through me. "What are you trying to do? What have you to hide that you are trying to incriminate Brandon?"

Andrew looked up at me sadly. "Poor Megan. Don't you know by now that he killed her? If you let him, he will do to you all the harm he did to Leslie."

I left him and ran upstairs to Jeremy's room. The boy slipped into his clothes reluctantly. His memory of encounters with Captain Mathews were far from happy, and he was not anxious to see him again.

By the time we went down, the coroner had arrived and Captain Mathews was in the hall, talking to him. The captain greeted Jeremy kindly and returned to the library with us.

"There's nothing to be frightened about," he assured the boy. "I'd like you to tell me in your own way what you know about that second pistol you mentioned at the time of your father's death."

Jeremy stood up so straight and tall that I was proud of his courage. His voice did not falter as he spoke.

"I tried to tell you, sir. I never fired the pistol they found. The pistol I took had ivory set into the grip. If you want to see it, it's hidden now in the brass candlestick in my mother's room. Maybe you've noticed that candlestick, sir?"

I shivered, remembering that Jeremy did not know how his mother had died.

The captain nodded. "Yes, I've seen the candlestick."

"There's a big hollow in the base," the boy told him. "The pistol is hidden there."

Captain Mathews spoke to the officer in the hall. I stole a look at Brandon and saw that he was frowning at Jeremy.

The police officer returned carrying the huge candlestick in both hands. It had been partially wrapped in a cloth and there was no candle in its socket now.

While we watched, the captain unscrewed the upper section from the lower. It turned, as Jeremy had said it would, though the

495

threads squealed faintly in protest until it came free, exposing a deep, shadowy cavity in the base of the stick. He set the top section on Brandon's desk and turned the base over. Nothing fell out. When he reached a searching hand into the hollow, he drew out some cloth padding that might have wrapped the pistol and kept it from rattling around. If anything had once been hidden there, it was gone now.

Jeremy told the captain the same story he had told me—of how he had gone to his father's room after Selina had confided her secret, and of how Miss Garth had come in and he had hidden under the bed. From beneath the counterpane he had seen her carry the candlestick into his mother's boudoir.

"Miss Garth will know about it," Jeremy finished. "She is the one who took the candlestick away."

But when the captain summoned Miss Garth to explain, she said she knew nothing of any pistol.

"Miss Leslie sent me for the candlestick. She had put it away in that room for some reason. I remember she put it there two days before Christmas."

Two days before Christmas, I thought, and remembered the touch of hands that groped in the dark, recalled the whiff of violet scent that had so frightened me. So it had been Leslie that evening in Dwight's darkened room.

"She sent you for the candlestick this afternoon?" the captain prompted.

"Yes, she asked me to bring it to her. So I carried it into her room and set it in its usual place beside the hearth."

"Did she tell you why she wanted it?"

Miss Garth began to sway a little. She put her hands to her temples in a distraught gesture. "No! I always sensed something queer about that candlestick, but I never knew what it was. She told me nothing. When I'd set it down, she asked me to go away and leave her alone. I—I never touched it again."

"The boy says there was a pistol hidden in its base. His sister claims to have seen Mrs. Reid take it out of the hiding place and put it back again some weeks ago."

"This is children's nonsense," Miss Garth said, shaking her head.

"I agree," said Brandon quietly.

Jeremy would have spoken, but there was an interruption from the door Miss Garth had left open. Andrew had roused himself and come into the library. The skin of his face looked yellow and drawn, and the dazed look had not left his eyes. He spoke with an effort.

"I've heard you mention a pistol hidden in the base of the candlestick. It wasn't in the candlestick today. It hasn't been there for some time. Mrs. Reid took it out several days ago and gave it to me to get rid of. She still had some notion of destroying evidence that might involve her husband in his brother's murder."

Jeremy's outraged cry made itself heard. "Uncle Brandon didn't kill my father. Of course he didn't!"

"Wait, Jeremy," the captain said. And to Andrew, "Where is the pistol now?"

"I have it," said Andrew. "I have it here."

He drew from the pocket of his coat a small pistol with an ivory-set handle and laid it on the desk before Captain Mathews.

CHAPTER 29

"THERE'S YOUR evidence," Andrew said. "That was the unloaded pistol Jeremy brought upstairs that day."

It was Jeremy who moved first. He slipped from my side and ran to the desk. Captain Mathews made no move to stop him as he picked up the small, deadly instrument and balanced it knowingly in his hand.

"This is the one!" he cried. "It's the pistol I took from the collection and carried upstairs that night. And it wasn't loaded, it wasn't fired. I know that now."

"Exactly," Andrew said. "The pistol Mr. Reid fired was cleverly substituted for the one Jeremy dropped."

"Uncle Brandon couldn't have fired at all!" Jeremy protested. "I'd have known if the shot came from across the room where he stood. It came from where I was standing. Close to me. That's why I began to think that I must have fired the pistol after all. Only I know now I didn't. Someone standing behind me held that other pistol and pulled the trigger. Someone hidden from Uncle Brandon by the curtains shot my father. And I know who it was."

In startled silence we watched as the boy replaced the pistol on the table. Without fear he looked at each person in turn, all about the room, and I found myself following his eyes. I looked at Brandon, on whose face bewilderment struggled with disbelief. Then at Andrew with his yellowish pallor. And at Miss Garth, who looked strangest of all—as if some restricting hand had closed about her throat, cutting off her breath so that it came in a choking gasp.

The captain reached for the pistol, turning it about in his hands, though his eyes did not leave Jeremy's face.

"It is best not to guess about a thing like murder," he said. "If you name a name, you must be sure."

Jeremy hesitated. "I don't know if I can be absolutely sure, sir. I didn't see the person. I never looked behind me at all. But the pistols could have been changed while Uncle Brandon and I ran to my father."

Miss Garth managed a strangled cry. "No—you mustn't listen to him! The boy is demented, unbalanced!"

"He is neither," said Andrew quickly. "But he is lying. He would do anything to save his uncle."

Jeremy flung a quick, scornful look at the tutor and leaned earnestly upon the desk, reaching a pleading hand toward the police officer.

"I'm not the one who is lying, sir. There's something I didn't tell you. When I went looking for the pistol today, I had time to open the candlestick before Miss Garth came in. The pistol was there. I still have a piece of the paper that was wrapped around it. I was in a hurry, so I didn't wrap it up again. I just dropped the pistol back in the cloth and screwed the top on the base. When I heard someone coming, I stuffed the paper in my pocket and hid under the bed. Here it is, sir."

From his pocket Jeremy drew a torn scrap of newspaper and handed it to the captain, who opened it on the desk before him.

"Yes," he said, "this might have been wrapped about the pistol. The date is here—the week of Dwight Reid's death." He looked at Andrew. "Have you anything to say about this, Mr. Beach? If the pistol was in the candlestick today, as Jeremy claims, then it must have been today that you had the stick in your hands."

Andrew said nothing at all. He stared at the pistol, the glazed look in his eyes again.

Miss Garth made a sudden violent gesture and would have left her chair, but Brandon moved to stop her.

"Wait," he said. "Give him a chance."

The governess fell back in her chair and began to weep uncontrollably, her handkerchief to her eyes. All her earlier self-control had vanished.

"A chance?" she moaned. "He gave my poor lady no chance!"

Andrew seemed not to have seen her movement toward him, nor to hear her words. He stared at the pistol on the desk as though it held his attention above all else.

"I never understood her vacillation about the pistol." He spoke as if to himself. "One moment she would threaten to use it as evidence against Mr. Reid. The next, she would plead with me to get rid of it entirely. I took it to satisfy her. It's true that she gave it to me today. She said it wasn't strong enough evidence to use against Mr. Reid. But I thought she was wrong."

The captain would have spoken, but Andrew turned suddenly to Jeremy.

"Who was it that stood behind you and fired a shot the night your father died?"

The boy answered without hesitation. "It was my mother," he said. "I know it was my mother because I caught the smell of her perfume. Like violets. That was the thing I kept trying to remember afterwards. But by the time it came back to me it didn't make any sense, because I thought I'd fired the gun."

Andrew made a brushing gesture across his face, but he spoke to Jeremy again. "Garth often uses your mother's perfume. How do you know it wasn't Garth?"

"Because her father was ill and she'd gone to be with him that night. She wasn't even in the house when it happened."

"That's true," Miss Garth said brokenly. "I wasn't there."

Captain Mathews fixed Andrew with his keen, steady gaze. "You are ready to admit that you were with Mrs. Reid this afternoon before she died?"

"Of course he was!" Miss Garth shrilled. "I see it all now. He even tried to fool me, but it was he who beat her so cruelly and horribly."

"What have you to say, Beach?" the captain urged.

Andrew shook his head as if he tried to clear his mind from some confusion of thought.

"I didn't kill her," he said. "I'd never have laid a finger on her. I was the one who loved her."

"She's dead," Brandon said grimly.

A long shivering sigh went through Andrew.

"Send the boy away," he said.

I took Jeremy to the door of the library. "Go upstairs, dear, and get ready for bed. Make sure that Selina is all right. I'll come to you when I can."

After he had gone, I closed the door and returned to my chair near Brandon.

Andrew had not moved and he did not look at any of us "You're wrong in what you think," he said dully. "If she couldn't have what she wanted, she wouldn't live. She died by her own hand."

The emotion had drained out of his voice, as though he had reached the limit of any ability to feel. No one spoke as his monotone continued.

"After Megan brought Mrs. Reid home from the ceremony this morning, I stayed on in the schoolroom, pretending to work on the portrait. I pushed a note beneath Leslie's door, saying I would come when I had a chance to slip in unnoticed. I wanted to know what had happened, and perhaps to comfort her. I didn't get to her until sometime in the afternoon. When Garth brought her the candlestick, Leslie didn't let her know anything was wrong. But she'd taken the laudanum even then. Enough to be sure of death. She told me when I went to her.

"The death of Brandon's father settled matters for her, I suppose. As long as he lived, her husband might stay with her to avoid scandal. But now she knew she couldn't hold him, though she must have brought up the accusation of Dwight's murder in a last desperate effort. Now I can understand why she always pretended devotion to Dwight, devotion to any cause that honored him. It was her own guilt she wanted to hide."

Miss Garth sobbed into her handkerchief. No one else made a sound.

"There could have been no saving her," Andrew went on. "At first I was wild with despair. I felt it was Reid who had killed her with his indifference and scorn. He was to blame for all her unhappiness. The drowsiness hadn't come upon her yet. Her thoughts were clear, and she spoke to me quite rationally. She told me there was a way in which Brandon Reid could be made to pay for all he had done to her.

"She sent me for a shirt from his room. He had already left the house by that time. She gave me the pistol and told me to get rid of it. Then she asked me to light the candle in the big stick on the hearth for the last time. I remember how she watched the flame while she talked to me.

"She told me what she wanted me to do and how I must do it. I had to promise— There was no other way to let her go in peace. Besides, I felt that Reid was her murderer in actuality and I wanted to see him hang for what he had done to her. He had all I wanted, and he valued it so little.

"She talked until the drug started to take effect. When her tongue began to slow, she told me to blow out the candle because she wanted it to be dark. I did as she told me and held her in my arms until she was gone. Afterwards I took up the candlestick."

He bent his head and covered his face with his hands. Behind the guard of his fingers his voice went on.

"After the first blow was struck, it wasn't hard to do. I closed my eyes and struck at Reid with every blow. I could take satisfaction in that. Afterward I took off his shirt that I'd worn and hid it in his bureau. I washed my hands in his basin. I had carried some of my painting equipment as a blind in going in and out of Leslie's room, lest I be seen, and I took it with me when I returned for my coat. I would have left the house if Kate hadn't chosen that moment to come to the door with a tray for Mrs. Reid."

The final telling seemed to have given him strength, for now he put his hands down and there was something like relief in his eyes. When he stopped, there was total silence in the room. The heavy silence of mingled horror and disbelief. Yet we had to believe. There was no doubting Andrew now. The laudanum would be found and his words substantiated—though if he had not spoken, the coroner's verdict would undoubtedly have been death from beating with the instrument of the candlestick.

Brandon moved first. He got up and went out of the room as though he could not trust himself to stay. The weight of the story we had heard lay upon us all, though now I had only pity for Andrew because of the dreadful road he had followed. Pity for Andrew and a slow burgeoning of relief for Brandon, as full realization came home to me. I, too, could stay in this room no longer.

"May I go to Jeremy?" I asked and when the captain nodded I

went past Miss Garth, still sobbing into her handkerchief, past Andrew, who did not look at me, and out the door.

Upstairs in his room Jeremy waited and I sat on the bed beside him, knowing that he must be told the truth. Not all the dreadful details, but enough so that he would understand that he was fully cleared and no one would ever point a finger of accusation at him again. He heard me through solemnly.

"What will become of Selina and me now?" he asked when I had finished.

It was Brandon who answered him from the doorway. "I'm going to send you and your sister upriver to your grandmother's for a while, Jeremy. Would you like that?"

The boy nodded, accepting the proposal with quiet satisfaction. I kissed him good night and went into the hallway with Brandon.

"There's a great deal to make up to him for," he said sorrowfully. "I've been blind from the beginning, and a fool to believe the evidence I thought my own eyes had given me. Do you think the boy will ever forgive me?"

"He won't consider that there is anything to forgive," I assured him. "Start with him as things are now. I think he'll want only to go on from here and not look back."

Brandon held out a hand to me. "Come, Miss Megan," he said, and led me into the empty schoolroom, where no fire burned, and sat me down in a chair.

"There are some things that the captain and Andrew Beach don't know," he said. "And needn't know. The true reason behind my marriage to Leslie, for instance."

"I know a little," I broke in. "Miss Garth said it was true that you married her to buy her silence, but there's no need for you to tell me more."

"There is need," he said. "But first let me say that if Leslie shot Dwight—and we know now that she must have—it wasn't because she wanted me. Not then. She had married him for his wealth and promising future. She had notions of flying high in governmental society. But after he managed to involve himself in a scandal of corruption that was about to break wide open, he had a change of heart and intended to make a complete confession. He sent for me to come home and stand by him while he faced what he had to face. Prison, perhaps, and certain disgrace. Leslie couldn't accept that. I can see now that her motive for what she did was clear by her standards. She would never have lived willingly with disgrace, and Dwight told me she had pleaded with him not to throw the matter open. After his death I wanted only to hush the whole thing up and spare my father the truth. There was no point then in making a scapegoat of Dwight, who had been only a weak tool and could no longer speak for himself."

I was beginning to understand. "And later Leslie used that over your head?"

He nodded unhappily. "With Dwight gone she had nothing to gain by secrecy. She could hurt my father cruelly if she spoke out—and all for nothing. If I married her she promised silence. So I bought her silence, but I bought it meaning to make her pay for it for the rest of her life. I did not dream of how heavily I was to pay as well."

He went abruptly to the window, where he stood with his back to me, staring down at the stables. I wanted to go to him, to put my arms about him, and offer the small comfort of my love. But he looked so stern and distant that I did not dare. Yet I must bring him back somehow to things as they were now—to a will to go on from here.

I stepped to the mantelpiece and picked up the pointer Andrew had laid upon it. Lightly I traced its tip along the colored map that hung against the wall.

"Show me," I said—although I knew very well—"show me where Thebes is located."

He turned from the window, smiling gravely, and came to take the pointer from me. "Why do you want to know, Megan?"

"Because you will be going there," I said. "And I don't want to be left here alone." For the second time I spoke the words I had said to him downstairs. "Take me with you, Brandon."

"Do you think I'd go without you?" he said. "When will you marry me, Megan?"

I knew there would be a great buzzing of gossip, but the children would be away with their grandmother and gossip eventually dies.

"As soon as you like," I told him.

How tender he could be, how very gentle. How surely his arms belonged about me, and how strong was the beating of his heart.

But we could not linger for our love now. He had to put me from him and go downstairs where his responsibilities as Leslie's husband must still be met.

When he left me I went into the hall and stood for a long moment, listening to the sound of his steps on the stairs. There were voices below, movement. As I stood in the shadows, Miss Garth mounted the steps slowly, mournfully, and went into her room. She did not see me, and I did not speak to her. I caught the whiff of violet scent in the hallway as she passed.

On the table beside my door was a candle I had left burning and I went to extinguish it. Violets and candlelight—always I would remember those two. "Blow out the candle," Leslie had said to Andrew.

I snuffed the flame with my fingers and went into my room. The scarab pin lay among other trinkets in a bureau drawer, and I took it out to hold in my fingers. Thebes, with Brandon beside me! I would see for myself those great figures of the queen, and all the other wonders. I would be with Brandon under the hot sun of Egypt, where warmth would renew and restore him, where the slow healing would begin that now must come to him. Somewhere there would be a home for us—a place where Jeremy and Selina could come and know that they were loved and welcome.

Though not in this house. Not ever again in this house on Washington Square.